Praise for *The Lottery Winner Widows Club:*

'An absolute hoot. Full of lovely Elly Vine's signature warm and wicked humour. Twisty, turny, funny and absolutely marvellous. This has WINNER written all over it!'
MILLY JOHNSON

'Brilliant! Riotously funny, gripping and twisty – and packs a real emotional punch too. The Lottery Winner Widows Club are the female friends we all need!'
CRESSIDA McLAUGHLIN

'Riotously funny! This story of mysterious deaths, sisterhood and secrets will make you laugh, cheer and buy yourself a lottery ticket!'
LUCY DIAMOND

'A truly original premise, which had me hooked from the start – a darkly funny tale with twists you won't see coming, and characters you'll be rooting for.'
SOPHIE COUSENS

'Joyous, dark and witty as hell. A devilishly funny celebration of female friendship and starting over. Warm but thrilling, pacy but deep, hilarious and poignant. Vine has given us a girl gang comedy-thriller with a delicious whiff of sulphur. This book made me laugh, weep and punch the air. An utter DELIGHT.'
EMMA JANE UNSWORTH

'A RIOT – uplifting, feisty and fun, with so much heart. It's a joy to read, but it packs such a powerful punch. This book is so good it's criminal.'
DAISY BUCHANAN

'A riotously funny romp of a read with a wonderful cast of characters and plot twists you will not see coming – I loved it!'
MIKE GAYLE

'Really enjoyed this! A funny and touching crime romp.'
CLAIRE McGOWAN

'A riotous romp through the bonds of female friendship with murder and (a lot of) money thrown in. Fun, funny and full of heart.'
ASIA MACKAY

'This is a super fun book about female friendship and solidarity. BRB, buying a lottery ticket and a spade so I can join this club!'
JULIE MAE COHEN

'The feel-good novel par excellence! Kickass women righting wrongs and reclaiming their own lives, all in fabulous style. Every character leapt off the page and the twists and turns of the story kept me guessing all the way. I bloody loved it!'
HARPER FORD

'Full of humour and deliciously deadly intent, I loved this colourful tale of murder, mayhem, friendship and self-discovery!'
KATE STOREY

'Utterly delicious – spiky, poignant and totally hilarious, I laughed and cried and could not put it down. If, like me, you grew up loving *The First Wives Club* but thought it needed more murders then this is the book for you.'
LAURA WOOD

'Such a joy! I love a story about cross-generational female friendship! This novel is a true escape – funny, twisty and heartwarming. I loved the time I spent with these brilliant female characters.'
LAURA PEARSON

'What a blast of a read – a deliciously fun and entertaining novel with a delightful cast of characters to root for. It's a winner!'
FIONA GIBSON

'An absolute slam-dunk – touching and wildly funny, with just the right amount of darkness. This fabulous and wholly bingeable tale of female friendship and brave new starts had me gripped from the first page – I adored it!'
ROSIE WALSH

'This book is a knockout! Dark and twisty, but packed with so much heart and genuine laugh out loud moments, I didn't want it to end. This feminist crime caper is an empowering, uplifting and throughly entertaining ride.'
KIRSTY GREENWOOD

'The funniest book I've read in a long time and a recommend-to-everyone book for me. You know how we always say 'I laughed out loud' but people hardly ever do? I ACTUALLY DID! A lot!'
CAROLINE CORCORAN

'This book had me HOOKED! A wicked plot, a fierce cast of characters and all of the charm and wit I've come to love in a Vine book. The twist shook me to my core and the entire book was an addictive, endearing joy from start to finish.'
OLIVIA BEIRNE

'A fabulously enjoyable romp full of badly-behaved women you can't help but root for, with a real heart lurking under all the Porsches and pink fizz. Everyone who reads this is a winner.'
P. J. ELLIS

'The perfect blend of darkness and humour. Fast-paced and hilarious with a twist that you never see coming. Absolutely delicious.'
KATE WESTON

'If anyone can put the fun in thriller it's Elly Vine! A hilarious, twisty and hugely satisfying crime novel. You'll be batting for Paula and co. from the off.'
LUCY NICHOL

'A darkly fun and funny read, with an emotional depth that I didn't see coming. The escapism I didn't know I needed.'
REBECCA RYAN

'*The First Wives Club* meets *Bad Sisters* in this effortlessly readable, laugh-out-loud funny crime debut from Elly Vine. With a page-turning story, a zany eye for the absurd and a killer twist, I was entertained from first page to last. But what left a lasting impression was its moving and insightful celebration of women who refuse to be overlooked.'
ZAC HAMMETT

'Hilarious, funny, surprising, warm and brilliant. A perfect read.'
SALMA EL-WARDANY

'A gripping, heart-wrenching and lively caper that will make you laugh, cheer and weep – sometimes all at once – packed with fabulous characters you'll long to drink champagne with.'
JUSTIN MYERS

'Excellent! Plenty of twists, turns and gasp-out-loud moments with bags of fun and warmth too. A true joy to read. Is it okay to consider joining my own Lottery Winner Widows Club? Asking for a friend . . .'
HANNAH DOYLE

'The perfect mix of comedy and drama, I adored it!'
JULIE HAWORTH

'This darkly hilarious ride through wealth, widowhood and female bonding is brilliant. If you binged *Bad Sisters* on TV, you'll adore this.'
KATE RIORDAN

'This is a deliciously dark revenge-fest, whose sharp wit and female camaraderie never underplays the dangers so many women face behind closed doors from the men in their lives. Vine takes a deadly serious issue and turns it into deadly action; we can't help cheering all the way.'
LESLEY McDOWELL

'Glam, sassy and oh so dark, combining witty barbs with characters that keep you turning the page. You're in for a treat with this humorous thriller that still keeps its edge. I am officially an Elly Vine fan!'
JACK STRANGE

'Reading this book is like winning the jackpot: heady, explosive and exciting in the extreme. It starts with a dead husband and went absolutely nowhere I expected until the triumphant ending. Elly Vine has created a pacy, hilarious thrill ride, full of glamorous settings and funny women who are hell-bent on revenge!'
KATIE MARSH

'Expect laughs, sobs and cheers in Vine's crime caper. Paula and the Widows might be my all-time fave girl gang. Hijinks, humour and heartache in bucketloads – I will be thinking of the Widows forever!'
LIZZIE HUXLEY-JONES

THE LOTTERY WINNER WIDOWS CLUB

Writing as Lucy Vine

Hot Mess (2017)
What Fresh Hell (2018)
Are We Nearly There Yet? (2019)
Bad Choices (2021)
Seven Exes (2023)
Date with Destiny (2024)
Book Boyfriend (2025)
Good For You (2026)

THE LOTTERY WINNER WIDOWS CLUB

Elly Vine

Copyright © Lucy Vine 2026

The right of Lucy Vine to be identified as the Author of
the Work has been asserted by her in accordance with the Copyright,
Designs and Patents Act 1988.

First published in Hardback in 2026 by Wildfire
An imprint of Headline Publishing Group Limited

1

Apart from any use permitted under UK copyright law, this publication may only be reproduced, stored, or transmitted, in any form, or by any means, with prior permission in writing of the publishers or, in the case of reprographic production, in accordance with the terms of licences issued by the Copyright Licensing Agency.

Cataloguing in Publication Data is available from the British Library

Hardback ISBN 978 1 0354 2850 2
Trade Paperback ISBN 978 1 0354 2849 6

Typeset in 11/13.75pt Sabon LT Pro by Six Red Marbles UK, Thetford, Norfolk

Printed and bound in Great Britain by Clays Ltd, Elcograf S.p.A.

Headline's policy is to use papers that are natural, renewable and recyclable products and made from wood grown in well-managed forests and other controlled sources. The logging and manufacturing processes are expected to conform to the environmental regulations of the country of origin.

Headline Publishing Group Limited
An Hachette UK Company
Carmelite House
50 Victoria Embankment
London EC4Y 0DZ

The authorised representative in the EEA is Hachette Ireland,
8 Castlecourt Centre, Dublin 15, D15 XTP3, Ireland (email: info@hbgi.ie)

www.headline.co.uk
www.hachette.co.uk

*For the real Ivy, Teddy and Audrey
(but also for Fleur, Dotty, Maze, Bruce, Vinnie, Floyd,
Ralph, Hades and Sir Douglas Butter Boy of Sawtry)*

PROLOGUE

Have you ever heard that seventy per cent of lottery winners end up bankrupt?

It's a common enough statistic, cited in most corners of the internet – but the fact is, it's just not true. Actually, studies repeatedly show jackpot winners have much improved life satisfaction and overall happiness.

Let's consider Edwin Castro, a man who, on 7 November 2022, bought a ticket at a petrol station in California. He won $2.04 billion, the largest lottery jackpot to date. What about the group a year later in October 2023, who took home $1.765 billion? Do we think their lives got better or worse?

Winning makes you one of the luckiest people on earth. It makes you rare; it makes you special; it makes you incredibly unique. The odds of winning the Lotto jackpot are one in 45,057,474. With the Powerball and Mega Millions lottery, it's around one in *three hundred* million.

So what would you do if you became a member of that blessed, tiny club? What if you woke up tomorrow having won that life-changing, mind-bending sum of money? And would you want to share it with someone undeserving?

I didn't.

1

Honestly, Paula really thought by the time she was sixty-one, she'd have learned a thing or two about having a normal conversation. But – standing here in her outdated, beige-coloured kitchen – she's realising now that she doesn't have a clue. How does one even *begin* to handle something like this?

She's on the phone – the landline – and staring at a suspicious patch on the ceiling in the corner. Is it a new leak coming through from the upstairs bathroom, or is it a shadow? She can't tell.

'. . . we know it must be a shock . . .' the man is saying down the line and his voice sounds awfully far away. '. . . it's been registered with the local authorities here, and we'll arrange for the paperwork, including a death certificate to be sent to you, of course . . .'

She wants to turn on the overhead light so she can have a proper look at that corner – the lamp isn't any use at all – but the phone cord doesn't stretch to the switch by the door. Tilly was probably right all those years ago, when she said they should get a cordless phone, but they were so expensive at the time. These days, of course, her daughter thinks it's absurd she and John even have a landline at all. But look here, isn't she using it right now?

Elly Vine

'... repatriation of the body is expensive, I'm afraid, but of course we'll make arrangements, if you'd like. It's possible his travel insurance may cover it.' The man pauses. 'Do you happen to know if he had any?'

Paula feels a familiar stab of fear at the mention of money. She shakes her head, then remembers he can't see her. 'I don't know,' she says simply.

'Sorry to ask this...' The man sounds awkward, and it is somehow more endearing in his light Austrian accent. 'But do you know if John had a... er, preference about his... remains? It is sometimes a more straightforward option to have the body – um, your loved one – cremated at a local crematorium and then transported back.'

This is, at last, something Paula can help with. She knows the answer to this one because John was always terribly clear. 'He *did* want to be cremated, yes!' she relays eagerly. 'He told me he didn't like the idea of his body being eaten by worms. He said that several times.'

There is a shuffling noise at the other end of the line and Paula wonders if she's said the wrong thing. Do people whose husbands have just died not talk about the body being eaten by worms? Has she messed up again?

'... and of course, there will be more documents for you...' The man has resumed talking, and Paula returns her gaze to the ceiling stain – or shadow, who knows? '... and I'll get that over to you as soon as possible, so you can apply for a Consular Death Registration in England. You can also contact the British Consulate if you would prefer a UK death certificate...'

'Gosh,' says Paula, because the idea of contacting the British Consulate sounds so grand. So unlike anything she's ever had to do before. But then, *this* has never happened before. Obviously.

'. . . and again, Mrs Sheldon, our most sincere condolences, as well as our deepest apologies it took us a few days to identify him and locate you . . .'

'Don't worry!' she says nicely, because it makes her uncomfortable when people apologise.

They say their goodbyes and hang up. Paula stares at the ceiling. Then back down at the phone in her hand.

Her husband of more than thirty years is dead. That's what the nice man with the nice accent said. John was in an accident; his car went off the road; it would've been very quick for him.

For John, she means, not for the nice man.

Paula wonders if she should've known something had happened. You hear about wives who somehow, intuitively *knew* something terrible had befallen their loved ones. Paula read something recently on Facebook about a woman who'd fainted at precisely 3.46 p.m., later discovering her husband had collapsed at his desk and died from a coronary at exactly that time.

Should she have known?

It had been a few days since Paula had heard from her husband. But that wasn't particularly unusual when he went to one of these work conferences abroad. The signal was often unreliable; he was busy with colleagues; he liked his space. She hadn't been worried at all, never mind sensing anything amiss.

It's true, she *had* tried to call him several times in the last few days, but only because of that thing she'd found out on Monday. The big, mad, incomprehensible thing she urgently needed to tell him about. But she hadn't been too concerned when he hadn't returned her missed calls.

Paula turns now in her kitchen to explain to John what's happened, and then remembers that she can't tell John that John is dead. Because he's dead.

Instead, she backs up, across the kitchen, letting the phone handset clatter noisily onto the faded orange floor tiles. She finds cupboards at her back and leans there for a few minutes, feeling the cool surfaces through her thin jumper. It's the cupboard with all the plates in it. Not *all* the plates, of course. The nice crockery is in the cupboard above the oven. John's always too worried they'll get broken, so they never use them.

He *was* always too worried. He can't be worried anymore. Because he's dead.

Paula considers sitting down on the floor, but she's not sure she'd be able to get up. Does it matter though? If she can't get up again? Why would she ever need to get up again?

She slides down, finding the frigid cold tiles beneath her, and then stares back up at that stain on the ceiling. She'd meant to turn the light on for a better look. But now the switch seems too far away and she was right before: standing up is going to be a complex negotiation. The stain – or shadow – will have to stay where it is. Unresolved.

'Mum?' It's her son, Seb, squinting at her from the open back door.

He looks so very young. Thirty *is* still young, she thinks, though she didn't feel it at the time. She had two babies at his age, whereas he's yet to learn how to use the washing machine by himself. Seb rubs his eyes and Paula notes how red they are, how tired he looks.

Perhaps he's been crying about his father? Except he doesn't know yet, does he? She's going to have to tell him. And Tilly. She wonders how she'll find the words and looks at the phone on the floor, wondering if 1471 still tells you the last number to ring. Maybe she can get the nice man with the nice accent back on the line to explain it all to her children.

'What are you doing on the floor?' he asks, looking a little alarmed. 'Did you get hold of Dad yet? Did you tell him the big news?'

'No,' Paula says softly.

It really is such bad timing that John's dead. Just when the biggest thing to ever happen to either of them – to anyone she's ever met! – has occurred. Just when she and John have won twenty-one million pounds on the lottery.

How is she going to manage this on her own?

And how in the world is she going to get up off the floor?

2

To: John.Sheldon1960@oldmail.com
From: PaulaJeanieSheldon1964@ptinternet.com
Subject: Some news

Dear John,

Oh my goodness, I've only just realised how funny it is that I'm sending you a Dear John letter! I'm sure you would laugh at me for that.
    Would've laughed.
    That is hard to get used to.
    Frankly, John, everything has been hard to get used to. These last couple of weeks without you in the world have been so . . .
    I'm afraid I don't have the right words.
    Seb would probably call the whole thing bananapants, but I know you never liked it when our children used made-up words. You would probably peer at him over your reading glasses and ask what exactly about the situation involves a banana or a pair of pants. And you can't argue with that kind of logic.

Although I did have a banana for breakfast this morning, if that matters.

You would no doubt find it strange that I'm writing you an email, of all things. When would I ever email you? Never! Not when I saw you every day. I can't remember the last time I really even used it, except to confirm my work schedule with Gary. The only emails I get are from Facebook about the community group page upset about potholes, and JustGiving because of that time Tilly ran a 5k.

Tilly's been taking care of everything since you . . . She's been calling people and letting them know. About what's happened. She's desperate to arrange your funeral, but we have to wait for your remains to arrive back in the UK before we can do that. I spoke to the nice man with the nice accent again about it yesterday, and he says it might be a few more weeks. Some of the paperwork has come through, but not your death certificate or your . . . ashes. I'm told they take longer to arrange.

Tilly cancelled your mobile phone contract yesterday. I didn't want her to do that, not yet. Not with so much going on that I need to talk to you about. But you know what she's like; she said it was important to get everything sorted out as quickly as possible. She said it would allow me to 'deal with all the tentacles of grief'. She really liked that analogy, but I'm afraid I don't. It just made me picture an octopus handing me a hankie. And you know how I feel about seafood.

Either way, I tried to ring you this morning. It's not like I expected you to answer, but I wanted to hear your *voice on the answering machine and I needed to tell you something. Of course, it was dead.*

Not dead. Just . . . not working.

I'll stop waffling, I know you hated it when I waffled.

The point is, John. We won the jackpot.

All those tickets. A lifetime of tickets! The same numbers on the same standing order for all these years. And we finally won.

Did you know, we've been playing the lottery since 1995? I remember that first ticket because I was pregnant with Seb at the time, and you held my arm so tightly and said to me that we were definitely going to win. You were right, as always. Just thirty years and one fatal car accident too late.

We talked so many times about what we'd do with the money, how it would fix everything. But we never really considered all the fiddly bits. It's been a funny old time since I got the notification on the app. Tilly called the helpline for large prize winners, and the operator scheduled an in-person meeting. Someone called Amy rang us back. She was very nice – her mum is called Paula, isn't that a coincidence? We had to go and see her at the office with our identification, where she talked to us about financial advisors and investments. It was all very overwhelming. If I'm honest with you, I didn't take much of it in. Thank goodness Tilly was with me. She made all the decisions, answered all the questions and filled in all the paperwork.

I was just back from that meeting when I got the call about you.

I haven't really been able to process anything since. Tilly says it's the grief. She said that thing about the tentacles again and I had to stop listening because I couldn't stop picturing clammy little suckers reaching for me.

If you're wondering how much we won, John, I'll tell you. It was 25 million euros on the Euromillions. I thought it would take a long time to sort, but it was only about a week. £20,725,250, just sitting there in our bank account. And there it still sits, I'm afraid, though Tilly keeps telling me I have to do something about it. It has to be moved or invested or something.

I'm sure she's right but I can't. Not yet.

Goodbye for now, John,

Paula xx

PS. The kitchen ceiling has another leak and I don't know what to do.

3

'WHERE'S THE BOLLOCKING WHISKY?' John's brother, Tom, hollers his question from inside one of Paula's cupboards. His huge pink head reappears moments later. He squints angrily at her across the room, awaiting a response.

'The cupboard under the stairs,' she bleats, wondering what John would think of his bullish older brother stealing their very limited supplies of expensive alcohol. Tom stands up, grunting and huffing, stalking through the kitchen and back out into the hallway. John's other two brothers – Pete and Leonard – both stand to follow. The three of them have always done things as a pack, usually leaving their youngest sibling, John, on the outside.

'Found it!' Tom yells, and Paula shoots an apologetic glance towards the non-family member in the room. The solicitor blinks back, looking vaguely alarmed.

'Shall we get on with this?' Tilly asks anxiously as the men pile back into the room, sourcing glasses and sloshing liquid.

The solicitor smiles uneasily. 'You know, we don't usually do these anymore,' he gestures around Paula's small kitchen. 'People always ask if there will be a will-reading, like they see on TV, but it's really not necessary these days.'

He takes a seat in John's chair at the head of the table and Paula feels panic rising in her chest. John wouldn't like someone else sitting in his chair, never mind a stranger. She makes a sort of strangled noise and her daughter turns in her direction. She reddens as John's three brothers exchange a smirk.

'You OK?' Tilly's wife, Misha, leans in closer. She's always been very kind, and Paula nods gratefully. She *is* OK. She just has to keep trying to remember that John is gone and it doesn't really matter who sits in his chair. It only *feels* like it matters.

'So why are we even here then?' one of the brothers booms, looking irritated, swigging from his amber drink. 'If this could've been a goddamned email, what are we doing here?'

The solicitor glances over at Tilly, and Paula understands that it is her daughter who has requested this.

'I just thought it would be better if Mum could hear all this,' Tilly says with self-assurance, 'y'know, out loud.' She looks around at the group, making pointed eye contact with Misha, then her three uncles, followed by Seb.

Paula stares down at her lap. She has been having a little trouble hearing things since she got that call about John. It's not that her ears are failing her, it's just that the words don't settle. They act like a fine snowy mist that melt into nothing the moment they land. She can hear the words OK, but she can't quite understand them. She can't internalise them. She's been having particular trouble with words that have been written down. Every time Paula tries to read, everything jumbles up in a confusing blur. Which is no doubt why Tilly's made this poor solicitor come all the way out to their house, instead of letting him send everyone an email.

'Do I need to be here?' On her left, Seb sounds bored, his tone childish. 'Can I go home?'

Elly Vine

When Seb says *home*, he's referring to the shed at the bottom of Paula's garden, where he currently resides. There is no running water and no electricity. Unless you count the very long extension lead he has running all the way from the main house, in order to power his game console. There's also a single bed, squeezed in beside Tilly's childhood chest of drawers. And a lot of spiders.

But Seb likes living there because he has – his word – 'independence' and can just about claim publicly that he doesn't live at home.

And it is, at least, a step up from his previous accommodation; a dilapidated, rusty old caravan on Paula's driveway.

Seb is thirty years old.

'Can we get on with this?' Tom booms, pouring himself, Pete and Leonard another quadruple whisky.

Tilly brightens. 'If everyone else is having a drink, maybe we should have one, too?' She doesn't wait for an answer, getting herself, Misha and Seb a beer – John's beer – and placing a tall glass of Malibu and Coke in front of Paula.

Paula stares at it. She can't stand Malibu and Coke. It's like drinking fabric softener.

'Thank you, sweetheart,' she says carefully. 'But I think I'll just stick to water.'

'Don't be ridiculous,' Tilly says cheerfully. 'It's your favourite and everyone else is having one!'

Paula nods, and takes a tiny sip of the fabric softener. It's horrible.

'So first off,' the solicitor clears his throat, 'I should say that John appointed his daughter' – he looks up from the page, pointing a flat palm at Tilly on his right – 'as his executor.

That means you are responsible for administering the estate and dealing with any assets, Ms Sheldon. We can talk this through in more detail after the will-reading.'

Tilly looks a little surprised and Paula feels a few eyes on her. She senses confusion from the room, but of course John appointed their daughter! Paula's always been hopeless with that kind of thing and Tilly is so very capable.

'It also means you're technically in charge of funeral arrangements, which I understand' – he pauses, glancing up for confirmation – 'hasn't taken place yet?'

Taking the lead, Tilly nods. 'We've had to wait a couple of weeks for the paperwork and we're still waiting on Dad's . . . remains.' She pauses to swallow. She's only two years older than Seb, but while he seems like a teenager, sometimes Tilly seems even older than Paula. 'But we're hoping it'll be soon.' She glances at Paula. 'We have it in hand.'

Paula nods, though she's done nothing.

'This is an informal process,' the solicitor continues, 'I'm just here to read out John's statement and wishes, and then help clarify anything. So, if anyone has any questions, please do speak up.' He leans back in John's chair. It creaks in the same way it did for John. Paula fights back that urge again – the one that wants to scream for the man to move. But people are allowed to sit in chairs. Even John's chairs.

'I'll crack on then.' The solicitor nods around the room, then clears his throat. 'I'll start with John's opening statement, which he wrote as follows: "Hello everyone, John here. It seems I'm dead, how strange. Hopefully I went peacefully in my bed at the age of 99, beside my loving wife, Paula."' Next to her at the table, Misha reaches for Paula's hand but she shrinks away from the kindness. Affection is only going to make all of this harder. The solicitor continues, '"I lived a good life. I tried to be a good man. I worked hard and made sure I provided for my wife and children. I hope I will be remembered fondly by one and all. Goodbye. See you when I see you. Love, John."' Paula stares down at the table as, across from her, she hears Tilly start to cry. Either side of her, both Misha and Seb sound a little sniffy, too.

Should Paula be crying? Probably. But if she starts crying now, goodness knows what might happen.

'I'll read out his estate bequests now,' the solicitor begins, and the room shifts a little with expectation. 'To his brother Pete, John leaves his collection of pool cues, along with his lifetime membership of the local snooker club.' Pete looks pleased with this and nods slowly, sipping his whisky.

'For his brother Tom, John leaves his clothes, along with his famous collection of belt buckles. His brother Leonard is to take possession of his stamps, his chess set, and the whisky under the stairs.' Tom and Pete exchange guilty looks, whisky in hand, as Leonard regards them with outrage. Tom quickly downs the remaining liquid in his glass.

The solicitor watches them for a moment, his expression bewildered, then turns in Tilly's direction. 'Er, to his daughter Matilda, John leaves his most treasured possession: a signed, framed photograph of Ronnie O'Sullivan and a first edition of Ronnie's autobiography.' Tilly releases a small guttural sob as he continues, 'And to his son, Sebastian, he leaves the fishing equipment out in the garage and his unfinished memoir, titled *Snookered*.' The solicitor adjusts his glasses. 'Apologies, I can see that name has been amended to *All Cued Up*.'

'That's not better,' Misha murmurs, but Seb looks pleased.

The solicitor continues, 'The rest of the estate – including the house and any other assets, financial, etc. – have been bequeathed to John's wife Paula.'

There is a moment of silence as the room digests this.

Misha leans forward gingerly. 'Is there nothing specific or personal for Paula?'

'Never mind that!' one of the uncles shouts. 'What about the lottery money? Does that mean she gets the lot?'

Paula's head whips around. Pete is standing over them, hands on hips, his empty glass discarded on the kitchen counter. Behind him, Tom and Leonard are listening intently, their expressions hard and menacing.

Paula can feel shock making her face slack. How do they know about the lottery win?

Every week, when they checked the results, John would turn to Paula and say, 'If we win, we won't tell a soul. Lottery winners don't make good friends.'

And of course he was right. He was right about everything. She had no intention of telling anyone about the win. No one beyond Tilly and Seb. She glances at her children fearfully. Seb is staring at the table, guilt painted clearly across his face. Tilly meets Paula's eyes, then rolls hers.

'Ah,' the solicitor says, and it's clear he, too, knows about the win. He removes his glasses and adopts a serious expression. 'From what I understand, the ticket was jointly bought, and even if it were John's ticket exclusively, it would still automatically become part of his estate. And – as I said – the will is very clear that it all goes to Paula.'

Pete takes a step forward. 'That's outrageous!' He waves his hands and Paula cowers, though he's at the other side of the table. 'What does she even need twenty million for? I've got three ex-wives and six stepkids.' He huffs furiously, waving at Paula without looking in her direction. 'John paid off this house years ago. She's living on easy street!'

Paula feels a stab of horror as Tilly jumps up, looking angry. 'Hey!' she says. 'You have no right to speak to my mother like that.'

Pete waves at the solicitor. 'I was talking to *this* guy, actually. We're *owed* some of that money. He was our little brother. We should be getting at least a couple of million each. She doesn't need it.'

Paula swallows hard. The truth is, they did indeed pay off their mortgage a long time ago. But then they had to re-mortgage when the roof needed re-doing. And then re-mortgage again a few years ago when a neighbour complained about the asbestos garage. They've long since run out of money. John hadn't had a pay rise at work in years and Paula never brought in much from her work at the care home. Maybe they could've just about made ends meet, if the bills didn't keep going up and things didn't keep going wrong with this old house.

She glances anxiously over at the stain on the ceiling.

Never mind *easy street*, it has been *quite difficult and stingy street* for a long time now. John had to count every penny in the last few years. It's why they played the lottery so religiously every week.

And now they... she has almost twenty-one million pounds sitting in the bank.

Tom and Pete are almost nose to nose with the solicitor, loudly debating the veracity of the will. Pete is hotly explaining how one of his stepkids urgently needs a new iPad. Apparently he is sick of the fifteen-year-old borrowing his computer for porn. The solicitor looks a little green.

Tilly gets involved.

Paula takes a long, deep drink of the fabric softener and stands up. She can't listen to this horrible nonsense anymore. She'll leave them to it; let them all shout it out. They can have the money if they want, she doesn't care. She doesn't want it.

Everything is so different all of a sudden, she just wants everything back the way it was. She wants John to be here, taking care of things like he always did. At the very least, she needs him here taking care of his shouty brothers.

As Paula mounts the creaky stairs, more than ready to hide in her bedroom for as long as it takes, she hears the front door bell. Somewhere in among the noisy din of men – and Tilly – shouting in the kitchen about how the tenth generation iPad isn't modern enough, Paula catches the sound of Seb opening the door and speaking. Curious, she turns back down the stairs, just as her son appears. He's holding a box and looking a little dazed.

'What is it?' Paula asks and he looks up at her.

He holds up the item in his hands. Paula stares at it. She suddenly knows what it is, what it must be.

'Dad's home,' her son says simply, gingerly putting down the box. The box carrying John's ashes.

4

The high-pitched wailing has not stopped all day. It didn't stop once as they brought in John's casket, it did not stop during the eulogies, and it has not stopped even here at the upmarket pub where they're hosting a wake. Not even as the wailer in question consumed five and a half cucumber and salmon sandwiches.

'Do you think she's all right?' Paula asks Tilly, concern in her voice.

Tilly huffs. 'Oh, she's bloody well fine, Mum. There's always someone at a funeral who makes everything about them. It's not actually about mourning, or even celebrating the deceased, it's about having all eyes and attention on *their* grief. She's a grief thief!' She regards her mum curiously. 'You should be the one crying, not her.'

'John did always say Bridget was prone to hysterics,' Paula whispers, glancing anxiously across the room at her husband's former secretary. As if on cue, Bridget's wailing inches up yet another octave. It is now that very special pitch employed by Bond villains to kill secret agents' brain cells.

Tilly winces at the sound, then tuts. 'That's sexist, Mum. You wouldn't call a man hysterical.'

Paula looks flustered, murmuring an apology. She's always saying the wrong thing around her daughter.

'Here,' Seb appears from the bar, holding two glasses. 'Mum, I got you your usual.' He hands her a Malibu and Coke and she sighs, accepting it. More fabric softener.

Seb swigs his beer, his eyes bloodshot. Paula would like to believe it's from the stress of the day. Or that maybe he's been up all night, weeping the loss of his father. Except that rather strong smell of marijuana wafting around him would indicate otherwise.

'Can we leave yet?' her thirty-year-old-going-on-thirteen son asks.

'No!' Tilly hisses at her little brother. 'There are still sandwiches to be eaten. And none of the uncles are even drunk yet. They'd be furious. Everyone has to have time to grieve properly.' Her eyes slide across her mother's face. 'Grief has tentacles, have I mentioned that?' Paula nods, trying not to grimace at the imagery.

'Ugh, fine,' Seb shrugs, then rubs his sore-looking eyes. 'Well, can someone at least tell that crying woman to chill?'

'John used to say there was no point trying to calm a woman down,' Paula observes solemnly. 'It's best to let her get it out of her system.' She shoots a fearful look at Tilly. 'Am I being sexist again?'

Her daughter nods disapprovingly, then sighs, placing a conciliatory arm around Paula. 'It's not your fault, Mum. It's your upbringing. You just agreed with everything Dad said. It's a generational thing.' She releases the arm, moving to face her mother. 'But it's high time you started embracing the new world. I know it's been a difficult time for you, but you're . . .' She raises an eyebrow. 'You're *rich* now, Mum! Super rich!'

She checks behind her shoulder for eavesdroppers before hissing, 'You've won the bloody lottery! This is your chance to have fun and enjoy your life. It's your chance to make friends and meet new people.' She waves her hands excitably. 'You can do *anything you want*. Absolutely anything! It's time for a fresh start. For an adventure.'

The background wailing drowned out some of Tilly's speech, but what she caught makes Paula fearful. She doesn't want a fresh start or an adventure. Losing her husband in a car accident was as close to being in a soap opera as she ever wants to come. And she couldn't care less about being rich. Yes, not having to worry about paying the heating bill will be very nice, and maybe she'll even be able to get someone out about that ceiling stain, but otherwise, she hasn't a clue about budgeting or how to spend her money. John always looked after all that. She wouldn't even know where to start with twenty-one million pounds.

'Look, I know your life has been on pause for the last month, while we waited for the ashes and made arrangements.' Tilly looks earnest. There are new wrinkles around her eyes that weren't there before all of this. 'But this is it, Mum. This is the funeral. After this, you're allowed – you're *supposed* – to start moving on. To start living your life again.'

'What life?' Paula asks, but she's drowned out by sudden yelling, over at the bar.

'Oops,' Seb nods towards the noise, blinking red eyes. 'Looks like the uncles are rectifying that sober situation.'

Paula follows his eyeline to where Pete, Tom and Leonard are roaring loudly with each other over what looks like more whisky. They're laughing over a childhood spent torturing one another.

'And then we held John's head down the loo and flushed it five times!' yells Pete, and Paula feels the room's eyes turning in the direction of the booming men.

'Bloody idiots,' Tilly murmurs, as twenty feet away, Bridget the Secretary is forced to wail even louder to outdo the uncles.

'Do you remember when he tried to hit us with an axe and we locked him outside in the garden?' Tom yells, delighted by the childish violence. He's wearing one of John's shirts, Paula realises. He took possession of her husband's clothes so quickly after the will-reading a week and a half ago. Paula keeps opening that side of the wardrobe to stare at the emptiness there. It still smells like John, but otherwise, it's like half of her has disappeared along with the shirts.

And that's when she found the notebook. Tucked away on one of John's shelves, previously buried under his Next T-shirt collection.

Her heart beats faster just thinking about it. About what it means.

She discreetly pats her coat pocket. It's still in there.

'You know what we should do?' the oldest, Pete, is shouting, looking excited. 'We should have a game of snooker in his honour!' They collectively look around the room, disappointment lighting their eyes as they find no trace of a snooker table.

'Not even a pool table!' Leonard cries, pouting.

Paula wonders, as she often has, how snooker and pool can be different things when they're both about hitting colourful balls. She would ask the brothers, but they didn't exactly leave on the best of terms after the will-reading the other week. By the end of their visit, Paula had been on the verge of transferring the whole twenty million, but Tilly overruled her.

'Let's do karaoke instead then!' shouts Tom, who has always been the biggest show-off. He's also got one of John's belt buckles on. The other two regard him sceptically.

'Did John actually like karaoke?' Leonard asks.

'Who cares?' comes the reply, as Tom downs his whisky in one and waves for another.

There is no karaoke machine, or indeed, even any access to a microphone, so the unsanctioned funeral karaoke begins, consisting mostly of the men shouting the words to Gloria Gaynor's 'I Will Survive'.

Which, honestly, feels far too on the nose for Paula's liking.

The widow and her children watch agape. Misha tiptoes towards them, looking mortified.

'Is this . . .' She waves at the singing 'Is this *OK*?'

'No!' Tilly replies firmly, taking her wife's hand as they all watch with horror. 'It's really not OK.'

'Should we do something?' Paula asks in a whisper.

'Yes,' her daughter says with determination, turning to face her. 'You should say something, Mum. You're the grieving widow. You need to tell them to stop! They're making a mockery of Dad's funeral.'

Beside them, Seb quietly joins in with the singing, his foot tapping. Across the room, Bridget's wailing is now in tune.

Paula gulps. Is it *really* her responsibility? Couldn't someone else be in charge today? She can't stand confrontation at the best of times and this is . . . a lot. John's brothers have always terrified her, and when they get like this, they're even harder to restrain.

Tilly tuts. 'Come on, Mum, it's time to stop being so agreeable and meek!' She waves a finger with authority, as Paula nods meekly, agreeing. 'They don't get to do this at my dad's funeral! Dad didn't even like his brothers that much.'

'He didn't mind them,' Paula protests diplomatically, afraid someone might hear them through the din. 'And people seem to be enjoying it.' She waves at the crowd, who are variously dancing and singing along.

Paula eyes the room now, wondering about John's work colleagues at the IT consultancy. He worked there for twenty-five years, and not one of them has made an appearance today. She shakes her head at the injustice of everything. They were the ones who sent John on the trip to Austria for the conference. They were the ones who pushed when he said he didn't want to fly. They're the ones who suggested John drive the twenty-plus hours across Europe. Paula is here today because of them. John's *not* here today because of them.

Perhaps his colleagues were too ashamed to be here. Perhaps there's an internal investigation going on. Perhaps people are busy covering for his absence. Or perhaps John just wasn't particularly popular. In her more generous moments, Paula can understand some of those reasons.

How different might things have been if he'd taken a train or hired a car? Or if someone else had been driving? What would've happened if he'd just... not gone? How different things might've been. How the same they might have been.

She reaches again into her pocket, stroking the thin cardboard of the notebook cover. John's notebook, containing all of his secrets. All of *their* secrets. She's been carrying it around since she found it, like some kind of security blanket.

If he hadn't gone on that trip, at the very least, she wouldn't be here in this dim room, watching his three brothers murder one of the best songs of her generation.

The singing gets louder and Misha squeezes Paula's arm. 'You OK?' she asks for the hundredth time in a low voice and Paula nods as enthusiastically as she can. But she suddenly feels very emotional. Her daughter-in-law's affection has made her miss her own long-gone mum. She was always good in a crisis. She would've given Paula lots of cuddles and helped her figure out what the hell she was supposed to do. But she's dead now, too, and there's every chance she wouldn't have come anyway. She never much liked John. No one was good enough for her only daughter.

Beside her, Tilly's had just about enough of her uncles. 'That's it,' she says with determination, grabbing Paula by the arm. 'Come on.'

Misha and Seb watch as Paula is marched across the room. As they approach, Leonard spots them and trails off, missing his cue to harmonise. Tom eyes his sister-in-law furiously, and then pointedly gets louder singing the chorus.

Paula stares at each of them, dumbstruck, as Tilly tuts. 'Can you lot stop this?' she shouts, trying to be heard over the racket. Tom ignores her but Pete eyes her angrily.

'Why should we?' he replies coldly. Paula can feel eyes on them. Anyone who wasn't watching before, definitely is now.

'It's my dad's funeral!' Tilly yells and Pete glowers back.

'It's *my* little brother's funeral! We're *celebrating* him.'

Paula reaches for Tilly. 'Come on, sweetheart,' she murmurs, desperate to get away from the escalating horribleness. For a long moment, her daughter and brother-in-law glare hotly at one another, before Tilly turns away at last. As they walk away, Pete shouts something at their retreating backs. It is louder than the argument, louder than the karaoke, louder than the room's low conversations. Every single person hears his words – acquaintances, relatives, neighbours, bar staff.

'You don't deserve the twenty-one million! I deserved to win the lottery so much more than any of you!'

Paula feels her stomach drop right out of her. She turns in slow motion to stare at Pete. His face is red and twisted, he's panting lightly. She catches a few gasps from the room's occupants and whispers of *lottery* and *twenty-one million*. All eyes are on her. She feels Tilly take her arm. Her heart racing, she reaches for the notebook, squeezing it tightly.

'Let's get out of here, Mum,' her daughter says and her voice is shaking slightly. 'The sandwiches are all gone anyway.'

Somewhere in the faraway distance, Paula notes that John's secretary, Bridget, is still wailing, as loud as ever. And who could blame her?

5

'We've got a surprise for you, Mum.' Tilly plonks herself down in John's chair across from Paula, then waves at Seb across the kitchen. 'Haven't we, bro?'

Seb trots over, holding a glass of lemon squash like he is nine years old. Paula wonders if she should ask him if he's going to the dentist and paying his taxes like other grown-ups. Although it's quite possible her son's occasional part-time work for his friend's food truck doesn't earn him enough to reach the tax threshold.

'We think it'll really cheer you up.' Tilly's still speaking and her words start to sink in. A surprise? Oh goodness, no! No, thank you. Paula's never much enjoyed surprises and there have already been far too many in recent months. Her husband of thirty-three years heading off on a business trip to the Austrian Alps and dying in a freak car accident, for one.

Tilly regards her mother with worried eyes. 'Are you looking after yourself, Mum?' She leans in, her voice softer. 'Have you had a shower today?'

Paula feels defensive. 'I had a bath last night,' she says, wondering if it actually *was* last night. The days have all been blurring into one a bit lately. Maybe it was a few nights ago? She's definitely had at least two or three baths since the funeral two weeks ago. At *least*. Would it be too transparent to give herself a sniff?

Tilly disappears into the hallway, reappearing with a carrier bag. She pulls out a pink jumper with a flourish. She holds it up, smiling widely. 'What do you think?'

Paula blinks at her. 'You bought me a jumper?' She's genuinely touched. She can't remember the last time anyone bought her something for no reason or—

'Actually it's Misha's,' Tilly shrugs. 'But you can keep it. I nicked it this morning for you to wear during your surprise.'

Paula frowns. 'So the jumper isn't the surprise?'

Tilly shakes her head, looking mischievous. 'Nope!' She places the jumper on the table in front of Paula. 'It's your colour and I thought it would look nice. You've been wearing the same blouses on rotation for decades.' She catches Paula's expression and adds hastily, 'Not that they don't look lovely! They do! But I figured you might like to start making a few changes.' She checks her watch again, looking excited. 'Come on, Mum, put it on. It's high time we celebrated you.' She clucks happily, gesturing at the jumper on the table. When Paula doesn't react, her daughter leans in closer, her voice conspiratorially low. 'You're going to love the surprise.' She nods at Seb who looks a lot less certain.

'Um, Tills, are we sure—' She cuts him off with a full-wattage big-sister glare. This works – it's always worked – and Seb concedes, giving a petrified thumbs up.

'Come on, Mum,' Tilly instructs, standing up, still scowling at her brother. 'Grab your coat.'

'I don't want to go outside,' Paula says mildly, but with something approximating stubbornness.

Tilly sighs and re-takes her seat, *John's* seat. 'Mum, we're worried about you.' She pauses, then reaches for Paula's hand. 'You've barely left the house since Dad died. It's like you're sitting here, waiting for him to come home and tell you what to do next. The funeral was two weeks ago and you've barely said a word since.' She squeezes Paula's fingers. 'I think you're in a slump – which is understandable after everything you've been through – but you need to *do* something. You need to start making the most of your life and enjoying your money. I bet you haven't spent a single penny of it yet, have you?' She shakes her head. 'Frankly, you might as well have given it to the idiot uncles. At least they would've enjoyed spending it.'

'On iPads and whisky,' Seb adds in a murmur.

Paula doesn't say anything for a minute. And then she picks up the pink jumper and pulls it on over her head. It's too small on her, and tight around the neck. The colour is too bright. She suddenly feels very claustrophobic.

Tilly smiles widely. 'It looks lovely, Mum!' she tells her warmly, then nods decisively. 'You ready?'

'Yes,' Paula replies, trying to smile, though she feels sick with dread.

Tilly leads Paula and Seb through the hallway.

Paula's head spins as she grabs for her coat, immediately feeling for John's notebook in the pocket. She can't go anywhere without it. What if someone found it? Really, she should burn or shred it, but she can't quite bring herself to do it.

Tilly's hand is on the door handle. She looks abuzz. Where could they possibly be going? Her daughter's right that she's barely left the house lately, but the outside world seems so far away at the moment. She's aware of how disconnected she is, but is there anything so wrong with that? What's so important about connecting with the world anyway? The world is horrible.

Tilly leads her out the front door and into the bright sunshine. It takes a moment for Paula's eyes to adjust to the sunlight.

A sudden burst of light explodes in her face and for a moment, Paula is certain she's having a stroke. She tries to recall the signs one is meant to check for. There's an acronym she's supposed to remember, she's sure of that. Except she can't remember it. Is it the ABCs? No, that's airways, breathing and something else. She can't remember that either. FAST – that's it! Face, Arms, Speech and . . . what's the T? Telephone? Do people even *say* telephone anymore? They say phone, surely? But FASP doesn't roll off the tongue so easily.

But it's not a stroke at all. It's people holding cameras, and the flashes are going off in her face, not inside her brain.

'What's . . .' Paula doesn't understand. Did her children hire photographers to sit outside her house? Five of them? There are men shouting at her, calling her name. Across her front garden, she spots a familiar face. It's Amy! The nice lottery girl whose mum is also called Paula. She's standing by the gate, smiling nicely. Amy waves them over, beaming, as Paula wonders fearfully what is happening.

'Here's the woman of the hour!' Tilly shouts to the men, waving at her mother with pride as yet more camera flashes go off. 'This is my lovely mum. No one has ever deserved to win the lottery more than this hardworking lady right here.' Her grin gets even wider and more oblivious. 'She's won more than twenty million pounds and she's *still* planning to go back to work at her care home!'

Paula looks at her daughter, frozen with horror. She looks back at the scene before her, caught in the glare. This is a . . . press conference? Some kind of public announcement about the win?

It can't be. They wouldn't. Surely they wouldn't? It was humiliating enough that John's brothers told so many people at the funeral, but these are strangers . . .

This is *awful*.

Seb touches her arm, smiling gingerly. 'Are you OK, Mum? Is *this* OK?' he asks softly. When she doesn't respond he adds, 'I know this is a lot. I didn't realise it would be so . . . We thought it would be one or two . . .' His Adam's apple bobs a little. 'But it'll be fun, I promise. And, like Tills says, it's time to start celebrating your good luck and enjoying yourself. You deserve all this.' He swallows anxiously when Paula doesn't reply, then gestures at Amy and a makeshift podium across the garden. 'Come on, we're supposed to be standing over there.' The photographers hover around, waiting. 'It's just a few minutes of telling the journos all about your lottery win.' He smiles encouragingly. 'The pink jumper looks very nice.'

A few minutes of . . . telling journalists?! *All about the lottery win?*

Absolutely not. No. This can't happen.

She can't talk to all those people! She can't perform for them or tell them about the money. She can't deal with them asking questions about what she might buy or what she might do. Or about her dead husband.

She lets herself be moved towards the podium. Men start shouting questions at her, crowding closer, yelling louder. She reaches into her pocket without thinking and squeezes the notepad.

Help me, John!

'Paula! Over this way! Tell us what it's like to win all those millions!'

'Mrs Sheldon! Givvus a smile, eh? What did you buy first, eh?'

'Paula! Who was the first person you called when you got the news about your win?'

It was John, she doesn't say out loud. It was John she tried to call. Of course it was John. He didn't answer. Because he was dead.

She blinks again and again as the flashes continue in her face. They get closer. There's a man practically in her face, shouting her name, asking questions. She can feel his hot breath. She can smell his breakfast.

Tilly steps into the foray, forcing a laugh as she tells everyone to step back and give her mother a moment. Paula doesn't need a moment. She needs this to not be happening.

John would never have let this happen. He would've protected her from this. From this press conference. He would've taken care of things – he would've taken care of *her*. Paula pictures her husband's face now, his image filling her vision, furious at this intrusion. Livid with their children for doing this to her.

She can't do it. She breaks free of Seb's grip, turning on her heel. As she does so, the notebook spills out onto the ground at her feet. She stares at it, frozen, then glances up at the photographers, the fear plain on her face.

One of them leans down to retrieve it. 'Here, love, you dropped this—' he begins, but she's already pounced on it.

'Don't!' she shrieks, her voice almost unrecognisable. The flashes stop. Everyone is staring. She swipes for the notebook, shoving it back into her pocket. For a moment she pants, regarding the strangers with pure panic, as they stare back at her. 'It's nothing,' she adds, glancing at Tilly and Seb, who are watching her with shock. 'It's nothing!' she says it again. The flashes begin around her again.

Tilly's face is full of regret as she reaches for her mum, but Paula recoils. Fear, rage and horror pool in her belly as she turns away. She runs at full speed back the way she came, back towards the front door. She has to get away, away from the cameras, away from the questions, away from her children. Away from all of it. She throws herself inside, slamming the door behind her. She leans against it, breathing like she's run a marathon, checking her pocket again.

This is all wrong. The whole thing. All wrong.

What have they done?

6

'But Mum,' Tilly sighs down the phone line – she always sighs after saying *Mum* these days. 'We talked about it with Amy, the Lotto woman. At that meeting? She asked if we were happy to go public with the news, and we said yes.'

Paula removes the phone from her ear to stare at it with outrage. 'We?! I never did, Tilly! I never would have!' Over the airways, she swears she can hear her daughter pulling a face.

'OK, fine, I'm the one who said yes. But you were sitting right there when we talked about it. You didn't say a word! You definitely didn't disagree or say no.'

'Oh, Tilly!' Paula tuts. 'I thought you knew I wasn't listening. It was all too much that day. I thought the pair of you were just talking about – I don't know! – legal thingys and financial advisors.' She shakes her head. 'I couldn't get my head around any of it.'

She stares across the kitchen, feeling hard done by.

Tilly sighs again, but this time with genuine remorse. 'Oh God, Mum, I'm really sorry. I thought it would be fun, telling the world about your amazing good fortune. You've been through so much and I've been really worried, I just wanted you to be celebrated!' She pauses. 'And I didn't realise it would be such a frenzy. Amy said there would be one or two journos. I thought you'd get a nice picture taken and a sit-down chat with someone. I had no idea there would be so many of them and that they'd be in your face like that.' Tilly's voice sounds a bit wobbly. 'I'm an idiot. I just thought it might be exciting, and maybe encourage you to finally start spending some of it! Get you in the media! Give you a bit of a distraction from, y'know, losing Dad.' Paula feels herself softening as her daughter continues. 'And I wouldn't have done it, but everyone at the funeral heard about it from the uncles anyway. Amy said the papers had your name and details. I think multiple people leaked it, the bastards.' Paula takes a deep breath, thinking again of what she'd seen earlier on her Facebook page, what people were saying. Tilly continues, 'I am sorry, Mum, but I guess there's no way of getting the genie back in the bottle now. You've been in all the papers for the last two days.' Paula's heart hammers in her chest at her words, and Tilly quickly adds, 'Not, like, the front page or anything.' She pauses, listening to her wife speaking in the background. 'Misha says it's page two at the most.' She takes a deep breath, which sounds suspiciously like another sigh. 'I was trying to do the right thing and I messed up. You were in a funk, refusing to leave the house. We thought this might help pull you out of things.'

Except now Paula can't leave the house at all, can she? Because there are journalists in vans lined up out the front.

Behind her, Seb wanders in from the back garden.

Paula only sees her son once a week or so, when he comes foraging for food. He also – very generously – leaves a large pile of washing in the utility room for Paula every now and again. Though, disconcertingly, it is mostly T-shirts, with hardly any pants in the mix. Paula hopes her son is, at the very least, turning them inside out.

'Is that Tills on the phone?' he asks, loading up the toaster with four slices of her wholemeal Hovis. He takes a clean plate straight from the dishwasher, ignoring the rest. 'Are you talking about the famous Lotto winner who threw a strop, screamed at everyone over a notebook, then stormed away from her own press conference and went into hiding? She's all over the internet, y'know. TikTok loves it.'

He chuckles as a faint sigh can be heard coming from Paula's phone.

'Oh Seb! It's not funny,' Paula cries, scolding. 'It's a disaster. I feel like I'm in hiding from the mob or something. There are journalists calling me constantly, and those photographers are camped outside the house. I can't even pop to the Londis for a loaf of bread' – she pauses to look a little pointedly at Seb standing by the toaster – 'without someone shouting at me that I'm the "sad Lotto widow" and asking me for money.'

Her heart races thinking of the onslaught of messages, calls from unknown numbers and random emails she's been getting. Yesterday, when the Sainsbury's delivery driver knocked, she almost had a panic attack thinking of the cameras waiting out the front. It only took about forty seconds to open the door, grab plastic bags out of crates and slam it shut again, but it was enough for the photographers to start. She can still see the flashes when she shuts her eyes.

She frowns, thinking of the other man standing out there with them all. He didn't have a camera and didn't seem to be with the photographers. He stood a little away from the rest just staring intensely at the house. Paula didn't recognise him, but something about him and the way he stared at her was frightening.

She wonders if this is what it's like to be Sigourney Weaver. To be *famous*. Well, no, thank you! Not even if it meant having all that lovely hair.

Seb reaches into the fridge, retrieving butter and Nutella as Paula follows him around, wiping crumbs. 'Never mind the incessant messages I'm getting from every distant relative I've never heard of, needing to borrow some money.'

Seb grins through a mouthful of chocolate toast. 'Ah, don't take it all so seriously, Mum. The fuss will die down. I think you should totally embrace all this mayhem – go out there in your new pink jumper and pose for the cameras!' He sprays crumbs as he talks. 'Maybe giving them an interview would actually help shake off some of the intrigue, too. At the moment, everyone's wondering about this mysterious woman who tragically lost her husband in a freak accident and had this incredible fortune with the lottery win at the same time. C'mon, you have to admit, you'd want to hear her story, too.' He waves the hand free of toast. 'Tell the world about your amazing luck. Have some fun.'

Paula knows her children are just trying to help, but if they tell her to *have some fun* one more time, she'll have them both adopted.

'I've got to go,' Paula says into the phone, catching some small squawks of protest from Tilly. She hangs up anyway, sinking heavily into a nearby chair. She suddenly feels very tired. Very tired and very small.

How has her life come to this? A dead husband, twenty million in the bank, an adult son living in the shed, and endless days spent hiding away from the internet comment sections.

From the other side of the room, Seb shouts a goodbye through a mouthful of toast, half slamming the back door. It bounces open behind him on its hinges. He never closes it properly. It drives Paula round the bend, but she doesn't have the energy to stand up and close it this time. Not now. Instead, she picks up the laptop from the corner, sits at the table, and reopens Facebook. It has refreshed itself since this morning, but there are still so many comments about her. So many acquaintances and neighbours she's 'added' over the years, all writing about her lottery win, sharing the same links to the same newspaper stories.

She pauses over one familiar name. An old friend from school, Lily. They haven't spoken properly in maybe thirty years. Not since the early days of Paula's marriage when she'd just had Tilly. She fell out of touch with so many people around that time.

On her profile, Lily's shared a headline about the 'Lotto widow', captioning it with a not-so-cryptic, 'Not everyone gets what they deserve.'

The tone is oddly threatening and it makes Paula's heart beat faster. Why would she write something like that? What does Lily know? She thinks again of John's notebook.

She stands up abruptly, shutting the lid of the laptop and going to fetch her coat. She'll go to work, that's what she'll do. They've given her indefinite compassionate leave after John died, but she needs something to be normal again. She needs to be busy and occupied. She needs to stop reading comments online and staring at her phone as it rings, wondering who this strange number belongs to. And she needs to prove to Tilly that she's fine. That she's getting on with her life.

Paula pulls on her coat and reaches for the front door. As she does so, the doorbell goes. She pauses, her hand frozen in mid-air.

It will likely be the photographers again. Journalists wanting to ask her questions about John and the twenty-one million. The door goes again and after a moment, she opens it, blinking rapidly at the two burly men standing on her doorstep. They don't look like photographers.

'Hello?' Her voice wobbles with uncertainty.

The larger man clears his throat and speaks in a low, growly voice. 'We're here to see John.'

She stares at them. They stare back.

'John?' she echoes faintly, swallowing hard. The man nods, his head round and heavy-looking.

They don't know. They haven't heard. They must be the only people in the country who haven't seen the headlines.

Paula opens her mouth to explain and then closes it again.

This is the first time she's had to tell someone that John's dead since that awful, horrible day with her children. Tilly informed everyone else who needed to know, and then of course, the newspapers told everyone who didn't need to know.

Apart from these two strangers.

Still she says nothing and they wait, looking at her curiously. She tries to gather herself. She just has to say the words. John is dead. John has died. I'm afraid John had a terrible accident and is no longer with us. He is late. He is of the past. He is a goner.

'He's not . . . He's not . . .' she tries to find the words but what comes out is only . . . 'here. He's not . . . here.'

The man narrows his eyes at her. It's very clear she's lying. Behind him, the second man – not nearly so large but still intimidating – waves at the group of photographers scattered about the roadside. They've been watching the exchange with interest. 'What's all this about?' he asks.

'It's nothing,' Paula replies in a high voice and they stare at her again. 'It's just a . . . neighbour,' she adds quickly. 'They've just won . . . *The X Factor*.'

'*The X Factor* isn't on telly anymore,' the second man says, his voice suspicious. 'It ended in December 2018, unless you count the two spin-offs Simon Cowell aired in 2019, *The X Factor: Celebrity* and *The X Factor: The Band*.' The large man regards his companion with surprise.

'Oh, um,' Paula tries to think. 'Maybe it was one of the other shows then. Erm . . . *Pop Idol* maybe?'

The second man snorts with amusement. 'Lady, that show hasn't aired in—'

'Never mind that!' the large man interrupts impatiently. It's clear he's in charge. And not a fan of reality shows. He steps a little closer, his face pursed and full of menace. He raises a finger, pointing at Paula's face. 'Tell John that Craig was here.' He pauses, his eyes dark and frightening. 'And tell him we'll be back.'

Paula stares at them as they slowly walk away, heading for a black car parked badly a way down the road. She feels fear creep across her skin.

She's never heard of a Craig before, she's almost certain of it. Is he from John's snooker club? Maybe he's a work colleague or an old friend?

No, not a friend. There was nothing friendly about his demeanour.

Paula shivers and pulls her coat tighter around her as she considers his final words.

They're coming back.

7

Paula stares up at the familiar building, fighting the mix of feelings bubbling up in her chest. She's worked at the care home for close to fifteen years and it's mostly been a happy time, a place of solace.

There were hard times, of course. Many of the residents were difficult, or rude or in pain. And Paula had been a witness to an awful lot of loss over the years. It was natural when you were dealing with older people, but it didn't get any easier. At Christmas, they'd lost three residents in one week! Two of them, Vinnie and Floyd, were among her favourites, always joking and offering up sweets. The third – Handsy Harry, shudder – was less of a favourite, but still, it was very difficult dealing with so much death all the time.

You'd have thought she might've been better equipped when she got that call about John.

Either way, her years working here have mostly been good. Mostly happy. It was somewhere Paula felt safe and normal when things were hard. But it's starting to feel like she'll never feel safe or normal again. Not after everything that's happened.

Full of trepidation, Paula takes a deep breath and pushes open the glazed double doors. The familiar smell of the place hits her immediately, almost making her dizzy. It's a mixture of musty hospital scents and lavender perfume. Paula rather likes it.

Approaching the reception desk, the young man gives her a double take.

'*Paula?*' He can't hide his astonishment.

'Hello, Sonny,' Paula greets him shyly, feeling self-conscious.

'What are *you* doing here?' The receptionist gapes at her.

'I'm hoping I can come back to work,' she shrugs, still smiling.

'But you won . . .' Sonny waves his hands, then whispers the rest, '*You won twenty-one million!* I saw all the newspapers – you're loaded!' He chokes a little on the words. 'Don't tell me you'd come back to this dump when you've got all that money in the bank!'

Paula winces at the description of her work home as a *dump*. Sonny has only been here a year and it's been clear from day one that he didn't think much of the place.

She swallows. 'I've just had a bit of time off. I was always coming back.'

Sonny squints at her. 'Didn't your fella die, too? Or was that someone else?'

Paula raises her eyebrows. 'Er, no, I mean, yes. That was my . . . fella. My . . . John.'

Sonny clucks. 'Oh, that's a shame. He seemed . . .' – he searches for a word – 'all right.'

'Thank you,' Paula replies politely. 'Er, can I pop through to see Gary? I need to get my name back on the schedule and get my pass reinstated.'

Sonny makes an awkward face. 'I better see if he's available, eh?' He waves self-importantly at the visitor area in the corner. 'Have a seat. I'll call through, see if he can squeeze you in.'

Paula nods, thinking how her boss, Gary, is *always* available. He's usually in that office playing Solitaire and delighted by any kind of interruption. As Sonny picks up the phone, Paula turns away. For a moment, the sight of this familiar, grey foyer takes her breath away. It all feels like it's from a different time – a different life. She can picture John here, meeting her from work, turning up to surprise her. She can see him vividly, laughing with residents Vinnie and Floyd, then scolding Handsy Harry for getting, well, *handsy* with his wife.

'Paula!' Gary's voice brings her back to the now, booming happily from across the foyer. He is as purple-faced and jovial as ever. He approaches her, his arms outstretched in greeting. 'Sonny says you're coming back, is it true?' He doesn't wait for an answer. 'I thought there was no chance we'd ever see you again after your good fortune!' He beams and Paula wonders if he remembers her husband also died. He continues, oblivious, 'But if you're sure, well, thank Christ for that! I don't know how we've managed—'

He is interrupted by a loud bang behind them. The main double doors crash open and three men carrying equipment suddenly fill the small space.

'Hey! Paula Sheldon!' She starts at the sound of her name and is caught off guard by a flash in her face. It blinds her for a moment as the same voice shouts playfully, 'Lend us a million quid!'

Another person yells, 'Are you coming back to work despite your win, Paula?' as a third asks, 'Or are you here to donate a few quid to your old mates? Good headline either way, love!' There is another flash, and then another.

They must've followed her here.

Paula's heart gallops as Gary bundles her away into his office. He is shouting something to Sonny who is delightedly throwing himself in the way of the photographers. The voices fade as Gary slams his door. He regards her, his face even more purple. He looks angry. 'For God's sake,' he blusters, taking a seat across from her. 'Are those bastards following you around?'

'I'm sorry,' Paula murmurs, mortification flooding in as her vision returns. 'I got on a bus. I don't know how they . . . I didn't realise . . . I'm so sorry.'

'It's not your fault, Paula,' he sighs. 'But you do understand we can't have you back right now. Not with all this going on.' She sees him swallow hard. 'Of course, we can have a chat when it all calms down a bit, but we can't have this media circus coming into the care home. It's supposed to be a calm, peaceful place for our residents. Relatives would complain. Imagine if someone had seen that ruckus out there!'

Paula is nodding and she can't stop.

'I understand!' she gulps. 'Of course I do! I'm so sorry.' She's standing up and Gary's expression flickers with guilt.

'I'm sorry, Paula—' he begins and she holds up a hand.

'No, no, please!' she says, backing away. She grabs for the door handle and makes a run for the exit. Thankfully, there's no sign of the photographers, only Sonny, back behind reception looking very pleased with himself.

She speed-walks for the door, reaching it as Sonny calls out to her retreating back, 'It's great to have you back, Paula!'

Work isn't a safe place. Her home isn't a safe place. So where is?

8

When Paula gets back home, she sinks down into her regular chair at the kitchen table and stares across at the spot where John sits. Where he's supposed to be sitting. She does that until her hands stop shaking and her breathing slows.

These last eight weeks – hearing the news, getting the money, waiting so long for John's ashes, then having his funeral and the press conference – it's all gone by so quickly. So much has happened and yet Paula feels like no time has passed. It's too fast; it's all moving too quickly. And she feels no further along.

She picks up her phone and opens the banking app Tilly downloaded on there. She logs in and looks at the money. It's still sitting in her bog-standard current account – much to the chagrin of Tilly, and of the bank itself, who keep trying to get in touch. But even there, where the interest rate is nothing of note, the money is earning hundreds more each day – thousands every week. It is unfathomable. In a few months, Paula will earn more from just the interest than she ever has or probably ever could from her job at the care home. It makes her feel a little sick.

'Helloooo?' A woman's voice echoes around the small kitchen and Paula's head jerks up at the sound. It is so unexpected – so wholly out of place and out of whack with Paula's universe – that for a moment, she assumes she's fallen asleep. But no, a tall, glamorous blonde woman with enormous sunglasses and a deep tan is really standing there, by the ajar door, smiling widely. She has big, white, Hollywood teeth, and there's a tiny bit of lipstick on her incisor, but otherwise her make-up – thick as it is – is immaculate. She steps inside, moving forward with confidence to offer up a hand for Paula to shake. Her nails are long and pointy, and baby pink.

'Hi, there! You must be Paula Sheldon? I'm Tina Edwina Fletcher. Call me Teddy for short, babe.' The accent is thick with American vowels. Texan?

Paula gapes up at her, blinking at the outstretched hand. She hasn't been called babe in – well, ever, probably. She's the wrong generation for babe. The wrong sort of person. She has the wrong constitution for babe, if she's being honest.

'Are you . . .' Paula swallows hard, a little afraid. 'Are you a journalist? Because I'm not—'

The woman's hand retreats as she shakes her head. 'God, no!' She looks horrified, grimacing and showing off those suspiciously straight teeth. Her statement earrings jangle with the movement. 'It's nothing like that. Though I saw all those jackals outside, ugh! They must be driving you mad, babe!'

Paula continues to stare, wondering if this is how she is to die. Murdered at the hands of a nice-haired lunatic, because her grown-up son didn't shut the back door properly. Again.

She doesn't know where she went wrong with Seb. He was such a clever, intuitive child; the one at nursery looking after the other children; the one checking in with everyone over dinner; the one cuddling Tilly when she banged her knee. And now he's . . . this. When Paula was thirty, she was a fully formed human being, wasn't she? And now she'll be leaving him an orphan, he'll be even more of a hopeless case. She'll have to haunt him until he gets his act together.

The woman examines her pink nails. 'I'm actually here because I'm . . . well, shucks, I'm like you.' The maybe-Texan pauses, looking Paula in the eye. There is something about the way she says this. Something Paula doesn't like.

'Let me get you a cup of coffee and we'll talk,' she announces with authority, moving swiftly around the kitchen, finding teaspoons and Nescafé like she's been here a thousand times before.

'What do you mean you're like me?'

Paula takes Teddy in. She must only be forty-something, one of those WAG types you used to read so much about in the papers. She's striding around Paula's home in the tiniest of skirts, the hugest of sunglasses on her face, with a confidence Paula's never felt. Imagine having the backbone to wander into a stranger's kitchen, uninvited! Just because adult sons don't know how to close doors.

This woman is *nothing* like her.

Teddy turns at last to face Paula. 'I mean I won the lottery too, babe.' The kettle hisses furiously from the counter and Teddy picks it up, filling cups with steaming liquid. She stirs too quickly, sloshing brown water all over the counter. She doesn't notice. 'Not as much as you, mind.'

Paula barely takes in the words, wondering again about the accent. It no longer sounds Texan. Now it's more like . . . Boston, maybe? Like she's come straight from the set of some over-ambitious police – sorry, *cop* – drama.

Wait – did she just say she *won the lottery as well*?

The woman brings the mugs over to the table, taking John's seat across from Paula and smiling that lipstick-stained smile again.

'Set For Life. I won ten thousand a month for thirty years.' She sips the too-hot coffee without reacting. 'Like I said, nowhere near your winnings – just over twenty mill sterling, wasn't it, babe? – but it'll do me!' She laughs dryly. 'It's enough to make me very happy indeed.' She looks down at the tight, pink skirt she's wearing. 'You see this? Six grand it cost, if you can imagine such a thing! Believe me, I know it's dumb. But' – she shrugs – 'if I get carried away with my spending one month, I know I've got another windfall coming the next! I love it.'

Paula tries to take in Teddy's words. This woman . . . won the lottery, too? Is that possible?

Her head spins. She hasn't got her head around her own win – hers and John's – and now another lottery jackpotter is here, sitting in her kitchen, drinking her coffee.

Paula doesn't even drink coffee! She only has that instant stuff in the cupboard for the builders who are always due over to fix leaks and never turn up.

Paula shakes her head. What's she doing here? What is this? Some kind of strange welcome to the lottery club? An initiation? Perhaps it's something Tilly's arranged, to help Paula come to terms with her win?

And how is it possible on God's green earth that such a small amount of material cost this woman six *thousand* pounds?

'What have you done with your cash so far then, Paula babe?' Teddy is looking at her through dark, tinted lenses.

Paula can just about make out thick, clumpy, black eyelashes. She's giving Paula alarmingly intense eye contact. 'It's been a couple of months, right? You must be having an absolute blast. How much of it have you spent so far?' She glances around the kitchen, disapproval at its mediocrity clear in her expression.

'Spent?' Paula is still trying to get a grip on this conversation. 'I haven't spent anything.' She looks down at the watery coffee on the table before her. It's gone four o'clock. She *never* has caffeine this late in the day.

She takes a sip.

Paula finds herself explaining. 'I can't spend it. It feels obscene – wrong. It all feels wrong. I can't do it. I don't want it.'

Teddy immediately tuts. 'It's not wrong, babe! You've *earned* it.' She raises an eyebrow and Paula gets the feeling she means something more by this comment. She's never been terribly good with innuendos or double entendre. Gary at the care home says confusing things sometimes and the meals-on-wheels lady always has to explain the joke to Paula. Not that Paula understands the explanations particularly well either. What on earth is pegging anyway and what's it got to do with the royals?

Teddy leans across the table, almost dipping a boob in her coffee. She doesn't seem to notice. 'Seriously, you have to enjoy the money, Paula. What's the point, otherwise? What was the point of all that . . . effort?'

'Effort?' Paula echoes, shaking her head, still trying to make sense of all this.

Maybe she was right in the first place – the woman's mad. She'd have to be to spend six thousand pounds on a skirt.

And for goodness' sake, who is really called *Teddy* anyway? Only mad people and reality stars. 'Look, I don't want to appear rude' – she pauses, aware this is a silly thing to say to a stranger who has made herself at home in her kitchen – 'but who *are* you? What are you doing here? I don't understand what this is.'

Teddy sits back, smiling enigmatically. 'Well,' she begins, then pauses. 'Me and a friend are putting together a group of . . . like-minded women,' she explains in a lowered voice, elongating her vowels. 'We're both lottery winners who've . . . lost our husbands. We're thinking of calling ourselves – are you ready for this, babe? – The Lottery Winner Widows Club!' She pauses. 'And we want you to join.'

Paula gasps. 'Widows? You mean . . .? Oh my goodness, has your husband passed away as well?' Her brow furrows. 'I'm so sorry to hear that. I know all too well how very difficult—'

Teddy shrugs. 'Not dead, not officially. He's *missing*.' She does air-quotes around the word missing. 'He's been MIA for two years now. Since just after the win.' She winks at Paula through her sunglasses. 'If you catch my drift.' She leans back now, smirking. 'But you know exactly what I'm talking about, don't you?'

Paula definitely doesn't know exactly what she's talking about. Not even vaguely, actually.

'Um, Teddy' – it's hard to say that name without feeling very silly indeed – 'what exactly are you implying?'

Teddy picks up her coffee again, taking a very loud slurp and leaving bright red lipstick marks all along the rim. It'll have to go in the dishwasher more than once, Paula's sure of it. Maybe even three times. 'I'm not implying anything, babe,' the woman says at last, looking Paula in the eyes. She leans back, reaching for the enormous sunglasses and removing them at last. Paula see the woman's eyes for the first time, bright blue and framed by long black eyelashes. Teddy grins, suddenly looking more like a movie star than a WAG. 'I'm telling you straight. I killed my husband after we won the lottery.' She leaves a beat before adding the literal killer blow: 'Just like you did.'

9

'Paula?'

Paula's head shoots up, a bewildered expression on her face. 'I'm sorry, what was the question?'

The man sitting across from her peers over grandfatherly glasses that seem deliberately chosen to soften a sharp face. He gives her a small smile through thin lips. 'I was asking what you've found hardest since you lost John?'

Paula tries to hide a smile. Lost. *Lost!* So many people have described his death like that. As if he's gone on a long walk in the woods without Google Maps on his phone.

Paula knows exactly where he is. He's in plot fifty-three of a grave site, about twenty miles from here. It's near a church, but it isn't technically a church graveyard, more of a field. The official church graveyard has long since run out of space thanks to too many ancient graves with leaning stones, featuring inscriptions and engravings you can no longer read. So John's ashes are buried in the grave-field next door. Sort of like an overflow car park for the deceased.

'Um,' she hedges, sensing impatience from her children, sitting either side of her. 'I suppose . . .' – she searches for something that will satisfy the counsellor – 'sleeping! Yes, sleeping. Sleeping is very hard since I . . . *lost* John.'

The counsellor nods gravely as Tilly reaches for her mother's hand, squeezing it with sympathy.

It's true enough that Paula's found sleeping difficult. But she's always found sleeping quite difficult. If she really had to put a pin in the hardest part of all this, it would probably be making decisions. Were they always so impossible? Just trying to get dressed in the morning feels painful. Jeans feel inappropriate for a widow, as do leggings. A dress feels too frisky for a cloudy Tuesday morning of mourning, while skirts feel too formal. Today, Paula's opted for a dark blue blouse, with some cropped, tan trousers, but it took her nearly two hours to decide. She ummed and ahhed for an age over a knitted cardigan, but ended up leaving it by the front door. She regrets that now.

Even before all this, when she wasn't addled with confusing grief, Paula found choices quite burdensome. Even an everyday mundane choice of what to watch on telly had to fall to John.

John would've known the answer about the cardi. He was very good with decisions.

'A lot of people find that, Paula.' The counsellor is nodding kindly. 'And grief can look different for everyone. You've stopped working, am I right? How has that been?'

'Just temporarily!' she says quickly, thinking with horror of last week's aborted attempt at returning to the care home. She remembers Gary's face as he told her to go. It was so humiliating. 'I'm just on leave, just taking a little bit of time. I don't know when I'll go back. But I will.'

'They don't mind?'

Paula shakes her head. 'No, no!' she says quickly. 'They've been very nice. They said to just let them know when I'm ready to return.' She thinks again of Gary and his horror. His reference to her bringing with her a *media circus*.

'Sometimes getting back to your usual routine can be a comfort,' the counsellor nods wisely. 'But there's no right or wrong, Paula, so you should absolutely take your time with it. There's no rush, especially . . .' – he looks awkward but it's clear he knows. He reads the papers – 'given that you have some . . . er, financial security now. You have options. Take a beat to decide what you want.'

Paula doesn't answer and he widens his gaze to include Tilly and Seb, asking her children what they've most been struggling with. Paula desperately tries to focus on their answers.

And fails.

After all, how on earth is a person supposed to concentrate on their dead husband, or on family grief counselling with a therapist called Gerald, when a stranger just accused you of murdering said dead husband?

Fancy that woman accusing her of such a thing! It's absurd.

Paula replays Friday's incident in her head, mentally re-watching Teddy as she moved around her kitchen in her tiny six-thousand-pound skirt. She sees her nice hair swishing around those monster-sized sunglasses, as she oh-so-casually talked about Paula killing John.

Paula wonders what she should've done differently in the moment. Of course, she tried very hard to deny it. She tried to tell Teddy she didn't do it and never would. She explained how much she loved John – dearly loved him! – but the woman wasn't having any of it. She kept smirking dryly and winking, if you can imagine such a thing.

And what about the woman's own confession? About her missing husband? Could she really have murdered someone and buried them under the patio? It's impossible to picture that glamorous woman with the confusing American accent in her expensive skirt, holding a spade, covered in blood and dirt. Apart from anything else, it sounds like an awful lot of hard work. Since John died, Paula has been worrying a lot about mowing the grass in her garden. She can't imagine how she'd cope if she needed to dig a big hole for a body.

And why on earth would Teddy tell Paula?

After the woman left, Paula had attempted to do the right thing. For once, she'd made a quick decision, picking up the phone and calling the non-emergency police line. 999 felt too dramatic and Paula isn't the dramatic sort.

'Hello, can I take your name?' the woman began.

'Oh! Yes, my name is Paula and I'm—'

'Hello, Paula, can I ask where you're calling from, why you're calling, and whether this is regarding you or someone else?'

'Yes, of course!' she'd paused then, before adding, 'I've forgotten the questions, I'm afraid.'

'OK, Paula, where are you calling from?'

'My house. In Surrey. Do you need the postcode? My children get very frustrated when I don't give them a postcode straight away. They just want to put everything into Google Maps these days, don't they? But I'm not so good with the newer technology. Tilly keeps trying to help me with Face ID on my phone but it never seems to know who or what I am—'

The woman on the phone interrupted her at this point. 'Paula, are you able to raise your arms above your head and has your face dropped on one side at all?'

'Oh no, I'm not having a stroke. I'm just not very good on the phone. I actually did think I was having a stroke recently! But it was just camera flashes going off. I remembered the letters you're supposed to check for a stroke though. It's ABC, isn't it?'

'Paula, can I ask why you're calling?'

Paula held her breath for a minute. 'I'm not entirely sure how to explain this.'

'I understand, Paula, but don't worry, I've heard everything before, believe me. There's nothing you can say that would embarrass me.'

'Right. Well . . .' – she took a deep breath – 'someone came to my house just now. The name was Teddy, I think. Although – for goodness' sake – that wasn't her real name. It was . . . Oh, darn it, I'm afraid I can't remember. I'm useless with names, you know. I'm constantly getting my children's names wrong. You'd think I could tell the difference between them. They're awfully different.'

'Who's different? Teddy?'

'No, no, Seb and Tilly. My children. But I'm ringing about Teddy.'

'Is Teddy a real person or a cuddly toy?'

'Yes, a person. Sorry.'

'Take your time, Paula. What's happened to Teddy?'

'Oh yes' – she cleared her throat – 'Teddy – I think it was Teddy. I'm fairly certain that was the name – Teddy's won the lottery, like me—'

'You've won the lottery?'

'I didn't mean to say that. Please don't tell anyone! I wasn't going to tell a soul because my husband, John, he always said people would take advantage of us, but he was in a car accident and died a couple of months ago. Goodness, can it be that long? Time goes by so quickly, doesn't it? And it took us quite a long time to get his ashes shipped over. And his brothers got drunk at the funeral and told everyone about the money, and then Tilly thought it would be a good idea to hold a press conference—'

'A press conference?'

'I know! Can you imagine anyone thinking that would be sensible? For goodness' sake! But that's when I thought I was having my stroke. And it's not ABC, is it? It's FAST, I remember now because I looked up the T. I thought it meant telephone but apparently it means Time. Which doesn't make all that much sense to me, what do you think? Are you supposed to check what time it is? How does that help? Anyway, I think Amy from the lottery talked Tilly into it. The press conference, I mean.' She paused. 'I was very upset and overwhelmed, and I'm afraid I ran away. And now the internet won't stop talking about me, and my children are insisting I go to grief counselling with them.'

'It does sound like you need someone to talk to.'

'That's not why I'm ringing! The reason I'm ringing is this Teddy woman—'

'Teddy's a woman?'

'Yes! It's a funny name, isn't it? I'm glad you think so, too, I thought I was maybe just being a fuddy-duddy. Tilly thinks I can be a bit old-fashioned about things, but it *is* a funny name for a woman in her forties, isn't it?'

'Paula, are you sure you're not experiencing any symptoms of a stroke?'

'No, no, I'm fine. This isn't about me. It's about Teddy. So anyway, Teddy said she'd won the lottery, too, and that she'd . . . done something to her husband. I thought I'd better call the police but it didn't feel like something I should be bothering 999 about. It didn't sound like it had happened recently either, but goodness, who knows? Maybe I should've called the emergency number, but I do worry about tying up the line. They're always so stern about that kind of thing and I wouldn't want to get it wrong or be told off. I'm so sorry, I know I'm rambling. My husband, John, used to tell me off for waffling, but it feels like I've barely spoken since he died. Sometimes it's so hard to talk to the people closest to you, isn't it? To be honest with them? And now I can't shut up, holding you up when you have crimes to be solving. But I really thought I ought to ring the police. Have I done the right thing?'

The woman on the end of the line paused for what felt like a very, very long time before answering.

'Paula, you've called the NHS non-emergency number, 111, not the police, who are 101.'

The woman had kindly offered to transfer her, but Paula felt too silly. The conversation had illustrated just how absurd she would sound reporting such a bizarre encounter. After all, what was there to go on? A strange woman whose nickname Paula wasn't sure of – never mind recalling her real name – had claimed she'd murdered her missing husband two years ago. Even if they took her seriously – and they were much more likely to think she was a crackpot – there wasn't anything they could follow up on, was there?

Although . . . there was an address. She could give them that.

As she left her kitchen yesterday, Teddy had insisted Paula must come to meet her friend. The one other member of this group she said they wanted to form. The Lottery Winner

Widows Club. That's what she'd called them. She said they had two more women to approach. Women who'd all won the lottery, who all had dead husbands. She'd winked again at that point. Teddy seemed to be a big winker.

Paula hadn't been able to take it in. She still can't now. More lottery winners with dead husbands? Surely not?

Teddy had written down her address in the Surrey Hills, not too far away from Paula's home. She'd then given her a time and date. Tomorrow.

She didn't have the first idea what to say – what would anyone say? – so agreeing seemed the best way to get the woman to leave. Teddy made Paula promise faithfully several times that she would meet them there.

But of course she wouldn't go. Paula's grieving! And in hiding from the press! She's barely left the house since John died, hardly even left her bed. All she's done for weeks is 'Netflix and Chill' – as Seb used to say. Although the last time she said that in front of him he got all pale and said she was using that expression wrong and no one even says it anymore. Then he said she also uses the aubergine emoji all wrong. So who knows? Either way, she's not ready to face the world yet – never mind socialising with strangers. She needs the world at large to calm down a bit, to forget about her, and for her to process what's happened with John and the lottery win. No one could deny it's a lot, for goodness' sake!

So what would possibly possess her to go meet strangers in the middle of nowhere? Not just strangers – quite possibly *murderous* strangers! It would be ridiculous to go. Why would she even consider it?

Curiosity, maybe.

And maybe to ask where Teddy gets her hair done. After all, it was *very* shiny and swishy – like a Timotei advert! – but that might just be an American thing. They all have nice hair on the Netflix shows she 'chills' with.

'Are you still with us, Paula?' The counsellor is smiling and his eyes are soft on hers. But Paula can see irritation twitching the corners of his mouth.

She's failing at grief counselling.

'Yes!' she replies too loudly, her face reddening. 'Sorry.'

'Don't be sorry,' he says nicely. 'Can you share with us what was going through your head?'

'Er . . .' She reaches for an answer. She can't exactly tell them that she was wondering whether to meet up with a woman with a silly name and nice hair and a confusing accent, so she could ask said woman's friend if she also murdered her husband.

Instead, she offers, 'Just . . . John. I was thinking about John.'

The three of them stare at her and it is clear from the crackly silence that they don't believe her.

The counsellor leans forward, his glasses sliding down his nose. 'Have you ever lost anyone before, Paula? What did grief look like for you previously?'

Paula looks down at her hands. 'I lost my mum and dad,' she mumbles at last. 'Quite a long time ago now. My dad first, then Mum not so long after, too. But that was fifteen years ago now. Ages ago.' She glances up anxiously at Tilly and Seb. 'But we weren't close, so it wasn't . . . I didn't . . . It wasn't anything like it's been for us since John died.'

'We never even met our grandparents,' Tilly adds helpfully. 'They weren't very nice to Mum, were they?' Paula looks away.

'We don't need people in our life like that!' Seb says defiantly and Paula's heart squeezes at his loyalty.

The counsellor asks Tilly and Seb about their own experiences of loss, and Seb starts to talk about their cat, Moby. Paula tries hard to listen as her son describes the small rescue centre they got her from, and how Moby spent the first six months hissing at anyone who tried to get close.

It's all very sweet, but Paula can only manage a few minutes of focus before her thoughts return to Teddy and the others. To these women she hasn't met. That she *could* meet.

But of course she won't! She won't go and see them tomorrow. It's ridiculous.

But what if she did? There is something gnawing away in Paula's stomach, a part of her that wants to go, that's *compelling* her to go and see Teddy again. To meet these women, to join this club.

Because maybe they might understand? How strange if they really were both lottery winners like her? What if they really had both lost their partners?

Maybe they'd understand. Maybe she could talk to them. Instead of blurting speeches down the phone to strangers on the NHS advice line.

She gives herself a small shake. Teddy was probably joking. Surely she was playing a prank. Paula will probably turn up at this random address tomorrow and find nobody there. It's just that American sense of humour. Those sitcoms Tilly was always watching as a teenager, they were full of . . . eh, women saying they'd killed their husbands? Oh, never mind.

'Mum?'

It's hardly likely to be true anyway. Teddy didn't really seem like the type to murder her husband. Not that Paula knows what *type* that would be. She's never met any murderers before. That she knows of. Because you just don't know what people might be hiding, do you? She's hidden enough over the years. John has too. Just look at the notebook.

She looks down at her hands again now, taking in the small bones moving under the thin skin. Maybe she would go. Just to see. Just to—

'*Mum?*' Paula jerks her head up, glancing anxiously around at her children. Tilly is looking at her penetratingly. With expectation. Seb is staring at her, too. But his expression is blank. He gets the same look on his face when he's playing those video games for hours on end. Paula's eyes travel up to the permanent dent in his unwashed hair, where a headset sits for days on end.

'Mum,' Tilly repeats, a hint of impatience. 'Gerald asked you a question.'

She frowns. Gerald? Who on earth— Ah, right, of course. She looks at the grief counsellor.

'Sorry! Just . . . you know, thinking about . . . John. Again.'

He smiles nicely. 'I was just saying, Paula, am I right in thinking you work as a carer? At a care home?' She nods vaguely as he continues. 'You must be around quite a bit of loss there?' She regards him blankly and then nods again, thinking of the three residents Vinnie, Floyd and Handsy Harry, all dying at the same time, at Christmas four months ago. How much more awful it must've been for their families, losing someone at that time of year. Gerald continues after a second, 'But being around loss doesn't mean you're equipped to deal with this on your own. Grief can come in many forms—'

'Grief has tentacles!' Tilly practically shouts.

Gerald ignores her. 'And it can make you feel very isolated sometimes, but you're not alone in any of this. You've got Tilly and Seth here.' Seb murmurs a name correction but the grief counsellor ignores him, too. 'As we continue to work together in these sessions, Paula, I want you to have a think about what you'd like to gain as a family from our sessions. And about what you think might help you process everything you've been through.' He pauses. 'It can really help to speak to someone like me, someone with an outside perspective.'

She nods at him, suddenly feeling brave.

She's made a decision. An actual decision!

She *is* going to speak to someone outside of her situation. She's going to see Teddy again and meet the mysterious other member of The Lottery Winner Widows Club. She's going to go. She's really going to go.

Tomorrow.

Maybe they'll understand. *Imagine* if they understood.

10

Paula takes the bus to meet Teddy, the smell of someone's curry following her from stop to stop. It's a pungent reminder that the twenty-one million currently burning a hole in her purse could buy her way off of public transport forever.

Not literally in her purse, of course.

In her purse she has only her bus pass, an old photo of Tilly and Seb aged five and three, and a handful of pound coins.

John always took care of their finances, especially when things got difficult and mortgages had to be taken out. So all their cards and accounts were in his name. After he died, Tilly spent a long time on the phone with the bank, getting things reissued for Paula, and it still gives her a jolt, seeing the name *Mrs P. Sheldon* printed there in that lumpy lettering. Despite that, she can't bring herself to use the card – she can't even bring herself to hold it. Not when she knows what it represents. All that money in one place! Twenty-one million pounds sitting on that little bit of plastic inside her pocket. It feels too frightening, like too much of a risk to have it with her. So the card stays at home, sitting there on her living room dresser, looking at her reproachfully.

What would it be like to splash out on a taxi, Paula wonders. What would it be like not to have to think about bus schedules and bus smells? To not have to check Google Maps over and over, anxiously waiting for the right place to get off? How would it feel to be reclining in the back seat of some kind of fancy saloon car right now, the feel of dark leather against her bottom? How nice it would be to escape this stale curry air, to have the window open a little. To feel cool wind on her face.

But not so much, of course, that it messes up her carefully arranged hair. It took Paula forty-five minutes to get it *just so* this morning, and it's thin enough already without being flattened by the air outside.

She wonders again what shampoo and conditioner Teddy uses.

A taxi would be nice, but Paula can't, not yet. She can't remember ever taking such a liberty, enjoying such a luxury. She doesn't feel worthy of it.

She glances down at her lap, where a slip of paper sits. She reads it again, though the words themselves are meaningless. It's the address Teddy gave her, written in the woman's sloping handwriting. Paula wonders about her again, feeling nervous. The woman is so dry. So American. So relaxed about murdering people.

Maybe going isn't the right decision after all. She felt so sure of herself after the therapy session yesterday – not that she shared it with the counsellor or her family.

Why *didn't* she tell Tilly or Seb about Teddy? Or about today's trip? Tilly, in particular, has been very worried about Paula's refusal to leave the house in recent weeks. She'd probably be delighted to see her finally getting out and about.

But Paula finds herself clamming up every time Tilly asks if everything's OK. Everything is obviously *not* OK – her life and her world have been turned upside down – but she can't tell her daughter that. She can't tell her the truth about how she feels or what she feels. Sometimes it's too hard to say these things to yourself, never mind anyone else. And Tilly has always been such a worrier, so overprotective. Of course her daughter means well, but it can feel a bit... claustrophobic. Especially since John died. Sometimes it feels like Tilly is the mum, not Paula. It feels like there isn't any room for Paula to think or speak when Tilly is already crowding in to anticipate her every mood.

She thinks again of how much she talked to the 111 operator. It was so much easier to speak to that stranger on the phone than to her own children. There's something wrong with that. With her.

If she was very honest with herself, a small part of her feels quite excited about having this secret. About this private new thing her family don't know about, strange as it all is. Paula's always given so much of herself over to her family, she wants this to be something just for her. She doesn't *want* them to know.

'Oh!' Paula leaps up, realising where they are. 'Excuse me, please,' she adds to the tall man beside her, who sat in the seat next to her despite the bus being empty.

She catches a loud tut floating over from the driver as she rings the bell one too many times and runs for the door. After all that obsessive map checking, she almost missed her stop. Too busy thinking about whether this is a good idea and whether Teddy's glossy hair is just the result of good genes.

Off the curry bus, Paula breathes properly at last, steeling herself for the twenty-minute walk. She spends the entire time staring down at her plimsolls, trying to work out how old they are. Has it been five years since she and John went to Clarks?

Probably more like fifteen. They're still comfortable enough – Paula does a lot of walking, especially with her job – but she has so much money now. Maybe she could buy an even more comfortable pair? Trainers and a taxi – goodness, it's a whole new world she's considering.

She is almost at her destination before Paula notices the overindulgent amount of greenery all around her. She's somewhere called Godalming in the Surrey Hills. It's an area that, despite having lived in Surrey her entire adult life, Paula has no knowledge of whatsoever. But it is undeniably beautiful.

Huge houses sit way back from the road, behind large black gates, surrounded by lush gardens. As she gets closer to the address, she can see only fields and high fences. Healthy-looking trees line the quiet, well-kept road. Paula can't see a single pothole. She wonders about the council tax.

She spots a pair of brass gates, which open magically on her approach. Paula walks through and down an extensive driveway, feeling more than a little dazzled. A humungous red-bricked mansion comes into sight, surrounded on all sides by endless green spaces; cultivated hedges, flower gardens, water features. Paula gasps at the sight of an enormous fountain surrounded by hundreds – thousands! – of perfectly positioned peonies. She and John once had a small pond in their garden, and it got so grimy, so fast. Moby the cat kept falling in trying to catch wildlife. They had to get someone to fill it in. *This* fountain looks like it's cleaned every day. The water is clear and algae-free. Untouched by creatures. It's like something straight off a film set.

This is where Teddy lives? Goodness gracious. It's beyond anything Paula could've imagined.

In the distance, she spots a small group of people gathered near what Paula assumes must be the front door. But it's grander than any front door she's ever seen. Apart from on that show, *Selling Sunset*. She and Seb watch the series together, and Paula likes it a lot, but she can't imagine how they get away with wearing those clothes to work. She tries to imagine how Gary would react if she came into the care home wearing one of those 'bodycon dresses'. It would've finished off residents Vinnie, Floyd and Handsy Harry long before Christmas.

Two women and a young man stand together in a loose huddle, a boisterous young dog circling them all at speed. As Paula approaches, she spots Teddy, taller than the rest, her hair still glorious, shimmering down her back.

She seems to be mediating some kind of argument between the man and an older woman who must be in her eighties. She's waving her hands in the air as he nervously pushes back gelled hair.

The raised voices reach her. 'I don't care what your rules say; she's coming in with us.' This is Teddy, speaking calmly now in her un-pin-downable accent. It sounds Southern again now.

The older woman is cackling, her fury full of mirth. 'Do you know how much collective wealth we have, Joseph?' She grins as she says this, enjoying the shock on the man's face. Across the gravel, she clocks Paula and shrieks, 'And that number just shot up by twenty-one million pounds!' She opens her arms in Paula's direction. 'Over here! Welcome, Paula!'

The dog barks happily.

'Um, hello?' Paula calls back, a lump forming in her throat. This is all . . . a lot. The gigantic house, the new people, a barking dog, everyone shouting, the lack of potholes. Paula's strength and resolve are both deserting her.

'Join us,' calls the older lady, oblivious to Paula's impulse to run. 'I'm Audrey Swift! That's Swift like the singer, but we're not related, so don't ask me for an autograph or we'll have *bad blood*.' She eyeballs Paula, waiting for an acknowledgement.

Paula stares at her, taking in the octogenarian. The woman is short and little, but vibrating with energy. As are her clothes. They're bright and floral, layered on with abandon. There are sweaters on top of shirts, on top of T-shirts, with a cardigan over the rest and a marbled scarf wrapped around Audrey's neck.

'Audrey Swift, like the singer, but not like the singer,' Paula repeats back to the older woman who looks miffed.

'I thought that was funny,' she mutters, then smiles brightly, throwing herself forward, scarf flapping excitedly in the wind. She folds herself into Paula for a hug and squeezes tightly. 'I'm *so* thrilled to meet you!' she murmurs as Paula freezes in the embrace.

'And this is Joseph,' Teddy calls out, pointing at the boy with gelled hair. 'We're just having a conversation about whether the dog can join us in the house or not.'

Audrey releases Paula at last, turning back to the argument as Teddy continues, 'Joseph, babe, you realise you're in violation of the human rights convention?' Her voice is dangerous. 'Section 48, subsection 8A. Would you like me to quote it to you, or shall we call your boss and I can quote it to him directly?'

Joseph pales, then sighs. 'Fine. You can take the dog inside. But please, please, please, don't let him touch anything?'

Audrey frowns. 'She's a she. And she can do what she likes. She's her own person.' On cue, the small scruffy creature ruffs with delight, then trots off towards the fountain to pee, bottom waving proudly in the air.

Joseph ignores this, turning his attention to Paula, his expression smooth. He hands her an A3-sized glossy pamphlet, clearing his throat. 'This is one of Surrey's finest rural estates,' he begins in a less whiny voice, and Paula stares at his hands, wondering if he gets a regular manicure. Surely no one naturally has hands so soft and pretty? The boy continues, 'The property is over twelve thousand square feet. It's surrounded by another sixty acres of gardens and woodland.' He pauses. 'And of course there's a maze.'

'A maze?' Paula repeats blankly.

'Obviously,' Audrey calls cheerfully from the back.

'The house is Victorian,' he continues, 'Grade II listed, but there is planning permission already granted for more developments by the south lake. Though the inside has all been done to a high standard. Sympathetic reno.'

'Reno?' Paula asks in a daze, wondering why he's directing all of this at her.

'It's posh white British boy for *renovation*,' Teddy explains.

The posh white British boy ignores this. 'There are also three staff cottages down that way.' He points towards a small lane Paula hadn't noticed, off to the right of the main house. 'The tennis courts and outdoor pool are also down there. There's another pool inside, where you'll find a sauna and steam room. In the basement, there's a fully equipped gym and a cinema room with a thirty-foot-wide screen.'

Paula gapes at him. What on earth is happening? Why is this man telling her about the house? Why was there a debate about whether the dog could come in? Has Teddy hired him to show her round for some reason? Is that what rich people do? Pay people to show off their mansions? She'd always suspected wealthy people were somehow a whole different species, but this is . . . unexpected.

Audrey circles another arm around Paula's shoulders but directs herself at the boy. 'We'll take it from here then, Joseph,' she says smoothly, shooing him away.

He takes a second, eyeing the dog coolly, but inevitably admits defeat. 'I'll leave you all to have a look around then. Any questions, let me know. I'll be out here.'

He wanders off in the direction of an outrageously shiny, electric-blue Range Rover, only pausing briefly to shout at the four of them about an EPC rating, as they move away en masse.

'What was all that guff about Section 48, subsection 8A of the human rights convention?' Audrey asks Teddy, while cackling to herself as she grabs for the end of her scarf, trying to get it under control.

'Made it up,' Teddy says smoothly, pushing her sunglasses up onto her head. 'It worked didn't it?'

'What's . . . happening?' Paula stares down at the brochure in her hand, eyeing the shiny pictures of this red-bricked castle before her. The name *Savills* is printed in a distinctive yellow at the top. 'Why am I here?'

Audrey gives her a squeeze. She's so soft inside the layers of cardigan. 'This lovely house here is for sale. We thought you might be looking to move.' She cackles again and you can hear years of smoking in the sound.

'What?' Paula stops dead, a metre from the front door, gravel kicking up at her feet.

Teddy turns to her, poker-faced. 'Like I told you the other day, it's time you started enjoying your win and having a little fun with it,' she says firmly, removing the sunglasses completely now and waving them at Paula. 'We thought taking a look around a little country manor might be a good place to start.'

Paula stares at her, wondering where to begin. Perhaps with the *little* part. 'So wait,' she stutters, 'this doesn't belong to one of you?' She glances between Audrey and Teddy.

'Oh lordy, no!' Teddy sounds more American when she's amused. 'I'm more of a city girl. I have a penthouse apartment in West London and a house in New York.'

Audrey puffs out her chest. 'I have a castle in Scotland, but it wasn't lottery money. It's been in my family for generations. The money I won just let me finally install central heating.' She pauses, hugging herself. 'It's been a godsend, I can tell you.'

Paula's head is spinning and she's fighting another impulse to make a run for it.

A house? For her? *This* house? This gigantic, listed Victorian estate with a *maze and servant cottages*? It's absurd. Who *are* these women?

And who would mow the grass?

Audrey loops an overly affectionate arm through hers. 'Don't be alarmed, my darling. Come on, I know you're going to love it.' The older woman leads her through the door, oblivious to Paula's distress. Or maybe just ignoring it.

'Pretty nice, huh?' Teddy's distinctive voice follows them into the entrance, but Paula's transition lenses have made everything dark. It takes a few more seconds to adjust and suddenly she's greeted by the hugest entrance hall she's ever seen. And Paula recently visited Guildford Cathedral.

'Oh, *my* goodness me!' She is horrified. For her? This is ridiculous!

The dog ruffs at their feet, bouncing around the cavernous room with delight. She pauses to scratch herself, sending hair flying over expensive-looking furniture. Wood panelling lines the walls, high ceilings drip with crystal chandeliers. Ornate mirrors line one wall, with floor-to-ceiling windows covering the other.

It takes Paula's breath away.

'This is so big!' she gasps, studying the brochure in her hand. 'There are *turrets*, for the love of God.'

Teddy tuts playfully, flicking perfect hair off her shoulders. 'It's only got six bedrooms.'

'*Six* bedrooms!' Paula shakes her head. 'Why on earth would I need six bedrooms?'

Audrey reaches for her hand, giving her a squeeze. 'To accommodate us when we're here! We can take it in turns to visit each other!'

Paula doesn't know how to respond. They've only just met, why would they visit one another? This is all so bizarre, she can't think or speak.

They wander through to a grand living room. Huge white sofas fill the room, facing an enormous fireplace. Floor-to-ceiling bookcases cover one side of the room, full of novels with suspiciously perfect spines.

'This is actually just the snug,' Teddy comments disinterestedly. She gestures with her sunglasses. 'The main living room is through there.' Paula follows her dumbly, focusing on the American's latest tiny skirt and wondering how much it cost.

A thought occurs to her. If a tiny bit of skirt can cost six thousand pounds, then . . . 'How much is it?' she asks, stopping dead before a painting and looking up at the mammoth landscape. It's twice the size of her.

'The picture?' Audrey asks, and Paula wants to laugh.

'This . . . place.' House seems like the wrong word for such an enormous property. 'How much does it cost?'

Teddy takes the brochure from her hand though the price isn't listed. 'They want eighteen million—'

Paula feels faint. 'Eighteen million? But that's . . . That's most of the money I won.'

Teddy laughs dryly. 'Oh hardly. You could definitely get it for fifteen.' She cocks her head. 'This is a steal. There's an apartment near mine in Knightsbridge that's currently on the market for eighty million pounds sterling.'

Paula feels faint. 'Eighty? As in . . . eight . . . zero?'

Audrey touches her arm gently. She smells like something floral. It is reviving. 'If you bought this place, you'd still have a few million left over as walking around money! That's still enough to get a few nice extras for yourself.' She brightens, her cheeks pink. 'Maybe a yacht!'

'Look, babe,' Teddy starts walking, and Paula follows as they move from room to room, 'this is what they call the honeymoon stage of sudden wealth, and you should goddamn enjoy it! We already talked about this. You *earned* it.'

There's that look again.

They fall silent, walking through the house – all eighteen million pounds' worth of it – in respectful silence. Teddy occasionally announces information from the floorplan, adding to the feeling that they are in some kind of museum.

'This is the turret sitting area,' she casually explains. Then, a few minutes later, 'Here's the spa.' Followed, oddly, by, 'Oh look, the chapel. The *former* chapel, I mean. In case anyone fancies getting married. Or re-married, I should say.' This elicits a huge peal of laughter from Audrey.

It takes them over an hour to finish the tour of the main house, and Teddy suggests in a far too casual tone that they check out the gardener's cottage, followed by the stable block. The four of them head out of a back entrance, passing through the largest utility room Paula's ever seen. As they make their way slowly down a path, moving to a soundtrack of bird song and dog yipping, Audrey once again takes Paula's arm. 'Twenty million, eh, my darling?' she says conversationally, thoughtlessly fiddling with her scarf. 'That's a lot of money.'

Paula sighs her acknowledgement, unsure how to feel about all this touching. She hasn't been touched so much in years, never mind by a stranger. Audrey seems to be a woman who touches everyone, always holding someone's arm or hand, always hugging and reaching for you, always using people's names. She is an excessively affectionate person. Paula finds it . . . unnerving.

The older woman continues, 'I'm actually the lottery loser of the three of us. I only won the Thunderball.' She giggles and her lovely wrinkled face creases into familiar laughter lines. 'All five numbers, plus the Thunderball wins you five hundred thousand! I'm practically a pauper in this trio.' She shrieks and Paula swallows hard. 'Luckily, darling, I already had money – the Swift family castle I mentioned, you remember?' Paula nods solemnly as Audrey grins cheekily. 'So you needn't worry about me keeping up. I can holiday in the Bahamas with the best of 'em.'

Paula turns to Teddy, who falls into step with her and Audrey. 'And Teddy won Set For Life?' she confirms, remembering their conversation in her kitchen. 'Ten thousand pounds a month for life.' For some reason, the statement makes Audrey cackle again. It turns into a cough and she stops to pound on her own chest, releasing some old tar build-up. 'Is that what Teddy told you?' She cackles again.

Teddy looks on coolly. 'I didn't want to frighten our new friend,' she says conversationally, examining her perfect pink nails.

'Frighten me?' Paula asks, thinking of how casually Teddy had spoken of murder during their first encounter.

Audrey is still laughing that filthy laugh. 'Teddy didn't win Set For Life, she won the . . .' She pauses, looking around herself with wide, furtive eyes as if people might hear. She hisses the next part, 'She won the *Powerball*.'

The way Audrey says this, it's clear to Paula this is meant to be a magic word. But she hasn't got the first idea what it connotes. Powerball sounds like some kind of laundry detergent.

At her blank expression, Teddy gives her a hard stare. 'Powerball? It's the American lottery?' She waves at herself. 'You didn't notice the accent? Or the white teeth?' She flashes them. Audrey removes her dentures and waves them at Teddy, 'Thesh Britishhh teeth are whitesh, too!'

Teddy gives her a withering glance then turns back to Paula. 'All I'm saying is that I'm not from the UK. I'm not even *allowed* to win the Lotto over here. You really should've figured that out. It's a good job we're not a group of detectives.'

Paula feels a surge of defensiveness. 'Well, you might've been born here! Or . . . Or you might've become a British citizen.' She trails off. 'So wait, how much *did* you win?'

Audrey hops excitedly from foot to foot, waiting for Teddy's reply. It takes her too long and the older woman answers for her, 'She won eight hundred million dollars!'

Teddy shrugs. 'Actually, it was a little over 774 million bucks.'

Paula feels the air vacate her lungs. 'Eight hundred million?' she gasps. It is an impossible figure. Impossible to fathom, never mind spend. No wonder Teddy spent six thousand pounds on a skirt. Why not six hundred thousand pounds? Why not six million? It would be a drop in the ocean of what she won.

Paula looks back at the huge red house in the distance. A mere eighteen million pounds. It must feel like chicken feed to Teddy.

'See, now, Audrey?' Teddy tuts, using her sunglasses to gesture. 'You've scared Paula.'

The dog barks.

'No, I'm not scared, I'm . . . fine,' Paula says faintly, feeling admittedly very scared. She pats her coat pocket, where she's still carrying around John's notebook.

Audrey chuckles and retakes her arm, leading the group down a path to a charming little cottage with its own white picket-fenced garden.

'Oh, isn't that lovely?' Paula says genuinely, taking in the sweet building before her. They make their way up a garden path flanked by hydrangeas, up to a country cottage door surrounded by white, pink and yellow roses. It's undeniably magical. 'This is part of the estate?'

Teddy nods, her nose inside the brochure. 'This would be for the house staff. It's a two bed.'

Paula shakes her head. 'I don't need staff.' She shakes her head again. 'I don't need a big house. I definitely don't need sixty acres! How would I even get around the grounds?'

Audrey looks excited. 'You could get yourself a little mobility scooter?'

'A scooter?' Paula is horrified. 'I'm only sixty-one!'

Audrey smiles, looking amused. 'You're being awfully uncooperative, Paula.'

Paula stares at her, feeling the edge of something she hasn't felt in such a long time: anger. She takes in her surroundings again; the endless greenery, the ostentatious wealth. It's like she's stepped through a magical portal-wardrobe into rich-people Narnia, and these women are acting like talking fauns and friendly lions are the norm.

'You should buy it!' Teddy shrugs, fiddling with a diamond bracelet on her wrist that probably cost thousands – tens of thousands! Paula imagines Teddy all in white now, wearing a twinkling tiara like the Snow Queen. She is – they both are – a whole different species. They have no idea who Paula is. They have nothing in common.

'No!' she says sharply, much more sharply than she'd intended. They're trying to take this decision away from her and she won't let them. She won't have it.

John's face suddenly fills her vision. She pictures him here, with her, viewing this ridiculous house. Then she pictures him dead in his car, covered in blood.

This should be her decision and these women are trying to force it. 'No, *thank you*,' she adds firmly.

Audrey and Teddy seem unfazed by her emotional reaction. 'Well,' Teddy says, 'if you don't want a mansion, what *do* you want?'

Paula considers this question as they return to the main house, her anger draining away. They pass across ornate floors that the dog takes a moment to wee on. For a while, she allows herself to imagine spending some of this money. Not just on small things like shoes and taxis, but on something real. What would she buy if she had no choice but to spend it?

She thinks of the bus that brought her here and the wait she'll have at a bus stop for it to take her home again. She thinks of that curry smell and the man who squeezed his rear end into the seat beside her. And she thinks of how he also smelled like food. Then Paula thinks of how she'd started to wonder if it was actually her who smelled.

John was the only one who ever drove – though she's had her licence all this time. For thirty-three years, he always had sensible cars – a Peugeot, a Volvo, a Ford Mondeo. She liked that last one, that Ford, but goodness knows it was now a total wreck. 'Unsalvageable' and 'mangled', the report she'd received read. Which was not a very nice image for Paula.

Across the hall, Audrey and Teddy debate the authenticity of another large painting by the front door.

'A car,' Paula whispers entirely to herself. 'I'd buy a car. I *want* to buy a car.' A feeling of excitement balloons in her chest, making her feel momentarily light-headed. She floats out of the mansion and into the bright sunlight, feeling heady and alive for the first time in a long time.

And it is only as Audrey gathers her up in an embrace to say their goodbyes, getting her scarf caught on Paula's glasses, that she realises she hasn't had a chance to ask Teddy about that other thing. About that other *big* thing.

She needs to know whether this new acquaintance with the American accent and the shiny hair really meant it. If she was telling the truth when she said she and Audrey had both killed their husbands.

11

The next morning, Paula is more than a little alarmed to find Audrey and Teddy waiting on her doorstep.

'We're going on a recruitment drive,' Teddy tells her cheerfully without a hello. There are new sunglasses on her head today. The leopard-print frames match the print on her low-cut top. Audrey bundles past Paula and into her hallway, 'Grab your coat, my darling, it's chilly out there today.' She doesn't wait for Paula to follow instructions, instead locating the coats cupboard and helping herself to the nearest hanging jacket. Audrey herself seems to be wearing two coats – as well as her signature flowing scarf.

'Are these the keys for your front door?' Audrey calls now, picking up a set by the door and herding a nodding Paula out into the front garden.

'Where are we going?' Paula asks dumbly, as Audrey helps her into the jacket. It's huge on her and she wonders whether to mention that it belongs to her son, Seb.

'I told you,' Teddy replies coolly, running long fingernails through blonde hair. 'We're recruiting.'

'Recruiting for what?' Paula shakes her head, following Teddy down the path. She scans the road. At least there are no photographers outside today.

Teddy glances back at Paula over her shoulder. 'For The Lottery Winner Widows Club,' she grins.

'I'm driving!' Audrey sings. 'You can sit in the front, Paula.'

This makes Teddy snort, and Paula understands her amusement when she spots Audrey's car.

There is no back seat.

It's a Jaguar E-Type classic. A flashy, silver convertible with the roof already down. Teddy throws long limbs into the passenger side, and pulls Paula in – along with her giant boy coat – and onto her lap. In the footwell beneath them, yesterday's dog yips. Audrey revs the engine, pulling violently out into the road and taking off at speed. The older woman's scarf flicks violently in the car around them, briefly blinding Paula as they launch over a speed bump.

Paula misses the curry bus.

'She's a beaut, isn't she?' Audrey yells into the wind as they hit the open road, her hair and scarf whipping up around her face. She surely cannot see a thing. 'It was my husband's car. He had it fully restored – no expense spared, of course. 1962 Jag, Series 1, the original 3.8 straight six. Four-speed Moss Box. Original Marston-style aluminium radiator, fifteen-inch Chrome wire wheels.'

Paula nods politely, with no idea what any of it means.

Audrey cackles. 'Of course I have no idea what any of that means,' she says. 'But he said it all the time.' She pauses to narrowly miss a tree before continuing, 'He refused to actually drive it so it sat in our garage for all those years! Turns out it's super fun to drive! And I can get it up to a hundred, easily. Shall we?' She glances around for approval. Paula tries to protest but she's frozen in terror. She wants to ask where they're going and what they're doing, but can't focus. Instead, she clings furiously to the car door handle as Audrey whips the steering wheel side to side, veering all over the small country roads.

Teddy sighs, shifting underneath Paula. 'Audrey, you're scaring our new friend again. Slow down a bit, can you? Haven't you already killed enough people?'

Audrey throws her head back to hack that laugh as Paula grips the door even harder.

Killed?

Paula had just about convinced herself Teddy's kitchen confession was a joke, so what does this mean? She really did it? They both did?

Audrey stops laughing at last, glancing over at Paula in the passenger seat. 'I think you're the one scaring her, Teddy,' she shrieks, but Paula feels the car's speed slow a little. 'I didn't realise you'd already told her the biggest secret of The Lottery Winner Widows Club.' She pauses. 'Are you OK, Paula darling? Don't be frightened, we only murder awful husbands. And you obviously know all about that, don't you, my darling?'

Paula glances wild-eyed over at Audrey who is – for once – watching the road. 'I didn't kill John,' she says, finding her voice at last. 'Did you two really... Did you honestly... Did you do it?'

There is quiet in the car, save for the sound of the roaring motor and howling wind. Beneath her, Teddy reaches forward to stroke the dog's ears. After another moment, she breathes out lightly into Paula's hair. 'My husband was a piece of shit. A gaslighting asshole. When I said I wanted a divorce, he said he'd never let me go and held my hand over an open flame.' She shakes her head, gripping her left fingers with her right hand. 'I look back at the me I was when I met him and can't believe it's the same person. I really thought he was my Mr Darcy. He turned out to be more Mr Asshole.'

'Mr Darsehole,' Audrey adds solemnly.

'Mr Dasshole,' Teddy agrees.

'No,' Audrey replies sternly. 'The pun doesn't work in your accent. It's Mr Darsehole or it's nothing.'

Teddy rolls her eyes. 'Whatever. Mr *Darsehole*.' She pauses and her breathing slows. 'I told him he'd never get to touch me again and then I caved in his temple. The rest of it you already know. Mr Darsehole's been under the patio a couple of years now.'

The driving gets worse as Audrey picks up the thread. 'My husband was ill for a long time.' She gives Paula a penetrating look, ignoring the road. 'When my children were young, he was ill. And when I say ill, I mean he was *sick*. He did things a father never should.' She takes a moment. 'I didn't know. I found out later, when we were already too old.' Clouds pass across her face, then she brightens. 'But it wasn't too late to do something about it. Because by then he was ill physically as well. His heart, such a shame. He needed a lot of looking after. He was on all this medication. It was hard to keep track of all of it, you know?' The car's speed picks up again as she continues, 'Do you know what happens when you take too much heart medication, Digitalis, Paula?' The dog barks and Paula rubs its ears. It is as much for her own comfort as the dog's. Audrey continues blithely, 'When you have more than ten milligrams of the stuff, you get all drowsy and dizzy. You start hallucinating and apparently some people see all kinds of fun colours! It sounds quite a nice experience actually, doesn't it? Oh, but then you die. Whoops.' She pouts, her eyes twinkling.

'Whoops indeed,' Teddy adds dryly. 'That was a little over five months ago, right, Audrey?' She nods. 'Then we met and decided to put together this club. The Lottery Winners Widows Club.'

'Do you think that sounds a bit bleak?' Audrey frowns. 'Maybe we should be The Lottery Winners Single Gals Club!' She cackles. 'You know I got myself straight onto Bumble after getting rid of Harold. But everyone I matched with immediately asked for money to save a dying relative or a pet. My daughter said it's quite a common scam and they target vulnerable old ladies. I was very upset she'd called me vulnerable.'

'Yes, it's called romance fraud,' Paula confirms. 'I saw a show all about it on Netflix called *Love Rat*.' She swallows. 'I've watched a lot of telly since I lost John. I haven't done much else.'

'I *like* the name, The Lottery Winners Widows Club,' Teddy says firmly.

'It's a bit clunky-sounding – maybe a bit long?' Paula offers. 'Perhaps The Widows Club would be simpler?'

'But that's the depressing part!' cries Audrey. 'We should at least emphasise the lottery win.'

'Do you even need a group name?' Paula asks quietly and Audrey jerks the wheel around a corner.

'Of course we do, my darling!' She shoots her a look. 'And it's *we*. You're a member now. You're one of us, Paula. There's no escaping us!' She says this gleefully, adding, '*We're* The Lottery Winner Widows Club! We're in it together.' The way she says this sends cortisol shooting through Paula. They're in it together. In *what* exactly?

'And hopefully after today, we'll have a couple more members,' Teddy says as Paula strains against the seatbelt.

'Is that what you meant before? About going on a recruitment drive?'

She feels Teddy nod. 'Yes, we've found two more women who won the lottery and offed their husbands. And we're going to see them right now.'

Audrey giggles, jerking the wheel round a corner. 'You wouldn't think there would be so many of us, would you, darling?'

Paula shakes her head, but it is not meant as an answer, just bewilderment. How did she get pulled into all this?

'It's only an hour to Buckinghamshire,' Teddy tells her. 'That's where Maisie lives. She actually went to prison for killing her husband after they won the lottery, but she was released on appeal. Lawyer error, I hear. Now she lives in a lovely big house in Beaconsfield, enjoying the high life.'

'How do you know all this?' Paula murmurs.

Audrey raises her eyebrows, her white hair wild about her face. 'We have our ways, my darling. And Maisie went really rather public about her situation.' She glances over, her eyebrows still high. 'As did you, Paula. You've not been terribly subtle with all this business, have you, eh?'

Paula coughs, choking on all the words she would like to say.

'And once we've convinced Maisie to join our group,' Teddy continues, 'we'll head on over to Cambridge. It's just over an hour to reach Ivy Kirk. She's been through a lot and she's only twenty-something, poor thing.'

'Poor thing?' Paula enquires, wondering what horrors this Ivy has endured.

Teddy tuts. 'Yes, poor thing. Being in your twenties is the worst.'

Audrey clucks in agreement, then continues after a moment, 'So what happened with your husband?' She nods at Paula. 'John, was it? Awful dickhead, I'm assuming?'

'Yes,' Paula begins, 'I mean, no! I meant yes, he was called John, but no, he wasn't a . . . thing head.' She sighs but it's lost in the noisy engine. 'Look, I really didn't kill him! I loved him very much. It sounds like you've both had a terrible time of it, and I'm sorry. But I didn't kill my husband. We were happy. He died in a car accident. I had nothing to do with it. I wouldn't . . . I wasn't even there or . . .' she trails off. The more she speaks, the more unconvincing she sounds. Why is it so hard to sound truthful when you know everyone thinks you're lying?

'Sure, babe,' Teddy says coolly. Paula can't see her face but she can hear the sarcasm in her voice. It's the same amused disbelief Teddy maintained around the kitchen table during their last conversation about John.

Audrey cackles again. 'OK, my dear, there's no pressure to tell us the truth. I know we've only just met and this is a lot. You take your time.'

Paula takes a deep breath. How can she convince these women that she didn't murder her husband? And should she even try? After all, she's trapped in a car with a pair of killers right now. On her way to see two more! Maybe it's better if they think she's somewhat capable of holding her own.

Also – and Paula's aware this shouldn't really be a factor – having to insist these women are wrong about her and John over and over is starting to get a bit... well, *awkward*... Maybe it would be less embarrassing to just let them think she murdered John? Since they clearly believe it anyway.

They drive in silence for a few minutes, the wind whipping through them, the dog whining happily at their feet. Paula wonders what kind of breed the dog is. It looks part Jack Russell, part Chihuahua? But the ears are pure spaniel. It's no good guessing, so instead she considers the two women they're going to see. Perhaps they're not really killers. Surely Teddy and Audrey have it wrong, like they do with her.

'What exactly is the plan today?' she enquires meekly, reaching up to try to pat down her mussed hair. 'Are we just going to knock on their doors and hope they want to talk to us?'

'It worked with you,' Teddy observes dryly.

'You didn't knock,' Paula points out but her words are lost on the wind. She picks up her volume a little. 'I was just thinking maybe you shouldn't go *straight* in with the murder-y part?'

Audrey veers too fast around a tight bend. 'But that's the fun bit!' she says happily. 'And it's what we have in common.'

'There's also the lottery,' Paula says quickly. 'We could just say we're millionaire winners, like them. We're lucky like them.'

'It wasn't luck,' Audrey says smoothly, with determination. 'I made it happen,' she nods with certainty. 'Every week I *manifested* it. I told the universe I was going to win and I did.' She flicks her loose scarf back over her shoulder. 'It wasn't even surprising when I got the message about winning. So, of course my husband didn't deserve any of it. *I* was the one who made it happen.'

Teddy tuts. 'Don't you think everyone who plays the lottery feels that way? We all tell ourselves we can make it happen by believing.'

The older woman waves her hands at the group. 'And look! It worked for all of us. Manifesting *works*.'

Teddy sighs, as though the logic is inescapable.

'But doesn't money make you ... unhappy?' Paula gives voice to one of the many fears that have plagued her since she met with Amy, the Lotto lady. 'Don't people say it ruins your life? That having money is a curse and you can't buy happiness?'

'What a bunch of absolute hogwash!' Audrey yells as the dog yips. 'Total rot. All of it. It's just the internet making things up and looking for the sad stories – the Michael Carrolls – in something that is bloody magical. People act like money is evil – like having it drives you to become a whole other person. As if having a few bob is suddenly going to transform you into a terrible gambler or a drug addict. I mean, for goodness' sake, my darling, cocaine is perfectly nice, but surely most of us couldn't get through millions of pounds' worth of the stuff?'

Teddy joins in, 'From my experience, I'd say money can *entirely* buy you happiness, babe. It can buy you all sorts of things – houses, cars, personalised pyjamas – whatever's your bag.'

'Bags, too!' Audrey sings.

'Of course, there are exceptions,' Teddy continues. 'You really need to have some level of happiness inside you already. Because, as we all know from that one horrible math teacher, it's no good multiplying things by zero.'

Audrey smirks, 'Not even seven zeroes on a big, fat cheque.'

'And after all, isn't being poor one of the biggest stressors in life?' Teddy shifts beneath Paula. 'Take that away and what do you get?'

'A chance to focus on other stressful things!' Audrey shrieks.

'Exactly!' Teddy nods. 'Finally your enormous forehead can get the attention it demands in every group photo.'

Audrey shrieks again and tries to reach over to slap Teddy, briefly veering onto the wrong side of the road.

Paula touches her forehead, suddenly self-conscious. 'Should I get a fringe, do you think?'

'Definitely. Everyone should have a fringe, that's what I always say,' Audrey nods from the driver's seat. 'But the point is, having more money allows you to do all the things you've always wanted to do and takes away the fear. You can carry on doing anything that already brought you happiness. Most lottery winners continue working, did you know that? They just work less. I still go to my ladies choir every week' – she pauses – 'we only sing Disney songs, isn't that the most wonderful thing you ever heard?'

Paula nods as Teddy makes a noise that would imply disagreement.

She considers what they've said. Does this win make her special? She doesn't feel special. The only thing she feels is broken and confused. But she felt that way before. This money just makes everything even more complicated.

If Paula were a better person, she'd give the whole lot – the entire twenty-one million – to a charity. She glances down at the dog at her feet. Maybe to an animal charity? She watches as the dog licks her own bits, then Teddy's hand.

Maybe not an animal charity.

But why *shouldn't* she try to enjoy this money and spend it on herself? You'd have to be an absolute saint to give away that kind of money. Paula is a nice enough person – she's not exactly going around punching people in the street – but she's also not a saint.

So why not splash the cash a little on herself? Why not buy herself a nice car with more seating options than this one?

She looks around at this small group of women. 'What was the first thing you bought with your money?'

'I booked a trip,' Teddy explains. 'Spent my first year after winning the money travelling around Italy and Spain.' She pauses. 'I don't recommend it actually. Too many English people living there. I only officially moved from New York to London a few months ago—'

'Oh?' Paula interrupts, jumping on the identifying clue. 'You're from New York?'

'Nope,' Teddy says smoothly.

'I bought a diamond necklace I'd always wanted,' Audrey jumps in. 'De Beers, 18k white gold, with combined diamond carat-age of 14.34.' She sighs dreamily. 'Gorgeous little blighter. Guess how much?'

Paula shakes her head, trying to fathom such a thing. 'I don't know,' she replies. 'Five thousand pounds?'

'Try fifty-eight thousand pounds!' Audrey tells her triumphantly. 'Isn't that ludicrous! Of course, I can never wear the bloody thing. My daughters won't let me. Too dangerous, they say. And it's not like I'm attending too many royal balls these days.'

Paula's head spins at the number, but something unfurls in her stomach. How . . . *exciting*. Just imagine being able to throw away such an enormous sum of money like that. Just imagine!

'So,' Teddy begins, 'if a house isn't something you want to buy right now, what *do* you want, Paula?'

Paula strokes the interior of the Jaguar. Terrifying as Audrey's driving is, it's also undeniably fun. Her insides are jangling with nerves but also a sort of thrilling feeling. She thinks about how she felt after the house viewing, when she considered the idea of buying a car. How wonderful that felt.

After a few seconds, she tells them in a whisper, 'A car.'

She can practically hear Teddy smiling. 'I know the perfect place,' she says. 'I'll make a call. We'll recruit our new members, then all go shopping together. It'll be a great bonding experience.'

Audrey nods. 'Today, Maisie and Ivy. Tomorrow, we help Paula buy a brand-new vehicle.'

A feeling blooms in Paula's chest that feels a lot like ... happiness?

12

'AND STOP PRESSING THE BLOODY RING DOORBELL!' The door slams in their faces and Paula, Audrey and Teddy stand in a row, silently blinking at one another.

'That didn't go very well,' Teddy says dryly and Paula nods in agreement.

'She said not to ring the bell,' Audrey rallies. 'But she *didn't* say we couldn't knock! Let's give it the old college try. Refuse to take no for an answer!' She raises her knuckles in readiness and Teddy stops her.

'That woman has had enough – we all have – of people refusing to take no for an answer,' she says carefully. 'Let's go. We can always come back another time.'

The group collectively turn back in the direction of Audrey's car.

Paula feels strangely deflated.

They'd been so confident, so sure that Maisie Bernard would listen, that she'd want to be a part of their group. But it was clear from the start that they'd made a mistake.

First off – and Paula isn't usually one to assign blame – Audrey really didn't help matters with the doorbell. It was one of those fancy Ring ones, and was definitely making a noise inside the house even if they couldn't hear it, but Audrey kept saying it wasn't working. She pressed it over and over, so of course, when Maisie eventually answered the door, she was wildly irritated. And then, before they could get a word in edgeways, she accused them of being from Neighbourhood Watch. Apparently, someone named Sheila from down the road 'had it in for her' and the three women on her doorstep were 'in on it' with her. Paula couldn't exactly follow what all the ins were, but it was obvious enough that Maisie wanted them to go away.

It took Teddy a few minutes to find a moment to speak, and when Audrey mentioned the death of Maisie's husband, it was immediately clear the woman was done with them. She didn't want to hear any more. She had nothing to say. How dare they come here? She'd even threatened to call the police, before slamming the door.

'What now?' Paula says quietly, feeling defeated as they climb back into the car. 'Do we head home?'

'No!' Audrey says with feeling. 'We can't do that! We're not far from Cambridge. This next gal will be much more receptive. Don't be put off, Paula, my darling.'

The dog in the footwell licks Paula's hand.

'OK,' Paula says obediently.

Exactly one hour and twenty-three minutes later, the three women find themselves outside Ivy Kirk's house and climb out of the car, this time, with much more trepidation.

Crossing the large gravel drive, Paula gapes up at the huge Edwardian property situated about a mile from Cambridge city centre. It's not quite on the scale of the eighteen-million-pound Surrey Hills estate they've viewed together, but it's still intimidating in its proportions.

'Maybe only one of us should knock this time?' Paula suggests anxiously, taking in the box hedges lining the borders.

Teddy nods. 'Maybe Paula's right. Our success rate *was* better when it was just one-on-one.' She waves towards Paula, who feels a foot taller, being referred to as a success.

'No,' Audrey says firmly, shaking her head and pulling her scarf tighter around her neck. 'All for one and one for all.'

'The Three Musketeers,' Paula acknowledges with warmth, remembering her dad reading her the story. She glances either side of her at these two strong women. Is she really one of them?

'I guess that makes Ivy our d'Artagnan,' Teddy murmurs, reaching for the large brass door knocker.

After a minute, there is movement inside. A small face appears at a side window.

'That was Ivy!' Audrey says excitedly and Teddy gives her an amused sideways look.

'How do you always know everything?' she asks and Audrey taps her nose.

'I have powerful connections,' she says. 'Think of me as your own personal Logan Roy.' Paula has no idea who this is, but Teddy looks alarmed. Audrey shrugs, adding, 'You can't deny, he got things done.'

'You are an interesting woman, Audrey Swift,' Teddy shakes her head.

Swift? It hits Paula that she has heard the depths of these women's darkest secrets – and yet, she'd forgotten her full name.

'Do we think she's going to answer the—' Teddy's question is cut off by a tiny young woman opening the door. She is wide-eyed and suspicious. Paula stares at her and she stares back, taking the three of them in.

'Yes, can I help?' she asks tremulously in a small voice. She frowns. 'Um, look, I'm sorry, if this is a God thing, I don't—'

'It's definitely not a God thing,' Teddy replies quickly.

'Or a Sheila from the Neighbourhood Watch thing,' Audrey adds.

'Sorry?' Ivy's delicate features screw up in confusion. Behind her, Paula can see a wide, open hallway with gleaming geometric oak flooring. A grand staircase winds its way up behind a grand reception hall.

'Ivy?' Audrey asks warmly and the woman's expression gets even more wary. 'You're Ivy Kirk, aren't you?'

'Er . . .' She glances behind her nervously, as if looking for help. 'Who—'

'Can we come in?' Audrey asks and the woman blinks at her in shock.

'Who are you?' Her voice is barely audible.

'I'm Audrey, that's Teddy and there's Paula over there, hiding at the back.' Paula squeaks a greeting as Ivy squints over at her fearfully. There is something about her that makes Paula's heart ache. She looks so small and vulnerable. So fragile. She's dressed in a T-shirt and jeans, projecting a 'bullied teenager hiding in a school library' energy.

Audrey continues cheerfully. 'We were wondering if you wanted to join this new club we're putting together. We have a lot in common, I promise. We want to help you.'

Ivy shakes her head. 'So this *is* a God thing. Um, look—'

'It's really not,' Teddy repeats firmly. 'Listen, Ivy, I know this is a little strange, us turning up on your doorstep out of the blue like this. We don't want to freak you out, babe, and of course I understand you won't want to invite a bunch of strangers into your house.' She shoots Audrey an irritated look. 'But if we could explain a bit more about who we are and why we're here . . .' She trails off, looking uncharacteristically unsure.

Ivy hovers at the door frame, looking puzzled and scared. She runs a nervous hand through short dark hair, wide grey eyes darting side to side. 'I'm sorry,' she says politely in her soft, sweet voice, hopping from foot to foot in thick bed socks, 'I don't think—'

Audrey moves closer and alarm crosses Ivy's face. 'Ivy, my darling, we're also lottery winners, like you,' the older woman tells her. 'And we've all . . . lost our husbands.' She pauses. 'In strange circumstances.'

Ivy, who seems to get smaller every time Paula looks at her, takes a step back, her face painted with sudden terror. Her mouth drops open and she glances at each of them individually again. Her eyes land on Paula and this time she stops to examine her closer. Recognition lights her face.

'I've seen you,' she says slowly. 'In the news, you're . . . you . . . you won . . .' Paula's face burns red, but any embarrassment fades quickly, as Ivy looks at her. There is something in the young woman's expression that is so familiar. As they regard one another, Paula's overwhelmed with a feeling of affection, of something like maternal instinct. She wants to reach for Ivy – so fragile and vulnerable – and bring her close. Paula can see what she's been through and suddenly wants nothing more than to look after her. To protect her.

Ivy slowly shakes her head, turning back to Audrey. 'But you've *all* won the lottery?'

Audrey nods eagerly. 'I didn't win all that much, a mere half a million. But Teddy here pocketed almost eight hundred million bucks, if you can imagine! Then Paula won her twenty-one million pounds a couple of months ago.' She pauses, looking at Ivy penetratingly. 'And you won three point eight million pounds, isn't that right? On the Lotto?'

Paula studies the young woman's face as she slowly nods. She is so young. Younger, even, than her own children. What would it be like to win so much money at such a young age?

'And your husband . . .' Audrey begins carefully. 'He died about a year ago now, didn't he? He . . . fell down the stairs, am I right?' Ivy's face has darkened, but she nods again. 'We understand,' Audrey continues, adding in a whisper, 'Better than anyone, we understand.'

Paula watches Audrey with wonder. How does she know all this? What secrets does she carry with her under that scarf?

Teddy clears her throat. 'Shall we come in or would you like to meet us somewhere? A coffee shop or—'

Ivy shakes her head again. 'I don't understand,' she stutters. 'I don't know what this is, or who . . . who . . . you are. But I'm . . . um, I'm trying to move on. I've put what happened behind me. I just want to live my life.' She swallows hard and Paula fights an urge to reach for her. She steps forward, out of Teddy's shadow.

'But can you?' she asks her softly. 'Can you move on? Can you live your life?'

Ivy stares at her. After a moment, her face crumbles. She swipes at her eyes, then opens the door wider. 'You better come in,' she whispers as a tear rolls down her cheek.

'The four musketeers,' Teddy whispers under her breath as they cross the threshold and enter the latest member of TLWWC's house.

13

To: John.Sheldon1960@oldmail.com
From: PaulaJeanieSheldon1964@ptinternet.com
Subject: TLWWC

Hello John,

How are you? Is that a silly question? I suppose it is.
   I'm having the strangest week. And I thought winning the lottery and my husband dying was a funny one.
   I think I've made some friends. They're lottery winners, too, like me. Like us. Their names are Audrey, Ivy and Teddy. Teddy has the most beautiful hair – it's even nicer than Sigourney Weaver's! They call themselves The Lottery Winner Widows Club.
   Ivy is the newest member of our group – we only met her on Thursday. She's got a lovely big house and we talked for a long time in her living room. She made me a peppermint tea and then complimented Audrey's scarf. Then Audrey said it wasn't a scarf, it was a pashmina, which I had to google afterwards. Apparently a pashmina is much fancier than a boring old scarf, and is

made with the finest cashmere wool. So then I googled what cashmere wool is and it turns out it's wool from cashmere goats. Don't ask me what cashmere goats are because I got a bit tired of googling after that and went to watch Selling Sunset instead.

I'm getting off topic.

So, like I said, all three of them have won the lottery, but they also – I think I should probably just blurt this out because I don't know how to bring it up naturally – killed their husbands. Which I know must seem very shocking to you, but they really did have their reasons. Poor Ivy is such a sweetheart and awfully young – only 27 – and her husband sounded like a really dreadful man. He used to hurt her, physically. He would beat her when he was drunk. Which was every night, by the sound of things. They were together for twelve years. They met when Ivy was only fifteen and he was in his mid-twenties. Which was hard to hear, I have to say. She ended up pushing him down the stairs a little over a year ago. And it's difficult not to think . . . good for you, Ivy.

I'm afraid they think I killed you, too. I've tried to explain, but they just don't believe me and it's getting too awkward to keep insisting.

Last week, they took me to see a house that's for sale. Though it's hard to imagine anyone thinking of such a place as a house. It was gigantic! Like Downton Abbey but with fewer servants kissing each other. I'm sorry, I know you hated that show.

It was beautiful and they couldn't understand why I didn't love it. And I don't know how to explain to them why it's so hard for me to see things change. They don't seem to understand that I'm grieving. And I'm not talking about my grief for your death. I mean that I'm grieving a life we might've had together with all this money. A life I thought we might be able to have one day. These women – these new friends – they don't understand that you and I talked about what kind of house we'd buy if we ever had that kind of money. It's hard to explain any of it. To anyone. Even to myself.

Maybe this is what Tilly means by saying grief has tentacles.

Although I really wish she would stop saying it.

I think about you a lot.

Paula

14

A loud knock at the front door makes Paula jump.

She's just sent John another email and is wondering if they give away unused email addresses like they do phone numbers. Surely not.

From her spot, sitting at the kitchen table, she glances anxiously out of the window. It's dark, gone eight p.m. Who would be calling round at this hour?

She gets up, something gnawing at her stomach, and heads for the door. As she reaches for the latch, she remembers.

We'll be back.

Her autopilot has the door open before she can register the fear she suddenly feels. The two men from a week and a half ago are there. Waiting. The same two men as before; as big and ominous as ever. But this time the larger one at the front – the one who'd referred to himself as Craig – is smiling. Widely.

'Paula!' He greets her by her first name like they are old friends. It makes that fear tickling the edges of her brain double down and her stomach drop. His tone is friendly, but his energy is chilling. 'Lovely to see you again. I know John's not in but can we come in anyway?' he asks, still smiling. Her mind goes blank, gripping on to the door frame. Everything inside her is screaming *shut the door and run away*. But she's too British to slam a door in someone's face.

She's alone in the house. Even if she could make a loud enough noise to reach the garden shed, Seb will have his gamer headphones on. He would never hear. And even if he could hear, there's not a lot he wouldn't sacrifice for a new top score.

'Oh! Well, actually, it's not a good time,' she says, forcing her voice to sound steady. 'We're having a family get-together right now, absolutely overflowing with people. So many ... tall, er, well-built male family members.' She swallows. 'What is this regarding anyway? Who are you?' She glances over her own shoulder, into the house, wishing she had more lights turned on. She still worries too much about the electricity bill, even though she could power the actual sun with her bank balance.

The large man, Craig, tuts. 'Well, now, Paula, I don't know what to believe anymore, since you lied to us the last time we came to see you.' He narrows his eyes and leans back on his heels. 'You said John was out, didn't you? But we now know he's dead, eh? We were a little late to the news, but we've seen the papers. Car accident, was it?' He tuts again. 'What a shame, nice man like that, fiery death.'

Paula swallows. 'I'm sorry,' she says. 'I didn't mean to lie' – she really didn't – 'but it's sometimes hard for me to say it out loud.' She takes them in, craning to see the smaller man standing behind Craig. He looks a bit bored. 'Are you ... Are you friends of his?'

Craig chuckles meanly. 'I wouldn't say that. Not exactly. More like business acquaintances.' He pauses and the nasty smile fades. 'He owed us a lot of money.'

'He... what?' Paula blinks. 'No, you're wrong, he... what?' She feels like she's been slapped. John owed money? To *these* people? How? Why? He wouldn't, would he? Yes, she knew there were loans and re-mortgages on the house, but John wouldn't have borrowed money from people like this. From people who would turn up on your doorstep with threatening smiles, calling you by your first name. He wouldn't!

Craig raises his eyebrows. 'They never tell the missus, do they?' He tuts again, as does the smaller man beside him, who has so far been silent. If he's meant to be some kind of henchman, he's not a terribly effective choice. He's not nearly as threatening as Craig himself, wearing a white hoodie easily two sizes too small, with 'University of Huddersfield' emblazoned across it. 'But either way,' Craig – who is wearing well-proportioned all-black with no logos – continues, 'it's the truth, I'm afraid, Paula, and he is way past due.' He sighs. 'I know he's conveniently dead and all that, but it's fine, isn't it? Because we know *you* have the money to pay us.' He winks. 'Like I said, we've seen the papers.'

'But I don't know anything about a loan!' Paula cries. 'John never—'

The large man raises a warning hand and she stops. 'Paula, love,' he says in that frighteningly low tone. 'I don't give a shit what you knew about or didn't. I'm telling you: he borrowed my money.' He smiles again. 'Liked a bit of snooker, didn't he, your John? Though it would appear he wasn't all that good at it.' Paula's mind is spinning. John was gambling? Is that what he's saying? Craig continues. 'We'll be back, and we're expecting you to have fifty thousand pounds in cash here, waiting. Clever move, getting himself killed like that, but John can't get out of this that easily. We want our money and we'll get our money.'

Paula puts a hand to her chest. *Fifty thousand pounds?* John owed these horrible people fifty thousand pounds? No, she can't believe it, she *won't* believe it. She stares at Craig, adrenaline coursing through her body as he keeps talking. 'No need to leave me your contact details, by the way, Paula,' he says breezily. He smiles at her, that same slow, horrible sort of psychopath smile, and pulls out his phone. He presses a few buttons and behind her in the house, Paula's landline starts to ring. He hangs up and the ringing stops. Smiling even wider, he taps the screen again and this time, the mobile phone in Paula's pocket starts vibrating against John's notebook.

Nausea pushes its way up her throat and Paula fights to keep it down and hold her ground. Everything in her is screaming to run. This man has her address and her phone numbers. What else does he have? What else does he know?

Craig turns to go, elbowing University of Huddersfield. 'Like I said,' he says, nodding as he walks off, 'it was very nice to see you again, Paula. And we'll be back. Maybe we'll come in next time – when you're not, y'know, having a *family get-together.*' He laughs as he walks off, the smaller man scurrying in his wake.

Paula stands in her doorway, watching them go, her whole body shaking. They're coming back, and they want fifty thousand pounds in cash.

15

Paula is immensely relieved to find it is just Audrey in the car waiting outside her house the next morning. For all her nice hair and expensive skirts, the idea of sitting on Teddy's lap again does not appeal.

'Paula, darling!' Audrey exclaims when she sees her, leaping out of the low car with ease and running up the front path, pashmina flying in her wake. She sweeps Paula up in her arms, breathing warm car air onto her neck.

'Hello,' Paula squeaks from inside the tight hug. It feels nice to be held this time, if unfamiliar. She realises how much she needed a hug after last night's horrible encounter with those men.

She's been up half the night, pacing the house, unsure what to do. She's still processing how she feels about it all, but she recognises hot, bubbly anger working its way through her veins. How *dare* these men turn up like that at her house? How dare they try to frighten her? And how dare they try to get her to turn on her husband like this?

Because of course there's no way it can be true. It can't be. John wouldn't do that. He wouldn't be so irresponsible. Yes, he played a lot of snooker but there was no money involved.

It's far more likely that these men are chancing their arm. They saw the news about her lottery win and are now trying to get money from her by besmirching John's good name.

She won't believe it, not without proof.

On the other hand, true or not, they seem serious about the money. But do they really expect her to get fifty thousand pounds out of her account and hand it over? To these nasty, threatening, grimacing strangers? And what would happen once they got it? How likely is it that these men – these *loan sharks* – will keep coming back for more? There's no way she can give it to them.

And apart from anything else, she's pretty sure the cash limit on her card is £250 per day. How long will it take Paula to gather together that vast sum at such a slow rate? She can't do the maths, but it must be months, surely. And that man Craig didn't seem like he'd be willing to wait months. Going into the bank, requesting such a large amount would no doubt raise a lot of red flags, too.

So what to do? She daren't go to the police, not with her new friends from The Lottery Winner Widows Club hanging about, and she can't get her children involved.

Because what if . . . what if John really did do this? No, it can't be true. Can it? If it were true – if there was proof – what then? It would destroy Tilly and Seb, knowing their father had done such a thing. It would destroy her.

And something else keeps ringing in her ears.

What that man, Craig, said as he left – what he said about John *getting himself killed*. She can't stop thinking about that. Is it possible . . . Is there any way that John did what he did . . . deliberately? What if he knew this was coming and—

She can't think it. He wouldn't. He *couldn't*.

Audrey releases her from the hug at last and they head back towards the car.

'Is it just us for shopping today?' Paula asks shyly, trying to put John and the debt out of her head.

'Gosh no. Four Musketeers and all that.' Audrey grins. 'We'll meet the others there. The showroom we're heading to is near where Teddy lives. And Ivy stayed with her last night. I was in a hotel near here.'

'Oh! I'm so glad Ivy is coming with us,' Paula says with genuine warmth. They may have only met a few days ago, but she felt an immediate kinship with the silent young woman all alone in the big house.

Paula climbs into the Jag, almost landing on the dog, who squeaks in protest.

'Oh, it's you again,' Paula says to her, then turns to Audrey. 'She's yours? I wasn't sure who she belonged to.'

'Of course she's mine!' Audrey exclaims happily, then adds, 'Paula.'

'Yes?' says Paula.

'No,' Audrey laughs. 'Her name is Paula.'

'What?'

'Her name!' Audrey reaches over and scratches the dog's head. Hair flies in every direction. 'My baby is called Paula. She's twelve years old, a Jack Russell Bichon Frise mix – a Jackie-B – and she doesn't like belly rubs. She has sensitive nipples.' Understanding, the dog rolls over, revealing six proud little nipples, buried in coarse, messy fur. Her tongue lolls out as she grins, one ear folded over in the wrong direction.

'Her name is Paula?' Paula asks, feeling a bit miffed. 'That's very confusing.'

Audrey grins widely. 'I know, but I can't help what her name is.' She reaches over to pat her hand. 'Never mind, eh, my darling? Here's what we'll do. We'll call her Paula the Dog from now on. How does that sound?'

For some reason, this offer really affects Paula the Human. She is not used to being put ahead of someone else. Not even ahead of *animal*-someone elses.

'Thank you,' she whispers and Paula the Dog yips in response, flipping back over and licking the gear stick. Paula the Human looks over at Audrey as she starts the car and they move off. She's starting to really like this overly affectionate woman with her layers of floral clothes and signature pashminas. How funny that they haven't known each other long, and yet, she already feels like one of them, like she has been granted unconditional access to their group, with a lifetime guarantee.

They sit in comfortable silence for a minute, heading in the direction of Central London. Paula wonders if she should double check Audrey has paid the congestion charge, but doesn't. Audrey is a grown-up. And she can afford the fine.

Of course, a part of Paula is frightened by all of this. These women have all confessed to killing someone. Each of them! Three women, all lottery winners, all murderers. She should be running a mile in the opposite direction.

But, Paula has to admit, she . . . likes them. She likes all of them. She can't help it. It's all so new, so different, so exciting. She understands why each of these women did what they did. She doesn't quite know why, but she trusts them all. And she's OK with what they've done. She wants to help them, protect them. There definitely won't be any more calls to the NHS non-emergency number.

Paula jumps in her seat when Audrey sighs beside her, reaching up to adjust her rear-view mirror. 'Columbo's back,' she mutters. It's the first time Audrey has sounded anything but totally delighted by life.

Paula strains to look behind them. In the distance, there's a dark non descript car hanging way back. She can't make out any person or persons.

'Did you say *Columbo*?' Paula is flummoxed. 'As in... the TV detective from the seventies?' She squints into the distance. 'The actor was called Peter something, wasn't he?' She cheers with the memory. 'I used to watch that show every week. I had quite a crush on him!'

'Well' – Audrey machine-guns her now-familiar cackle – 'this Columbo hasn't got the lazy eye, but he has got an old beige mac. And – most annoyingly – he's got Columbo's dogged determination.'

'Determination to do what? Why is he following us?'

'He's not following us. He's following *me*.' She reaches over and pats Paula's hand reassuringly. It is not reassuring how long her eyes are off the road. 'He thinks I killed my husband. Which, of course, I did, but he doesn't know that. Not for sure anyway.'

Paula's head whips round, straining to see the car behind them, then – instinctively – she ducks way down in the seat. 'Are you serious?' she shrieks, half-hiding behind her seatbelt. Paula the Dog gives her a withering look.

'Don't worry, my darling,' Audrey says happily. 'He can't see you or anything much of anything from this distance.' She gives Columbo a happy little wave in the mirror, which makes Paula sink even lower in her seat. Audrey glances over, looking amused. She has her tweed coat collar popped, her pashmina tucked inside. It makes her head look tiny. 'He hasn't got an iota of proof. Paula darling, you mustn't panic. He's just a bit obsessed. It's nothing to worry about.'

'Are you sure?' Paula squeaks.

'Absolutely! He turns up every now and again, asks all the same questions and then goes away. Goodness, it's been four months or so now since Harold died. The police don't have the money or the resources to log a neighbourhood mugging, never mind endlessly pursue an eighty-one-year-old over the death of her very sick husband. He'll go away soon!' Audrey reaches over again and this time she squeezes Paula's hand hard. 'And we'll lose him in Central London traffic in a mo, you'll see.'

Paula tries to sneak another look in the wing mirror. The car is so far back, Audrey surely can't be certain who it really is following them. What if it's . . . What if it's the loan sharks?

'I promise, it's fine,' Audrey says again. 'There's nothing to worry about.'

Paula finds herself reassured and she sits back up.

'OK,' she says at last. 'If you're sure, I trust you.'

She feels Audrey's eyes on her. 'I am sure,' she replies, then adds with warmth, 'Thank you.'

They pass a sign about ULEZ and Paula again stops herself asking about the charge. She trusts Audrey.

It doesn't take long for them to lose the car, and forty minutes later, they crawl past Piccadilly and on to Hyde Park Corner. Paula stares out of the window in awe at the giant stone buildings on Knightsbridge, full of luxury stores and five-star hotels.

'We can pop into The Lanesborough for a drink after car shopping, if you fancy?' Audrey comments, revving the engine as they dawdle through traffic. Paula nods dumbly, looking up at the huge white Regency hotel. 'They're absolute darlings in there,' Audrey continues, chunky gold bracelets jangling on her wrist. 'Buchanan on the door is the nicest chap you'll ever meet, and the head concierge, Simons, can get you anything at all at the drop of a hat. Did you know they also have a butler service for your room? Although you'll never get Amos; he's far too in demand.'

'Butlers?' Paula repeats dumbly, trying to imagine such a thing.

'Or The Ritz isn't far from here,' Audrey waves in a direction behind them. 'It can be a tad touristy, but you can't get away from the fact that they truly know how to do old-world glamour. Their afternoon teas are *legendary*. The dining room is Michelin-starred but personally, I'd pick a freshly baked scone with Cornish clotted cream over almost anything, wouldn't you?'

Paula tries to remember the last time she had a scone. Or Cornish clotted cream. Or even cream. She can vaguely remember Tilly and her wife, Misha, offering her some Coffeemate in her hot drink once. She said no. It was a bit too decadent for Paula. Even coffee feels a bit too exciting.

'We could make a weekend of it sometime!' Audrey says excitably, twirling her pashmina between fingers that should be on steering wheels. 'Afternoon tea at The Ritz, then some cocktails at The Laney, followed maybe by Dinner by Heston Blumenthal. His restaurant does a Sunday roast with the most tender beef you've ever tasted, I guarantee it. And his potatoes! Oh my darling, they're so fluffy, I snuck some home with me and used them as pillows on my four poster.'

She cackles at her own joke, then hacks a cough. 'We'd have to stay the night at The Ritz, of course, but that's no problem. They keep a suite available for me when I'm visiting. Although it seems a little silly now we have Teddy around the corner.'

'How much does a room at The Ritz cost?' Paula asks, her brain jumbling with the confusing image of a roast potato pillow.

'Oh, the Deluxe Suites start at around three and a half.'

'Three and a half what?' Paula is genuinely baffled.

Audrey shrieks, 'Thousand pounds, my darling!' She glances over. 'Don't look so shocked. The Lanesborough's royal suite costs twenty-four thousand pounds a night.'

Paula swallows hard.

'To be fair,' Audrey muses, 'it *is* a seven-bedroom, 450-square-metre apartment with views over Hyde Park and Buckingham Palace Gardens. Amos the butler let me have a sneaky peek once. Not to be sniffed at.'

Paula's head is still spinning as they turn onto Park Lane, pulling up in front of another tall white building. This one is glass-fronted with huge shiny cars parked up inside, glinting in the cold sun.

She spots Teddy and Ivy just inside the door. Ivy sees them first, waving excitedly and looking perkier than Paula remembers from last week. Maybe she's a bit of an engine head. Seb calls himself an engine head, but that mainly seems to consist of racing Mario cars with other grown men via a headset on a computer.

A tall man appears from nowhere as Audrey leaps out of the car. She throws her car keys at him, thanking him by name. He smoothly slides into the driver's seat, as Paula scrambles out. She wonders how Audrey has so much grace at eighty. Is it a rich thing? Will she learn? Does she want to?

The valet whisks the Jaguar away as Audrey bundles Paula inside.

'Let's spend some of your millions!' she says with glee as they enter the biggest car showroom Paula's ever seen.

Time to buy a car.

16

Paula is having fun. She's actually having fun!

'Look at this one!' Teddy calls out across the room. Her perfect hair is today pulled back behind her ears, showcasing statement earrings that are bright gold and round, with a large stone in the centre. They look heavy and painful. But beautiful.

She stands back, waving towards a low sporty car in a flashy red. Paula, Ivy and Audrey all gather round to ooh and aah over the Porsche.

It turns out, buying a very expensive car is a very different experience from buying a fifth-hand 2011 Ford Mondeo. This place gives new meaning to 'high end'. Paula, Audrey and Ivy are the only customers here, but it feels like that was supposed to happen, rather than the result of the cost of living crisis finally hitting all the millionaires.

On hand to help, they have a stunningly beautiful personal sales person called Francesca, who does not call herself a sales person. She is apparently a *consultant*. As such, she hasn't given them the hard sell, but hung back respectfully for the two hours the ladies have already been there. When they want answers, Francesca materialises from nowhere, offering expert details about engine sizes, paintwork, interiors, and the various bespoke, customised features.

And she hasn't said one word about Paula the Dog. Not even when she went round sniffing each car wheel in the room and looking at us with intense disappointment at the lack of interesting smells.

This is, apparently, what money buys you.

'How much is that one, do you think?' Paula muses, admiring the distinctive lettering at the back.

Francesca appears, silently and seamlessly. 'The Porsche Taycan Turbo starts from eighty-six thousand, five hundred and fifty-five pounds.' She says this like it is not an incredible sum of money.

Paula instinctively draws back. There is no way she could spend that kind of cash on a vehicle. Not on anything! It's offensive!

She swallows, reaching into her overcoat, her fingers finding John's notepad, as well as the shiny new bank card slipped into its pages. She very nearly left it behind again today. It was only as she saw Audrey pull up, that Paula remembered to fetch it from the living room. She traces the lettering on it now, letting her forefinger follow the shape of her name inscribed there. For some reason, it makes Paula feel a little emotional.

That card represents an awful lot, after all. It represents a kind of freedom. A freedom from years of turning lights off as she followed her children from room to room. Freedom from constant worry and fear about mortgage payments. Freedom from hole-y socks and shopping for clothes in charity shops.

These kids today, they all seem to think it's cool and hip to shop second hand. Tilly is constantly yelling about something called Vinted, as if it means something to Paula. They all act like they're single-handedly saving the planet by wearing a jumper someone died in.

And maybe they are?

To Paula, wearing second-hand clothes from her local charity shop always represented something like a failure for her. She couldn't afford new, not even as she got old and saw people she once knew buying bigger and bigger homes. She *had* to shop for second hand and didn't like the things she ended up buying. But they were a cheap means to an end.

And now she has more than twenty million pounds sterling sitting in her bank account. Twenty million *pounds*. Just sitting there. By pure luck!

Why shouldn't she spend some of it on something ridiculous? It's got to be better than giving all of it away to a loan shark called Craig.

Francesca continues in a tone that is professional and somehow unintrusive. 'It combines the classic Porsche silhouette with a modern all-electric design. It has a panoramic glass roof, with lateral Aircurtains and deploying door handles—'

'What are Aircurtains?' Ivy asks in a too-low voice from the back.

'It has six-piston aluminium callipers on the front, and four-piston at the back, LED four-point headlights, a sixteen-point-eight-inch digital display, with Direct Touch Controls—'

Paula can't hear any more nonsense words. 'And if I bought this . . .' she interrupts hesitantly, feeling oddly brave. 'If I bought this car here and now, what then? How does this work?'

Francesca smiles a small, perfect smile, like a cat eyeing the dazed mouse under her paw. 'Well, first we would talk about any customisation you might want.'

Paula raises her eyebrows. 'Customisation?'

'Paint colours, wheels, interiors, specific tech. We can even discuss the kind of seat stitching you want.'

'Wow,' Paula breathes. *Seat stitching.*

Teddy sounds amused. 'I'm sure Paula has very specific thoughts about seat stitching.'

Francesca nods, giving nothing away. 'Then we would handle all the paperwork for you, arrange the registration and have the car delivered wherever you'd like it in the UK. Or indeed, anywhere in the world.' She pauses. 'If it was something you were keen to do, I could also arrange to fly you out to the factory where the cars are built, for an extra-special delivery experience.'

'That is almost certainly not something Paula or any of us would be keen to do,' Audrey sniggers, flicking her pashmina over her shoulder.

'No, thank you,' Paula says carefully. Audrey's right; she doesn't want to go to a car factory.

Francesca moves infinitesimally closer. 'We will also arrange for you to be included in our special client car membership, which means you get invited to all kinds of exclusive racing events – including Formula One – on us. As a thank you for your custom. It also gives you access to our concierge maintenance service, where you have an on-call expert available to you twenty-four seven. We would regularly collect your car for a personalised check with one of our experienced mechanics as well.'

'Well, that all sounds very . . . nice,' Paula says, nodding slowly, feeling like a fraud. It feels like she is playing a part.

And not very well. She wants to be good at this. She wants to be cool like Teddy, taking all of this in her stride. She is suddenly very aware of her clothes. She must look very drab and unfashionable. Why hasn't she got herself a six-thousand-pound skirt? Or, at least, a six-thousand-pound pair of trousers, since her varicose veins are not for display. She glances over at Ivy, feeling grateful that she also looks overwhelmed. Ivy seems even younger to Paula today, still dressed in her jeans and T-shirt. Her hair is pulled back in a sweet, bouncy ponytail and it reminds Paula of the long-gone days when she would do Tilly's hair for her.

She makes eye contact with the sales consultant. 'I will have a . . . think.'

Francesca smiles that enigmatic smile. 'Of course. Please take your time, there's no rush. I'm here if you need me.' She moves away across the wide expanse of marble floor.

'I had no idea cars were so expensive,' Paula whispers to the group, though Francesca has disappeared inside her office.

Audrey is amused by this, as she seems to be by so much. 'My husband, Harold, was obsessed with cars,' she says. 'He used to talk endlessly and tediously about the most expensive vehicles in the world. There's a Rolls-Royce somewhere out there that costs thirty million dollars, did you know that? The Rolls-Royce La Rose Noire Droptail. He called it "a piece of driveable art".' She snorts, her white hair wobbling with amusement. 'Absolute drivel. I should've killed him there and then just for that.'

Paula winces at her casual reference to murder.

Audrey continues with her lesson. 'They have another one called the Boat Tail that's only twenty-eight million dollars.

Or you can get something called a Pagani Zonda HP Barchetta that's eighteen point five million.'

'How do you remember these things?' Paula murmurs in awe. She can't remember anything. Yesterday she called her elbow an arm-knee.

Audrey grins, tapping the side of her head. 'It's not quite a photographic memory but it's close enough.' She looks away. 'Though there's plenty I'd love to forget.'

Teddy fans herself with her hand, long, pink nails flapping. 'I always quite liked the look of those Bugatti cars. I saw one in the US that looked like the Batmobile. It was only sixteen million dollars.'

'What kind of car do *you* own?' Paula asks her curiously. Teddy is, after all, the richest of the group, by quite a long way. And today she looks even richer. She's wearing tailored trousers that taper in such a way as to emphasise the bottom she seems so proud of. On her top half, she's wearing a luxe, cashmere jumper, topped with a Burberry trench coat.

Teddy half-smiles. 'I live in London, babe. Why would I need a car? I use a Knightsbridge car service that operates near my apartment. The chauffeurs get me wherever I need to go.' She pauses. 'Or I just – y'know – take an Uber! I might be ridiculously wealthy but I'm still a human being who appreciates a car turning up in thirty seconds flat.' She makes a face. 'Although my star rating has been dreadful ever since Paula the Dog arrived in my life.' She glares down at the scruffy mutt.

Ivy steps forward, looking at Paula kindly. 'Which car do you like best?'

Paula scans the room, her eyes returning again and again to the Porsche.

'She wants the red sporty one!' Audrey crows.

'But it's eighty-six thousand pounds!' Paula says, a little horrified.

'Don't forget that extra five hundred and fifty-five pounds.' Teddy is amused again.

'That's the *starting* price,' Audrey reminds them. 'If you want it in red or if you're getting any of that clever seat stitching thingy she mentioned, you'll probably need to find at least another twenty grand or so.'

Paula shakes her head with determination. 'It's too much. I can't.'

'Don't be ridiculous,' Teddy says, hands on hips. 'Firstly, you have twenty million.'

'Nearly twenty-one,' Ivy murmurs.

'And secondly,' Teddy continues, 'it's time to start enjoying this money.' She grins. 'You know, when I won, one of the first things I did – after killing my husband, of course – was to go to Vegas. I stayed in a penthouse at The Bellagio and spent sixty grand in the casinos.' She shrugs. 'It was fun, but to be honest, I prefer Great Yarmouth. The arcades are so much better and, holy crap, babe, don't get me started on the mini golf. It's *fantastic*.'

Paula nods, but she's trying to imagine how an American would even know about Great Yarmouth. The Brits have tried so hard to keep it a secret from the rest of the world.

Audrey joins in excitedly, 'I went on holiday, too, I took my parents on a cruise. They were absolutely mad about the on-deck water park. Ooh, we should go on a cruise together one day! What do you think?'

The other three regard her blankly. 'Your *parents*?' Teddy asks at last in a stunned voice. 'Like, you took them . . . in an urn?'

Audrey huffs good-naturedly. 'No, and I don't like what you're implying. I'm only eighty-one, thank you. We Swifts live until we're at least one hundred and twenty.'

Ivy straightens up, preparing herself to speak. She does so quietly. 'The first thing I bought after I won the money was a boat.' She looks around the group proudly and Teddy gives her an encouraging nod. 'I'd always wanted one. Much more than a house or a car or holidays. I always loved being on the water. It felt so free, and I loved the idea of having that freedom whenever I wanted.' She looks down, fiddling with a small silver ring on her middle finger. 'Being in the middle of the ocean away from everything is the best thing in the world.'

This is the most Ivy has spoken since Paula met her, and she resists an urge to reach out and give her a hug. Audrey puts up no such fight and gathers the younger woman up in her arms.

'I bet it's a lovely boat!' she says, patting Ivy. 'With an awful lot of freedom. We'll all have to go out on it sometime. Forget the cruise, we'll go on a yachting trip, eh, Paula?' Paula the Dog barks at this and Audrey nods at her. 'You too, my darling.'

Paula the Human smiles. 'I'd like that.' She turns to face the big red sports car again, nodding to herself. 'Oh my goodness.' She takes a giant breath. 'I think I'm going to buy it.'

'Francesca!' Audrey calls out, waving towards the office. The older woman is giving Paula no chance to change her mind. The sales consultant is with them in moments.

'Have you made a decision?' she asks and the four women all nod in unison.

Teddy steps forward. 'She only won twenty-one million on the lottery, so we've ruled out the Rolls-Royce La Rose Noire Droptail,' she says smoothly, turning to Audrey and Paula to offer a casual wink. 'But we'll take the Porsche here.'

'Not in red though,' Paula adds quickly.

'God no,' Teddy nods, 'because she's not a fifty-seven-year-old man who's compensating for being too embarrassed to approach the pharmacy counter in Boots to buy Viagra.'

'Of course,' Francesca nods, unfazed by Teddy's long-winded analogy. 'If you'd like to join me in the office, we can go through everything.'

'I want it in sky blue,' Paula tells the group. 'I've always wanted a sky-blue car.'

She turns to follow Francesca, when her handbag starts to ring. She pulls out her phone. 'It's Tilly,' she says conversationally.

'Your daughter,' Audrey says and it's not a question. She seems to know everything about everyone. She seems to know all their stories before they've even entered a room. She's probably hugged them all already, too.

'Hello, Tills, are you OK?' Paula answers and even she can hear the weird, fake tone in her voice.

'Mum? Where are you?'

Paula tenses. 'Has something happened?' She's suddenly picturing Craig and his friend going to her daughter's house, grabbing her and Misha, hurting them.

Tilly makes an apologetic noise. 'No, no! Sorry, I didn't mean to scare you. I just . . . I'm at the house, and Seb doesn't know where you are.'

'No,' Paula agrees, feeling unsure. She doesn't want to explain.

'Well?' Tilly's using her worried voice. 'Where are you?'
Paula pauses before answering carefully. 'I'm in London.'
'London?'
'Yes, I'm . . . shopping.'
'You're *shopping*?'
'Yes.'
'Oh.' Tilly sounds nonplussed. 'Well, I suppose that's good. I've been telling you to spend some of that money, haven't I? Have you bought anything nice? You could do with a new shower curtain in the bathroom, y'know. If you're near John Lewis or anything.'

Paula swallows. 'Yes, that's a very good thought, Tilly. I'll get on that. And maybe a new bath mat, too.'

'Great!' Tilly pauses. 'You should get something fun, too,' she tells her encouragingly. 'Maybe a new handbag or a fancy coat! You deserve it!' There is a long silence before her daughter continues, 'Um, Mum? You know you're acting a bit weirdly, don't you?'

'Am I?'
'Yes.'
'OK.'

There is another heavy pause on the line between them and Paula waits anxiously. At last, Tilly sighs heavily. 'You're coming to the next session tomorrow with Gerald, aren't you?'

'Gerald?'
'The grief counsellor! Our next family session is tomorrow. It's every Tuesday, remember?'

'If that's what you want, then of course, Tilly.'

'What *I* want?' Tilly sighs again. 'OK, whatever, yes, I want us to continue with the family grief counselling.' Paula doesn't reply, and when Tilly speaks next, there is hurt in her voice.

'Right. I guess I'll speak to you soon then. Enjoy . . . London or whatever.'

'Thanks, Tills.'

Her daughter hangs up and Paula feels a beat of worry pulse through her. She knows her children are concerned. They have every right to be, but she doesn't want to share any of this just yet. She doesn't want to share The Lottery Winner Widows Club. She's not quite sure what to make of it herself yet.

As she puts her phone away, she notices she has a text. She doesn't know the number but opens it anyway. The message is only five words long.

Can I have some money?

She blinks at the message, reading it a few more times.

Paula doesn't understand, but it makes her feel funny. Is this the loan sharks again? It doesn't sound like them. They've already made their demands in person and that was only yesterday. This doesn't sound like Craig or his reality-TV-fan cohort.

But if not them, then who? And how did they get her number? Perhaps it's meant to be funny? Is it a prank? She's certainly had enough messages, calls and emails from distant relatives over the last couple of weeks, since it all went public about her lottery win.

'Are you OK?' Ivy asks quietly as they file towards Francesca's office.

'I just got a bizarre text,' she confides.

Ivy frowns. 'Can I see?'

Paula hands her the phone and Ivy quickly scans the odd words.

'That is a bit disconcerting,' she admits after a moment, handing back the device. 'But I don't think you should worry. When I won the lottery, I got a lot of weird messages, too. Random strangers would call me at work and email my family. There are lottery obsessives out there with no boundaries.' She shudders, fiddling distractedly again with that silver ring. 'They feel entitled to you and your winnings. They act like you're now a celebrity or public property because you had this huge bit of luck. I'm sure it's just one of those creeps. It'll die down. It did for me.'

Paula nods, feeling marginally better. She puts her phone away in her bag and straightens her shoulders, trying to shake off the strangeness of the message. Ivy's right, it's probably just some lottery fan. And people win the lottery every day; there's bound to be some other jackpot winner soon for the internet and the weirdos to obsess over. They'll soon lose interest.

She takes a deep breath, joining the group in Francesca's office, where all kinds of exciting paperwork no doubt awaits her. She fingers the notebook and the bank card in her pocket again, thinking about what it means for her. And what it apparently means to others.

The money suddenly feels very heavy in her pocket and she doesn't know if that's a good or a bad thing.

17

Paula is hiding in the loo. It's not terribly dignified but it's better than being out there. With them. With Gerald.

This second session with the family counsellor has so far been even more awkward than the first. The man keeps talking about mutual support and identifying emotions. He must've said at least four or five times that he wants to *facilitate dialogue*. Which honestly just makes Paula want to scream.

Would that be considered facilitating dialogue? Or would it be him demonstrating *active listening*?

And they've talked so much about John.

Tilly has cried twice today, talking about her dad. Both times she was telling a story from her childhood. She told Gerald the counsellor about a Christmas Day where the star attraction was the brand-new video camera under the tree. Tilly cried buckets as she described rehearsing a version of *Sleeping Beauty* all day with Seb, and how John laughed his head off filming their efforts. Then she talked at length about a birthday spent at a theme park, where, she says, her dad had nearly cried from fear in the queue for the biggest roller coaster, but didn't run away. Tilly smiled through tears, describing how he threw up afterwards, but went on again when she begged.

Paula remembered both days vividly. They were good days.

But when the focus had turned to her – when Gerald had asked her to share some of her own favourite memories – she had stuttered, panicked, then excused herself for a loo break.

It was hard enough talking about John in the last session, before she found out about the fifty thousand pounds. About the loan sharks. About what he might have done.

About what she now knows he definitely *has* done.

Paula's spent much of the last two days rooting through John's things, looking for proof of this fifty thousand pound loan. Looking for proof that he couldn't really have done this to her or to their children, that surely he never could. But late last night she found a slip of paper, tucked into a pile of unopened junk mail. It listed games played, alongside names Paula vaguely recognised from the snooker club, and the sums and sums of money he'd bet. It took her only minutes to understand that John's losses added up to that horrible, outsized figure the loan sharks were asking for.

And at the top of the sheet of paper were five letters written in damning capitals: CRAIG. His name was underlined twice, and Paula could feel her husband's fear in those scrawled strokes.

So now she knows. And Paula doesn't know where to go from here. She's been awake all night, questions racing through her mind. She's surprised to find that she doesn't feel surprised, but she does feel pain. Pain at the betrayal – not of her, but of their children. How could he do this to them? And how could he not have told her so they could deal with this together? How could he leave her with this huge, awful thing to cope with all alone? She's been shocked by the rebellious strength of her feelings; by the pure fury she feels towards John. She's disgusted with him. *Disgusted!* Appalled that he could do this to her – to the family.

And then the guilt arrives, because how can she be angry with him when he's dead?

The worst part is that there's nowhere to put the anger or the guilt. She can't talk about John here, with Tilly and Seb – and Gerald – not without thinking about his lies. She can't talk about him without thinking of the cash envelope she's started putting together, that so far has only around one per cent of the total she needs. She can't tell them. She knows how much it would hurt them and she can't do it.

So she's hiding in the loo. Paula stares at herself in the mirror, wondering how much more of the session she can get away with missing. They're nearly at the end, maybe she can ride it out in here.

She pulls at the bags under her eyes, wondering if there is anything that can be done there. She looks old. She always looks old. She might even look older than eighty-something Audrey Swift. Though it's hard to see Audrey properly when she shines all the time, with so much joie de vivre and so many layers of floral clothes.

Could Paula get away with a pashmina? Probably not. She might manage a scarf from M&S but a pashmina made from cachemire goats just isn't her.

She sighs, looking away. This is why Paula tends not to look in mirrors. In her head, she's still young. She's perhaps thirty-two-ish. It was a good age to be, an age where she felt like she was a grown-up to the outside world but not too grown-up yet on the inside. Either way, her face no longer matches the way she feels. It hasn't for a long time.

But Audrey is twenty years older than Paula, and she doesn't seem to mind that fact. She is the youngest old person Paula has ever met.

Paula takes a deep breath, looking at her reflection again. She takes in her sun spots and laughter lines, and decides to be kinder to the person looking back. She is going to be more Audrey.

Which also probably means facing up to things that scare her.

With a resigned sigh, Paula turns away from the mirror again and heads back in the direction of the therapy room. She pauses for a moment outside the door, hearing Tilly's raised voice. She and Seb are talking to the counsellor and her daughter sounds upset.

'What's wrong with her though? Why is she so . . . cut off?'

There is a pause before Gerald replies, 'It's likely your mum still hasn't processed what's happened yet. But that is completely normal! Everyone deals with grief in a different way. You need to give her more time. Be patient with her.'

'You don't understand, this *isn't* normal. Not for her! This isn't . . . her! She's not herself. Is she, Seb?'

Seb's reply is sarcastic, 'Oh sure, yeah, because she reacted sooo differently when her last husband died suddenly in a horrifying car accident.'

'Shut up, you idiot.'

'I mean, c'mon, Tills,' Seb's voice is lower – less invested. 'She's just trying to cope or whatever. Just because she's being bananapants weird lately, doesn't mean there's something more going on. She's just – I dunno – sad about Dad or whatever.'

'But *is* she?' Tilly cries. 'Because she doesn't seem that sad to me.' She gulps, sounding like she wants to cry. 'This doesn't feel like grief at all! I'm so worried about her. She doesn't cry. She doesn't seem sad or morose. She's not depressed. She doesn't even get angry. There are no tentacles, Seb!' Paula can hear her daughter shift position in the room, turning to Gerald. 'What are the seven stages of grief again?'

Seb interrupts, 'Isn't it twelve steps?'

Tilly angrily sighs, 'Shut up, Seb! It's seven, right, Gerald?'

Paula's daughter always has to be right. Especially around her little brother.

'Um.' Paula can sense the counsellor's discomfort through the door. 'Well, it's actually five stages. I think, Seb, you're thinking of AA? And, Tilly, maybe... deadly sins? Or wonders of the world?'

'Oh.' Tilly sounds embarrassed. 'OK, but I was closer. Twelve steps was way wronger, Seb.'

Gerald clears his throat. 'The five stages of grief are thought to be denial, anger, bargaining, depression and acceptance. Although I would argue that grief is a much, much more complicated—'

Tilly interrupts, 'See! Mum's not doing any of those! Where's the secretive weirdo stage?'

Secretive weirdo? Paula doesn't much like that description of herself. Has she really been acting so oddly? She's just been getting on with things, hasn't she? Trying to make her way in this new world. And hasn't she always kept certain, difficult things to herself? Maybe Tilly doesn't know her as well as she thinks she does.

It occurs to Paula that her children are only just noticing her now. And they seem to be discovering they don't really like what they're seeing.

Behind the door, Paula's phone buzzes.

It's Audrey, sending a video of Paula the Dog doing something called the 'zoomies'.

Buying a car together yesterday has been quite the bonding experience. Teddy even created a new WhatsApp group for them all. It's named TLWWC. Paula still thinks it's a rather silly name, too clunky and awkward. And, for goodness' sake, where are all the apostrophes supposed to go? Surely they warrant at least two or three? Paula's mother was an English teacher, she'd know the answer. Teddy doesn't use any at all, which surely can't be right, but she's the one who seems very set on the name – even after Paula brought up the grammar issue – so it seems they're stuck with it.

Either way, it's been a nice distraction. It seems not an hour can pass without one of them sending some funny picture or Facebook meme. Many of them, Paula is well aware, Tilly would probably tell her off about, for being inappropriate or sexist towards men, but they still make Paula chuckle.

She steels herself and opens the door.

Seb startles in his seat, looking guilty. Tilly looks upset and vaguely annoyed.

'Your tummy OK?' she says pointedly and Paula dips her head, reddening. She hid in the bathroom for too long.

'I'm afraid we're at the end of the session for today,' Gerald says, giving Paula a regretful look over his grandpa glasses. Tilly sighs. Paula knows it's directed at her, but she's relieved all the same. They've signed up for six of these sessions, which means she's a third of the way through already. Paula gathers her bag and coat, pleased with her quick maths.

They head out to the car park where Tilly's Mini Cooper waits. A strange silence hovers around them as they all pile in and Tilly asks the sat nav to take them back to Paula's.

'Do a U-turn,' instructs the sat nav and they do.

After a few more minutes of loud directions cutting through the tense silence, Seb leans forward from his middle seat in the back. 'Can we have some music on? Olivia Rodrigo, please?'

Tilly ignores him. 'You know, Mum,' she begins carefully, 'you missed a meeting with the financial advisor yesterday? The one Amy from Lotto set up for you? And I've messaged you twice about meeting with a solicitor and tax specialist. I know it's all pretty boring, but it needs doing. You can't just let all that money sit there in your Club Lloyds account.'

She'd missed an appointment? That's not like Paula.

'It's not like you, Mum,' Tilly says, glancing over, her brow furrowed.

'It might be like me,' she replies with a hint of defiance. Tilly is driving so slowly and carefully. Why has Paula never noticed how dull her driving is?

'Look,' her daughter begins again, and it hurts Paula's heart to hear how much she's having to try. 'I get it, I'm annoying and overbearing.' She sighs. 'And if you don't want to keep doing the grief counselling sessions, we don't have to.'

'Don't we?' Paula asks hopefully.

'Yes, we do!' Tilly answers. 'That was meant to be rhetorical, Mum! They're important! We talked about how important they are. You really need to start opening up because I'm worried we're losing you, too. Losing Dad like that, it's knocked all of us off our axis . . .' She frowns at the windscreen. 'Axi? Axises?'

'Axee,' Seb says with confidence from the back seat.

'Anyway.' Tilly ignores her brother's input. 'What I'm trying to say is, please, can you give it more of a chance, Mum? The counselling? Gerald? It's not going to help you or us as a family if you won't share anything during the sessions.' She shoots Paula a slightly amused look. 'Or if you hide in the loo.'

Paula stares out the window. She wants to help her family, and she's aware she's letting her daughter down. But she doesn't know how to be the person Tilly wants her to be. She doesn't know what to say.

On her lap, her phone buzzes again. It's from the TLWWC WhatsApp group. Another meme from Teddy. She seems very keen on the theme of wisdom coming hand in hand with age. This one describes how women over forty are powerful, strong, and no longer 'give any fucks'.

Paula covers her mouth to stop from laughing. She very much likes the idea of it. She waited eagerly over the years to start caring less, but it never happened. She is sixty-one and unfortunately still gives a multitude of effs. She still cares about how she looks, how she feels, what she does. And goodness, she cares more than ever about what other people think of her. Even – *especially* – strangers.

Tilly pulls up at a red light, glancing over. 'Who's messaging you?' She says this conversationally but it alarms Paula. She hastily turns her phone away. 'No one,' she says quickly. 'I was looking up the plural of axis for you.' In her hand, the phone buzzes again, rather undermining the lie. Paula wonders how one might turn that noise off. Usually she'd ask Tilly, but that seems out of the question right now.

A quiet hangs over them for a few seconds. Paula breaks the awkward silence. 'I've got the answer!' She looks up from her phone. 'The plural of axis is axes.' She pauses. 'But I can't remember now why we needed to know it.'

Seb leans forward. 'It was because Tills said we'd been knocked off our—'

Tilly emits a strangled noise. 'Does it really matter?' She pulls up at another traffic light and turns to face her mother. 'The point is that it doesn't feel like you're really listening to me. To either of us.' She gestures at her brother in the back seat. 'Something's going on with you, Mum. It's obvious. And I want you to feel like you can talk to us. Please? If not to Gerald, then to us?'

'Tilly, love.' Paula turns to face her daughter, the seatbelt straining against her chest. 'I know you're worried about me, but you don't have to be. I'm your mum. I'm the same mum I've always been. It's not your job to worry about me. And there's nothing to worry about anyway! Nothing at all. I'm fine. I'm doing OK. Everything's the same. The house is the same; the garden's the same, though it needs mowing. And I'm very much the same as I've always been.' She laughs, then gestures to Seb over her shoulder. 'Your brother's the one you need to worry about changing. I caught him looking at a jobs website the other day. Can you believe such a thing!'

'Hey!' Seb pouts in the back seat. 'A person can evolve, can't they? I thought it was about time I started thinking about my career trajectory now I'm in my thirties.'

'Career *trajectory*?' Tilly grins over at her mum, the mood in the car softening. 'Is there a natural next step from serving hot dogs part-time?'

Seb harumphs as Paula smiles. 'The point is, my children,' she says determinedly, 'you have nothing to fret about, so please stop. I'm the same mum I've always been. I haven't changed and that's that.'

Tilly pulls up outside Paula's house. 'OK.' Her daughter takes a deep, slow breath. 'I get it. I'm sorry for giving you a hard time. If you say nothing's going on with you, I believe you.'

A man with a clipboard approaches Paula's open window and for a moment she recoils, thinking it must be Craig again, or maybe one of the lottery obsessives, here in person to demand cash.

'Paula Sheldon?' he asks politely as she nods back nervously. 'I'm just delivering this for you.' He turns proudly to reveal a brand-new sky-blue Porsche Taycan Turbo, sitting on the kerb, sparkling like a *Twilight* vampire.

Whoops. So much for being the same as always.

18

'No, Paula doesn't like that.' Audrey is shaking her head into the phone glued to her ear. 'Nope, she doesn't like that either. Nope. Find another way, please, Belinda.'

'What don't I like?' Paula wanders over to join Ivy, who is listening intently to the phone conversation.

'Paula the Dog,' Ivy explains, starry-eyed at the very mention of the darling little pup. She's wearing a shirt today instead of her usual tee, and the effect is endearingly like a young child playing dressing-up.

Teddy continues, 'Audrey's on the phone with the groomer. They want to wash her but apparently Paula the Dog doesn't like that. Audrey wants her dry-cleaned in some way. Dry-cleaned in a way that also won't go near her sensitive nipples. It's quite an involved process. I'm not sure how they've managed before now.'

'Oh, I wondered where Paula the Dog was today,' Paula the Human says. 'I thought perhaps even your eight hundred million wasn't enough to persuade Gucci to allow dog hair on the premises.' She waves around at the luxury store they've been ransacking for the past forty minutes. The store is empty of customers, bar them – just like the car showroom last week – and Paula wonders if this is what money really buys you: an escape from other people.

Audrey ends her call as Teddy leads the group over to the shoe area.

'Here we are, Mrs Fletcher.' A staff member trails behind them. She holds up a pair of shiny burgundy leather boots, presenting them like they are a fine jewel. They look to Paula more like something you'd wear to stables for horse riding. 'Size nine and a half.'

'It's *Ms*,' Teddy says icily, pointing her sunglasses at the woman. 'Not Mrs. Yuck. And no need to shout my shoe size to the whole world.'

Given it's only the five of them there, including the disinterested sales assistant, this seems like an overstatement, but Paula can't help sneaking a look down at Teddy's feet. She's been so caught up with the woman's lustrous hair and expensive clothes, she'd never noticed the size of her feet. They are, admittedly, quite large. But they suit her.

Teddy accepts the boots, examining them close up, then taking a seat to try them on. 'I'm going to have to call my wealth management team at this rate,' she guffaws, flicking that luscious hair off her shoulder. 'I've spent so much today, they'll be having a meltdown.' She sighs happily, pulling up the zip with long, orange nails. 'But what's the point of winning the lottery if you don't then spend it in the most ridiculous way possible?'

'Are they expensive?' Paula asks, then looks fearfully at the staff member. Is it considered gauche or embarrassing to mention money in a place like this? The girl doesn't visibly react, but Paula's pretty sure she senses a disapproving energy.

'Of course they're expensive!' Teddy says. 'One thousand, seven hundred and fifty pounds.' When Paula's eyes widen she quickly adds, 'But they're cheaper than most things I've bought today. They really shouldn't let me loose on Old Bond Street. God, I *love* being stupidly rich.'

She pulls a dark-coloured credit card out of her purse and hands it to the young woman. The assistant practically bows as she takes it and Paula catches a glimpse of the name on the credit card. Tina Edwina Fletcher.

'I keep forgetting Teddy's not your real name,' Paula says.

'Tina. Teddy for short.'

Paula frowns. 'But Teddy's not shorter than Tina.'

Teddy laughs at this. 'You got me. OK, the truth is, I spent a lot of years working in a law office surrounded by a lot of moron men failing upwards in every direction. And having a guy's name on my email address sure helped me out over the years. You wouldn't believe how many people assumed *Tina* was a receptionist and *Teddy* was the boss.'

'*You* worked in a law office?' Paula can't help giving Teddy another once-over. The huge earrings, the short skirts, the big, shiny hair ... they don't exactly scream white-collar professional. 'Like ... as a *lawyer*?' She suddenly remembers Teddy at that house viewing, quoting some obscure made-up legalese at the estate agent.

Teddy clocks the tone. 'I hope you're not making assumptions about me, Paula? It took me a lot longer than it should've to prove myself, thanks to my tits, but by the time I left, I was one of my firm's most in-demand lawyers. I had all the biggest accounts and the highest billables. They begged me not to go.'

Paula blushes a dark red. She feels terrible because of course she made assumptions. What did she think of Teddy after that first meeting in her kitchen? A WAG, that's what she internally called her. It's becoming very clear that Teddy is so much more than that. She is dry, funny and – clearly – incredibly smart.

'Sorry,' she mutters and Teddy laughs.

'Forget it, babe. We all make snap judgements. I quite like them actually, because then I get to prove everyone wrong. I like other people being wrong.' She pauses, then continues, 'The truth is, I didn't wear any of this stuff in the office.' She waves at herself. 'I forced myself into a little grey, pantsuit box, the box they wanted me to fit into. I thought pretending to be one of them – pretending to be *like* them – was the only option I had. And maybe it was. But I can't tell you how liberating it is to have this money. To be able to be whoever I want to be after all this time. To spend like an absolute beast whenever I want.'

Paula smiles at this. At the idea of money letting this woman be free to be whoever she wants. Goodness, it even let her be a woman again. Paula feels like she understands Teddy a little more now.

As they leave the shop, Audrey is back on the phone, debating Paula the Dog's diva demands. Paula looks around at her friends, feeling abuzz with dopamine from all the spending. She can't believe how much she's bought today. She got herself a beautiful new camel-coloured trench coat, two new dresses, one long and one something Teddy called midi, three pairs of trousers, a new blouse, some T-shirts that Ivy liked, and – maybe most excitingly – a new pair of trainers to replace her Clarks plimsolls. Honestly, her shopping haul list feels like a designer *Hungry Caterpillar.*

Oh, and because Tilly mentioned it last week, they also popped into John Lewis so she could pick up a new shower curtain and bath mat.

She feels unleashed! And she didn't even buy as much as Teddy or Audrey, who seemed to be competing to spend the most money in one outing.

And yet, none of the group is weighed down with bags because the staff arranged to have it all delivered directly to each of them at home.

As they head down the beautifully maintained, pedestrianised streets of Old Bond Street, Ivy is almost mown down by a man and woman walking past at speed. The man hisses furiously at the woman with him, grabbing her, his grip white on her arm. 'You're humiliating me,' he says to her in a low voice as she stares at the ground, her face pale.

It happens in just a few seconds and then they're gone, but the group dynamic shifts around Paula. Both Teddy and Audrey have encircled Ivy, who is visibly trembling, her young face contorted with fear. Teddy's hands are shaking too, but Paula can see that it is with rage, not fear. Audrey pulls Ivy close, murmuring kind, reassuring words.

After a moment, Paula realises she is holding her breath. She releases it slowly, her heart pounding.

'Asshole,' Teddy says a minute later, staring off after the couple. Then she repeats the word three more times. Audrey moves Ivy with her across the road, walking like they're in a three-legged race. They make it to a black bench and all sit in a line, all four of them holding hands.

It takes a minute, but Ivy at last straightens up, looking at Audrey. 'I've been attending that support group you suggested.' She nods at the older woman, speaking in that quiet, soft voice of hers. 'For women like me. Women who've been through . . . domestic abuse. We meet twice a week and all we do is sit around talking about what we've . . .' She swallows. 'The stories, the awful, bloody, brutal stories . . . they really get under your skin, you know?' She blinks around at the others and Paula's reminded again that Ivy is only twenty-seven and she's already been through so much. Ivy continues, 'I think about it constantly. I dream about the women in the group. Sometimes I can't remember what really happened to me with my husband, and what happened to Christina or Kuba or Ayesha or Megan.' She takes a ragged breath. 'I feel so helpless all the time. Most of them are still in those relationships as well. Still getting beaten up most nights, still getting abused, and they can't see a way out.' She inhales deeply. 'I want to help them so badly.'

The group lets the words settle over them in silence, taking it in. People wander past, chatting about their lives, swinging shopping bags, pulling coats tighter around them as the breeze picks up.

After a moment, Ivy says almost under her breath, 'I wish we could just . . . *do* something.'

There is a loaded pause before Audrey offers in a low voice, 'What if we can?' She continues, almost too quietly for Paula to hear, 'What if we can use what we've learned, use our money and our know-how to help other women? Women who are trapped in the same way we all were?'

Paula leans closer. 'What do you mean?'

Teddy narrows her eyes at Audrey. 'Use our powers for good? You mean help other women . . .' she hisses the next part, '. . . get rid of their asshole husbands?' Audrey nods and, after a moment, Teddy slowly smiles. 'I love it.'

Paula leaps up off the bench. 'Hold on,' she says, sweat breaking out on her forehead. 'You're not talking about . . . You don't mean—'

'It's OK, my darling, don't get upset,' Audrey says. 'We're just talking.' She waits for Paula to slowly sit back down. 'But think about it for a minute. We've all been there, and there are so many women out there who need help, who need *our* help.'

Teddy's face is set in a hard expression. 'We have the money, the resources, and the know-how. I'm a lawyer, for God's sake! I know what it takes to get away with this kind of thing. We have time on our hands and first-hand experience of what these women are going through. We could make such a difference. Nobody's looking at us. Nobody would suspect us—'

'Wait.' Paula is really panicking now. 'What about Columbo? There is someone looking at us! Or at Audrey, at least.'

They all look to Audrey, who shrugs. 'OK, yes, the police officer investigating my husband's death is still hanging around.' She nods at Paula. 'He was following us in the car last week. And the other day he turned up at my daughter's workplace to ask her a few questions about me and Harold. It was . . . unpleasant.'

Paula shakes her head. 'Even if we wanted to help these women – and of course I do! – we can't risk doing anything with a police officer hanging around, surely!'

'He doesn't scare me, and don't call me Shirley.' Audrey sounds positively jolly. She pauses to take Paula's hand. 'Look, he has absolutely nothing to go on with Harold and he's running out of options. Plus, he has no idea about any of you. And even if he did, we became friends long after Harold's death. He'd never be interested in any of you with regards to the case.'

Teddy fixes her with a look. 'Maybe we can hit him with a harassment suit. I'll get my lawyer hat back on and call the station, get him to back off.'

Audrey looks amused. 'How thrilling! But there's no need for any of that, darling; he's got nothing at all. And I can stay in the background of things if it makes you all feel a little better. I'll help with planning and orchestrating, but avoid anything that might draw suspicion.'

'But— But—' Paula splutters, as Ivy interrupts her.

'I have a list,' she says with steel. 'I started making notes after the support group sessions, writing a journal . . .' She smiles shyly at Audrey, who gives her an encouraging nod.

'Go on, my darling.'

Ivy nods back. 'Audrey thought it might help me sort through my feelings, and it really has. But it's turned into a lot of unhinged raging about the men these women talk about. I've got a list of what they've done.' Her face is wearing an unfamiliar expression. 'And names. I've got a list of names. Of the ones who are doing the worst things. I know stuff about them . . . about these men. I've been listening. We could find them really easily, don't you think?' She looks to Teddy, who nods, then Ivy turns to Audrey and Paula in turn. 'We can save these women.' She nods in the direction of that long-gone couple. 'We can help women like her.'

19

Paula has just decided that people use the word *breathtaking* way too frivolously. The scenery is breathtaking; that painting is breathtaking; the bungalow on *Escape to the Country* is breathtaking – just look at the kitchen island!

Because they've just arrived at Teddy's apartment, and it is *actually* breathtaking. It has very literally taken Paula's breath away. She continues to struggle for breath as she passes through the grand entrance hall and into a large, open-plan kitchen. It is pink. Pink marble tops, pink cupboards, pink table tops. Even pink – no, wait, hold on. Paula looks closer but can find no evidence of an oven or hob. Does Teddy not cook?

Reading her mind, Teddy presses a button and cupboard fronts open smoothly by themselves to reveal a variety of fixtures and fittings. There they are! Hidden by magical cupboard doors! How clever. It all looks brand new and shiny. So maybe Teddy doesn't in fact cook.

When Audrey casually referenced Teddy's flat in west London, this was not what Paula pictured. She's never seen, or even imagined, a flat this size before. It goes on for ever, down corridors and through giant well-lit spaces.

'Here's my room,' Teddy calls out from down another long passageway. Paula passes through a large dressing room, noting an ensuite bathroom off to the side. She peeks a head in. The ensuite is practically the size of Paula's whole house. She gasps her astonishment as they enter the bedroom itself. Windows line the entire wall, featuring dramatic views of London's greenest spaces. At one end of the room sits the biggest bed Paula's ever seen, and a TV spans almost the whole facing wall.

'This bedroom must be forty square feet!' Paula gasps. 'How do you even watch that TV? I'd have to wear my glasses in bed and have the subtitles as big as my head.'

Teddy shrugs. 'To be honest, I mostly just bring my laptop into bed with me and watch my reality shows there. I don't think that TV has ever been turned on. I wouldn't even know where the remote control is.' Paula shakes her head in bewilderment. All this luxury. It's sort of . . . silly?

They wander through another three bedrooms, each immaculately decorated and practically untouched. Everything is neatly tucked away, everything is high-end, and everything is still mostly all pink.

'How big is this flat?' Paula can't keep the awe out of her voice.

'Just under nine and a half thousand square feet,' Teddy confirms, respect in her voice. 'It's more than ten times the size of the place I had in New York, before I won the money.' She smiles broadly and winks. 'But obviously I've held on to that house. Can't have anyone digging up the back garden now, can I?'

Ivy and Audrey giggle at this, and Paula swallows hard, wondering how seriously to take all their jokes. At least it sounds like she's been sensible about the body. It's reassuring, somehow. They might talk about death with a light tone, but the group apparently take covering it up seriously.

But were they really being serious back then, on that bench on Old Bond Street? They can't honestly be considering... Paula shakes her head as the group moves on through to the back part of the apartment. Just as they seem to be reaching the end of the tour, another room materialises.

'They call this a *cinema room*.' Teddy rolls her eyes. 'But it's basically just another big living room.' She pauses. 'Although most living rooms don't have a bar.' She gestures across the wide expanse to an area that is essentially a Wetherspoons in its own right. A large mirror across the back wall showcases a fully stocked selection of every type of spirit on the market, along with a variety of beers on taps. There are large glass-doored fridges either side, with an array of pink and white wines, along with champagnes and Proseccos from every region.

Paula is so busy examining the choices and wondering if it's too early to ask for a drink, that she almost misses the best part of the room.

'Oh my,' she gasps, wheeling round as Teddy pulls back enormous bifold doors. They open out onto a huge, secret terrace out the back. She, Ivy and Audrey all step out into the sunshine, looking around at the large hedges and the array of potted flowers and plants surrounding them.

'There's a *pool*?' Paula is incredulous, taking in the small outdoor infinity pool, shimmering away, hidden among the plants.

'Sure,' Teddy says, following them out. 'But this is still the UK. I can get in there *maybe* twice a year on selective July dates. Even when I whack the heating on high, all night.'

Paula nods dumbly as they all take a seat around a table under a large cream umbrella. She sinks into the comfy seating, aware that she's never before experienced such luxury outdoor furniture. Usually it's all shiny wicker, cobwebs and pointy bits.

They bask in the cold sunshine for a moment, and Paula closes her eyes.

'So,' Audrey says cheerfully after a moment. 'Murdering men.' She turns to Ivy. 'Where is this list of yours? I don't suppose you've got it to hand?'

Ivy smiles sheepishly. 'You'll think I'm terribly Gen Z, but yes. I keep my journal on my phone.' She pulls it out, tapping a few things and handing it across to Audrey, who starts reading closely.

'Bastards,' she mutters after a few minutes, handing it along to Paula, who starts to read, then stops. It's too awful. Ivy's listed names in bold, and beside them are words like 'Drugged and raped her in her sleep', 'Put her in the hospital because she didn't reply to a text for half an hour', 'Told her he would kill her if she ever tried to leave him.' It is too much for Paula. She's lived a sheltered life, she knows this, and this is beyond anything she could imagine, or ever wanted to.

Her silly little worries suddenly seem so ridiculously insignificant.

She hands the phone to Teddy quickly, feeling bile sloshing around in her stomach.

'So who's first?' Ivy interrupts her reverie.

Teddy looks up from the phone. 'Can we get them all together in a room and shower them with Novichok?'

'The tennis player?' Paula blinks.

Teddy frowns. 'You might be thinking of Novak Djokovic? Novichok is a lethal nerve agent.'

'That would be ideal,' Audrey agrees. 'Though getting hold of that much Novichok might be a little tricky. Unless anyone here has an *in* with the Russians?' She pauses, then nods towards Ivy's phone – towards the list. 'What about that dreadful piece of shit, Dominic Shipman?' Paula feels waves of panic overtaking her as Ivy nods enthusiastically.

Her voice is clear and confident as she answers, 'He's a monster. His wife, Gemma, has tried to escape him so many times and he always finds her. They have two children and he's started on the little boy now. She tried to get a restraining order, but he's a police officer and they cover for him.'

Teddy shakes her head, her lip curling in disgust. 'Ugh, of course they do. The blue wall of silence. They won't stop one of their own. We have to take matters into our own hands if we want this man stopped.'

The four of them all stare silently at one another. Paula's heart is racing. Are they really having this conversation? She should leave. She should leave *right now*.

She doesn't.

Dominic Shipman. Paula steels herself and takes back Ivy's phone. She reads the two lines of notes Ivy's made.

Partner of Gemma, two children. Violent, horrible, abusive, a bully, a drunk – and works in police. Broke her arm twice, recently slapped little boy. Escalating.

Paula thinks about that final word. Escalating. He's escalating. What might he do next? To their children? His poor wife,

Gemma. How could anyone do that? To someone they love? She can't fathom it.

This is a bad man.

'He deserves to die,' Ivy says darkly, her eyes flashing. Some of her youth has fallen away and she suddenly seems much more like a grown-up.

'Right. Well, that's that then,' Audrey says. She slowly starts unravelling the pashmina wrapped tightly around her neck. It's the first time Paula has seen her without it and it adds to the surrealness of the moment. In a serious voice, the older woman adds, 'He'll be our first.'

Paula's chest tightens at the words. *First.*

Hearing about this horrible, evil man, all she can think is how much he obviously deserves to die. How much Gemma and her two young children need to escape him. And yet the idea of actually doing it . . .? She can't! Can she? Of course she can't!

'Ivy, babe, do you know anything else about him – where he lives, whereabouts he works?' Teddy has her thoughtful face on. She's slipping into high gear, into lawyer mode, making a plan.

Ivy looks thoughtful. 'I can find out. Gemma mentioned he's renting somewhere from a friend.'

'OK,' Teddy nods. 'That's good.' She looks down, her expression serious. 'Right, firstly, I think we need to do some surveillance. Although, Ivy, it might be a good idea to put some distance between yourself and Gemma for now. We're unlikely to be suspects if none of us have any connection to the man, but it would still be better to give her some space.'

Ivy nods and Teddy looks around the group. 'We need to make a plan. Brainstorm some ideas. Decide where and when.' She keeps nodding and Paula finds herself nodding along, then stops. What's happening right now? Teddy's still talking but her voice seems faraway. 'What do we know about planning a murder? What do we need to watch out for? How do most people get caught?'

'DNA!' Ivy interjects, wild-eyed. 'We need to be careful about DNA.'

Teddy nods. 'Right. I guess that's a good place to start. Ideally we would do this somewhere that has a lot of DNA from strangers. That way, if we leave any traces, there will be too much of it around to locate us.' She looks blank. 'What else?'

'Disposing of the body?' Audrey offers, and Paula thinks how odd it is to be able to see her neck, though it's a very nice neck. And what an odd word *neck* is.

'Ideally we would get rid of it.' Teddy looks thoughtful, then smiles dryly. 'I know better than most people that no body means no investigation. Did you know around six hundred thousand people go missing in the US every year?'

Audrey snorts. 'I should've shipped Harold's body off to the States. That would've stumped Columbo!'

Paula's stomach flips. 'I should think a lot of people get caught because the police are already familiar with them. So maybe Audrey should stay away from this completely? With a police officer watching her every move? I know I said it before but maybe none of us should be—'

Teddy interrupts, fixing Ivy with a determined stare and ignoring Paula's fearful babbling. 'The best way to avoid a murder investigation would be to make it look like it wasn't a murder.' She leans closer. 'Is this Dominic guy a drug user? He could overdose or something.'

Ivy shakes her head. 'I don't think so. Gemma says he drinks a lot, but I don't think he does anything harder than that. I don't know for sure though.'

'That's where the surveillance comes in.' Teddy nods.

'I could ask her?' Ivy offers and Teddy shakes her head.

'No, don't ask Gemma anything else about him for now. We don't want to raise any suspicions.'

'You know . . .' Audrey looks excited. 'I once read that the best getaway vehicle to escape a crime is a bike! I've got a lovely bike!'

Paula opens her mouth again to object – especially about the cycling part, murder is bad enough, for goodness' sake – but is interrupted by a loud buzzing. They all jump, then Teddy laughs.

'It's my front door,' she says, standing up.

'Don't answer it!' Paula says, her voice full of terror.

'Why?' Teddy looks puzzled.

'What if it's him – Dominic Shipman? Or Columbo? Or maybe the entirety of the police force? Maybe they heard us? Seb always says our phones are listening to us and I have been getting an awful lot of targeted ads about visiting the Austrian Alps ever since John's car crash.'

Audrey cackles that throaty cackle, throwing an easy arm around Paula. 'God, it's times like this I wish everyone still smoked. That would soon relax you, my darling.'

Teddy pats her on the shoulder gently. 'It's not the police, babe. Chill out.' She throws her sunglasses onto the table with abandon and disappears back inside the apartment.

Ivy leans closer, resting a hand lightly on Paula's arm. 'Are you OK?' she says in a low voice.

Paula nods slowly. 'Just a little bit on edge, I suppose.'

Ivy cocks her head. 'Have you been getting any more strange messages? Y'know, like that one at the car showroom, asking for money?'

She hesitates, wondering how much to share. Yes, there have been more odd texts from unknown numbers. But what about the rest of it? Should she tell Ivy about the men – the loan sharks who haunt her thoughts? How she lies awake at night wondering if they're about to turn up at her door? How she's been stashing cash every day, feeling increasingly helpless and frightened as it amounts to nowhere near fifty thousand pounds? Should she tell Ivy about the phone calls from breathy no ones who hang up after a few seconds? And those texts, all asking for money.

Apart from the last one. That last one . . . was different.

If she were braver, she'd message back telling them off. Maybe she'd even call the number to tell them to stop. If she didn't have a bunch of murderer friends and loan sharks on her tail, she might've even considered calling the police to report it.

At last she nods gloomily and Ivy looks stricken.

'That's horrible,' she says with sympathy, her eyes wide. There is something in her expression, and Paula regards her quizzically. After a moment, Ivy leans closer, placing a smooth little hand on Paula's gnarled old fingers. Did she ever have young hands like Ivy's? 'Um, Paula, have you been online much at all? I wondered if you've seen—'

A sound behind them stops Ivy mid-sentence. It's Teddy. She's reappeared with—

'Oh my goodness, *Tilly*?' Paula leaps out of her seat. 'And *Seb*? What on earth are you two doing here?' Paula is flabbergasted to see her children standing before her in this

Knightsbridge penthouse apartment. Do they know what they were just talking about? Do they know about the debt? Do they know about . . . But how could they?

Seb gives her a grin. 'Surprise, Mum.'

'What is . . . What are you . . . I don't understand. How did you find me?' Paula asks in a strangled voice.

Tilly eyes are wide, taking in the huge expanse of greenery around her on the roof terrace. 'I used Find My Phone,' she answers in an awed voice. 'It was already set up on your computer at home.' She pauses, looking now at the stunning views and at the infinity pool. 'What *is* this place?' She regards her mother in stunned silence. 'You haven't bought something else huge without telling me?'

Behind them, Teddy snorts. 'Babe, your mom couldn't afford this.'

Paula stands back, waving towards the gathered group of women. 'Um, Tilly, Seb, this is Teddy. This is her home. And that's Audrey and Ivy.'

Teddy nods, Ivy waves shyly, and – predictably – Audrey dives in for a group hug.

'It's *so* lovely to meet you, my darlings!' she says, smooshing them into her bosoms. 'I've heard so much about you, Tilly and Seb.'

Paula is aware this isn't true and she feels ashamed. She should've talked about her children more but something inside her wanted to keep these two worlds separate. She wanted to protect her friends and her children from each other. But look how well she's managed that. They're *here*.

'Er . . .' Tilly's alarm is plain on her face, as she tries to extricate herself from the Audrey hug as politely as possible. 'Nice to meet you, Audrey, was it?' Audrey nods happily, releasing them both at last. Tilly's brow is furrowed deep as she makes eye contact with her mother.

'Mum, what is all this? Are you OK?' She leans closer, speaking in a stage whisper. 'Have these women . . . kidnapped you? Do we need to get you out of here?'

'No!' Paula answers in a strangled tone. 'They haven't kidnapped me! They're my . . . friends.'

Tilly stares at her for a moment, taking this in. Then she turns to the group. 'And . . . um, how do you all know my mum?'

Paula regards the others fearfully, as Audrey speaks up. 'Your mum knew my husband,' she lies smoothly. 'She was his carer before he died a few months ago. And I got back in touch when your dad passed away.' She reaches for Seb's hand, squeezing it and looking with sympathy to Tilly. 'I'm so sorry for your loss.' The moment passes and she waves towards Teddy and Ivy. 'Then I introduced her to my pals here.'

Tilly still looks baffled taking in the three women – their ages spanning more than half a century – but Paula notes her shoulders relaxing a little. She's bought the story. Audrey is a very accomplished liar, Paula thinks, only slightly worried by the revelation.

'Would you like something to drink?' Teddy asks, as they all move inside to congregate in the ginormous kitchen. 'Tea? Or something stronger?' She finds mugs from a pink cupboard that appear from seemingly nowhere.

'Er, sure,' Tilly says, and Seb nods eagerly. 'Tea, please,' says Paula's daughter as Seb simultaneously requests a beer. They gather together at the large kitchen island and Audrey makes conversation, firing questions at Tilly and Seb, as Teddy moves about the room, playing host.

'And you're married to Misha, is that right?' she throws out to Tilly, barely waiting for an answer before moving on to Seb. 'And you live in the shed, don't you, my darling?'

He colours, shooting an embarrassed look at Ivy, the only other person in the room close to his age, before quickly offering, 'Well, yes, I do right now. But I've actually been looking at places to rent. And I had a job interview the other day!'

This is all news to Paula and she blinks in surprise at her son. Is he finally growing up? Goodness, wouldn't that be a revelation? Paula always felt he was capable of so much more than playing games in a shed. He was such a bright child, so intuitive. But when those teenage hormones swept in, he became subdued and uncommunicative. Fifteen years later and he hasn't made much progress on that front. Until now, it would seem.

Tilly titters awkwardly. 'It sounds like you know a lot more about us than we do about you . . .' There is an edge to her tone and Paula jumps in.

'So, Tills,' she begins nervously, 'what are you . . . Why is . . . Why were you looking for me?'

Her daughter takes a sip of tea. 'I was worried. I turned up at the house to pick you up, and Seb didn't know where you were. Again.' She shoots him an angry look as her brother stares down at his drink. 'That mad, flashy car you've bought wasn't in the driveway, and I keep having this dream that someone sees it outside your house and realises you're super rich. They decide to steal the car and kidnap you and—' She stops suddenly, sounding a little choked up and Paula reaches for her.

'I'm sorry, sweetheart,' she murmurs into her daughter's hair. She smells like fruity shampoo. It suddenly occurs to Paula that her daughter's fears might not be so far off the mark. What if those loan shark men do come back and see the car? Maybe she'd better clear the garage and park it out of sight. Paula draws back, regarding her oldest. 'I didn't mean to frighten you. But pick me up? What were you picking me up for?'

Tilly cocks her head. 'Our next session? We're supposed to be at the grief counselling.' She checks her watch. 'Right now, actually. They'll charge us for it.'

Paula gasps. 'Oh my goodness, Tills, I'm so sorry! I completely forgot.' *What with all the murder chat* – she doesn't add.

Her daughter huffs in response and it's clear her concern has turned into irritation. Paula suddenly feels a little defensive.

Of course it's not fair or right that she missed their appointment – she feels bad about that – but does Tilly really need to be kept in the loop about everything she's doing? She wonders what her daughter would make of her mother and these new friends planning the murder of a man named Dominic Shipman. The idea makes Paula want to do it after all. What would Tilly think of that?

For that matter, what would the Paula of a few months ago have thought?

After a moment, Tilly takes a deep breath, steadying herself. 'It's not just the flashy car, Mum,' she says slowly, looking anxious. 'There's another reason I panicked . . . Um, have you seen the stuff online?'

Paula glances at Ivy, whose eyes are wide and alert. 'No, why? What do you mean?'

Tilly swallows. 'You haven't checked your Facebook lately?'

Paula shakes her head again, fear creeping up the back of her neck. 'What is . . . What's going on?'

Her daughter shuffles closer. 'OK, look, it's not a huge deal and I don't want you to panic, but someone wrote an article last week . . .' – she pauses – 'about you.'

'About me?' Paula is confused. The lottery winner widow stuff had died down, hadn't it? Why would anyone still care?

Tilly looks around at the group of people she doesn't know, all listening intently. 'Shall we talk about this in the car? Or at home?'

Paula shakes her head quickly. 'No, it's fine, tell me.'

She sighs, looking a bit annoyed. 'Mum, it's kind of a *private* matter.'

Seb takes a sip of his beer. 'Stop making it into a massive drama, Tills. It's not that big of a deal.' He looks directly at Paula. 'It was just some rubbish online about how weird it was that Dad died just as you won the lottery. They thought it was suspicious and then with the way you reacted at the press conference, running off like that. They said it was like you had something to hide. They suggested . . .' He glances away awkwardly. 'Whatever. Anyway, the story got shared a bit and some idiots on the internet – a small handful of idiots – have been getting carried away with some stupid conspiracy theories.'

'Conspiracy theories about . . . me?' Paula asks, bewildered.

'Mostly just on Facebook.' Ivy moves closer. 'And no one even uses Twitter anymore.'

'X,' Audrey corrects. 'As in, the *ex*-social media website that only misogynists frequent these days.'

'I'd better go.' Paula turns to her friends, suddenly feeling very sick. She has to get out of there. She needs to go home and google herself. She has to figure out what all of this means. She splutters a thank you to Teddy for having her, and the group exchange awkward hugs. Paula, Seb and Tilly head out via the ornate lift, as Seb gleefully volunteers to drive Paula's car back home. She hands over her keys, her head spinning, and follows Tilly out onto the street, staring down at the pavement before her. She's suddenly feeling very exposed and frightened by the outside world.

Seb didn't say the words back there, but Paula got the inference.

It's no longer just Audrey, Teddy and Ivy who think she killed John. It sounds like the rest of the world thinks so, too.

And now that final text she received yesterday makes sense. The one from the unknown number who'd previously just asked for money.

I know what your friends have done.

20

To: John.Sheldon1960@oldmail.com
From: PaulaJeanieSheldon1964@ptinternet.com
Subject: Secrets and lies

John,

I don't know why I'm writing this. After everything that's happened – after I found proof of your gambling – I didn't think I ever wanted to speak to you again. But here I am.

    The trouble is, you were my whole world. And I suppose I always knew I wasn't yours, but finding out about this secret you had – this £50,000 you owed – has hit me very hard. I don't know how I'm supposed to forgive you.

    And with all of these things online now . . . it's awful. People are calling me a murderer, John! They keep pointing to things from the press conference as 'evidence' of my guilt. How I acted so suspiciously; how I snapped at the photographers; the look on my face when I ran away. Even the pink jumper I wore is apparently proof, because, 'what heartbroken new widow would wear such a tight pink sweater'.

It wasn't even my jumper, John! Tilly brought it for me to wear – it was Misha's.

And of course, everyone's asking questions about the notebook I dropped. Your notebook, John. The one I found. It took me a while to understand what it all meant – all the numbers and dates – years of them in there – but I do now. And I can't exactly explain it to the world, can I?

Although, in one way, the renewed media attention has been something like a blessing. The photographers are camped back outside our house again, and your friend Craig sent me a text message saying they can't risk meeting with me while I'm being so closely watched by the entire world. He said the moment the noise dies down, he'll be back to collect the money – the £50,000. I don't know what to do, I've barely gathered together a few thousand so far.

I think he and his friends are still watching me from afar. I've had some more hang-up calls and strange messages on my phone. I tried unplugging the landline, but there were several voicemails when I checked. And hearing those minute-long, silently crackling recordings was somehow even more frightening than the rest of it.

I've kept all this from Tilly and Seb, of course. They can't know the truth. It's causing such tension and distance between us. It's yet another thing I have to keep from them. I don't know how to make it better between us. Tilly just seems to be getting more and more worried about me. She thinks I'm having a breakdown, and

Elly Vine

I don't know how to make her understand. Every time I try to reassure her, she seems to get more suspicious. But there are things I just can't tell her.

Oh John, I don't know. Things have been so strange since you died, and they've been getting even worse since I met my new friends. But Tilly was the one telling me to get out there and have fun after your accident! She kept telling me to find and make a life for myself. Now she seems upset that I actually am.

I think she had this image of what she wanted from me as a widow. She wanted me to fold in on myself and disappear with grief. But I don't want to disappear. I feel like I was disappearing for a long time, even before all this. Audrey, Teddy and Ivy have made me want to . . . I don't know, reappear. I can't let them go. I can't.

Paula

21

'There he is,' Ivy gasps. The women all flatten against a wall.

Across the road, Evil Bastard, Dominic Shipman, is emerging from the pub. *Evil Bastard* is how Teddy is referring to him. Paula thinks it's a bit much.

'I can't see anything,' Audrey whispers loudly from the back. Paula ducks her head, trying to get out of the older woman's way. 'No, my darling,' Audrey tells her. 'I mean I literally can't see anything. I haven't got my glasses on. You're all blobs.'

'*You're* all blob,' Teddy mutters childishly.

'Are they in your handbag?' Ivy offers more helpfully. She might be the youngest of the group by a couple of decades, but she's probably the closest to an adult.

'No,' Audrey shakes her head. 'I don't like how I look in them. I want to be gorgeous at all times.' She flicks her pashmina over her shoulder and smiles mysteriously.

'You look more like a hippy art teacher in that scarf,' Teddy tells her dryly.

'It's not a scarf!' Audrey retorts. 'It's a pashmina.' She eyes Teddy's pink coat and coiffed hair, up in a loose bun tonight. 'Better than looking like Barbie with a pink tequila hangover.'

'You two!' Ivy scolds as Audrey and Teddy smirk at one another.

'The point is,' Audrey continues breezily, 'I want to make an effort for our special evening outings together.'

'Special evening *outings*?' Paula raises an eyebrow. She wouldn't exactly call these past few days spent following Dominic Shipman around . . . *an evening outing.*

Plans have stepped up a gear since their discussion last week on Teddy's rooftop terrace, sitting around on that expensive outdoor furniture. The TLWWC WhatsApp group has been alight with messages. But gone are the memes about ageing disgracefully. Now they're all murder themed. 'Feeling stabby' says one, while another reads, 'I'm the quiet neighbour with the big chest freezer!' A third warns, 'Don't annoy me, I'm running out of places to hide the bodies.' That one comes from Teddy, who follows it up with a quick, 'Actually, that's not true, there's still plenty more room in my back yard.'

There are also the messages that Paula mostly doesn't reply to.

If we go for an overdose, where does one buy heroin these days?

These days? Does that mean you once knew?

Oh darling, I've lived a long time. The sixties were a magical era.

What if we just ran up to him in the park and whacked him over the head with a brick, then ran away?

Audrey, you have such a violent streak.

Or I could strangle him with my pashmina!

He's not worth wasting a good scarf on.

It's a PASHMINA.

Do we need to make sure the ex-wife is nowhere around or at least has an alibi? I'd hate to kill him and then have her blamed?

I'm seeing Gemma at the support group today. I'll see what I can find out about her schedule.

Be subtle about it, Ivy, keep your distance as much as you can.

I think we should just go for something simple, like a burglary gone wrong. We break in, smash him round the head with a baseball bat. Get out of there. What do you think?

I'm not sure we're really capable of bashing someone's brains in. Not when it comes down to it.

We could wait until he's asleep, turn all the gas knobs on full blast?

I like that!

It could work?

It's better than my next suggestion, which was going to be inviting him up to my castle in Scotland, then arranging some kind of country shooting accident.

Maybe that'll work for the next one!!

Has everyone got gloves by the way?

I've only got fingerless gloves, would that work?

No.

I have some spares! Oh hold on, they're mittens. No good?

No.

I've got proper gloves! And I have the matching pashminas if that helps.

It doesn't.

OK, well, I'll bring them anyway. Just in case it gets chilly.

I found out from Gemma the name of the pub Dominic goes to every night. Shall we case the joint tonight?

How lovely! I've always wanted to be a stalker. You don't get much of a chance up in Scotland.

It is, oddly enough, a welcome distraction for Paula, who is under orders from Seb to 'stop looking at the internet.' She was really quite shocked after she'd rushed home last week. She had opened Facebook to find hundreds of friend requests from strangers, and almost as many messages. Seb didn't let her read them all, but they mostly seemed to be from people she didn't know, accusing her of killing her husband for the money. It was bizarre and harrowing. And it hasn't slowed down since. Neither have the journalists, calling and emailing, harassing her for an interview.

Across the road, Dominic staggers off down the street into the dark. He's oblivious to his surroundings and free of any safety concerns in the way that only a forty-something straight white man gets to be. When he reaches the crossing, he pauses and checks his watch. Instead of turning left in the direction of his car, Dominic heads right.

The women silently glance at one another. This is new. So far, he has very much been a creature of routine. He leaves work, goes straight to the pub – sometimes with friends, sometimes on his own – where he gets extremely drunk, and then he goes home to sleep it off.

Tonight though, he apparently has a new idea.

'Should we keep following?' Ivy asks anxiously in a whisper.

Paula shrugs. 'Whatever you think. We're at your beck and call.'

Audrey squints at her. 'Who are Beck and Paul? I thought it was Dominic and Gemma?'

Teddy shakes her head, rolling her eyes at her. 'She said *beck and call*. Listen up, you deaf old bint.'

Audrey shrieks with amusement, then covers her mouth. 'My hearing is perfect, thank you. It's my eyes that are shot. It's Paula's fault for mumbling.'

'I don't mean to,' Paula mumbles.

'I think you speak at a very nice volume,' Ivy says kindly and Paula smiles at her gratefully.

En masse, they make their way down the darkened streets

after the Evil Bastard. It's only just after ten p.m., but the streets are mostly empty. It's the middle of May, but unseasonably cold. People seem to be holding off breaking out the early summer socialising for now.

Dominic stops after a few minutes, lingering by a lamppost. He stares out across the road at a steakhouse. It looks busy.

'What is he doing here?' Teddy hisses. 'Is he going for dinner?'

Audrey brightens. 'Ooh, shall *we* go for dinner there? I'm starving.'

'I'm a pescatarian,' Teddy comments, shaking her head.

Audrey pouts. 'I'm an Aquarius, what's your point?'

'I don't believe in horoscopes,' Paula adds helpfully.

'For the love of—' Teddy begins but stops when she sees Ivy's expression. She's pale and trembling.

'What is it?' Teddy asks urgently.

'Gemma,' Ivy whispers softly, her voice trembling. 'I remember Gemma saying she works at a steakhouse one night a week.

'Shit,' Teddy says in a low voice. 'What do we do?'

'We wait,' Audrey says firmly. 'If we have to step in, we step in. But we shouldn't blow our cover unless we have to. Let's watch and wait.'

Paula can hardly breathe as she watches him watching the restaurant entrance. After a few minutes, a woman emerges. It's Gemma. Paula recognises her from the social media photos Ivy's shown them. She's laughing with a colleague – a man – and they turn together to lock the door behind them. Paula's eyes flick to Dominic a few feet away, waiting by his lamppost. Even from this distance, she can see his breath is getting faster, his chest rising and falling. He's furious.

He steps forward, into the light, blocking their path, and Gemma's entire expression and body language change. The terror on her face is obvious.

Beside Paula, Ivy reaches for her hand, and they squeeze each other hard, fighting an urge to run towards the woman.

Dominic starts shouting immediately. She's a slut, she's a cheat, a bad mother for leaving the kids at home. The male friend steps in front of Gemma protectively. There is more shouting, more horrible, cruel insults thrown. Dominic tells Gemma he's going to take the children. She won't get custody. She'll never see them again. She shakes her head, fighting her instincts. It's clear she's in survival mode, hunched in on herself as she waits for this to be over. The man with her says he will call the police and Dominic laughs at this. Eventually, he turns to leave, calling his wife a whore as he goes. Gemma and her friend – as well as the four women hiding in the shadows across the road – all watch him go, holding their collective breath.

No one says anything for a while. Not even as Gemma and her friend hurry away in the opposite direction.

Ivy is the first to speak, and she does so quietly. 'I don't think letting this man peacefully die in his sleep from gas poisoning is enough,' she says.

'Agreed,' Teddy replies quickly.

'What do you want to do to him, Ivy? What would you *like* to do to him?' Audrey asks and Ivy narrows her eyes, considering this.

'Pushing my husband down the stairs felt pretty good,' she answers solemnly, fine lines appearing around her eyes.

'Let's do that again then,' Audrey says with delight, and Teddy nods with determination.

'We'll follow him home from the pub one night – make sure he's really drunk and everyone's seen him staggering about. Then we'll break into his house and push him down the stairs. Everyone will assume the drunken fool fell.'

They all look at one another and nod.

When Paula gets home an hour later, her phone beeps with a message in the group WhatsApp from Ivy.

I messaged Gemma. She's going away on Friday for a whole week. She'll be in Cumbria staying with her parents. We should do it while she's there with a decent alibi.

The replies come thick and fast.

Sounds like a plan.

Next week it is.

Paula is the last to respond.

I'm ready. Let's get that Evil Bastard.

22

'Whoops!'

'Oof!'

At least two people have fallen on top of one another, but Paula isn't quite sure who.

'Shhhh!'

That's definitely Teddy shushing everyone, so it's likely those currently on the ground, flailing about in the mud, are Audrey and Ivy.

'Is everyone OK?' Paula whispers into the darkness and Teddy shushes furiously again. Honestly, the shushing is a lot louder and more obnoxious than any other noise they're making.

'We're fine!' Audrey calls out at a normal volume. 'You all right on the ground there, darling?' Paula's eyes adjust enough to see the older woman picking Ivy up off a patch of grass. She squeaks her confirmation.

Paula sighs, wondering if it's too late to back out.

They are four reasonably intelligent women – Teddy's a lawyer, for goodness' sake – and they have a really quite solid plan that they've gone over many times. Plus! Several of them have already gotten away with murder! This should've been straightforward. Easy, even. And yet, just a few minutes in, everything is already going badly wrong.

The plan started off OK. They'd followed Dominic Shipman home from the pub, as agreed, with Audrey tutting the whole way from the passenger seat about his terrible driving. He'd been all over the road, speeding over potholes and not once indicating, which Audrey was outraged by. Which seemed a bit hypocritical to Paula, but she didn't say anything. Once he'd pulled into the driveway, narrowly missing a phone box, they'd quickly turned off down a side street – away from any streetlamps or nosy neighbours. Then they'd sneaked over to the Evil Bastard's house, finding their way around the back and into his garden, moving with ninja-like stealth. And that's where . . . everything started to implode.

'Do we really have to wear these on our feet?' Ivy asks in a whisper as she brushes herself down, wiping grass off her black jeans.

'Yes,' says Teddy, who has assumed the role of de facto leader. She does in most situations, Paula's noticed.

Ivy is referring to the booties they're all wearing. They're the kind of thing estate agents wear to cover their shoes during viewings. It was one of the many genius things they thought of, to stop them leaving footprints at the scene. They're also wearing gloves to avoid finger prints. That is to say, all of them *apart from Audrey*, are wearing gloves. Audrey's wearing mittens – much to Teddy's irritation – but she insisted they work just as well as gloves and she won't take them off. There was nearly a full-blown fight about it in the car. Oh, and they're also all dressed in black, so no one can see them in the darkness.

All very clever and sensible, they congratulated each other beforehand.

Except it turns out those protective shoe thingys are incredibly slippery, gloves mean you can't feel anything in your fingers, and – who would've guessed – wearing black and being out past midnight means not only can they not be seen, but they can't really *see*.

Paula is trying to stay positive though.

'I know the booties are a pain,' Audrey says in a kind voice, 'but we can't risk leaving any evidence we were here, can we?' She pauses. 'Plus, I got them on Amazon Prime same day delivery and I couldn't *believe* how quickly they turned up! Same day! Isn't that amazing? They are clever, aren't they, these delivery people?'

'I ordered some new lightbulbs the other day,' Paula tells her excitably. 'It must've been gone eleven o'clock at night and they were on my doorstep by the next morning.' She sniffs. 'It was actually a little bit annoying because I wasn't there and they were soaked through and useless from the rain by the time I found them. I shouldn't have selected that "leave in my safe place" option. My front doorstep never seems to be much of a safe place.'

'Can we have this conversation another time?' Teddy asks, her tone strained. 'Literally any other time when we're not standing in the back garden of a dangerous man, ready to commit murder?'

'Of course!' Paula says brightly. 'Is it time to go in, then?'

'I think we should give him another two minutes,' Audrey warns. 'Make sure he's had plenty of time to get into bed. How unfortunate would it be if we bumped into him while he was brushing his teeth?'

'Do you think he brushes his teeth before bed?' Paula asks. 'I bet he doesn't. I don't think bad people brush their teeth twice a day.'

'I only do it once in the morning,' Audrey tells her defensively. 'On the other hand, my teeth do go in a glass overnight with a cleaning solution.'

'So,' Ivy begins in a small voice, 'I know the plan is to wait for him to go to sleep, then creep upstairs where we get his attention with a loud noise. We lure him to the top of the stairs, where we all shove him, but . . .' She clears her throat. 'How are we actually going to get inside to do all that?' She wipes some more mud off her jeans. 'We didn't make a plan for that. We can't really smash a window, can we? It would look a bit suspicious.'

'Hmm,' Teddy says, using her best authoritarian voice. 'That's a good point. We can't really force the door either. It might alert the idiot inside that we're here.'

Audrey tuts. 'He might not hear us. He looked awfully drunk, leaving the pub. He's probably passed out without brushing his teeth, dead to the world.'

'He soon will be,' Teddy says darkly.

'But we're trying to make this look like an accident, like he fell,' Ivy points out. 'Why would there be a smashed window, or a forced door?'

Paula tries to interrupt but they continue talking over her.

'We can't risk it!' Teddy says firmly. 'We'll have to figure something else out.'

'If I could just—' Paula begins.

'Look!' cries Audrey too loudly. 'There's a drain pipe. We'll just climb up and find an open window.' She takes a step forward, immediately slipping over again in her estate agent booties. From the ground, she rallies. 'Someone pick me up, then give me a leg up!'

'You're being ridiculous, you mad old bat!' Teddy cries.

'I *love* being ridiculous!' Audrey says with delight. 'I *pride* myself on being ridiculous.'

'You actually think you could shimmy your way up that drainpipe?' Teddy asks archly. 'You think you can . . . what? Use your art teacher scarf to loop through that tree branch up there, and then Tarzan your way up?'

'It's a pashmina!' Audrey's voice is shrill, then she grins. 'You lot have no idea how strong and nimble I am. I did some pole dancing in my day and I'm more flexible than you can possibly imagine.' She winks at Ivy who turns a bit green. 'Just ask my ex-lovers, they'll tell you.'

'OK, great,' Teddy says cheerfully. 'Get over here, I'll give you a leg up. Come on, old woman.' She leans forward, linking her fingers together as Audrey excitably clambers on, grabbing for the plastic pipe.

'Ugh, it's wet!' she cries and Teddy rolls her eyes.

'It's a *drainpipe*.'

Ivy reaches forward, ready to catch the octogenarian when she inevitably falls. 'Maybe we shouldn't . . .' she attempts as Audrey throws another hand upwards, pouting as she finds only moss and muddy leaves.

'Just listen to me!' Paula says with determination, taking herself by surprise. Everyone turns to look. Audrey steps back down. They regard her expectantly. 'I think,' Paula continues in a softer tone, 'that we should probably just go in through this unlocked back door here.' She pauses as they stare at her with surprise. 'I tried the handle, it's open. Drunk idiots don't tend to bother with security that much.' She sniffs, thinking of Seb. 'Drunk idiots and thirty-year-old sons.'

In silence, they file inside, Audrey shooting one last longing look up at the drainpipe before they enter. They find themselves in a utility room of sorts. A dirty mat welcomes them, with coats and shoes piled up underneath a boiler in the corner.

The group takes a moment, listening to the house around them. There is no noise, no movement, no nothing.

'He's got an Ideal Boiler like we have at my house!' Paula whispers and Teddy shoots her a look. How is she to know what's relevant and what isn't?

They move out into a small hallway. There are several doors – several rooms – coming off the hall, and the group exchanges a look, wondering which way to go. They need to find the stairs. *He's up there right now*, they silently communicate, fear and adrenaline zigzagging between them.

Paula takes a left, happening upon the kitchen. It's bigger than her own and has a darling little island in its centre, flagged by two stools. She likes an island. Maybe she'll get one of her own in the future. If she hasn't given all her money away to loan sharks. She turns to say as much to Ivy and finds herself all alone.

Pure terror spikes through her. Where have they gone? Did they find the stairs and go up without her? They're supposed to be in this together. She's supposed to be one of them, how could they abandon her? Should she run away? Should she hide? Should she—

'Paula?' Teddy's impatient tone is clear, even in a whisper. 'Don't go off on your own, babe, we're supposed to be in this together. Don't leave us.'

Paula feels warmth move through her as she rejoins the other women. They didn't leave her. They were just in the living room.

Silently, they move through the rooms, and Paula thinks about the last time they explored a strange house together. The eighteen-million-pound mansion in the Surrey Hills. It was almost a month ago, but feels much longer. So much has happened in that time. They've bonded a lot in such a short period of time. Death and money will do that, Paula supposes.

At the front of the group, Audrey makes a noise. She stops short and Ivy crashes into her.

'Have you found the stairs?' Teddy hisses from beside Paula.

'No, my darlings,' Audrey sighs. In the dim light, Paula can just about make out her friend's silhouette. 'I'm afraid there was something rather crucial we forgot to check when we made this plan.'

'Beyond lucking out with an unlocked back door?' Teddy asks dryly in a low voice.

'Yes,' Audrey nods. 'When we decided to push the man down the stairs, we probably should've checked he lived in a house with them.'

'What?' Paula whispers and Ivy waves before them at the kitchen. They've come full circle.

Audrey sighs. 'My darlings, we're in a bloody bungalow.'

23

They've stood around in worried silence now for several minutes. Paula's anxiety is notching up and up and up and up.

'So, what now?' she says at last in a low voice.

They all look back the way they've come, towards the direction of the one closed door in the single-floored home. It must be Dominic Shipman's bedroom.

Audrey pulls off a mitten, a strange expression on her face. 'Now,' she says, 'we're out of options. So you guys get out of here, while I go in that room and smash his head in with a baseball bat.'

Teddy tuts. 'You've seen too many Tarantino films.'

'What's a Tarantino?' Audrey asks innocently. 'Some kind of spider?' She makes a face. 'I don't like spiders, but I don't mind a bit of blood and brain splatter.'

Teddy frowns. 'Audrey, do you think you might be a tiny bit of a sociopath?'

'More than likely!' Audrey nods happily.

'We don't even have a baseball bat with us!' Paula hisses desperately, as the older woman makes her way back through the kitchen.

'I saw a poker in the living room,' Ivy offers helpfully. 'Would that work?'

'That'll do,' Audrey says cheerfully.

'Two sociopaths,' Teddy murmurs from the back.

'Hold on.' Paula clings to Ivy's arm. 'You were the one who said we wouldn't be able to do something like this. You said it would be too violent! That we couldn't physically or mentally go through with it!'

Ivy nods. 'I know. But we've come this far! And we may not be naturally violent people, but he *is*. And if we let him continue, he'll just keep hurting Gemma and her kids, and whoever else he might meet. He has to be stopped. We have to try. If Audrey thinks she can do it, we have to let her try.'

Audrey turns to the group, looking directly at Paula. 'Please leave,' she says sincerely. 'I'm already under suspicion. If this goes wrong, it'll just be me who goes down. I'll be out in twenty years and still have a decent couple of decades of my life to live.'

'We can't let you go to jail!' Paula says too loudly. Teddy puts a reassuring hand on her shoulder, but Paula shakes it off. 'No!' she says. 'It's not happening.'

Audrey shrugs happily. 'I don't think they'd put me in prison anyway. I'm in my eighties! I'll plead dementia or osteoporosis. One of the old lady things.'

'No, Audrey,' Paula says again, standing in her way, shocking herself with her strength. 'There has to be another way. We're not letting you sacrifice yourself.'

Audrey stares her down in the dark, but Paula holds her ground, her heart hammering in her chest. She's accepted that her friend is going to kill this man. She knows it's really happening. They're all going to kill him. They're not just accessories to the crime here; they're fully complicit. This is really happening. But she's not going to let Audrey casually volunteer to get caught. Not if she can help it.

After a minute, Audrey sighs, her shoulders sagging a little. The adrenaline has drained away. 'OK, my darling.' Then she brightens. 'Oooh, how about this then – I'll suffocate him! I'll get a plastic bag and stick it over his head until he dies. Then I'll call the police and tell them my lover has died during a sex game gone wrong.'

Beside her, Paula hears Ivy swallow hard. 'Your . . . lover?'

Audrey nods, leading the group through to the kitchen. 'Yes indeed. I'll say we've been casually dating for a while. We met in that godawful pub he frequents every night – what was it called?'

'The Three Stags,' Teddy confirms.

Audrey nods. 'Right, and I'll say we got experimental and he asked me to suffocate him. Then whoops, we got carried away and he died.'

'This kind of defence *does* regularly work for men in rape trials,' Teddy points out, looking thoughtful.

'Well, perfect!' Audrey replies with delight, opening a drawer. It's full of cutlery. She tuts.

'What are you looking for?' Ivy asks as Audrey opens another.

'A bag.'

Paula peers about the kitchen. 'Surely the carrier bags inside another carrier bag will be in a cupboard, not a drawer?'

Audrey shakes her head. 'No, a Tesco bag's no good! Too big and holey. We need one of those freezer bags. Sturdy but suffocating. That's the kind of thing they use on TV.' She roots around in another drawer, yanking out a ziplock bag triumphantly. 'Here!'

Paula frowns. 'Do we know what sort of head Dominic has?'

'Big,' Ivy says confidently, then scrunches her nose. 'He has a big forehead at least. Or maybe his hairline is just receding?'

'This is why everyone should have a fringe,' Audrey replies, sounding confident. 'Smallifies the head.'

'Is smallify a word?' Ivy asks curiously.

'Either way,' Paula tries to retrieve the conversation thread. 'I'm not sure you'll be able to get a freezer bag over his head. That barely looks big enough to suffocate an ear.'

Audrey holds the bag up to the moonlight to examine it. 'Perhaps you're right,' she acknowledges. 'So we need a bigger, head-sized freezer bag.'

'I don't think he has any of those.' Ivy is peering into the open drawer. It is mostly tinfoil and a collection of wooden spoons.

'What about one of those on-the-spot delivery services?' Audrey looks inspired. 'You can get a Tesco Whoosh delivery, can't you? We could have head-sized freezer bags here in under twenty minutes.'

'Is that the same as Sainsbury's Chop Chop service?' Ivy asks as Paula blinks at them both in confusion.

'Hold on!' Something has dawned on Paula and horror creeps up her spine. 'Er, where is Teddy?' Audrey spins on her heels, scanning the room in a panic. No sign of Teddy. She turns back and the three of them all stare at each other with fear.

'She wouldn't?' Ivy breathes in a low voice. 'She can't have gone in there on her own? She wouldn't do it without us . . .'

They move as one, in a blur, Audrey still clinging on to the too-small freezer bag. It's dark as they run through rooms, trying to find the bedroom. Paula quickly loses her way. She spins around, trying to work out where she is and where Ivy and Audrey have gone. She can hear noises around her. A loud thump. Someone nearby is groaning. Her heart is banging loudly in her chest now as she turns one direction, then another. Terror makes her fast but confused, and she finds herself circling an unfamiliar space. Her knee hits something soft. A sofa! She's in the living room. Where is everyone else? The groaning gets louder. Who is that? Teddy? Audrey? Ivy? Could it be... Dominic? Where is *he*? He must've heard them by now. Has he got one of her friends? Is he hurting them? Is he calling the police? Should *they* call the police?

Paula swallows hard, her heartbeat pounding out of her chest. Retracing her steps, she finds the groaner. It's Ivy. She's on the ground in the hallway, bathed in dim moonlight.

'I tripped,' she says simply.

'Are you all right?' Paula's voice is high and scared. 'We have to find the others. We have to get out of here!' She reaches for Ivy's hand, and the younger woman winces.

'I think I've sprained my ankle.'

'Can you walk at all?' Paula asks, looping an arm under Ivy's to take her weight.

'I think so. But where are the others?'

'I don't know,' Paula whispers back, her heart beating faster again.

Suddenly, the overhead light floods on.

'There you both are!' Teddy calls out down the hallway in a loud voice. Ivy and Paula stare at her, frozen. Audrey appears at Teddy's shoulder, looking dazed.

'What's happening?' She looks up at Teddy. 'Did you leave us? Did you put the light on? Is he dead?'

'Nope,' Teddy says and Paula wonders which question she's answering. She blinks around her at the suddenly bright space. Audrey approaches, noticing Ivy's injury. 'Oh my darling! Are you OK?'

'I slipped on a step,' Ivy replies. 'It was my fault.'

'What is a bungalow doing with a bloody step anyway?' Teddy mutters. 'The whole point is that they don't have steps, surely.'

Audrey frowns, pulling off her own booties. 'It's not your fault, Ivy! Nothing is your fault. It's these bloody shoe things! Do you think I can return them to Amazon? They're a hazard! I will be leaving a strongly-worded three-star review.'

'Three stars?' Ivy smiles through her pain.

'Well, I don't want to damage anyone's reputation,' Audrey explains. 'You hear so much about cancel culture these days, don't you? I wouldn't want to be part of anyone getting a cancellation.' She considers this. 'So maybe I should give them four stars? Maybe four and a half? What do you all think?'

Teddy shakes her head. 'So you have no problem bashing someone's head in and getting brain matter on yourself, but you don't want an online bootie company to be at risk of getting *cancelled*? An internet term that is mostly made up and never really happens?'

'Humans are complicated,' Audrey shrugs. 'And I will certainly flag how absurdly slippery the boots are in the comment section.' She pauses, remembering where they are and why they're here. 'Hold on, what's going on? Shouldn't we be making a run for it?'

It is Teddy's turn to shrug. 'Nah. He's not here.'

'*Not here?*' Ivy bleats, sounding upset. 'How can you be sure?'

'Well,' Teddy begins slowly, 'my first clue was when you lot all started shouting at each other about freezer bags and the size of Dominic Shipman's head. There was absolutely no chance anyone would sleep through that – not even an unconscious drunk – so I made an educated guess and went to have a look in the bedroom. No sign of the Evil Bastard. Bed hasn't been slept in. So I thought it might be easier to just put the light on, since we've made such a hash of things here anyway.'

'Where is he then?' Ivy asks, frustration in her voice. 'We followed him back here from the pub, didn't we? Where is he? Is he hiding in the basement or something?'

'I'm pretty sure bungalows don't have basements,' Teddy observes dryly. 'Would sort of defeat its purpose, wouldn't it?'

'It had a step,' Ivy points out with a hint of defensiveness.

Paula gasps. 'Oh my goodness, I know what's happened! We parked down the road and came around to the back garden. We must be in the wrong house!'

Teddy wanders towards the front door, looking out of its small window pane.

'Nope,' she says again, tiredness in her voice. 'It's not the wrong house. Right house. But he's not here.' She takes a deep breath, gesturing at the door. 'He's still in the car,' she continues, rolling her eyes. 'I can see him out there. He parked up in the drive, like we saw. Then – it would seem – the drunken idiot passed out on his own bloody steering wheel.'

24

'Maybe we should've just opened the car door and bashed him in the face with the poker there and then,' Audrey offers, shifting in the plastic seat.

'In front of the neighbours?' Teddy enquires, archly. 'And I'm not sure the angle of the poker would've been particularly effective inside a car. It's probably quite hard to beat someone to death inside a confined space.'

'I know the freezer bags were too small,' Audrey offers thoughtfully, 'but maybe I could've tied two together and pretended we were doing our sex stuff in the car?'

Teddy's sigh comes by way of answer.

'Is it just me,' Ivy begins anxiously, 'or are we, like, *really* bad at this? Like, super, aggressively awfully catastrophically bad at the whole thing?'

'It's not just you,' Teddy inhales heavily. 'I thought we'd be a lot better at murder. All that planning and talking things through, and we couldn't even *find* him.'

Audrey places a comforting arm around Ivy. 'We'll regroup, my darling, and have a rethink. We just need a better plan.'

Paula leans a tired head on Teddy's shoulder. 'At least I let his cat out as we left,' she offers and they all smile at one another. That is something.

They're at a private clinic in London, positioned somewhere between Teddy's apartment and the scene of their nightmare visit to kill Dominic Shipman. As they drove away in what should've been the getaway car, Teddy put in a call to her concierge doctor service about Ivy's foot. Paula listened in amazement as Teddy's *on-call* private doctor offered on loudspeaker to meet them at the apartment *in the middle of the night* to assess the injury and arrange treatment. There was talk of a private X-ray service arriving in a mobile unit with a radiologist and a physio on board.

Paula thinks of her next-door neighbour, Samira, who had to wait six months to find out a bone in her knee was broken, and that she needed an operation, having made things worse by walking on it the entire time. It is astonishing stuff, money.

Ivy refused the doctor's offer though, insisting they head straight to a clinic instead. A private one, but an A&E nonetheless.

They're using the waiting time – minimal though it is – to dissect what just happened.

'Can we try again?' Audrey asks.

'How?' Paula blinks.

Audrey takes a minute to consider this. 'We could go to the pub he drinks in and start a fight with him,' she suggests hopefully. 'Then one of you could kill him in an act of self-defence.' There is silence at this, so Audrey continues, 'Or could we trick someone else into murdering him? Or pay for it?' She looks around the group, her eyes landing on Paula.

'My darling, you must know a contract killer? Or is he based solely in Austria? We could fly him in. Does he have a website?' She waves her hands as Paula's mouth opens and closes. 'Or are there apps for things now? You can find a handyman in the blink of an eye. Isn't there one for snipers?'

Paula tries to think of what to say. It's been a while since she last tried to convince them she didn't kill John. Maybe now is the time? Maybe she should be looking them in the eye as they sit around waiting in this A&E, and convince them once and for all that she didn't murder her husband.

Perhaps this is the time for all of it: the truth about John, about the loan sharks, about the notebook she's been carrying around for weeks now. Paula takes a deep breath and . . . nothing comes out.

What if they reject her? What if they turf her out of the group when they realise she's not really one of them?

Ivy looks down at her swollen foot but says nothing.

Teddy is staring off into the distance, a strange look on her face.

'Or . . .' Audrey is still murder-spitballing. 'Or . . . maybe I could trick him into getting in my car and then drive the whole thing into a river! I'll make sure the child locks are on, so he can't get out, and meanwhile, one of you could be on hand to rescue me!' She looks around again. 'Who's the strongest swimmer here?'

'We can't,' Teddy says abruptly. 'That whole thing was a total disaster. And' – she gestures at Audrey's bare hands – 'Audrey's prints are all over that house now. If something suspicious or violent happens to him, they might investigate. It's too risky.'

'But there must be something we can do!' Ivy cries, and Paula lays a reassuring hand over hers.

'It's all right, sweetheart,' she tells her. 'We'll think of something. We can't kill him right now, but there will be some way we can help your friend Gemma...'

'What if we made him think the mob have put out a hit on him?' Audrey offers excitedly. 'We could give him a fake passport and get him a place in Australia or something.'

'That wouldn't be a punishment!' Ivy sounds so upset. 'We are *not* rewarding that evil monster for what he's done.' She swallows. 'Plus, then he'd just find someone over there to do this to. We can't inflict an abuser on Australia. He'd ruin just as many lives over there.'

'But he'd have to contend with a lot more big spiders,' Audrey mutters.

Teddy stands up abruptly, stalking away and out of the sliding entrance doors.

The group watches her go with confusion. 'Did I upset her?' Ivy asks at last, in a quiet voice.

Audrey shakes her head. 'It's not you, my darling. You must stop assuming things are your fault. She's just upset. Teddy is someone who needs space and time to process things. That's OK. We're all different. She'll be fine. We'll just give her a minute. We all move at our own pace when it comes to trauma and recovery. Half the time we don't know what might trigger us. Teddy knows what's best for her, I believe that. She'll talk to us when she's ready.'

Ivy takes a deep breath. 'That's true, I guess.' She nods kindly at Paula. 'You never speak about your husband.'

Audrey jumps in protectively. 'Yes, but Paula lost John much more recently than the rest of us. We've had a lot of extra time to process things.'

Paula feels at a loss for words. Her mouth opens and shuts. She doesn't know how to get through to them. 'I didn't kill John,' she manages to get out at last, but even she can hear how unconvincing it sounds.

Ivy smiles, and rubs her on the back. 'I told myself that for a long time, too. I kept insisting on it. I think I even partly convinced myself. But it was important in the end to be honest, at least with myself.' She pauses. 'And it's fine, there's no rush to open up to us. Just know that we're here when you do want to tell us the truth.'

Paula takes a second, then nods slowly. 'OK,' she sighs, because what else can she say? Maybe she doesn't want them to believe her anymore. Maybe it doesn't matter.

A nurse comes by, smiling broadly. 'Great news, Ms Kirk,' he says to Ivy with impeccable bedside manner. 'A doctor has just had a thorough look at your X-rays and she says it's not broken!' He pauses, then adds, 'Yay!' and you can tell he has had extra training in being human for the rich people who come here. 'I'm sending you home with some painkillers and strict instructions to rest up for a few days, OK?' He looks faux-stern. 'But of course, if the swelling or the pain get any worse, please call us right away. I'm leaving you with our direct number here at the clinic and we'll make sure you're seen right away if you need to return.' He glances at the group. 'You'll look after her, won't you? Make sure she doesn't lift a finger – and definitely not an ankle – and ring us if you're worried.' He smiles warmly.

Wow, Paula thinks, remembering her neighbour again and the waiting lists.

'Thanks for choosing our clinic today.' The nurse offers up a handful of small plastic packets. 'Here are some biscuits for you all to enjoy on your journey home.'

Wow.

They thank him and start to gather their belongings, when Teddy reappears, her eyes wild.

'I've got to go,' she says. 'Right now.'

'No, Teddy!' Paula cries out, reaching for her friend. 'Don't leave like this. Ivy's been discharged. We can all leave together. Don't be upset.'

'Please stay!' Ivy says at the same time. 'Talk to us, you can be sad about Dominic Shipman *with* us. We're here for you.'

'We want to look after you!' Audrey adds to the noise. 'We're your friends. We'll get you a fringe. You'll feel much better.'

Teddy grins, shaking her head. 'No, you guys don't understand. I went outside to call the cops.'

The group draws back, shocked by her words. Teddy shakes her head again. 'Don't panic, I wasn't reporting TLWWC for murder.' She laughs dryly. 'I called them about a drunk driver I saw earlier.' She lets the words sink in before continuing, 'I told them how I witnessed a man leaving the pub and then saw him driving off. I explained seeing him weaving in and out, nearly hitting every lamp post on the street and then I told them how I followed him to his address as I was very concerned he might kill someone. I told them how he is currently parked up on his own driveway, passed out, slumped over his own steering wheel.' She takes us all in, her voice triumphant. 'The police might be able to cover up domestic abuse for one of their own, but they won't be able to ignore drunk driving reported from a lawyer. I've already called a couple of former colleagues to attend the scene as witnesses. One of them is part of a review panel investigating police corruption. Maybe this will finally get him off the streets. At the very least he'll lose his licence, which might make it harder for him to harass poor Gemma.'

Ivy looks up at her with big, watery eyes. 'Thank you, Teddy,' she says in a quiet voice.

'I have to go to the police station right now to give a statement,' Teddy adds proudly.

'Go!' Audrey instructs joyfully, though Paula can see she is feeling emotional, too. Teddy quickly hugs each of them excitedly, dashing out to catch her taxi. She's taking action; she's doing something to help Gemma.

Paula feels so much better.

'Come on,' Audrey says kindly to Ivy, helping her limp out of the clinic and out into the cold night air. Paula stops for a moment as they reach the car, taking in all the darkness around them. Teddy's getting the abuser arrested and they don't have to kill him.

'Thank you,' she says to Ivy and Audrey sincerely, wondering when she was last out with friends at this hour of the night. Certainly not in decades. Probably never, if she's being honest. She was never much of a night owl or a wild party animal, not even in her youth.

'For what?' Ivy says, looping an arm through hers and nuzzling in. Paula shakes her head, unsure what she meant. This has been the most exhilarating night of her life. There were so many highs and lows. So many joyous and terrifying firsts for her. *And* on top of all that, they've actually managed to help someone who needed it! Not to mention punish an Evil Bastard who deserved it. Her whole body is abuzz with adrenaline. It has all gone wrong tonight, but also so right. And for the first time in her life, Paula was right there, at the heart of the action, wearing silly estate agent booties. They deserve at least a four-star review on Amazon for that.

25

To: *John.Sheldon1960@oldmail.com*
From: *PaulaJeanieSheldon1964@ptinternet.com*
Subject: *Counselling*

Oh John, Tilly's so upset with me and I don't know what to do. T

Paula stops typing, pausing over the letter T.

She wants to talk, she *needs* to talk, but it no longer feels like John is the only person she can talk to. There are others. Her friends.

She hasn't had close friends in years. Sure, Paula used to have people in her life, when she was young, people she worked with or went to school with. But life happens. Things got in the way. Some moved, some argued, some had more than two children and were therefore never heard from again. Either way, everyone drifted apart. Long ago.

But it seems that, somehow, Paula now has real friends again.

She picks up the phone. She wants to speak to her three friends, right now.

Opening their WhatsApp group, Paula taps the call icon. Seb showed her how to do this a while back, but this is her first chance to have a go for herself.

'Call TLWWC group?' it asks and she feels a calm settling over her even at the question.

Ivy is the first to answer.

'Paula, are you OK?' The concern in her voice is evident.

'Oh! Yes,' Paula blusters, feeling a little silly. She's forgotten that Ivy's generation panic about unsolicited phone calls. 'I'm sorry to ring. I just wanted to talk. How's your foot?'

She hears Ivy move, settling into some kind of seat. 'Don't say sorry, that's really lovely. It's nice to hear your voice. And yes, my foot is almost back to normal, thank you for asking.'

'Hellooooo?' Audrey booms into the receiver. 'Darlings? What is happening on my phone?'

'It's a group video call,' Ivy explains nicely.

Audrey crows, 'Oh, how *thrilling*. I didn't know you could do that. Isn't the modern world such a joy? I know I'm still young – I plan to be the first one in my family to get to a hundred and fifteen, you know – but I do sometimes wish I could be born right now, so I could see for myself the whole, wild future unfold. It's going to be so exciting. You should've seen me when *pagers* came out!' She cackles. 'Ooh, I know! We'll have to arrange a group call the next time we're planning a M-U-R-D-E-R.' She laughs joyously again.

'Well, it can't go any worse than the last attempt.' Teddy has joined the call during Audrey's speech.

'I think it worked out perfectly,' Paula says, smiling to herself at the thought of last week's absurd antics.

According to Teddy's lawyer friends, Dominic Shipman is currently sitting in jail after his arrest for being drunk in charge of a vehicle. And for aggravated assault. It turns out that when the officers arrived to breathalyse him, a newly woken Dominic got belligerent. He punched the woman trying to arrest him and the situation quickly escalated, with backup being called for. He is now facing major charges for assault on a police officer and for resisting arrest, as well as the original drink-driving offence. And he's been formally suspended from the force. At last.

All in all, that horrible, horrible man – the Evil Bastard, Dominic Shipman – is now potentially facing years in jail, thanks to Teddy and the rest of the group.

Paula has felt strangely alive and full of joy ever since. She hasn't done anything so . . . well, *silly* in years. Probably ever! And yes, OK, she wasn't terribly keen on the kill-y part of things, but that didn't happen after all. And if it had, wouldn't he have deserved it?

It's funny how quickly you can come round to a way of thinking.

Either way, she had fun – she's *having* fun. And one cannot underestimate how important fun is at her age.

Paula self-corrects. She *was* having fun. Until today. Until the latest family grief counselling session with Tilly and Seb.

She sighs and Ivy pipes up, 'Paula, are you sure you're OK?'

Paula nods into the phone, feeling a bit emotional. 'Yes. Well, I'm not sure, if I'm being honest. It hasn't been the best day. Tilly is upset with me. I don't know what to do. She feels distant lately and I can't fix it.'

'Grown-up children are so much harder than children children,' Audrey says solemnly. 'My two girls are in their fifties and I haven't a clue what they're thinking half the time. You should see the partners they've chosen! It's like they were brought up with no imagination whatsoever!'

'What happened?' Ivy asks Paula softly.

'Goodness knows!' Audrey replies. 'I have told the girls they can do miles better and they deserve the best, but neither of them ever listens.'

'Er,' Ivy sounds awkward, 'Audrey, I was actually talking to Paula. I was wondering what happened with her daughter, Tilly.'

'Oh, sorry, darling. Maybe these group calls aren't all they're cracked up to be after all. Terribly confusing.'

Paula inhales deeply, trying not to get upset. 'We've been having these grief counselling sessions once a week, you remember?' She adds sheepishly, 'Though I may have missed the odd one . . .' Paula pauses. 'Anyway, Tilly doesn't think I'm sharing enough.' She pauses. 'Or reacting in the right way, I suppose. She wants more grief tentacles from me. She thinks I'm repressing my feelings, which is leading to . . .' Paula pauses, trying to remember the odd wording her daughter used. 'It's leading to trauma and something called a psychosomatic effect on my body.' She hesitates again. 'I think it's something to do with sleep.' Paula sighs. 'She wants more from me, but I don't think I have it in me to give it to her. And this counsellor keeps asking me questions about John and my feelings and my life now – and I don't have answers for him either. And there are just things I can't talk about.' She looks across the kitchen now, towards the drawer where she's keeping the money. The money for Craig and his cohort. She has several thousand in there now, but it's not enough. Not nearly.

'Maybe you need a different therapist,' Teddy says. 'You can't just assume the first one to come along is the right fit. It can take a while to find someone you gel with.'

Audrey nods, her face mostly nostrils on the screen. 'She's right, I went through fourteen therapists before I found Gráinne.'

Teddy shakes her head. 'That's too many. That's a you problem, Audrey.'

'Gerald is nice enough,' Paula says begrudgingly. 'I don't think this is his fault. I'm sure he's doing a good job. And it really seems to be helping Tilly and Seb! But it's not helping *us*. My daughter seems to be getting further and further away from me with every session.' She takes another deep breath. 'Today, Gerald asked me to share some nice family memories and my mind went blank. I have such a dreadful memory at the best of times, and put on the spot like that, I couldn't think of anything. Then Tilly got sad, so I said what about that nice Christmas with the new video camera where they performed *Sleeping Beauty*, or the day at the theme park when we went on the biggest roller coaster. She looked so upset and said that those were *her* memories – the ones she'd shared during a session a few weeks ago – and of course I know that. But I didn't know what else to say. I couldn't think of anything. I didn't mean to steal her memories. She was crying and said it feels like I don't care about her or her dad. It was horrible.'

There is an understanding silence on the phone as they digest this.

Paula sighs. 'Then Seb tried to defend me and that only made things worse. Tilly ended up running out. Seb went after her, and it was very awkward with just me and Gerald sitting there. I ended up asking him if he was a fan of *Strictly Come Dancing*, just to say something.'

'And is he?' Audrey enquires.

Paula shakes her head into the phone. 'No, so then I *really* didn't know what to say to him. Imagine not liking *Strictly Come Dancing*! What's not to like?'

'I use the same fake tan as the professional dancers,' says Teddy.

'Do you really?' Audrey sounds thrilled. 'Where do you get it, my darling?'

'I'll send you a link,' Teddy says with authority. 'I'll send you all a link.'

'Can you send me a link to your shampoo as well?' Paula asks anxiously, and Teddy shrugs.

'Sure, I guess.'

'Have you thought about talking to your daughter about their dad?' Ivy asks in that nice way of hers.

'What do you mean?' Paula frowns.

'I mean . . .' Ivy trails off. 'Maybe they should know the truth about him?'

'The truth . . .?' Oh, for goodness' sake, she means the murder thing. Again. How many times does Paula have to tell them? It doesn't feel like there's much point in denying it at this point – not again – especially since they're so certain she's lying.

She reaches for a truth, if not *the* truth: 'I don't think Tilly's ready to listen to anything I have to say these days.'

'What about Seb?' Ivy suggests. 'He seemed a bit more open to things. He seems very kind.'

'Maybe,' Paula says lamely. Is her son kind? He certainly used to be when he was little. He had a lot of emotional intelligence and sweetness; Paula had great hopes for him back then. But lately, she's been so focused on the whole him living at home and playing silly games thing, she forgot to check if Seb is a nice person. Maybe he is. She *hopes* he is.

The trouble is, of course, that Paula now has this other big secret hanging over her head. This group – her friends – are murderers! How can she be honest with her children about anything while she's keeping this enormous, gigantic, *illegal* thing from them? Never mind her own participation in attempted murder.

'Will we . . .' she begins hesitantly. 'Do we think we're . . . Are we done with the murdering now, do we think?' She adds hopefully, 'We weren't very good at it, after all.'

'It was only our first go as a group!' Audrey cries. 'We'll get better. We just need some practice.'

'There were certainly a lot of obstacles we hadn't considered,' Teddy adds carefully.

Ivy smiles shyly. 'Well, I have another name on my support group list, if we do want to try again . . .'

'I'm game!' Audrey says, gamely. She has a new floral pashmina on today and Paula wonders if the last one got too drainpipe-y during their visit to Dominic Shipman's house.

'I don't know if it's a good idea,' Paula tries valiantly. 'What about the police officer, that Columbo man investigating you? What about the weird messages I've been getting on my phone and online from strangers? It feels like we're being watched.' She doesn't say the truth, which is that it feels like *she's* being watched.

'Pish posh,' Audrey tells her. 'I haven't even seen Columbo in a week or so. I think he's given up on me. And the messages have calmed down a bit now that you've made your Facebook private, haven't they, Paula? Teddy got the article about you taken down as well, isn't that right?' Teddy nods, but Audrey doesn't wait for a reply from Paula before continuing, 'Ivy darling, tell us about this awful man who needs a good baseball bat around the head.'

There is a rustling on the line as Ivy moves about. 'His name is Owen Max. He's a serial abuser.'

'What else do we know about him?' Teddy's voice is serious.

'That's all I need to know!' Audrey pronounces.

Teddy tuts. 'I meant more, like, what do we know about him that we might be able to use?'

'Well,' Ivy sounds reticent, 'he's a professional bodybuilder. He's . . . big.'

'He sounds far too dangerous,' Paula gasps. 'We can't!'

'Danger is my middle name!' Audrey says gleefully.

'He could *really* hurt one of us. We can't!' Paula says with heavy emphasis.

'Actually, my middle name is Meredith.' Audrey's voice is thoughtful. 'But I never much liked that. Danger is far better. Audrey Danger Swift.'

'Paula, stop panicking,' Teddy instructs calmly. 'Audrey, have a day off.'

'It's too much of a risk,' Paula cries, still very much panicking. 'We got lucky with Dominic Shipman, but what if they start looking into who reported him? What if they link her to Ivy and back to Gemma? Columbo's coming after Audrey and the world is still calling me a murderer. Not to mention I've got Cra—'

She stops short of mentioning Craig and his henchman, and Audrey helpfully distracts the group. 'It's funny that more parents don't actually give their children the middle name Danger, isn't it? It would be *so* funny! I wish I'd thought of it when I was having my girls. What a waste. Harold and I went with the middle names Janice and Margaret. Very tedious. No wonder they've ended up making such boring life choices.'

'We'll have to think of something different for this guy, Owen.' Ivy ignores both Paula's protests and Audrey's bizarre tangent. 'We can't confront him. Not even all four of us combined could push this guy down the stairs or get his head into freezer bags tied together. And we can't keep getting men arrested like we did with Dominic.' She makes a noise akin to a growl. 'Even though Owen's been accused of sexual assault by so many women. *So many.* Only two per cent of rape cases ever end up going to court, do you know that?' She sounds enraged.

'I do know that,' says former lawyer Teddy. 'Why do you think I obsessively played the Powerball lottery? It wasn't so I could kill my husband and move into an overpriced apartment with a pool I never use. It was so I could get away from the terrible justice system I worked in.'

'You could've got a new job,' Paula mutters, but Teddy doesn't hear her. Or chooses not to.

'I think we should talk more about this,' Teddy says loudly. 'Let's do something fun together this week, where we can properly hatch a plan. A better plan this time.' She pauses. 'And it'll be good for you, Paula. Distract you from this argument with your daughter and from any remaining internet troll stuff.'

'I've got something fun we can do,' Audrey says. There is mischief in her voice. She leaves a dramatic pause, which – Paula thinks – is *so* Audrey. 'I reckon,' Audrey begins, 'we should get on a private jet and go on holiday to Saint-Tropez.'

'To plot a murder?' Paula says, incredulous.

'Yes, my darling!' Audrey laughs. 'Why the hell not?'

26

Paula didn't expect to feel so disappointed with her own decision.

She's sitting at her kitchen table, staring into space, wondering if the house has always been so . . . silent? She's spent the morning cleaning and tidying, trying to keep herself distracted. She's trying not to think about her friends, all packing their suitcases and laughing about who'll take the communal hairdryer, and whether they need special foreign plugs.

But *of course* Paula couldn't go traipsing off on holiday with them. Of course she couldn't! With practically no notice! In the midst of a big falling-out with her daughter? And so soon after John's death!

Everyone on the internet apparently already thinks she murdered him. A trip to Saint-Tropez would really be the icing on the troll cake. And what about everyone else? What would the neighbours think of her sudden disappearance? The telltale sunburn upon her return would be the talk of the street. She's already getting funny looks over her new Porsche.

But why should she care what strangers and neighbours might think?

If Paula's being honest, she's never really much liked this area anyway, or the people who live here. John was the one who chose this town. He was the one excited about the sturdy former council house, with its modern interiors and functional garden. He was the one delighting over the size of the double garage.

Obviously, Paula has made it her home over these last thirty-three years, but she never felt particularly attached to it – or to the small but busy town on her doorstep. And good Lord, she despairs over the number of arguments its inhabitants seem to rejoice in starting on the town's Facebook page. It's enough to make anyone want to move.

Maybe she *will* buy somewhere new. If she can't have a glamorous holiday somewhere hot with her friends, maybe she can spend the next week distracting herself browsing Rightmove. She could start working out where she might live next. What kind of place would she need? What kind of place does she *want*? Certainly not that Surrey Hills mansion the group took her to see almost two months ago now. Paula's not interested in anything like that. It was too big, too showy, too expensive. And gosh, it was also so very cold! She might have twenty million in the bank, but the idea of the heating bill on that place is enough to make her shiver.

But she really *did* like the sweet little cottages that came with it – the so-called servants' cottages round the back. Perhaps Paula could find something like that?

She smiles to herself at her kitchen table, imagining her very own country cottage with low beams and a huge open fireplace. The door frames would all be stooped and the wooden doors would have those sweet little latches. There would be gardens and flowers visible out of every window. It would be situated somewhere beautiful and peaceful, where no one on Facebook gets cross on a daily basis about the new speed restrictions.

Mind you, those new speed restrictions around here *are* ridiculous.

She sighs, imagining Audrey, Teddy and Ivy packing suncream and hats, preparing for their no-expense-spared trip to Saint-Tropez. Just *imagine*.

But she can't go. And that's that. She's already made her decision and she stands by it. It was a silly idea and it's just not the right time. Plus, have you seen how expensive suncream is these days? Eyewatering! And also literally eyewatering actually. The cream always gets in Paula's eyes and makes them sting.

No, Paula needs to be at home right now. She needs to sort things out with Tilly. She needs to work out a solution to the problem with the loan sharks. She needs to figure out what she's doing with her life. She needs to decide if she's really going to help the rest of TLWWC get rid of this bodybuilder man, Owen, when they get back.

She sighs and stands up, filling the kettle and flicking it on just for something to do.

Maybe it'll be good to have a bit of space from her new friends. It's all been so full on and intense since she met them. They've seen so much of each other, spoken constantly, almost killed people together. It's a lot for a brand-new friendship.

Paula pours herself a peppermint tea and sits back down, absent-mindedly opening the laptop on the table before her. She selects the already-open tabs for Facebook, X and Threads, feeling guilty. She promised the group that she'd stop looking at social media – and she has! Under her own name, at least. It turns out you can sign up with a fake name incredibly easily. What did Seb call it? *Lurking*. He also said something about *doom scrolling*. Which admittedly sounds a bit horrible, but Paula has mostly found the lurkiness and the doominess to be quite entertaining. There is so much nonsense out there to distract her from the world. As long as she specifically avoids the nonsense out there about her.

On Threads, someone has shared a funny anecdote about a Conservative MP who didn't know the difference between Wales and Scotland. Someone else has done an entertaining breakdown of the latest sexcapades in *Bridgerton*. And there's a storm brewing over a rich kid from *Made in Chelsea* complaining about being forced to pay tax.

It's all relatively amusing, and it works, for a moment, to help Paula forget.

But after a few minutes she can't resist the pull any longer. She clicks the search box and types in the words 'Paula Sheldon'. After a second's hesitation she adds 'Lottery' and hits return.

It shows the 'top' comments and Paula wonders how someone out there decided these were the best, of all the horrible things people are saying about her.

Did you know that lottery winner Paula Sheldon is a CARER for old people? Anyone else thinking ANGEL OF DEATH???? #DefoKilledHerHusband

Good for mother Paula Sheldon getting rid of that sugar daddy just to take his money!!! And have you seen that new car?! She SLAYED and then she SLAYYYYYYYED. #BuffyTheLotterySlayer

Can't stop LOLing at that vid of lottery winner Paula Sheldon running away from her own press conference in her slutty pink jumper. She must've been crapping herself after offing her hubby!!! And wtf was with that notebook? Clearly full of her murder-y plans.

Soooooo, we're just expected to believe that woman Paula Sheldon happened to win the jackpot on the lottery and also just HAPPENED to lose her husband within a week in MYSTERIOUS circumstances??? Why are the police not on this??? Why are they so useless???

I would totally kill my husband too if I won the lottery. That would teach him to leave his protein powder all over the worktops every morning. Team Paula Sheldon!!!

Did you hear lottery killer Paula Sheldon even had karaoke at the funeral for her husband????? I know someone who was there and apparently they sung I Will Survive. Sounds like she was really sad, doesn't it? What a joke. It couldn't be any more obvious she did it.

Has anyone else read this stuff about the lottery winner whose husband 'mysteriously died', like, seconds after they won, like, £50million?!!!!!! #PaulaSheldonKilledJohnSheldon

Paula feels her whole body flush. The cereal she had for breakfast curdles in her stomach. She takes a sip of the herbal tea, hoping it will be calming. Her hands are shaking on the handle.

It's not even accurate! It was twenty-one million, not fifty. She starts to reply, clacking furiously at the keyboard . . . and then stops herself. There's no point. It would only lead to more suspicion, more anger, more mean-spirited accusations.

She's about to exit the website when she stops, reading one more comment at the bottom of the page.

I personally know Paula Sheldon VERY WELL. And I know for a fact what she did to her husband. The truth will come out. #LotterywinnerPaulaSheldon #PoorJohnSheldon

She gasps, re-reading the comment several times. What on *earth* is that? Who is this person? She clicks on the profile but there is no other information. No other comments or tweets. Another lurker.

Could this really be someone she knows? Someone currently in her life?

For some reason, it reminds her of the texter. The one who kept asking for money and then wrote, 'I know what you did. Everyone knows.' She hasn't heard anything more from them since. Not on text anyway. She thought they'd got sick of tormenting her but maybe they just moved online.

Paula sits back in her chair, her head spinning with possibilities. Things have changed so much in the last few months, it's hard to picture herself before all this. Before John died, before she won all that money.

The lottery. The stupid lottery. It's all the fault of those silly random numbers. She's starting to wish she and John had never played in the first place.

It occurs to her then that they must still be playing, every week. They've had an automated direct debit paying for a rolling subscription all these years. The same numbers, the same Euromillions Friday game. It didn't occur to her to cancel it after the win, what with everything else going on.

Paula exits the websites and instead pulls up the lottery site, bookmarked at the top of the page. She logs into her account.

There it is, the subscription, same as ever. It looks like they even won another two pounds forty recently.

Paula scans the page, her eyes landing on the six numbers ranging from one to fifty. Always the same numbers. Every week for thirty years. Except . . . oh.

The lottery numbers. The ones they've played every week for three decades. The same ones they've been playing since the time the lottery was still called the lottery. The numbers.

They've been changed.

Paula brings a hand to her chest; it's shaking. Her heart is thumping hard and frightened. How could they have been changed? It was always the same numbers. She knows them off by heart. She and John had chosen them carefully in those early days – they were all meaningful in some small way. Her birthday, his birthday, their wedding date – all the special numbers. How could there be new ones here now? Who could've changed them?

Is it possible there's a fault on the website? Paula clicks refresh and waits breathlessly for the numbers to reappear. The new numbers are still there, unfamiliar and strange.

Only a handful of people know about her lottery numbers. She mentioned them in the family grief sessions, and she's told Audrey, Ivy and Teddy.

But why would any of them change them? And how? Why?

Paula clicks through a few settings, finding a log of the numbers played. She can see clearly now, the numbers were changed just over a week ago.

She definitely didn't do this, so who did? Perhaps the lottery people did it? Maybe once you've won the jackpot, they automatically change the numbers for you?

She shakes her head. That seems implausible.

But how else could it be done? Who would even have access to this laptop?

Yes, the back door is always unlocked because of Seb living in the garden, and yes, the computer sits in the same corner of the kitchen, on the countertop, always unlocked. All of Paula's passwords are auto-filled in because how is anyone supposed to remember them otherwise. So it would be easy enough if you were really motivated.

Could someone really have let themselves in here and done this? What if one of the creeps who've been messaging her online came here? What if it was one of the lottery obsessives? What about those photographers, or the journalists in the vans outside? Could they? The most likely culprit is, of course, the loan sharks – Craig and his friend. They've so far been avoiding the house because of the photographers outside, but they could've sneaked in here one night. The thought fills her with horror.

But why would they?

Why? Just to scare her? Just to send some kind of message?

The thought Paula doesn't want to think hits her: what if it wasn't a stranger. What if someone she knows did this to torture her? She considers that tweet she read earlier.

'I personally know Paula Sheldon VERY WELL' they've written.

What if—

Suddenly there is a noise at the back door and Paula is on her feet, grabbing for the nearest weapon before she can think.

It's Seb. He's standing in the doorway, frozen with shock at his mother's wild expression. His eyes travel to the large wooden spoon in her hand, raised and ready to strike.

'Mum?' he says in a wobbly voice, like he's not sure. 'Sorry, I didn't mean to scare you.'

Elly Vine

Paula lowers her weapon, her breathing slowing. 'Sorry, Seb. I . . .' She can't find an explanation for him. Or for herself. 'I was just having a moment. I thought you might be an intruder.'

Seb's shoulders relax as he moves into the kitchen. 'If I were a burglar, I'm not sure a wooden spoon would've done you much good,' he points out nicely.

Paula stands up straighter. 'This is a very expensive wooden spoon from M&S actually. I think it could withstand a couple of hard heads.'

'I stand corrected.' Seb gives her a small smile. 'I'm glad you'll be well armed with defensive wooden spoons when I'm away next week.'

Paula blinks at him and he raises his eyebrows. 'You remember the course I'm going on? I told you about it?'

'Of course I remember!' Paula says emphatically, though this is entirely news to her. 'The course!' She pauses to swallow, willing the guilt not to show on her face. 'The course, of course! I hope of course that the course won't cause you to be too . . . coarse!'

Seb beams, 'I'm not sure the *cause* part worked in there, but well done on the rest.' His warmth makes Paula feel terrible.

'Will it be . . . long days on the . . . course?' she fishes, hoping for more information to assuage the guilt.

Seb nods, then his face falls. 'Look, Mum, Tilly didn't want me to say anything about this to you, but I don't want to blindside you when—'

He's interrupted by his sister's appearance behind him at the back door. She sounds intensely annoyed, 'Oh cheers, Seb, glad I can count on you for help.' She shoots him daggers and he looks down at his feet, red-faced.

'Help with what?' Paula asks fearfully. 'What are you doing here?' She starts, checking her watch. 'Are we supposed to be at a counselling session?'

'No, Mum, it's a Monday,' Tilly says really slowly, enunciating her words. She's looking at her mother penetratingly, an expression of genuine concern lighting her features. She continues, speaking in the same exaggerated way. 'And do you know where you are right now?'

Paula tuts. 'Yes, Tills. I haven't lost the plot entirely. Days are just a little difficult. Who keeps track of Mondays?'

Her daughter nods, then moves to sit down at the table, opposite Paula. After a moment, Seb goes to join his sister. They are both sitting across from her, and Paula suddenly feels like she is being interviewed for a job. What is this? Has Tilly come to apologise for storming off last week? She doesn't look very sorry, watching her mother carefully now from the other side of the table.

'We wanted to talk to you,' Tilly begins in a fake-sounding tone. 'Me and Seb. Together.'

Seb looks at her askance. 'God, Tilly, is that meant to be your soothing intervention voice?'

'*Intervention?!*' Paula echoes with alarm. 'Intervention for what? I only have the odd glass of champagne when Teddy and Audrey make me. They're both very insistent. Ivy and I hardly really drink—'

Tilly elbows her brother, then reaches over and places a hand over her mum's. 'Ignore him. Look, Mum, I'm very sorry for getting so upset with you during the counselling session last week. That wasn't fair or right. I want you to know we both love you very much and want what's best for you.'

'Am I dying?' Paula asks fearfully. Surely she'd have noticed if she was?

Seb snorts. 'Hope not.'

'You're not helping,' Tilly snarls at him. 'Look, the fact is, you're not yourself, Mum, and we want to know why. You've been secretive for weeks. Months! You bought a bloody sports car. You refuse to speak up in counselling. You carry that weird little notebook around everywhere you go. You suddenly have these new friends out of nowhere that we know nothing about. I mean, who *are* those women? Why does that tall American one wear such tiny pink skirts and have such enormous earrings? You have a lot of money now, Mum, and Dad isn't here to look after you – to protect you – and I'm worried these strangers are preying on you somehow. Have you given them any money? Have they asked?'

Paula tries not to laugh. 'Teddy has eight hundred million dollars in the bank, Tills.'

Tilly stares at her, then nods nicely like you would at a child making up stories.

'OK, Mum, sure she does.' She sits back. 'What about that twenty-something pretty one? What is she doing hanging out with a bunch of women more than twice her age? She seems totally out of place, in those band T-shirts and old jeans. What's she after?'

'I like the band T-shirts,' Seb mutters as his sister continues, not waiting for a response. 'Or the older one with the scarf? She seems completely doolally.'

'Well, yes, she is a bit,' Paula acknowledges, then adds in a whisper, 'And it's a pashmina, Tilly. They're made from the wool of cachemire goats.' Tilly doesn't reply and the three of them all fall silent.

Paula's been trying to avoid attracting attention to the Widows Club and their murder-y antics, but all she's done is make them a bigger, stranger, more intriguing thing in Tilly's eyes.

Her daughter leans back, a dark cloud passing over her face. 'The stuff online . . .' She pauses. 'The mean comments and the . . . the theories.'

Paula swallows hard. 'Theories?'

Tilly fixes her with a concerned stare. 'I know you don't want to think about it – I don't want to think about it either – but you must have seen what people have been saying about you. About you and Dad. There's no way that's not getting to you. It's horrible. Misha's been blocking and reporting accounts left, right and centre.'

Paula inhales and stands up, bustling around the kitchen picking up expensive wooden spoons and putting them in drawers. 'I really do appreciate the pair of you worrying about me, but there isn't anything to be concerned about. I've made some new friends; Teddy likes expensive tiny skirts; I've bought a car. What's so bad about all that? I did win the lottery after all.' She wheels on Tilly. 'And you're the one who told me I should start spending it and having fun! You told me to start having adventures.'

Tilly stands up, too. 'Yeah, but I guess I thought you'd maybe start slow! Like get yourself a new coat and a fancy handbag! Some new hand towels for the bathroom. Not go straight out and buy a hundred-grand car! You've gone from zero to a hundred in a hot minute.'

'A bit like the new Porsche,' Seb mutters dryly.

'I love my new car!' Paula cries, suddenly feeling very hard done by. 'I don't regret buying it – not for one second.' She nods decisively. 'And I'm going to buy myself a house somewhere, too!' She falters at Tilly's expression, then pastes on a smile. 'And I've decided I'd like to buy the two of you a home each, as well.' She's hoping this announcement might break the tension, distract her children from this so-called intervention rubbish.

It works with one of them.

Seb breaks out into a huge grin. 'Woah! Are you serious, Mum? I've been looking at rentals lately, and blimey, I can't believe how expensive everything is!'

Tilly scowls, but Paula continues, undeterred. 'I am serious, Sebby. Of course, it'll take a bit of time. You'll have to find the right place and then it'll be a few months for the purchase to go through, but you could be out of the shed by Christmas.' She pauses. 'And of course there'll be a budget. I'm not offering to buy you each a five-bedroom mansion. I think a two- or three-bed should suffice.'

'Mum!' Tilly's voice cracks. 'It doesn't feel like you're listening to me! I don't need a house. I just want my mum back.' She breaks now and hot tears spill out onto hot cheeks. 'I want you to be honest and tell us what you're hiding!' Paula says nothing and Tilly's voice gets even louder. 'I'm starting to think . . . I don't know. It feels like you . . .' She breaks off, pursing her lips shut like she's decided against saying whatever it is. But then she changes her mind, spitting the horrible words that come next. 'It feels like you're happier without Dad.'

Paula stares at her, saying nothing.

'Well?' Tilly says, her voice now raised, her face getting redder. 'Because it seems like you might be! You're suddenly this whole other person I know nothing about, with all these weird new friends and a weird new car. It's like you're . . .' Her eyes flash and it's clear she is finally saying the things she's wanted to say for goodness knows how long. 'I haven't seen you *once* cry about him. You're not sad about Dad's death at all, are you?'

Paula mutters a protest, 'Tilly, grief has tentacles . . .' she begins and her daughter makes a noise somewhere between a groan and a scream. There are more tears, her face wet, as she continues. 'Just admit it! Admit you're happier without him! Mum, tell me the truth. Are you happy he's dead?'

Paula feels like she's been slapped. Her mouth gapes open as her children stare at her, waiting for an answer. An answer she can't give them. Everyone in the room stays frozen, holding their breath, waiting.

Paula opens her mouth, 'I—'

The doorbell cuts her off. Tilly stares at her, still waiting. Seb is stock still, a haunted look on his face.

Paula turns for the hallway and her daughter calls after her, 'For God's sake, Mum, please just leave it. Come back and talk to me about this!'

She ignores her, reaching for the front door and opening it wide.

It's Craig and his friend. The sight of them makes Paula's head spin. Quickly, she steps outside, pulling the door shut behind her.

'My children are in there,' she says and her voice comes out all strangled and terrified. Craig smiles wolfishly.

'Well, that's OK, we can do this out here.' He turns to nod at the empty road in front of the house. 'Look at that, Paula, the photographers are gone.' He pauses and adds in a menacing tone, 'At last.' He smiles again. 'We've been more than patient. And very generous in waiting for the money, Paula, but it's time. John owed us. *You* owe us.'

Paula shakes her head. 'I have . . . I have some of it! I didn't know how . . . I couldn't just go into a bank!' Craig's face hardens into a scowl, and she quickly adds, 'But I do have some! I have nearly ten thousand pounds, I think.' She shakes her head. 'But it's in the drawer inside. I can't go back in right now . . .' She trails off, wondering whether it would be better to face Tilly's wrath or Craig's.

He sighs. 'Believe it or not, I'm actually a nice guy, Paula. So here's what I'm going to do.' He inhales a long breath. 'You have one more week. And I don't give a shit if you have to go into the bank with a gun and hold the place up – maybe shoot a cashier or two. You're going to be paying up at that point. Otherwise, we're coming back here with sledgehammers.' He holds up his hands. 'I don't like saying that, for the record, but it's the job. And it's not even your knees we're going to break, Paula. It'll be your kids in there.' He pauses, smiling that Cheshire Cat grin again. 'Seb and Tilly, isn't it? Tilly and her wife Misha have a nice flat they rent, don't they? Although I don't know how they manage with all those stairs.' His grin gets wider. 'They certainly won't be able to manage them anymore, if we don't get this money.' He leans closer. 'Now go back inside, Paula, bring me that ten thousand pounds and then I'll see you in a week for the rest.'

Paula slowly nods, her mouth dry, her whole body trembling. She reaches for the door, barely able to turn the handle. Her hands don't feel like her own. She makes her way inside quickly, heading into the kitchen, where Tilly and Seb are still sitting, waiting. Tilly's head is on the table, resting on her arms.

'Mum?' Her daughter looks up, her eyes red and watery. Paula walks calmly over to her junk drawer in the corner of the kitchen. Calmly, she retrieves the fat brown envelope stowed away in there. Then, after thinking for a second, she also picks up her passport, slipping it into her handbag.

'What are you doing, Mum?' Seb asks and she turns back to her children.

'I'm sorry I'm not acting the way you want me to, Tilly,' she says, her voice calm. 'I know I'm getting it all wrong, but how is anyone supposed to get it right in a situation like this? Why do you get to decide what the right reaction is?'

Tilly stands up, she looks angry now. 'That's not what I'm saying,' she says gruffly. 'But my life is in ruins and you seem totally fine. Better than fine.'

Paula stares at her for a long moment. 'I'm not fine,' she says after another second. 'But I don't need you to keep analysing my every move – my every utterance! – and dissecting what's right or wrong. I'm finished.' With that, Paula turns away, walking back out into the hallway and away from her children without another look. She wants to be away. Away from all of it. Away from all the accusations and fear and suspicion. Away from Craig and his horrible, horrible threats. Away from John's ghost in this cold, broken-down house.

It turns out, she is going on holiday after all.

27

Paula can't remember the last time she was this sweaty. She's not really a sweaty sort of person. She said this to Seb recently and he made a joke she didn't understand about Prince Andrew and Pizza Express.

But the sweating has been worth it – as was the horrifyingly expensive taxi – because Paula's made it to the airport just in time. And, after much joyful and excited shouting, she, Audrey, Teddy and Ivy are about to board an actual private jet!

Except... who knew private jets could be so... so... well, *underwhelming*.

'Here we are!' Connie, the aggressively happy air steward, announces. She waves across the concourse, across the blackened tarmac, to where the small, unimpressive plane sits. It is very... It's... hmm, it is very *new* looking, Paula concedes, taking it in. And it is a very shiny metallic. In a sort-of sensible black colour. But otherwise, it is not terribly *un*like every other plane she's seen before on the telly.

Connie gesticulates some more, waiting for applause from the group, like she's done a magic trick. Audrey coos politely and nods excitedly, but Paula can tell she's not entirely buying Connie's enthusiasm either.

They move towards the small boarding steps, Paula trailing behind Teddy and Ivy as Connie pauses, smiling some more. 'Can I just re-check your passports?' she asks and Audrey gathers everyone's documents, passing them to Connie, who looks them over. Still smiling.

Smiling is clearly a big part of her job description.

Paula can't believe she's really here. She came. She's going *on holiday.*

Audrey, Teddy and Ivy had looked so shocked to see her appearing from nowhere in the airport like that. She must've been a total state, all red-faced and befuddled, but they didn't hesitate to gather her up into the biggest cuddle. For a moment, Paula forgot about all of it – about all of the horribleness – and let herself be swept away by their excitement. She let herself feel happy. Just for a moment.

Before her, Connie struggles with the passport pages, her perma-smile faltering. From her angle, Paula strains to see, wondering if Paula the Dog has a passport of her own and whether Teddy's will finally reveal the answer of where she's really from. The American sounds very LA today.

Instead, Paula catches a glimpse of Audrey's passport in Connie's hands. The steward is checking the picture and it's funny to see her friend so straight-faced in the image, staring dead-eyed at the lens without her signature pashmina. It barely even looks like the real Audrey, who always appears to be shiny and happy. Paula's eyes travel down the page and there is a half-second before Connie shuts the passport, where she thinks she sees something. Something jarring and confusing. Paula frowns, wondering if she imagined it. It was such a quick look, maybe she got it wrong.

They head up the steps and on board, as Paula considers what she did or didn't see. What would it mean? She shakes her head, trying to dislodge the thought as they file inside the jet.

It is just as underwhelming there.

Paula's not sure what she expected from a private jet but she certainly expected . . . more. So much is made of them by pop stars on Instagram and angry students on the M25 who don't want the world to explode before they're fifty. She expected at least a glitterball or some Abba playing. But no. The cabin is quite claustrophobic, with low ceilings and miniature windows. The lighting is dim and yet too fluorescent; it hurts Paula's eyes.

She takes a seat towards the back as Audrey chatters away loudly to the group about the Michelin-starred food she's pre-ordered for their 'din-dins'. They all buckle up as Connie wades through the safety information and no one listens. Some things don't change whatever kind of plane you're on.

As they begin rumbling along the runway, Paula tries to persuade herself to join in with the rowdy fun. Being around these women usually lifts her out of herself, makes her feel light, but today there is too much. Too much going on and too much to fear. The noise in her head is loud and frantic as she watches the landscape of London get further away out the window. As they pass through fuzzy clouds, she mentally orders herself to let go of all the horrible feelings. She tries to picture all of the darkness as a solid, tangible thing she can throw away. She orders herself to release all the confusion, all the cruelty, all the things she doesn't quite understand – or doesn't want to understand. She closes her eyes and tries to imagine it. She takes the murders, the loan sharks, the accusations, Tilly's worried face, and turns it all into a blob of blackness she can launch into the sky out of the window.

This is a holiday after all, and Paula hasn't had a proper holiday in so long. Even that family wedding they all went to in Spain six years ago wasn't exactly what you'd call *relaxing*. They'd had a panic trying to get her passport renewed before leaving, and once there, John's brothers spent the entire week getting very drunk and shouting angrily about Spanish people speaking Spanish.

She visualises throwing it away. All of it. She watches the blob of awfulness flying through the air and away from the plane. Paula takes a deep breath, letting it go, trying to find the zen and . . . it doesn't work. The blob is still there. Paula's whole mid-section feels like it's blocked up. Like there is tar clogging all of her vital organs.

Tilly hates her. Her own *daughter* accused her of . . . well . . .

There has been so much shouting, so many accusations, never mind all the glaring and sulking Tilly's directed at her over these last few weeks. But there is something else Paula keeps wondering. How strange it is to Paula that apparently her daughter thinks she's happier without her husband, but hasn't once asked *why*. Shouldn't that be important? If she really is happier without John around, shouldn't her children want to know *why*? In her coat pocket she feels for the notebook. John's notebook. Apart from her passport and the clothes on her body, it's the only thing she has with her today. She thinks of the numbers inside. Rows and rows of numbers. Numbers that reveal the truth about her marriage.

Perhaps this was a mistake after all. She shouldn't have come. She regards her friends with sudden fear, watching Audrey sloshing champagne into glasses as she soliloquises about the bars and restaurants she wants them to visit. She describes a particular bit of beach no one but the A-listers know about, and Paula wonders what makes it so special. Does it have magical celebrity sand that is easy to walk on and doesn't get in all of your stuff so you're tasting it for days?

This is no time for a holiday. This was the wrong decision. She shouldn't have come.

'I haven't got any knickers!' She shouts this too loudly and the women all turn to face her. Even Connie looks over, her smile wavering.

'I didn't bring anything, no luggage at all, what am I going to do?' Paula asks with urgency. 'I haven't got any underwear, Teddy! Apart from what I'm wearing, I have nothing. Nothing else at all. No toothbrush. No hairspray.' Paula glances longingly at Teddy's hair. 'No nothing!' She makes eye contact with Audrey and is filled with the sudden certain knowledge that Audrey will insist on lending her some knickers. And probably her pashmina, too. Her voice starts to shake. 'We need to go back. I need to go home. Can we turn around? Is that possible on a private jet? Can we knock on the cockpit door? Text the pilot? I hate to ask, but I really can't go to France today. I can't go without any knickers, what would they think? Can we go back, please? Please? We have to go BACK!'

Ivy moves quickly from her seat, coming to sit beside Paula. 'Hey,' she says softly, reaching for her hand. 'Don't worry about your underwear. We'll work it out.' Paula stares at her. There's no way she'd fit into tiny Ivy's pants, never mind the indignity of borrowing a twenty-something's jeans and T-shirts.

Teddy joins them, crouching at her feet and speaking in a low voice with a serious expression. 'Listen, Paula, everything is OK. You're OK.' She removes her signature giant sunglasses before gesturing at Ivy and Audrey. 'We're here with you. We've got Ivy's yacht waiting for us. It's going to be a *relaxing* time, a *fun* time. Or it's meant to be. So if you don't feel like you'll be able to enjoy it' – she nods her confirmation at the other two – 'then we will turn this crappy private jet around and all head home right now, OK?' A few feet away, Connie looks a tiny bit offended.

Paula feels tearful looking up into Teddy's wide beautiful eyes. Her hands are trembling. This feels like too much. She feels like she's been holding her breath since leaving the house, since the fight with Tilly, since the terrifying threats from Craig. She's been holding her breath and holding herself together. But she's not sure how much longer it will be possible. She can feel herself on the edge, about to fall apart. Her edges feel frail and dusty, ready to disintegrate at any moment.

How has her life come to this? Her husband is dead. There are goons threatening to hurt her family – a family who all hate her and think she's a bad person. She's got no job and everything she knew of her old life is gone.

'Is there something else, Paula?' Teddy asks kindly, her brow furrowing as she takes in Paula's face. 'Has something happened? Why did you change your mind about coming?'

Paula feels her eyes welling up and she stares down at their clasped hands, unable to speak. Teddy squeezes them tightly, waiting.

'Tilly said . . . Tilly accused me of . . .' But she can't bring herself to say it. She can't bring herself to even *think* about what her own daughter said to her. 'Tilly and I had another big fight,' she finishes lamely. The group says nothing, waiting patiently for her to reveal more. Paula looks down at her own lap. 'Her and Seb both seem to have this idea of me . . . They don't *see* me. They never have. I'm just their one-dimensional mother with no life of my own. And now that I'm starting to find a life and enjoy myself . . . they don't like it. Or maybe they just don't understand – I don't know. I feel like my children have no idea who I am.' She pauses, staring out of the tiny window at the clouds below. 'But I'm not sure *I* know who I am, so why should they?'

There is silence in the cabin as they all wait. Everyone holds their breath.

Paula inhales deeply and turns to face them. 'I'm sorry. I'm OK. Let's keep going. We don't have to text the pilot.' She looks over at Connie. 'It's not a crappy private jet. It's lovely.' She swallows. 'Let's go to the South of France.'

Everyone smiles, relieved, as Audrey leans in. 'Well, thank buggery for that! I've got us booked for dinner at Club 55 on the beach. It was a favourite of Joan Collins, don't you know!' She cackles, so very much like Audrey, and Paula – at last – smiles a genuine smile. And so does Connie.

28

They land at an airport that Teddy coolly reports in a lovely French accent to be the *'aeroport du golfe de Saint-Tropez'*. A limo is waiting for them outside, and they travel the fifteen kilometres to their hotel at speed. Audrey and Teddy chat over each other the whole time, wondering where to get Paula a toothbrush and knickers. Thankfully, it hasn't yet occurred to Audrey to share.

Paula is distracted, still unable to shake the doomed feeling she's brought with her across the Mediterranean. So she opens the window and sticks her head out, silently pleading with the French sunshine to do its job. Paula the Dog joins her, her tongue lolling out of her mouth as they both let the warm wind whip up hair around their faces. Even feeling as she does – and even with Paula the Dog's hair flying into her mouth – Paula can acknowledge this is something like a dream. Until . . .

'I feel sick,' Ivy says suddenly from the other side of the car. She leans forward to speak to the driver. 'Pull over, please, sir? *S'il te plait? Monsieur? Er, je suis . . . mal?*'

He nods, understanding and quickly pulling over. Poor Ivy opens the door, throwing herself at the foreign ground, and then throwing *up* on that foreign ground.

'Too much champagne?' Audrey climbs out, rubbing Ivy's back as Teddy and Paula hover at a distance.

'She's only had one glass,' Teddy points out. 'She fakes drinking when you aggressively top everyone up. She always does.'

'Excuse me,' Audrey smirks. 'I was making Connie the air steward aggressively top everyone up, *actually*.'

'Car sick,' Ivy mumbles, her face hot and sweaty.

'You've been in my car plenty of times!' Audrey points out.

'You go really, really fast,' Ivy pants. 'It helps.' She collapses onto a grassy bank. 'I just need a minute. I'm sorry, everyone.'

'Don't be sorry, my darling!' Audrey tells her loudly. 'It'll give Paula a chance for a wee.' Everyone looks to Paula quizzically and Audrey hastily adds, 'Paula the Dog, I mean. Sorry, darling.'

Paula the Human steps away, thinking about how she does actually need a wee, but will probably wait. She takes in the scenery and her breath slows. It is so beautiful here. *So* beautiful. They are high up, looking down at endless rows of beautiful yellow, pink and orange buildings, dotted higgledy-piggledy across the landscape. The sea stretches out beyond it, covered in small white boat-shaped dots. A large port snakes out into the water, with what looks like a small lighthouse at the end. Paula suddenly wants to run towards it. She wants to dive fully clothed into the emerald sea and swim and swim and swim.

She won't though. It's not her.

'*Ah non, est-ce que tout va bien?*'

Paula turns towards the lyrical syllables, finding a debonair older man in a hat, regarding Ivy prone on the grass.

'She's fine!' Audrey leaps into his path and he steps back. 'I mean, *elle va bien, merci.*'

'British?' the man asks with a smile. His teeth are startlingly white against his deep, deep tan.

'*Oui!*' Audrey says, offering him her hand. He kisses it, looking more and more amused.

'How charming,' he tells her in that swoony accent. 'Have you just arrived?'

'*Oui,*' Audrey repeats, her eyes laser-locked on to his. 'We're on our way to our hotel right now. Do you have any recommendations for anything we should see while we're here? We haven't the first idea about this place!'

This, from a woman who spent the plane journey itemising every single building in Saint-Tropez.

'I'm actually feeling a lot better now,' Ivy says, sitting up. 'We can get going.'

'Not yet, darling,' Audrey tells her. 'You're still very pale indeed. You stay seated on the ground there. It's the best place for you.'

Ivy eyes the pool of sick beside her with discomfort. 'Is it?' she asks, but Audrey ignores her. Her gaze is focused.

The Frenchman considers her question. 'Well, you must see the citadel,' he says after a moment, 'and the Saint-Tropez market. Pampelonne beach, perhaps? Cape Camarat? Oh!' Inspiration strikes. 'You must see the Château de la Moutte!'

Audrey inches closer. 'That all sounds fascinating!'

They are all things she has already told the group they should see.

'*Mon nom est Antoine,*' he offers, and Audrey introduces everyone, barely turning as she waves, half-heartedly acknowledging her friends.

'These three are not as cultured as I am,' Audrey tells him. 'They just want to sit by the pool and gossip about men.' She titters as Teddy rolls her eyes. 'Would you be interested in taking me to see the castle of Moutte? Maybe tomorrow?' Audrey flutters her eyelashes and he beams.

'*Merveilleux!* Wonderful!' he says. 'I would be honoured.'

They grin at one another, swapping numbers as the rest of the group pile back into the limo.

As they drive away, Audrey squeals, reaching over to cuddle Ivy. 'Thank you, my darling! You did splendid work.'

'Oh!' Paula looks between them. 'Was that all a set-up? You spotted him and faked your . . .' She trails off at Ivy's face. She is very pale and sweaty.

'Not fake,' she says in a quiet voice. 'Definitely not fake.'

'Not everything is a plan,' Audrey says. 'Just most things. And either way, it worked out perfectly!' She smacks her lips with satisfaction as Ivy sticks her whole head out of the window. Paula the Dog loyally joins her.

'Look, we're here!' Teddy points out the front windscreen. They catch Ivy murmuring, 'Thank God,' as they pull into a car park.

The hotel is lovely. The Cheval Blanc Saint-Tropez is small and boutique, sitting on the water with its own jetty. Not to mention its very own beach. The inside – which the concierge, Gerard, calls an 'intimate maison' – is smaller than Paula expected. Much more low key and minimalist than the large ceilinged London hotels Audrey talks about. The concierge shows them round, and they walk from room to room in awed silence. There are only thirty bedrooms, but Gerard says each is themed around 'thoughtful elegance'. By which it's clear he means *money*.

When Teddy informs Gerard that Paula has come without a suitcase, within an hour, someone has filled her room with everything one might need for a holiday in the South of France. And quite a lot of things she would never, ever need. For example, in what world might she have use of a week-to-view calendar on her holiday, or a toastie maker? But she is impressed nonetheless.

In her room, Paula takes a minute to brush her teeth, admiring the shininess of the bathroom and the room itself – sorry, the *two-bedroom Sea Suite*. It must be a thousand square feet, with two expansive bedrooms, a dressing room and its own private garden terrace. Moving past her king-sized bed and out onto the balcony, Paula looks out over the Mediterranean, admiring the deep greens and pale blues. There are boats in every direction and Paula thinks of Ivy and of her deep-seated need for freedom.

It's a beautiful distraction, but everything that's happened isn't far from her thoughts. The way Paula left without a word, Tilly and Seb will be even more convinced of what they said. And what is she going to do about the money she owes? She shouldn't have come here. It doesn't feel right. Nothing feels right. She just wants to be at home in her own bed, under her duvet, where she can cry and cry and cry.

She checks her phone, hoping there might be a message from at least one of her children. But there is nothing, only messages from Audrey and Teddy in the TLWWC WhatsApp group. Audrey wants them all to know that Antoine has already been in touch about their date, and she's hoping to fix that twenty-five years and five months dry spell imminently. If they know what she means. Teddy's reply asks about dinner and studiously ignores any mention of Audrey's sex life.

She's also asking in convoluted metaphors, what they're going to do about sexual predator, Owen.

Elly Vine

Paula's heart beats fast as she backs up across the room, sitting heavily on the sprawling bed. She doesn't even take off her shoes, climbing under the covers and holding them over her. She squeezes her eyes tightly shut. She came here for an escape from everything, to hide from the danger and the horror. But she's brought everything with her here to paradise. There is nowhere to hide.

29

Several hours later, Paula jerks awake at the sound of persistent knocking on the door. For a moment she freezes in the unfamiliar surroundings. This isn't her home. Where is she? Who is making that noise? Have they come for her?

'Paula?' It's Teddy's voice. She sounds worried.

They're in Saint-Tropez. They're on holiday. She's with her friends.

Groggy and tangled in the silk sheets, Paula reaches automatically for her phone. She has several missed calls and message notifications.

'PAULA? DARLING?' That's Audrey now, and she's shouting.

Paula fights the heaviness in her limbs, clawing her way out of the bed to the door and pulling it open.

'I'm here, sorry,' she says quietly, and Ivy is in her arms before she can say anything else.

'I was worried,' she murmurs into her ear. 'You didn't answer.'

'I'm sorry, sweetheart,' Paula says in the same low voice. 'I was asleep.'

Ivy releases her at last and Paula swipes at her swollen eyes.

'Are you OK?' Teddy's usually cool, unaffected gaze is earnest and frightened.

Paula nods quickly. 'Of course. Shall we go to dinner?'

Audrey tuts. 'We missed our reservation, I'm afraid.'

Teddy waves an angry hand at the older woman. 'Never mind that, it doesn't matter.' She turns to face Paula, frowning. 'Something's going on with you, Paula, please talk to us.'

Paula shakes her head vaguely. 'No, no, nothing. It's just . . . you know, Tilly and . . . well, you know. It's all a lot.'

Teddy stares at her, waiting. Ivy does the same. Audrey fiddles with her phone, ever the sociopath.

She should tell them. She should tell them everything. She should tell them the truth about John and the loan sharks and how she's living with this paralysing fear.

She opens her mouth.

And then closes it again.

She can't.

'Let's go for dinner,' she says simply. 'I'm sure we can find somewhere to eat.'

The women exchange a look.

'Paula, please,' Ivy begins, sitting down and pulling Paula down onto the bed with her. She encircles an arm around her friend's shoulders. Paula pulls away, standing back up and grabbing for her coat. It's in a pile at the foot of her bed and as she tries to turn it upright, something clatters to the floor.

It lands at Teddy's feet. She reaches for it as Paula's eyes widen. It's John's notebook. It's fallen out of her pocket.

'Give me that!' she says in a high pitch as Teddy regards her with shock. Paula swallows and shakes her head. 'Sorry, I mean, can I have that back, please?'

'What is it?' Teddy asks, holding firm to the thin notebook. Paula resists the urge to grab it and make a run for the door. This is all too much.

'It's . . . It's just a . . . Nothing,' Paula finishes lamely. 'Just a notebook, nothing.'

Teddy stares at her and then down at the unassuming grey pad in her hands. 'Is it yours?'

Paula blinks. 'Um, no,' she admits. 'It was . . . John's. I found it after he died. Can I have it back? Please?'

Teddy takes a second and then, reluctantly, reaches out to hand it back to Paula. It is Ivy that stops her.

'Paula,' she says with determination. 'There's clearly something going on. Something you want to tell us about, but can't, for some reason.' She pauses, her sweet expression perplexed and vulnerable. 'Please. You can trust us, please believe that.'

Paula swallows hard, looking at her young friend. Another long moment passes.

'OK,' she says hoarsely at last. She turns to Teddy, who is still holding out the notepad. She nods towards the book without taking it. 'OK.'

Teddy frowns and then nods back. She moves to the bed, taking a seat there. Inhaling deeply, she opens its pages. There is silence in the room as Paula watches her friend making her way through the scribbles inside. She looks up at last, still frowning.

'I don't understand,' she says simply. Audrey moves to sit beside her as Ivy takes Paula's hand, squeezing it.

'What is it?' Audrey asks, taking the notebook and scanning its contents for herself. She shakes her head. 'It's just pages and pages of numbers. The whole notebook, it's full of them. What does it mean? Are they dates? Times? Something else?'

Paula's breathing is ragged as she fights back a confusing bundle of feelings. She has to stay steady for this. If she's going to tell them the truth of it all, then she has to stay clear-headed and present.

'It's both,' she says at last. 'I found it not long after John's accident. It took me a while to understand what it meant, but you're right: it's pages and pages of times and dates, going back years. I sat up all night, trying to put it together, and when I did, it all fell into place.' She takes a deep breath. 'It's my . . . It's a list of my . . . movements.'

There is silence in the room again, but this one is not full of expectation. It is dawning understanding. It is disgust.

'John was . . .' – Ivy swallows – 'tracking you?'

'Everything I did, for years,' Paula nods. 'Everywhere I went, he documented.' She moves to the cabinet where tall bottles of expensive-looking still and sparkling water stand side by side. Carefully, she pours herself a glass, amazed that her hands are not shaking. They have done every time she's thought of the notebook over these last few months. Every time she thought about anyone finding it. She takes a long sip and looks out of the window and into the distance. 'I've been telling everyone – and myself – that I loved him and that we were happy. I even believed it some of the time.' She turns to her friends, eyes wide. 'Honestly, my whole life was turned upside down by losing him. I had no one and nothing, and I missed him so much. My John was the centre of my universe.' She swallows with some difficulty. 'But the trouble with that is that he *made* himself the centre of my universe. He made it so I had nothing else. He never left me alone, never let me have any freedom or choices. I belonged to him.'

Paula takes another long sip of her drink trying to steady her breathing. The last thing she wants to do right now is cry.

Ever since she heard the news about John's fiery car crash, she has been trying not to cry. She didn't want to cry because the tears would not have been for him or his death. They wouldn't have been for their lost love or their many years of marriage. Any tears she wanted to shed in the last few months would've been for herself. They would've been for the thirty-three years John had stolen from her. They would've been for the friends he stopped her seeing. For the family she barely spoke to because of him. For the day she got a call to say her mother was dying, when he wouldn't let her go visit to say goodbye.

'He took so much from me,' Paula continues in a shaky voice. 'Not long after we got married, I told him I wanted to be a nurse, but he said I was too stupid. I think he wanted me to stay a carer, working in a care home because then he knew exactly where I was all the time. He would turn up there a lot, to check I was where I was supposed to be, I suppose. He was making notes about my routine even then. He was very jealous, too, and would fly into rages about me speaking to any other men. I think it suited him that I spent my working days around older people who were less likely to show any interest in me.' She pauses. 'Although the irony is that a lot of those elderly men were very handsy. They were much worse than many younger men.' She turns back to the window and continues after a moment, 'He didn't want me driving, though I used to love it when I was young. He said it was because I was such a terrible, dangerous driver, and then he said I'd end up crashing with our children in the car. I believed him. I thought I was a danger to everyone around me.'

'No wonder the first thing you wanted to buy was that car,' Audrey murmurs, standing up and coming to stand beside Paula. She takes her arm, squeezing it hard.

'I love my car,' Paula says fiercely before looking down. 'He didn't let me have any money.' She can barely hear herself speak, as the thoughts and realisations come faster. 'He gave me a few coins for the bus every day but I couldn't have my own credit card or access to our joint account. He told me we were hard up, so I couldn't question anything. He took care of the mortgage and the bills. I never even knew how much things cost until he was gone. Tilly had to sit down and go through it all with me. She got me access to the account and ordered me my own card. But I think she just thought I was a hopeless, clueless idiotic little woman. Like I'd wanted, or asked, for John to take care of everything.'

'So Tilly and Seb don't know any of this?' Audrey asks nicely.

'No,' Paula shakes her head. 'And I've tried so hard to keep them from knowing. I didn't want them to have to carry that; I wanted to protect them.' She takes another deep breath. 'How could I tell them how unhappy I'd been, or that their father was a cruel, selfish man who followed my every movement' – she waves at the notebook on Teddy's lap – 'and wrote it all down so he could more easily control me.' She pauses. 'Their father wasn't a good person.'

'He was an abuser,' Ivy quietly corrects. Paula looks at her searchingly.

'But there were times when he was lovely!' she says, suddenly defensive. 'He would say sorry for being... he called it *grumpy*, and I would think, "Oh, maybe everything will be good again, like it was in the early days." And he would be kind and sweet and affectionate. There *were* times when we were happy! I wouldn't have kept going if there hadn't been some kind of hope to cling on to through the bad times. But as the years went by, those nice moments got fewer and further apart.' She pauses. 'You know how films have a soundtrack? I always felt like my life had a soundtrack, but it was this constant low hum of misery, of . . . dread.'

Paula sits down on the bed now, the air thrumming around her. Her friends gather about her. They all sit there, at Paula's side, silently acknowledging all the sadness, the misery, the denial – the abject horribleness of it all.

Ivy reaches for her hand at last. 'Paula, just because someone doesn't hit you, doesn't mean they're not an abuser. Coercive control can be just as real and damaging as violence. It's against the law, the things he did to you. He was a controlling, abusive monster, just like my husband.' She gestures to Audrey and Teddy. 'Just like all our husbands. Just because he wasn't violent, doesn't make him any better or different.'

'It's insidious and nebulous, that kind of torture,' Teddy says in a low voice like she knows. Like she really knows. 'It makes you question everything, especially your own sanity. It's all too easy to blame yourself, but it was him. Not you.'

Paula hesitates, then nods. 'I think I know that now. I didn't used to know. I used to think it was normal. A normal relationship! Maybe a bit old-fashioned compared to other, younger couples that I'd see treat each other kindly and equally. But I thought we were mostly normal enough.' She sighs. 'I was lying to myself for a long time. Really, I suppose,

I was lying to myself until I met all of you.' She shakes her head. 'The fact is, I wasn't just trying to protect the children; I was trying to protect myself from the truth, as well. And he was so good at making me feel like everything was my fault!' She sighs heavily. 'The strangest thing is that I missed him so much! For weeks I reached for him every morning when I woke up. I sent emails telling him about my day, telling him I missed him.'

'I missed my husband, too,' Ivy admits. 'I hated him – I still hate him – and I'm glad I did what I did, but I still thought – *think* about him so much. You don't always have to miss someone in a nice way.' Audrey and Teddy are both nodding.

Paula stares down at her feet. She's wearing new trainers, but she suddenly wishes she had on her comfy old plimsolls. She has to tell them the rest now, too. 'And he owed money,' she whispers. 'A lot of it. Men have been coming to my house since he died, asking for it in cash. Bad men. I don't know what I'm going to do.'

'Oh, Paula,' Ivy says in a low voice. 'I wish you'd told us.'

Paula regards them solemnly, meeting Teddy's eyes. 'Right from the beginning, none of you believed me when I said John and I were happy. You kept saying you would wait for me to tell you the truth. And I thought you meant about killing him, but I realise now that you meant about our relationship ... You knew I was like you. That I was a ...' She can't finish her sentence.

Audrey does it for her. 'A domestic abuse victim?'

'Survivor!' Teddy corrects defiantly. 'A domestic abuse *survivor*.'

'I think I prefer the term victim,' Ivy says quietly. 'Survivor implies I've overcome what I went through. That I've won, that I've beaten it, that I've moved on, somehow.' She looks down. 'But I haven't. It's a part of who I am. I didn't survive it; I'm ... damaged. I can't call myself a survivor, like it's some big, triumphant result. I escaped him, but what my husband did is part of who I am. For ever, I think.' She swallows. 'I know I didn't make it out unscathed.'

'My darling,' Audrey says, but it is soft, accepting. There is no argument.

'I am healing though,' Ivy adds brightly. 'You've all helped me be happier and more open again. I accept this version of me and I've even started to like it. One day I might even love me. And maybe one day I might even be ready to meet a new partner. Someone kind instead of cruel. A cheerleader instead of a controller. Someone who will love me properly.'

'*We* love you,' Teddy says with strength. 'And you're free. We all are. We've escaped the men who did those things.'

'I'll never escape John,' Paula says fiercely, her voice choked. 'It doesn't matter that he's dead; I'll never be free of him.'

'Of course you will!' Audrey says, and Paula shakes her head. She thinks about the loan sharks – about Craig and his small henchman – turning up on her door step. About the threats he made just before she left to find the group at the airport. She thinks of what he's going to do to her children, to her friends, to her life. About how John did this.

She'll never be free of him.

30

'We should sail to Italy,' says Audrey from her deckchair. 'We can go around the Amalfi Coast, head for Lake Como, then just keep going.'

Paula's not sure how serious Audrey's being. She's also not sure of her geography. But then the older woman throws her head back and starts cackling. Teddy and Ivy join in, and so does Paula, though the idea of never going home somehow seems very appealing right now.

It's the first time she's laughed in days, she realises. She feels better for it. It is a nice, bubbly feeling in her chest. It pokes a hole in the horrible, oppressive sadness.

It has been a quiet few days since Paula's confession. Cosseted away in the South of France, her friends have kept her close and kept her peaceful. Instead of the loud, fancy dinners and wild celebrity bars Audrey had promised, the group has mostly spent long, sedate days on Ivy's boat. They've given her a lot of space, a lot of affection, and a lot of support. They've let her talk when she wanted to talk and been silent when she needed that instead. They haven't pushed.

They know her, Paula realises. They understand how this works. They've all been there. Paula feels a long way away from the world, away from her children, away from the goons who've been keeping her up at night, away from everything. She knows Craig is coming back and everything is going to come crashing down, but right now, she feels only cocooned and protected; she feels loved.

'We can't just sail away,' Ivy smiles over at Audrey. 'We can't leave without Paula the Dog and she gets so seasick. We can't abandon her at the hotel doggy daycare for ever.'

'That's true enough.' Audrey smiles.

All around them is glorious, endless water. Paula shields her eyes, trying to see an edge to the blueness, but it's too bright. The sun bounces off the waves in all directions. She can still see the sun when she shuts her eyes.

Ivy's boat is lovely.

Yacht! She has to stop calling it a boat. Teddy has corrected her several times. Yacht, yacht, yacht.

Paula doesn't know much about boats, but this one seems to be particularly nice. It's large but not Simon Cowell with Sinitta in tow large. There are two decks; one with a spacious suite downstairs for sleeping, and another that features a large living area above. But it is the sun deck out the back where the group has spent the majority of the last few days. There has been an awful lot of lying around talking, while drinking endless glasses of champagne topped up by the few discreet crew members that otherwise keep their distance.

Paula adjusts her swimsuit and the towel underneath her. It's thick and soft – another no-doubt-pricey item provided by her obliging hotel concierge. As far as Paula's concerned, this is the epitome of luxury. The apex of fancy trips. She keeps expecting a member of the royal family to appear out of nowhere. It has been the kind of dream holiday Paula didn't know was possible. Everywhere Paula looks there is money being brandished. People are walking around, displaying their wealth with expensive watches, shiny handbags, and perfect, perfect hair. It's like everyone in Saint-Tropez is coming directly from a hairdresser. Even Teddy's lovely hair somehow pales in comparison.

At least, with everything going on, Paula hasn't had much of a chance to worry about her thin hair. Plus, hats seem to be a big thing over here.

'Did you know,' Audrey begins conversationally from underneath her own huge sunhat, 'that there is a villa you can rent by the night up in the Les Parcs complex of Saint-Tropez. It's on the water, only really accessible by helicopter or by ship via their private port. It's about twelve-thousand square feet, with nine bedrooms and nine bathrooms. It has mountain and sea views, plus its own waterfall. And it only costs sixty-two thousand euros per night to rent.'

Paula gasps, covering her mouth.

'Isn't it funny that this used to be a cute little nothingy fishing village?' Teddy says, adjusting her sunglasses.

'And it's visitors like us that have come along and ruined it,' Ivy points out, to which they all nod solemnly.

Paula sits up, feeling the warmth of the sun move across her body as she shifts position.

'But oh!' Ivy sits up on her towel. 'I know what we can do to even out our universal karma.' She reaches for the suncream, layering it on her legs. 'Kill a vicious deviant called Owen.'

'Let's knock the sexual predator's block off!' Audrey suggests playfully.

'Sounds good to me,' says Teddy.

They fall silent again as Paula holds her breath, hoping this is just talk. And hoping that talk is now over.

Ivy sits forward. 'I went through his Facebook page last night, looking for ideas. He's a smoker. Could we dip his cigarettes in arsenic or something?'

'My new lover, Antoine, is a smoker,' Audrey says conversationally. 'It's disgusting.'

'Didn't you used to smoke?' Paula asks curiously.

'Of course I did! Forty a day for fifty years!' Audrey says proudly. 'But then I got emphysema and had a double lung transplant. Had to pay for each of them privately, of course. I still need regular oxygen therapy though. Smoking is *disgusting.*'

'So, you find your beau, Antoine, disgusting.' Teddy shakes her head. 'And yet, since we got here, you've gone over to his place every night after we've said goodnight. I'm not sure I get it.'

'Does that mean you're not seeing him again after today?' Ivy asks nicely.

Audrey blinks at her. 'My darling, of course I am.' She smiles at Ivy and Teddy. 'Did I not mention twenty-five years and five months? Thanks to that man, that figure has at last been reset, and I intend to take full advantage of him for as long as possible before we fly home. I can put up with some yellow fingers.' She wrinkles her nose at her own words.

'Yuck.' Teddy makes a face. 'I've sworn off romance for ever.'

Ivy smiles at this but changes the subject. 'He's not the next Mr Swift then?' she asks as Audrey regards her with confusion and then revulsion.

'Darling, no!' she cries, and Paula finds herself relieved. It's not that she doesn't like Antoine – or his yellow fingernails – but a part of her was afraid of what might happen if Audrey were to fall in love now. Especially with someone who lives in a different country. If Audrey wanted to stay here, what might happen to their group?

It all feels a little fragile. This holiday – and the last few months – have felt like living in some kind of magical bubble, and Paula's so afraid of the moment when it might burst. She's never known friendship like this before, and she's only now realising how much she missed out on. She loves them. She needs them. Especially with the rest of her world disintegrating like it is.

Over the last few days, she's told them so much about her life with John – and about her life *without* John. They talked about the fifty-thousand-pound debt, about Craig stalking her on her doorstep, about discovering the proof of John's gambling, about the phone calls and the threats. Teddy extracted every last detail regarding the loan sharks. Paula even found herself describing the second henchman's too-small University of Huddersfield hoodie and his interest in the history of *The X Factor* – and Teddy promised she would take care of it the moment they left Saint-Tropez. She got very fierce about it and said neither Craig nor any of his sidekicks would be hurting anyone Paula loves. It has reassured her no end, and honestly, Paula feels a little silly for not bringing it up sooner. Of course Teddy can make the problem go away. The woman is a force of nature who could solve anything and everything. She could probably sort out world peace if she didn't keep getting distracted by tiny skirts and oversized sunglasses.

'Do you have a way of obtaining arsenic?' Teddy asks Ivy suddenly, and everyone regards her with confusion. She sighs.

'You know, to poison Owen's cigarette? Your suggestion?' The young woman shakes her head.

'Well, what about some other kind of poison?' Audrey chimes in from her sun lounger. Despite the heat, she's still wearing a pashmina, but this one is, at least, a little lighter. 'I once considered putting some mushrooms in Harold's dinner, but I haven't got the first idea how to tell the difference between chestnuts and a death cap.' She pauses. 'And to be honest, it all felt a bit too Agatha Christie for my liking.'

Teddy tuts. 'On second thoughts, poison just feels a little bit sexist, don't you think? Everyone assumes it's all we women are capable of, don't they? That's why I quite liked the baseball bat idea. It's so brutal, it's so . . . *men*.'

Ivy looks thoughtful. 'But maybe it's OK that the four of us aren't capable of the same things as men. I think the problem is more on their side. I think we should probably be working towards men not being capable of hitting someone with a baseball bat either, rather than trying to meet them at their level?'

'Quite right,' Audrey nods determinedly. 'Male violence is not something we should be aspiring to. We should stick to female violence as much as possible. And there's nothing wrong with a bit of poison, if that's what we're left with. We just need to find some.'

Teddy picks up her bag. She pulls a laptop out and starts tapping away.

'I'll do some research. It's usually not a great idea to google how to kill someone,' she comments casually. 'But I think we'll be OK. If Columbo comes a-calling for me, I'll just say I'm writing a book.'

Paula dislikes the reminder of Columbo – yet another thing hanging over their heads – but tries to put it away and focus on the towel underneath her. If the bubble is going to burst – if the police are coming for Audrey, if her daughter is going to cut her off for good – then she might as well enjoy a little sunbathing while she can.

Beside her, Teddy taps away on the keyboard at speed. 'Does anyone want to check their emails while I'm online?' she offers after a minute.

Paula takes the proffered computer, a tiny bit of hope lighting up in her chest. OK, so she hasn't had a text or WhatsApp from Tilly since their fight, but maybe she has an email. It's possible, isn't it? She can't remember her daughter ever sending her an email, but there's a chance. Maybe she wanted to send something too long for a text. Is there still a character limit on messages?

She logs into her email account wondering what she would do if Tilly has sent her an email. Is she ready to forgive her? Of course she is. They just need to talk things through and find some peace.

She has only one email and Paula opens it quickly, before she has time to register who it's from. And when she does, she feels everything around her go dark.

* * *

To: PaulaJeanieSheldon1964@ptinternet.com
From: John.Sheldon1960@oldmail.com
Subject:

Hey honey, I'm home.

31

Paula drops the laptop.

It slides off the sun lounger and skids off towards the edge of the boat. Part of Paula wants it to tip over and into the sea, never to be seen or heard from again.

But the email would still be there.

'Whoops,' Audrey says loudly as Ivy hops up, retrieving the computer and examining it for scratches.

'Sorry, Teddy,' Paula says almost under her breath. Her voice is shaking and far away. It doesn't even feel like her speaking.

'Oh God, don't worry about it, babe,' Teddy replies, waving her hand. 'The amount of times I've nearly drowned a device . . .' She pauses. 'But mostly it's been in a toilet, not the Mediterranean ocean.'

Paula doesn't reply and Teddy sits up straighter, immediately sensing something has happened. 'What is it, Paula?' she asks, standing now and moving to sit at Paula's side. 'Was it a message from Tilly or Seb? Or the loan sharks?'

Paula shakes her head numbly. A coldness is creeping through her, spreading upwards from her toes and into her chest, despite the hot sunshine overhead.

The group watches her carefully, waiting. She looks up at them at last.

'It was... It was an email,' she begins as they stare. 'From... John.'

The group glance at each other and Paula wonders if they think she's mad. Maybe she *is* mad? Maybe her dead husband's ghost heard her finally reveal his secrets and has leapt at the chance of haunting her.

Quietly, Teddy takes the laptop from Ivy and opens it. She blinks hard at the screen, her face quickly contorting with rage.

'This is sick,' she mutters. 'Disgusting.' She looks over at Paula, shaking her head. 'It's someone's idea of a horrible joke. It must be.'

Paula blinks at her, something unfurling. Could it be a joke? Could it really be someone playing a nasty prank on her? Who would do that? The person behind the texts? Behind those tweets? The person who changed her lottery numbers?

Because it can't be real. Surely it can't be... John. John's dead. They had the paperwork. They got his ashes. They had a funeral. He's dead.

But who else would have access to his email account?

Audrey and Ivy crowd Teddy, reading over her shoulder. Ivy recoils in horror.

'It can't be real?' she says softly. 'There's no way, is there, Paula?'

'No! Of course not. I... I don't know,' she says, her mind racing. 'I mean *no*. Definitely not. Of course it isn't real. This is someone who's got into his emails or...'

'People can clone email addresses now, can't they?' Teddy directs this at the youngest of them. Ivy nods half-heartedly.

Audrey suddenly looks determined.

'Call him,' she tells Paula. 'See if it really is him. You've still got his mobile phone number, haven't you?'

'I can't,' she shakes her head. 'Tilly cancelled his contract. She sorted everything, shut everything down. His email was the only thing I had left. The only way I had left to . . . speak to him.'

'OK, well . . .' Audrey waves her hands, searching for an answer. 'I don't know, let's maybe send him a Zoom invite!'

'Teams is much better,' Teddy says smoothly.

'Nonsense!' Audrey says as Teddy pulls a face.

'Listen to me, old woman, Zoom has a forty-minute cut-off. Teams has thirty hours! It's very obviously the superior video chat tool.'

'You're a video chat *tool*,' Audrey mutters, grabbing for the computer. 'And do we think it'll take longer than forty minutes to ask John if he's really alive?'

Paula feels so far away. Her friends' voices sound a million miles away. Like strangers shouting across the water.

Audrey starts tapping away at the keyboard. 'We're doing Zoom because that's the one I know.' She glares at Teddy. 'Stop trying to make me learn new things.'

The whirring of the computer sounds strange and alien as Paula stares down at her left hand. At the plain gold band still sitting there, stuck on that finger. She hasn't even *tried* to take it off.

Is John alive? He can't be. So who's done this? And why?

There is a fraught silence as Audrey presses send on the video invite email, and Ivy sits heavily back down beside Paula.

'There's no way, right?' she says almost in a whisper. 'You identified the body, didn't you? You saw him?'

Paula looks at her, trying to ground herself in Ivy's sweet, young face. She feels so far away, so frightened. Then she shakes her head. 'Well, no, they never asked me to . . . He died so far away. In Austria. On a work trip. They said it had all been sorted out over there. They never asked me . . . He was with a work colleague. They said his body had been identified. It was too . . .' She's stuttering. She takes a deep breath, trying to level her thinking. 'They had him cremated over there. They said it was simpler. It was a man with a nice voice . . . They sent over paperwork. There was a lot of paperwork! It was real . . . It couldn't be . . . I can't . . . I don't understand how . . . I had . . . paperwork.'

Teddy shakes her head slowly. 'Was there a death certificate?'

'Yes!' Paula says, then swallows. 'Or . . . I don't know . . . I think so. There were a lot of documents.' She shakes her head, trying to remember. 'I couldn't understand a lot of it. I know Tilly was chasing things, but . . . I don't know.' She finishes lamely, 'I thought there was.'

'Leave her be,' Ivy murmurs at Teddy and there is steel in her tone. 'This can't be real. Stop putting mad ideas in her head. Of course this email isn't from John, that would be . . . insane! This isn't . . . It can't . . . There's just no way . . .'

'Holy cow,' Audrey interrupts, breathing hard from behind the computer screen. 'It says someone has requested to join the Zoom meeting.' She looks up, blinking hard at Paula. 'Do we accept?'

32

'Hello, Paula, love.'

John says this with such joviality, so seemingly oblivious. He leans into the camera, those familiar nose hairs magnified by his close proximity. 'You look very tanned. Off somewhere enjoying my money, are you?'

Paula stares at him with abject horror.

How is this possible? She says this over and over, but only in her head. Although it more than warrants saying out loud.

John is alive. He's right there in front of her on the screen, looking the same as ever. He's really alive. He's alive, right here, right now.

But not just right now. He was alive all this time. He was alive.

He grins, continuing, 'I'm glad to see the house is still here,' he looks about him, and Paula notices for the first time that he is sitting in their kitchen. At their kitchen table in their home. He's in Surrey this very second, back in the place where they spent thirty-three years. 'I was half expecting you to have knocked it down and built some fancy-pants mansion in its place!' He laughs, then frowns. 'You could've at least got the new ceiling stain sorted.' He sighs. 'I thought you might've sold up.' Still, Paula says nothing as he carries on, 'But that was never really *you*, was it, Paula? Not one for the flashy things, are you? Lucky for me, or there might not be any of that twenty-one million left, eh?'

She still doesn't answer and this time he sighs with frustration.

'Come on, love, aren't you pleased to see me?' She can't bring herself to react. He squints at the screen again, trying to see past her, but the blank white of the boat's stern behind her fills the entire screen. 'Where *are* you, anyway? Are you on holiday? Hopefully not gone to Turkey to find yourself a toy boy!' He laughs at this, and she feels the coldness in her chest again. It fills her lungs, travelling up her throat and out of her mouth at last.

'What did you do? How did you . . .? What . . .' – she gulps – 'happened?' Paula wants all of this to sound furious, but it comes out softly, almost grateful.

He makes a face like a naughty schoolboy who knows he's been caught out. 'OK, yes, I'm sure it's pretty obvious at this point. I faked my own death. Guilty!' He holds his hands up, then laughs. 'No canoes were involved at least.' He waits for Paula to say something but she can't. She physically can't. 'I've been over in Austria, waiting for things to calm down. I was steering clear of anything I thought might be traceable for a while – y'know, phones, computers – but I was watching the news of course. Wanted to see whether my death had been reported and whether anyone was suspicious.' He puffs out his cheeks. 'And holy cow, I got the shock of my life when I saw we'd won the bloody Lotto jackpot! I couldn't resist a quick look at my emails then, and you'd confirmed it all. Phew!' He shakes his head in disbelief. 'Obviously, that changed everything. I knew I had to come back to life. It took a bit of time, but ta-dah! You can understand that, surely.'

'They called me though.' Paula is shaking her head. She still can't accept what's happening. 'The authorities over there, the man with the nice voice, he said—'

'Oh yeah,' John nods, 'that was my mate, Danny. Good lad he is. He was great on the phone, wasn't he? He's always been good at accents. I bunged him a few quid.'

'But the papers they sent over, the documents . . .'

He shrugs. 'They were easy enough to fake. AI can help you do anything these days. Even fake your own death!' He smiles and the sight turns Paula's stomach. 'Then all I had to do was post over a box of ashes.' He chortles. 'Don't worry, it was just a bit of burnt wood. No actual dead bodies were harmed in the making of my dead body.' He laughs heartily.

The questions come properly at last. Smaller ones first. 'Where have you been, John? What have you been doing?' Then the bigger ones. 'How could you do this? Why did you do this? *Why?*'

He sighs. 'Oh Paula, do we have to go over all of that right away? I'm alive! It's a miracle! I'm back from the dead, and we've got a new chance at everything. A new life ahead of us. We have money! Millions! This is our chance to start anew, Paula. We can start again and forget everything that's gone on before all this mess.' He smiles that familiar *John* smile. 'Come on home, love, and we'll start planning how we're going to spend the money!'

She shifts in her seat, suddenly aware of eyes on her. Not John's, but TLWWC's eyes. She doesn't have to look up to know Ivy, Teddy and Audrey are all listening and watching, just a few feet away. They are waiting for her to react to all this. Waiting for her answer.

The Old Paula would've accepted John's response. She'd have waited to deal with it properly in private at home – and then never dealt with it properly. The Old Paula would've let him brush it under the carpet, nodded and shut up. But this newer Paula's been through too much in the last few months. She can hear the voices of her friends in her head. Teddy's voice telling her not to take 'shut up' for an answer. Audrey's voice telling her she is worth more than being dismissed like this. Ivy's soft, sweet voice telling Paula she deserves the truth.

'No,' she says at last. It's just her own voice now, but it's unfamiliar. Quiet and steely. 'No, John, I need to know. You need to explain it. How long had you been planning this for?'

He laughs. 'Quite a long time, to be honest! I can't believe you didn't notice! But you never did notice very much, did you, love?' Paula burns with humiliation.

Were there signs? Did she really not see anything? It occurs to her that if he'd planned this – in detail – that means he'd planned to leave her penniless and in debt. He knew the loan sharks would be coming for her once he was gone. He could've taken out a life insurance policy or something, but he didn't. He had no idea they'd win the lottery. And he didn't care.

John sighs impatiently. 'For God's sake, Paula, let it go! You know very well you and me . . . we weren't working. We weren't happy. We hadn't been for a long time. And Bridget was making a big stink about coming clean about it all, and I know you would've made a fuss about the whole thing.'

'Bridget?' His secretary? The one wailing for hours on end at the funeral?

His next sigh is even more put upon. 'Yes, yes, come on, Paula, let's not play games. I know she must've told you about us after I . . . well, died. Sort of.' He's not looking at Paula as he continues, examining his watch instead. 'Me and Bridget, we'd been having . . . you know, *a thing*. A *nothing*, really. Very casual. It barely went on for a few months. It meant nothing. But Bridget wouldn't let it go. She was obsessed and desperate! Crazy psycho. Kept saying we had to come clean to you and her husband. But I know you would've overreacted, and I bet you would've told the kids. I couldn't face any of it – you, Tilly, Seb. Never mind Bridget's husband! Brick of a man he is! Never out of the bloody gym. And . . .' – he huffs a deep breath – 'well, there was also a bit of snooker debt I hadn't exactly dealt with.' He doesn't pause to dwell on this. As if she wouldn't know about the debt by now. As if those awful men wouldn't have come for their money even after he'd gone. John continues blithely. 'It seemed easier to have a clean break.' He chortles. 'That wasn't a snooker pun by the way!' He waves his hands. 'It was easier to just . . . you know, disappear. I had this international bank account I'd kept quiet, so I just thought we could all start again. Fresh start for you, fresh start for me. Everyone's happy.' He pauses. 'But now we can have a fresh start together! With twenty million!'

Paula blinks hard, trying to take all of this in. John was cheating on her. John was sleeping with that poor woman. No wonder Bridget was so upset that day at the funeral. She wasn't trying to steal her grief thunder after all. There were no grief tentacles. John lied and cheated and *faked his own death*. And now he just wants to return to the family home like nothing's happened, to start all over.

She still hasn't said anything, so John gets going again. 'You know, you should be thrilled I'm back. There are some hilarious rumours about you online! Have you seen them? Everyone thinks you've offed me!' He laughs like this is brilliant. 'At least me returning to the land of the living will shut them up.' He wrinkles his nose, looking mischievous. 'I have to admit, I had a bit of fun on social media, winding those armchair detectives up. I told them I knew you and hinted that it was all true! Isn't that funny?' Paula doesn't answer, so he adds, 'C'mon, Paula love, I did *want* to tell you I was alive! I tried dropping a couple of hints. I sent you a few text messages asking for money.' He catches her horrified expression. 'You don't have to look so grumpy about it, Paula; it was meant to be funny! And I changed our regular lottery numbers so you'd know I was still around. I thought that was a dead giveaway.' He chortles again. 'Another great pun. I should save all these for my memoir, *All Cued Up*.' He shrugs again. 'To be honest, it was mostly a bit boring being dead, I had to entertain myself somehow! But I'm back now and we have the world at our feet. It'll be great. We'll tell everyone the death thing was just a mistake. You got sent someone else's documents, or I had amnesia. Something like that. No one's going to look too closely. It's not like I had life insurance or anything like that. And we can get my little bit of debt paid off. Bob's your uncle. New life for us.'

He smiles, waiting for her to answer, but she can't. She can't process any of this. Instead, she reaches for the laptop lid, slowly bringing it down and closing it. The video disconnects and she breathes out, realising she's been holding her breath. He's gone. John is gone. Again.

Except he's not gone.

There is silence and at last Paula looks up.

Teddy, Audrey and Ivy have all been sitting across from her, listening and watching. They all look as shell-shocked as Paula feels.

Teddy clears her throat, staring at Paula penetratingly. 'Oh my God,' she says at last. 'Oh my God. So you really, actually, totally *didn't* murder your husband. Oh my God!'

'No,' says Paula, shaking her head. 'But I should've done.'

33

They don't really talk properly until they've docked. From the boat – *yacht* – they walk slowly to a quiet nearby café. They hold hands in a row, upsetting passers-by who want to use the pavement.

'That was a lot,' Teddy comments quietly, after they've bought expensive hot drinks and taken a seat in the corner.

'I can't get my head around it.' Paula is barely audible, her mind racing. 'He's *alive*.' She takes a deep, shuddery breath.

'I'm sorry we didn't believe you,' Ivy murmurs. 'About murdering him, I mean.'

Paula shrugs and the small gesture takes a lot of effort. 'I didn't kill him, but I did want to.' She scrunches up her face. 'At least, I did in hindsight. I didn't realise it at the time. I was so deep inside it all, inside the life I knew, that I didn't realise how unhappy I was. How trapped. And the truth is, it really has been awful since he died.' She corrects herself. 'Since he pretended to die. I was struggling so much. I didn't even know what to wear when I woke up in the morning because he chose everything.' She pauses. 'But it's also been wonderful. The freedom was a bit terrifying and overwhelming and difficult, but also so . . . nice. Especially after I met all of you. You made me realise I can have a life of my own. I can make choices for myself. I get . . .' She trails off, staring down at her shaking hands before continuing, 'I get to decide on my own happiness. I don't have to walk around on eggshells for ever. I don't have to spend the rest of my life always wondering what kind of mood John might be in. I don't have to tie myself in knots trying to say the right thing to fix things. I don't have to live in fear that the man in the coffee shop looked my way, or that Vinnie, Floyd and Handsy Harry at the care home talked to me too much that day.' She shakes her head. 'John was so possessive, and the silly thing was that he was the one having an affair!' Paula glances wide-eyed around at her friends. 'I feel like such a foolish old lady. I didn't know he was sleeping with her.' She pauses. 'Poor Bridget, I hope he was kind to her.'

'I doubt it,' Teddy says in a low, sour voice.

Paula stares out of the café window. People wander past, arm in arm, laughing. Look at all these people on their magical holiday without a worry in the universe. None of them seems to understand that the world has just ended.

A group of young women pile into the café, taking the noise level up a notch as they laugh and order cake in lovely French.

Paula turns back to the three women. 'You know, when I won the lottery, the first thing I thought was how different life was going to be. I tried to ring John over and over that day, to tell him the news. I told myself he would be so happy – so much happier – and that he would like me more. I thought the money would solve everything.' She shakes her head. 'But I know so clearly now – it's so obvious! – that things wouldn't have been – wouldn't *be* different. If anything, they would be worse, because with all that money he could control me even more. He would stop me working or going out, and I'd be even more trapped.' She swallows. 'After I won the lottery money, everyone kept asking me why I hadn't quit my job. My boss laughed at me when I asked for some time off, like it was totally absurd that I might come back. But for a long time, that job – my work – was the only little bit of freedom I had from John. We needed the money, and so I *had to* go to work. But he won't let me out at all now we have twenty million pounds. I'll be even more of a silly little submissive mouse, even more afraid of my own shadow than I am now.'

'You're not a mouse.' Audrey moves her chair closer, circling an arm around Paula. Paula feels the warmth of her friend's skin through her loose T-shirt. Even after all these weeks of open affection from Audrey, Paula still finds it a shock. John so rarely touched her. 'You are a strong, brave, kind woman, who got through years of this.' Audrey waves her free hand with enthusiasm. 'Look at you! So many people wouldn't have made it through what you've been through. You're amazing! And we love you.'

Teddy and Ivy nod at this.

The French women at the counter start shrieking with excitement as their cakes are plated up. They move towards a table at the back, leaving one of the group behind, still waiting on a drink. The woman stares down at her phone, her face going slack without her friends around. Paula wonders if it means something. That we need other people at our side – we need friends – to keep us alive and moving.

'Can I ask you all a question?' she begins hesitantly. 'How did you know ... How did you know I was ... like you? That I was ... the same as you? That my husband was like your husbands?'

They look at her, three sets of kindly eyes watching carefully, considering this.

'You think we can't see it?' Audrey replies at last. 'You think we can't see the pain? It's clear as day.'

'It is?' she says helplessly.

They nod. 'To us,' Ivy whispers. 'We know it because it's the same as ours.'

'Plus,' Teddy says, 'there are other more obvious . . . signs. For one thing, you don't have any friends! None of us did before Audrey brought us all together. It's something a lot of abuse survivors – or victims – have in common. We were all isolated from loved ones. A lot of abusers do that.' She pauses. 'You didn't notice the way we've all clung to each other desperately, even though we've only known one another a few months?'

'I guess I was so far removed from reality, I missed it. I'd forgotten what friendship looks like,' Paula shrugs. 'Plus, John had me thinking I was so unlovable and unlikeable, it never occurred to me anyone would want to be my friend.' She thinks of all those old faces on Facebook she hadn't spoken to for years. She thinks of her family, of her mum.

She stares up at the cake board above the counter, trying to work out which of the options would contain the most chocolate. She needs chocolate right now. She doesn't speak French but she has a feeling gâteau au chocolat would do the job.

Paula leans her head on Teddy's shoulder. 'Can we hold off killing that man Owen for a while?' she whispers at last. 'Because there's someone else I want to add to Ivy's list.' She draws her eyebrows together, determination lighting her face. 'I really do think John deserves to be a priority. He deserves to die.'

Ivy looks anxiously to Teddy, then back again. 'Are you sure you want to do that? I mean, you're not actually a killer, Paula. Are you sure this is something you want to do?'

Paula looks at her. There's something else she wants to tell Ivy. Something she wants to tell them all. Something very small but very important. She's thought about saying it so many times since John died. She opens her mouth, then closes it, her heart beating fast. Ivy reaches for her hand, squeezing it. Paula feels her friend's body warmth and it makes her feel strong.

She's going to say it.

Paula leans forward. 'Can you call me Pauline, not Paula? It's my name, what my mum and dad called me, but John didn't like it. He said he preferred Paula, so that was that. I had to go by what he wanted all those years.'

They stare at her for a beat, then Teddy shakes her head in disgust. 'OK, yeah, John definitely deserves to die.'

'So you'll help me?' Pauline asks, and they all nod with enthusiasm.

And now, Pauline – formerly Paula – allows herself to cry. She hunches over in that café and cries and cries and cries. The group of women with the cakes look over anxiously, but still she doesn't stop. She lets the tears run down her face. And they're still not for John. They're all for her. The tears are for Pauline the brave, the survivor, the victim. For Pauline, the woman she's going to be from here on out. For Pauline the soon-to-be husband killer.

Ivy holds her as Audrey fetches some gâteau au chocolat. Pauline continues to cry, imagining John's blood dribbling out onto the carpet at home.

They need a new carpet anyway.

34

Pauline hates to sound ungrateful, but private jets really aren't all they're cracked up to be.

She was underwhelmed by the last one and this one is even more... well, it's just quite... how does she put this? *Uninspired.* She's surrounded by cramped, beige interiors and rows of grey seats. And that's it! Of course, there are a lot fewer seats than you'd find on an EasyJet plane, and an awful lot more legroom. But Pauline's only five foot two; she's never wanted for legroom in her life.

At least the last jet had Connie and sofas.

Gosh, has Pauline already become spoilt? How exciting.

Perhaps, she decides, they save the really exotic, *glamorous* jets for the Hollywood stars. Perhaps Sigourney Weaver is flying about on the truly lavish ones; the ones that have jacuzzis and snooker tables.

Not that she'd want to play snooker anyway. John and snooker... yeugh. He played it every Wednesday and Thursday evening with his friends.

Before he faked his own death, that is.

Will he resume his snooker playing now, she wonders, like

none of it ever happened? Will he resume his life? Their lives? She can't let that happen.

'I still can't believe John's really alive,' Pauline says out loud for quite possibly the hundredth time since yesterday's Zoom meeting with him.

In a seat across the aisle, Ivy shoots her a look of genuine sympathy. Behind them, Audrey shouts, 'Not for long.'

'How am I going to tell Tilly and Seb?' Pauline says, shaking her head.

'You won't have to, darling,' Audrey points out. 'If we can get to him before he tells anyone else, no one ever has to know he survived the Austrian Alps.'

Teddy nods. 'It's actually the perfect crime. As far as the world knows, he's already dead. We just need to get rid of the body.'

'What if he's already told them?' Pauline asks anxiously. 'Seb's only out in the shed in the garden. He may well have already come in and seen his dad. He would be so shocked! I want it to come from me, if he has to find out.'

'How often does Seb come in the house?' Teddy leans forward.

Pauline is struck by something her son said just before she left. 'Oh wait! He's on a course! He's away for a week.'

'A course?' Audrey cocks her head. 'How exciting! For work?'

Pauline has no idea. All she remembers is saying the word *course* a lot. 'Yes, for work,' she confirms, hoping this might even be true.

Ivy smiles softly to herself. 'Good for Seb.' Then she nods. 'Plus, John's said he's hiding out, staying under the radar until you're back, right?'

John has been bombarding Pauline – or Paula as he's still calling her, of course – with messages since his return to the family home. He has demanded she return immediately so they can 'begin their new lives together'. He has also promised they'll tell the children together – and the world – about what he's calling 'the wonderful miracle'.

Pauline shifts around uncomfortably in her seat, trying to find an angle that doesn't make her behind quite so sweaty. She is unsuccessful.

She checks her watch, feeling a little queasy. She took some travel sickness pills after they took off, but they don't seem to be working. It's odd that she was perfectly fine on a boat all week, and yet being on this journey home has made her feel so poorly.

Maybe it's less to do with the flying, and more to do with what she's flying home to.

From the back, Teddy crows happily, 'Pauline, babe? We're all sorted.'

She cranes around to look at her friend. 'What's sorted?'

Teddy smiles, throwing her phone into a huge, brown leather bag that no doubt cost five figures. 'Those pesky loan sharks. I had a quick chat with your man Craig before we boarded. My finance guy has just messaged to confirm he's paid them off. They won't bother you again. They send their thanks and best wishes.'

Pauline gapes at her. All these weeks of fear, all this time wondering what she was going to do and how she was going to cope. And Teddy's solved the whole thing in a few hours.

She smiles a watery smile. 'Thank you,' she whispers, and Teddy winks.

She sinks back into her uncomfortable seat, the weight of weeks of fear and worry finally lifting.

Is it always so freeing to just ... say your problems out loud? Granted, not many people have a pal with eight hundred million pounds in the bank, but even without Teddy's surreal bank balance, admitting the issue – getting it off her chest – had already made Pauline feel a thousand times better. Who knew having best friends was so important?

She checks her watch again.

Not much longer until they land, and then straight back to Surrey to see John. Not *see* actually – back to Surrey to *off* John.

Pauline giggles childishly to herself at the thought. She's never said *off* before. Well actually, she *has* said off, of course she has. Just not in reference to murdering someone.

Something has happened to Pauline overnight. She feels so different and she can't quite pinpoint why. She really should be miserable and in the absolute doldrums about all this. Her awful husband is back from the dead and wants all their money, just as she's starting to enjoy spending it. Her children aren't speaking to her and thinks she's a terrible person. And everyone on the internet thinks she's a murderer. Never mind the police on her friend's tail. Oh, and she might be about to throw up into a paper bag if they don't land soon.

But she's *not* miserable. She's happy. Happier than she's been in ages – years! Perhaps even decades. Five days in the South of France with TLWWC has transformed her into a whole new woman. No longer is she meek little Paula, terrified by everything and everyone around her. Now she's Pauline. Pauline with a brand-new Porsche, a new group of friends and a whole new set of underwear courtesy of a helpful French concierge.

Oh! And she's got a *tan*! She hasn't had a tan since she was a teenager!

Pauline is fearless. Pauline is a winner. Pauline is a member of a murder club who kill misbehaving husbands. And Pauline's husband is about to get what's coming to him.

Paula the Dog barks from her seat beside Audrey.

Pauline reaches over and strokes the pup, always careful to avoid the sensitive nipples. She can have that old name. She's welcome to it.

For the first time in three decades, Pauline feels like she's taking control of her life. So many choices have been made for her over the years, foisted upon her. Now she's making some for herself and it feels . . . good. Really good.

Up at the front of the plane, the disinterested steward twitches the curtain. Their previous stewardess, Connie, had to fly to Canada for a VIP client, according to Audrey, so she wasn't available for their plane ride home today. It's a shame. Pauline liked how much she smiled. She's going to do more smiling herself from now on. Be more Connie, Pauline tells herself. She considers making it her new motto, but then remembers she's already changed her name once this week. People might get confused.

The new steward peers out at the group disapprovingly, daring them to ask for something. The young man seemed *very* displeased by their arrival on board earlier. There was a great deal of sighing and tutting over the fact that they weren't dazzling celebrities in designer gear. Pauline's fairly sure Sigourney Weaver wouldn't get this kind of tutty treatment.

To be fair, Teddy *is* in designer gear, but you wouldn't necessarily think it to look at her. Her clothes mostly look like very thin pieces of pink material stretched around body parts. Very expensive pieces of pink material. Of course, Pauline likes the clothes a lot. But just on Teddy. They wouldn't work on her.

Audrey takes out her earphones. 'Have we made a decision about the . . . plan?' She eyeballs the steward. He's still fifteen feet away, still on his phone, still beyond disinterested. Despite this, Audrey leans closer to the group, whispering, 'We need a code for talking about this. How about we say . . .' – she pauses, then her eyes widen – '. . . *cook* instead of kill?'

Ivy smiles. 'Good idea!' She turns to Pauline. 'So then, what, er, *meal* are we cooking for John tonight?'

'I get what you're doing there,' Audrey says, 'but that doesn't actually make sense. You just asked what meal we're killing for John tonight.'

Teddy shuffles closer in her seat. 'I think it's fine to take some liberties with the code, Audrey. The code is not set in stone. You only just made the code up, babe.'

'Well, assuming no one knows he's back from the dead yet,' Pauline muses, 'the actual, er, *meal* we cook doesn't really matter so much, right? It's all about getting rid of the . . . leftovers.'

'Quite,' Teddy nods, looking faintly amused. 'So what are our options? Do you have any woods near your house, Pauline? Maybe we could get John to . . .' She glances over at the steward. Not a flicker of interest. 'Maybe if John was willing to come to the woods, we could have a . . . *picnic*, and then bury the . . . er, leftovers.'

'Are there bears in the woods?' Pauline asks, suddenly feeling less brave.

'No, but there's a lot of pope shit!' Audrey cackles confusingly.

Teddy shakes her head at Pauline. 'No bears. Or pope shit. There's nothing to worry about like that. Although bears would be handy to get rid of evid— leftover picnic food.'

Audrey looks inspired. 'Ooh, if we're going to the woods maybe we could pick up some mushrooms. You know' – she narrows her eyes – 'the Agatha Christie kind of mushrooms. For his din-dins?'

'John doesn't like mushrooms,' Pauline explains. 'He says they're too slimy.'

Teddy sniffs. 'Audrey, we're only going to the woods to dispose of . . . leftovers. We don't want to go to the woods to get Agatha Christie mushrooms and then return to the woods later with John's bod—' She sighs. '*Leftovers*. That would be far too much of a palaver.'

Pauline shakes her head, feeling confused. The code is starting to take on a life of its own. 'Well, I don't think the woods are any use anyway. They're too far away. I'd suggest the back garden, but Seb is always in his shed.'

Audrey looks disappointed. 'Oh, what a shame. I was hoping I could get some soil while we're out there. My local Dobbies has shut down and I need to re-pot some plants. My passion flower's roots are getting wildly out of hand. They keep threatening to strangle Paula the Dog.' Paula the Dog yips fearfully.

'I've got an idea!' Teddy says brightly. 'What if we parcel him up in bubble wrap, secure him carefully in a crate and have him sent special delivery to New York? We can then fly out and bury him beside my dead husband!'

'You weren't using the code there at all,' Ivy points out nicely.

'Not at *all*,' Audrey adds for emphasis, shaking her head.

'Oh, he's not listening.' Teddy waves her hand at the steward. She's correct; he is not.

'He's not very friendly, is he?' Pauline says. 'The steward, I mean.'

'If we crash into a snow-covered mountain, we'll eat him first,' Audrey pronounces.

'We're not passing any mountains, are we?' Pauline asks anxiously.

'Not unless you count the plastic mountain at the mini golf range in south London,' Teddy says dryly.

'Sounds dangerous,' Audrey murmurs with excitement.

'Anyway,' Pauline tries to get them back on track. 'I say we just stick to what we know. What's actually worked for us so far? Definitely not baseball bats.' She looks at each of them in turn, listing out each successful murder. 'Tripped down the stairs, overdosed on heart medication, and—' She pauses, looking at Teddy quizzically. 'What did you do again?'

Teddy fills in the blank. 'I shoved my husband. He hit his head on the corner of the coffee table as he went down.'

'Excuse me?' Audrey peers at her. 'You told me you caved in his temple.'

'I did cave it in!' Teddy exclaims. 'Via the coffee table.'

'That's barely manslaughter, for goodness' sake,' Audrey tuts.

Teddy raises an eyebrow. 'He took ages to die. I could've called for help, but I didn't. And then I buried him. It's definitely at least unlawful disposal of a dead body. But I'm pretty sure they'd get me for murder, too.'

'OK, darling.' Audrey holds up her hands. 'This is not a sociopath competition.'

Teddy mutters, 'You would win if it was,' and Audrey nods agreeably. She would.

'Does John have any health issues or a drink problem we know about?' Ivy asks. 'They were both helpful in our ... situations.'

Pauline considers this. 'He takes a lot of vitamins, does that count? Can you overdose on vitamins?'

'I don't think so, babe.' Teddy shakes her head. 'They mostly just come out when you wee. I'm not sure they do much at all, good or bad.'

Pauline sighs. 'In that case, I'm going to have to push him down the stairs, aren't I?' She pauses. 'At least we know for sure I have stairs in my house. And I will have surprise on my side. There's no chance in hell he'd ever see it coming. I've barely said boo to a goose in thirty years.'

'Why would anyone say that to a goose?' animal lover Ivy murmurs, but they ignore her, regarding each other seriously and giving a collective nod.

'It's a plan, Paula.' Teddy's face falls. 'Sorry, *Pauline*.'

Pauline smiles. 'There's no need for an apology, I understand. It's going to take some getting used to.'

'But it's important,' Teddy says fiercely. 'And I want to get it right. John chose your identity for you for so long. *You* get to choose who you are in this life. This is your choice and I want to get it right.' She pauses. 'Maybe I should stop being Teddy and go back to Tina? Screw the patriarchy!'

Audrey groans. 'Oh darling, please don't. It's too confusing for me. I'm eighty-one. There are too many name changes going on as it is.' She reaches for her dog's chin, giving it a big scratch. 'I'm probably going to have to come up with a new name for Paula the Dog now anyway. It's rather soured now I know John was a fan.'

Teddy shrugs. 'Fair enough. To be honest I never much liked the name Tina anyway. Teddy is much cooler.'

Ivy looks alarmed. 'Tina Turner's the coolest woman to ever live.'

'I'd say that's a fair assessment.' Teddy nods. 'And I'm not very cool, so I better stick with Teddy.'

'Thank goodness!' Audrey calls out.

Over the tannoy, pilot Stan informs everyone there is just a few minutes until they land. He tells them the local time in the UK is eight thirty p.m., and describes the weather as 'British'. He laughs for a while then and Pauline wonders if they should perhaps add him to Ivy's kill list.

Pauline really is a changed woman.

'Let's have one last drink before we land,' Audrey calls out to the group, waving to the angry steward. Pauline adds her cheer to the chorus of excitable replies and feels Ivy reach over to give her shoulder a reassuring squeeze.

It's strange to think Pauline's only known these women for a relatively short amount of time. It feels like she knows each of them intimately. But, she supposes, that's what happens when you're around this much death and money.

Pauline squeezes her arm rest, thinking about the hours ahead.

She can't wait.

35

For *this* murder, The Lottery Winner Widows Club have tried to learn from their previous mistakes.

Gone are the slippery estate agent booties. Long gone are the awkward gloves no one could open any doors with. And it's broad daylight as the four women approach Pauline's house. They've come straight from the airport, which – as Audrey pointed out – means they have their luggage in the car, ready for a speedy getaway should everything go disastrously wrong. They've taken almost no precautions this time, but there's also a lot less reason to *be* cautious. After all, why wouldn't Pauline and her friends be at her house? There's no reason their finger and shoe prints wouldn't be all over the place.

Pauline pauses on the porch outside the house for a moment, her hands shaking as she regards the familiar front door. The paint at the bottom is chipped and peeling, the wood starting to splinter. Last year she asked John about buying some paint and filler to fix it herself, and he laughed at her. The idea of her being anything but useless was hilarious to him.

'Are you all right?' Ivy asks softly. 'Sure you want to do this? We could wait a bit, have a big think about it all, if you want?'

'She can't wait,' Audrey says quickly. 'It has to be done before anyone else finds out he's back.'

'I'm fine,' Pauline answers. 'I'm scared, but he deserves it, he really does. Let's do this.' She roots around in her handbag for a key that has languished down there for what feels like an eternity. It's hard to believe she's been away for less than a week.

'Hello?' Pauline calls out nervously as they enter. There is silence in the house and she turns to the others, unsure what to do next.

'Do you think he's gone out?' Ivy asks, mirroring Pauline's anxious tone.

'Maybe,' she whispers back. 'Or maybe he just didn't hear me. He's a bit deaf in his right ear.'

'That might be quite useful,' Teddy nods. 'He won't hear us coming.'

'Should we split up to look for him?' Pauline asks and Audrey shakes her head.

'Splitting up is *never* the right thing to do, my darling. You don't watch any horror films, do you? We'll stick together and make our way round the house. We're not leaving you or anyone.'

Ivy takes Pauline's hand. 'We'll *always* stick together.' She nods at the stairs in front of them. 'Let's look up there first.'

They creep up the steps, Pauline silently thanking the previous owners who so thoughtfully installed the thickest carpet known to man. Sure, it might be bright orange and forty years old, but it turns out it's also ideal for creeping up on unsuspecting husbands who were supposed to be dead.

Teddy takes the lead and they walk, single file across the landing. Pauline's bedroom door is closed and she searches her memory, trying to recall if she'd shut it before she left. It all feels like a million years ago, so much has happened since she last slept here.

They stop in a huddle outside the door, each of them attempting sign language about their next move. Eventually, Teddy rolls her eyes and turns decisively for the door. Pauline gasps lightly as she moves the door knob, opening the door in slow motion. She places her face at the crack, then backs off, closing the door silently.

'He's in there,' she mouths. 'He's fast asleep.' She pauses. 'What do we do?'

'We can't really push him down the stairs like this,' Ivy says in a low whisper as Audrey nods.

'We can smother him though,' Pauline says with determination. She disappears into a room down the hall, returning a minute later with a large blue throw pillow, featuring a smiling giraffe. They got it at a Blue Diamond.

'Is this a good idea?' Teddy says nervously, and if Pauline didn't know better, she'd say there was trepidation in her voice.

'No,' she shakes her head. 'But I'm doing it anyway.' She lets herself quietly into the familiar bedroom. It smells like John in there and for a second her head spins. It's been so long since she smelled that smell. It almost knocks her off her feet.

John is lying under the covers of her bed, breathing heavily with his mouth open. He always slept like the dead. Ironically.

Looking at him lying there, in the spot that has become her personal space – hers and hers alone – Pauline feels only revulsion. How did she ever believe he loved her? Or that she loved him? The way he loved her wasn't love. She realises now that this man is not capable of real love. He is a cruel, horrible person who only cares about himself.

She thinks of all those times he said she was ugly, that no one would ever love her but him. She thinks of the time she saved up her bus money by walking to work for months, so she could buy new pyjamas. And how he'd marched her back to the shop to return them because they were 'too fancy for the likes of her'. She thinks of how he would buy food she didn't like, then claim he had no idea salmon made her ill. She thinks of how he always gave her a Malibu and Coke at family gatherings, knowing full well she thought it tasted like fabric softener.

She stands over him now, holding the pillow. She wants to do it; she has to do it; she needs to do it. She raises it up over his head, staring down at his cruel face. Even sleeping, he is smirking. She *needs* to do this. This will solve everything. She can't let him back into her life. He will ruin it all. He is poison; he is a disease; he is a vampire.

She thinks of their life together and all the casual, daily cruelty. He deserves this. She raises the pillow higher.

Then she thinks of Tilly and Seb. She thinks of those happy memories Tilly shared in family grief counselling with Gerald.

She wants to do it.

But she can't do it.

She brings the pillow back down. It sags at her side.

She looks up after a moment. Audrey, Teddy and Ivy have all entered the room and are watching her nervously in the dim light.

'I can't,' she whispers. 'I hate him, but I can't. I'm just not capable. I keep picturing Tilly and Seb's faces.'

Ivy nods solemnly. 'I don't think we're cut out for murder, you guys.'

Beneath them on the bed, John stirs, and they glance at each other with panic.

'Run!' Audrey squeals, and they do as instructed, thundering down the stairs and towards the front door, the panic turning to squeals of hilarity.

They don't stop running when they get outside, heading at full pelt down the road towards Pauline's car, giggling as they go. The fear has turned to hysterical relief and they all pile into Pauline's car, breathing heavily.

'Why do so many of our plans end up with us running for our lives?' Pauline asks, panting hard.

'I *did* once suggest we could cycle away from our crime scenes...' Audrey points out and they all nod their acknowledgement.

There they all sit for a minute, the adrenaline slowly draining away. From this distance, they watch the peeling front door, waiting for John to appear. Surely he must've been woken up by their maniacal exit?

Nothing happens. The door stays shut. Eventually Teddy pipes up from the back seat. 'Pauline, you can stay at mine until we figure out what to do.'

'Are you sure?' Pauline is ridiculously grateful, though that enormous, pink penthouse apartment intimidates her a little.

'Of course I'm sure,' Teddy replies.

'I'd offer,' Audrey titters from the passenger seat beside her, 'but the Scottish castle is a bit of a trek.'

Pauline grimaces. 'I may have to take you up on that if all of this goes to hell. I might need to get as far away from all this as possible.'

They continue to watch the front of the house for a few more minutes. There is still no sign of John.

From the back seat, Ivy suddenly sighs. 'I know some of us are literally already murderers, but I don't think we've got it in us to be serial killers.'

'I don't either,' says Pauline as Teddy shakes her head sadly.

'I really thought this was the best way to help people,' she murmurs, staring out of the window. 'I thought I was strong enough to do it.'

'I don't think it makes us weak that we can't,' Audrey replies after a moment. 'I don't think we're bad people because we can't bring ourselves to kill anyone.'

'It *is* disappointing though,' Teddy says. 'I really did want to *want* to do it.'

'And offing John would've been such a handy solution to this whole mess,' says Pauline. They fall silent and eventually she reaches for the ignition. 'We can't sit here for ever. We better go.'

They fiddle about with seatbelts, and Audrey reaches down into the footwell to place her handbag. Immediately she knocks it over, spilling the contents everywhere and laughing at her own clumsiness. Pauline reaches across to help her retrieve things, picking up Audrey's passport first.

The passport.

She remembers that moment at the airport on their way to Saint-Tropez – that glimpse she got of her friend's photo page. There was something . . .

The name. Was that right? She can't be sure. But five days later, Pauline's head feels clearer, and something occurs to her. Something clicks. Something that has been niggling and wriggling at the back of her brain all week.

She opens up the passport and stares at it. She didn't imagine it. She wasn't wrong. There it is. The name.

She stares at it for a second or two longer, trying to convince herself she's wrong. Perhaps – after everything they've been through – Pauline's mind has finally snapped. Maybe she's seeing things. Because if this means what she thinks it means . . .

No, it can't be right. Except there it is, laminated right there on the most legal of legal documents.

At last, Pauline looks up from the page, everything she thought she knew shifting. Audrey is staring at her, and Pauline stares right back.

Teddy strains against her seatbelt in the back. 'What's the hold up, babes?'

Pauline doesn't reply. Instead she holds Audrey's eye contact. The moment stretches on, until at last Pauline clears her throat and speaks.

'I know who you really are.'

36

The car ride to London mostly passes in total silence.

For the first few minutes, Teddy and Ivy try to ask questions – what's going on? What did Pauline mean? What happened with the passport? – but Audrey and Pauline both refuse to speak. They exchange looks but neither of them says another word until they pull up outside Teddy's apartment building.

Audrey stops in the foyer to greet the security concierge by his first name. Pauline watches carefully as this old woman she doesn't really know asks after the man's wife and newborn. She reaches for a hug as they pass. It is very Audrey, thinks Pauline.

Or it would be very Audrey, if Audrey were really Audrey.

Upstairs, they file into Teddy's oversized living room and take a seat, the energy around them edgy and confused. The room feels too big, everyone sitting too far away from each other. Pauline wants to reach out and hold all their hands, but there's too much distance, too much she doesn't understand. Instead, her gaze moves from Ivy to Teddy, landing on the woman she knew before today as Audrey Swift.

But she's not Audrey Swift, is she? There is no Audrey Swift. None who is a part of The Lottery Winner Widows Club, at least.

This eighty-something woman sitting across from her, her back straight and tall, her white hair pinned back – her real name is Audrey Meredith Woodbead.

She watches Audrey carefully now, as the older woman takes a deep breath.

'So,' she begins, then pauses. 'Actually, I'm going to get a cup of coffee. Does anyone else want a drink?'

'Let me,' Teddy says, standing up and crossing the room.

There is more silence as Teddy jabs at her fancy coffee machine, slotting pods and positioning mugs. Audrey stares at the ceiling, fiddling with her fingers, as the machine hisses into life. She's nervous, Pauline suddenly realises. She's never seen Audrey nervous before. But then, she doesn't know this woman at all, does she?

How many times has she openly lied? How many times has Teddy pointed out she's a sociopath?

'Here,' Teddy returns with a tray, handing out steaming mugs that, one by one, they each immediately put to one side with disinterest.

'Audrey?' Pauline nudges after another moment.

'I just need to pop to the loo—' Audrey starts to stand up.

'Audrey!' The sharpness in Pauline's tone stops her.

'OK, my darling, OK!' Audrey says, sitting back down. 'Though you forget I'm over eighty; my bladder isn't what it was.' She takes a deep breath. 'My surname – as you now know – is not Swift. Or, at least, it *was* Swift a long time ago, before I got married. My real surname is Woodbead and has been for fifty-seven years. My real name is Audrey Woodbead.'

'What?' Ivy shakes her head, her face slack and baffled. 'I don't understand, why would you give us a fake name?'

Audrey doesn't reply. She's still looking directly at Pauline. 'And my husband was Harold Woodbead, as you now know.' She dips her head but maintains the eye contact. 'But you probably mostly knew him as Harry.'

Pauline stares back. After a moment, she whispers, 'Handsy Harry.'

Teddy looks between Pauline and Audrey. 'She knew your husband?'

'I did,' Pauline confirms, swallowing. 'I looked after him at the care home, where I work.' She pauses. '*Did* work.' She sighs a big, shaky breath. 'Harry was a resident there for many years. He died at Christmas.' She swallows again. 'I knew he had a wife – we all knew he had a wife – but we only ever heard about Mrs Woodbead from Harry. She never visited. Neither did his two daughters. He didn't talk about them often, not about any of them. He said there had been a falling-out – a family rift.' Pauline shakes her head, remembering something. 'You said this,' she wheels on Audrey. 'You told the truth! That day my children, Tilly and Seb, turned up here and wanted to know who you all were' – she shakes her head again, unable to look at Audrey anymore – 'you told them I'd worked with your husband at the care home and that's how you knew me. I thought at the time it made you a good liar.'

Audrey says nothing.

After a moment, Pauline continues, 'And when Harry died, I was the one who found him and called an ambulance.' She swallows again. 'And the police, since it was unexplained.'

'I did go to the care home once,' Audrey suddenly speaks. She directs her words at Teddy but she's still talking just to

Pauline. 'The day I dropped him off. But I suppose you weren't on shift.'

Ivy shakes her head in pure confusion. 'I don't... So why...' Ivy can't find the right words.

'When he died,' Audrey continues, and now she is looking at Pauline. 'I knew I needed to find you. I only had your name from the report, but *Paula Sheldon* came up with about fifty million results on Google.' She sighs. 'I do miss the days of Yellow Pages, you know, much more convenient.' She pauses, then smiles tightly. 'I had no idea what to do, but then a picture of you appeared in the newspaper. You'd won the lottery and become a widow all in the same week! And it was pretty obvious to me that you'd killed your husband.' She pauses and the strange smile gets wider. 'Or so it seemed at the time.'

'Wait.' Ivy holds up her hands, her face screwed up. 'Why would you need to find Pauline? What am I missing?'

'That's what I'd like to know,' Pauline says coldly. 'Why this elaborate... *scam* to befriend me? Why all the lies? Why pretend to like me and—'

'I wasn't pretending!' Audrey interrupts, looking wounded. 'I adore you, Pauline. I love all of you. You are my friends, my dear, dear friends.'

Teddy leans closer, her expression unreadable. 'But you only started this group – you only brought us together as The Lottery Winner Widows Club – as some kind of... *cover* to find Pauline?'

Audrey looks down at her feet. 'That's how it started.'

'Did you even win the lottery?' Ivy's voice is barely a whisper.

'Of course!' Audrey is indignant. 'But it wasn't *quite* what I said. It wasn't half a million, it was thirty-two pounds.'

'So the Scottish castle . . .?' Teddy's face is darkening.

Audrey brightens. 'That's real! My family really does have money. I've been paying my own way with you all, haven't I? I told you I didn't win as much as the rest of you. I just . . . well, I just . . . exaggerated. I'm still a lottery winner, like you three. Technically.'

Teddy scoffs at this, furious indignation clear on her face. Ivy looks disappointed and confused.

Pauline puts her head in her hands. 'But *why*? Why did you need to find me so badly? What's this all about?'

Audrey sighs. 'Because, my darling' – her breathing is ragged – 'I didn't really kill Harold. I meant what I said before. I hadn't seen him in years, not since I dropped him off. The moment I found out what he'd done to our daughters – the abuse – I dumped him in a care home as far away from Scotland and our family as possible.' She nods at Pauline. 'That meant Surrey, I'm afraid, where you had to look after that disgusting, creepy little man.' She shudders. 'No wonder you called him Handsy Harry, quite apt.' She looks down. 'But stowing him five hundred miles away wasn't enough for my youngest daughter, Nina. She couldn't let it go. We tried therapy and medication, but she couldn't . . . I couldn't help her. None of us could help.' She nods, and it's clear she's trying not to get emotional. 'I didn't know what she was planning until after she'd done it. She knew what medication her father was on. She knew what too much would do to him. I don't know how she got hold of it, but she did. Then she went down to see him at the care home and force-fed him that overdose of Digitalis. She's the one who watched him die. My daughter killed him. She did it.'

There is silence in the room.

'Your daughter?' Teddy's eyes are wide. 'She ... so you didn't ...'

'But,' Pauline is still confused, 'how am I—'

Audrey sighs, looking at her intensely. 'My darling, *you saw her*. You were the only one who knew she was there in his room that day. And you saw her leaving after she'd done it. I needed to find you and work out what you knew. Make sure you weren't going to tell anyone it was my child, my Nina. I had to be sure that no one was asking you questions. That you hadn't told Columbo anything.'

Pauline screws up her face. 'But I didn't! I don't remember seeing anyone ...' She shakes her head, trying to remember that day from so many months ago when Handsy Harry Woodbead died. They'd just lost fellow residents Vinnie and Floyd the same week and she'd been so sad about their deaths. It was a busy day. It was always busy at the care home. There were so many people who needed things, so many hands to hold, so many medications to check. That day – it was a weekend when Harry died – a Sunday. She'd been working all weekend and she was tired. Her feet hurt. She remembered the plimsolls pinching her little toe where her socks had a small hole. She remembered sighing when her boss, Gary, asked her to go and check on Harry.

Nobody on the staff much liked Harry. He was leery and creepy. He always smelled bad, even immediately after a bath. But, as the biggest pushover on staff, Pauline nearly always ended up being the one running around after him. She always ended up being the one groped by him.

There *was* a woman there that day ... a redhead with an accent. Was she Scottish? Pauline couldn't recall. She'd asked what room Harry Woodbead was in. But Pauline doesn't remember seeing her leave, and she certainly didn't think anything more of it. Not even after she found Handsy Harry dead.

Pauline worked at that care home for twenty-five years. She was used to finding dead bodies. No, not *used to*, because you never really get used to something like that. But she had seen enough of them not to scream or run about the hallways making a fuss, like some of the newer staff members sometimes did.

He was in bed. He looked peaceful enough. He was even smiling a little.

She checked his pulse and went to inform her manager, Gary. Gary had called the authorities. Everyone thought he'd taken the meds himself, ended things. There were whispers that Harry must've been storing them up to take all at once. At the time she'd felt only fear that she'd be in trouble for not double-checking he was taking them as prescribed. Someone with a badge had come and asked Gary questions, but only because it was standard procedure. No one had asked her anything particularly interesting or followed up afterwards. She hasn't even heard from the care home since she's been on leave. Shouldn't Columbo have been in touch if he'd been assigned to the case and thought it suspicious?

The man clearly isn't as good as his TV namesake.

Pauline shakes her head. 'I wouldn't have been any good as a witness. I didn't see anything.'

Audrey's nostrils flare. She breathes out heavily, her relief obvious, those donor lungs working hard. She looks up after a moment and her eyes are clear. 'I thought as much, my darling, but I couldn't take the chance. I had to protect my daughter. I couldn't protect her before, when she was young, but I had to this time. At any cost. I had to *protect* her! I wasn't going to risk anyone thinking she was the one who'd done this. She has a life. She has a partner and a job. She deserves to live.' Audrey nods, mostly to herself. 'So I told anyone who'd listen that I killed him. I even took the empty bottle of Digitalis that Nina used, and I've kept it as evidence – evidence against myself. I was more than prepared to take responsibility. I *am* more than prepared. It's why I haven't been too bothered by Columbo following me around, asking questions. As long as he leaves Nina alone and focuses on me. I . . . I have to protect her.'

She falls silent, her heart racing. Pauline feels frozen in her seat. The air in the room has vacated and it hurts to breathe.

Audrey is not who she said she was. She has lied to Pauline from the start. She has been moving all of them like chess pieces since day one. Setting up the group with the sole purpose of finding Paula. Just so she could keep her quiet! And then pretending to be someone else for months; pretending to be a jackpot winner to win their trust. The group sit dumbly for a minute, processing; trying to make sense of this.

After a moment, Ivy reaches for Audrey's hand. 'I think I understand,' she says softly. 'You were protecting your child.'

Pauline stands up, her chest tight. She has always taken everything lying down. She has been steamrollered her whole life, staying quiet and subdued and mousey. But she won't do it anymore.

'Well, I don't understand!' she explodes and Ivy looks up at her with shock. 'You lied to me. To all of us! You manipulated everyone and only befriended me so you could . . . *control* me. Do you know how familiar that sounds? It's what John's done to me for years! Controlling me – *using* me! You're just like him!' The anger feels unfamiliar but hot and good in her belly. She whirls around on her heels, looking for the front door. Her mind is racing. She has to get out of here, away from these women. Tilly was right all along: there was – there is – something wrong and weird about this group of women. And it's not just that they've won the lottery and killed their husbands. Some of them haven't even done that! She trusted them. She trusted Audrey! She thought they were her friends. She thought that she finally had a safety net, a security blanket that she could— Goddammit, where's the front door? She's all disoriented in this absurdly giant place.

'Pauline . . .' Ivy stands up, too, her face full of regret and upset. She steps towards her, reaching for her friend, but Pauline puts up a warning hand.

'Don't!' she says, her voice high and choked with emotion.

'I agree with Pauline,' Teddy says furiously. 'You're a liar, Audrey. The whole point of this group was that we could trust each other – rely on one another – when we'd all been screwed over time and time again. You lied about so much. You lied about your own name, for God's sake! How would we ever believe anything you ever said again?'

Audrey hangs her head. 'I'm so sorry.'

'Sorry isn't good enough!' Pauline explodes again. 'I'm done with this, and I'm done with you.' She finally locates the right corner of the room, storming towards the door to leave. She's almost shouting as she reaches for it – something Pauline can't remember ever doing before. 'Don't message or call me,' she yells. 'I don't want to hear from any of you. Just leave me alone. I'm done with The Lottery Winner Widows Club. For good. Stay out of my life.'

She slams the door behind her, hoping they heard every word, because she means it. She's never meant anything more in her life. She's done. She's done with all of it.

37

Pauline checks into a hotel five minutes from her house in Surrey, where she stays, avoiding the world and ignoring her problems, for the next few days. All the bravery she'd found on the trip to Saint-Tropez – all that New Pauline energy – has deserted her. She is absolutely wretched; bereft, broken, hollowed out. Paula again.

She still has her luggage from the holiday, though she barely changes out of the hotel bathrobe, moving from the bed to the door to fetch occasional room service food. And then back to the bed again.

She sees there are messages and calls coming in on her phone. Lots of them. Some are from Teddy, Audrey and Ivy, but most are from John, demanding she return to the house immediately. He wants to make a plan, relaunch his life, to start spending their millions. His impatient tone gets more and more shocked. His disbelief at her defiance gets more and more pronounced.

On day four, John decides to take matters into his own hands, having had enough of his silent, defiant wife.

He calls a press conference.

Pauline reads the message from the hotel's king-sized bed, horror growing with every passing word.

> It's time to come home, Paula. I'm announcing my return to the press today. It's happening outside our house in an hour. I know your new little group of friends are supporting you, wherever you are, but enough's enough. Perhaps you've forgotten that you told me all about those women in your emails to me? All about Teddy, Audrey and Ivy. I know all of it. I don't want to have to talk about what I know and what they did. It's time to come home, Paula. We'll be waiting for you.

She throws the covers back, feeling proper feelings for the first time in days.

She told John everything about the group! She wrote it all down! How could she be so stupid, so thoughtless? She thought it was safe, that he was dead, that those emails were just for her. She had no idea he could... that he was...

Pauline frantically pulls on her clothes, her heart pounding in her chest. She has to get home; she has to speak to John; she has to stop him saying anything.

She reaches for her belongings, throwing them back into her suitcase and looking around for any errant items. However angry she is – however let down she feels by her friends right now – she has to protect them. She can't let John put them in danger.

She has to go back to him.

The press conference has already started when Pauline pulls up outside the house. She parks her new car behind a row of vans and climbs out, her whole body shaking. Slowly, she makes her way along the pavement, catching glimpses of John between the parked vehicles. Behind rows of men holding cameras.

There he is.

John. Standing in front of their home, smiling widely.

Her deceased husband is announcing his return to the world. Floating above her own body, she can just about make out his voice as she crosses the road towards him. He was not dead after all, he's explaining, as cameras flash. He was merely ill and misidentified. He lies smoothly to reporters, describing months spent stuck in a hospital in the Austrian Alps. He had a vent down his throat preventing him from telling the doctors who he really was. Thank God he finally recovered enough to be sent home to his loving family . . . and to the surprise twenty-one million pounds waiting in his bank account.

He talks about how relieved he is to be back, and how thrilled he is to be suddenly wealthy. No one questions the veracity of his story, instead they ask him what he'll buy with the Lotto millions and he jokes about getting a new tie. With a kindly, serious face, he adds that the truth is, he's planning on spending it all on his beloved family. Every last penny.

He is flanked on either side by a pale Tilly and a red Seb. They look beyond shell-shocked.

'Where's your wife today, Mr Sheldon?' one of the men calls out and something flickers across John's face. Irritation. He opens his mouth to respond and then he sees her. Standing there, thirty feet away, at the end of their driveway. A smile spreads across his features.

'Speak of the devil.' He reaches an open palm in her direction and the swarm of journalists turn en masse. The flashes begin and Pauline covers her face with the back of a hand.

'Please!' John calls out. 'Leave her be! All of this has been a lot for my little Paula.' He continues with emphatic concern, 'My poor, fragile wife, finding out her husband was alive all this time and stuck in a hospital eight hundred kilometres away! It's been very hard for her.' He frowns. 'Especially after so many online armchair detectives made all those cruel comments about her. Unfounded, evil comments from social media investigators who had no right.'

He says this last part with such fury, shooting angry looks at the journalists who have provoked it, like he is a loyal and devoted partner.

Pauline stares at John, feeling numb.

It's too late now. It's all too late. She should've taken her chance to kill him when she had it, because now it's over. It's too late to do anything about him – about his return. She's trapped. Everyone knows he's back. He's told the world. He's told the kids. She'll have to be his wife again. She'll have to go back to being controlled and mocked and – a term she has newly learned from Ivy – *gaslit*. She'll have to go back to being Paula again.

As the reporters shout more questions, Pauline finds herself moving towards the front door. She needs to get away from all this noise, all those penetrating stares, all that *John*. She finds the handle at last and quickly pulls the door shut behind her, leaning against it and allowing herself a little cry.

She'd come so far . . . She'd been feeling so good – so *new*. Yes, she felt anxious and frightened a lot around the other women, but in a positive way. It was exciting! She was doing brand-new things and discovering for the first time what kind of person she was, underneath all that John-ness. She was figuring out things she liked – like cars – and things she didn't like – private jets – and it felt good. It felt right! For the last few weeks, Pauline's body has been zinging with adrenaline and excitement. John's death had given her the chance to finally feel alive for the first time in decades. And now he's back from the dead, it's like he's killed her.

She stumbles through to the kitchen, collapsing onto a chair and sinking her head onto her arms.

She hears the front door open and close. 'Mum?'

It's Tilly. It is the first time she's heard her daughter's voice since their fight. Since before Saint-Tropez. Since before Pauline found out about John. Since before Audrey's confession. Since before.

The sound reverberates in her ears and she sinks further into herself. But then she stands up. She can't ignore her daughter, no matter what's gone on. She's missed her so much. She needs to see her.

And then she's there, in front of her. Tilly's kind, warm, infuriating, judgemental, overbearing face. The sight of her fills Pauline's heart with love.

'Tilly,' she says simply.

'Mum!' She sounds so relieved, though her skin is ashen. 'He's back. He's really back. Did you know? Where have you been? What's—' Tilly starts crying quietly and Pauline reaches for her, wrapping arms around her oldest child. Tilly continues speaking into Pauline's shoulder. 'He called us this morning and we rushed over here. It's a miracle.' She's mumbling through her tears. 'It was all just a mistake, Mum. He's fine! He's OK.' Pauline lets her speak, afraid to breathe. 'Everything is OK now. Everything will be all right. Dad's home.'

'I know, Tills. I know.'

There is a pause and Tilly pulls out of the hug, looking at her mother with fearful eyes. 'Is it . . . Are you . . .? Oh, Mum, I'm so sorry about our fight. I'm so sorry I accused you . . .' Her voice breaks again. 'I'm really sorry I said that . . . thing. I didn't mean it. I could never mean it! Not really. I think I was having some kind of breakdown or . . . I don't know, *something*. Maybe it was a delayed reaction to grief. Those grief tentacles reaching out and pulling me down. Or maybe I'm just a crappy person. But there's no excuse.' She shakes her head. 'I can't believe I said it and I hate myself for it. Of course you're not happier without Dad. Of course you're not.' She breathes out slowly, trying and failing to regain her composure. 'I've been so worried about you, Mum. I've not slept a wink since I said those awful things. I've kept Misha up all night talking about you, wondering what I should do. I've felt terrible.' She pauses, smiling a watery smile. 'But it's all fine now, because Dad's back! He's back. He's not dead! Our lives can go back to normal.'

'Normal,' Pauline repeats faintly. 'OK.'

'It's all going to be all right, Mum,' Tilly says again with emotion. 'It'll be even better than it was before. John and Paula Sheldon, reunited after all these months. We're getting so many messages! No one can believe it's real! It's like a love story!'

'Yes. Like a love story,' Pauline repeats robotically, hating the words. But a part of her knows this is true. It is like a love story. Because – after everything she's been through and seen – she knows better than most that not all real-life love stories are romantic. And even fewer have a happy ending.

38

'Paula's home at last!'

Pauline winces, not just at the sight of her should-be-late husband, standing there in their kitchen, but at hearing that name. The name he gave her. 'You took your time!' He grins at her, waiting for a reaction. She freezes, unable to move.

'Come on, Mum!' Beside her, Tilly throws herself forwards, bundling her mum and dad into a group hug. From her position, looking out into the hallway, she can see John has left the front door swinging wide open. Outside, cameras are still flashing, journalists shouting.

The neighbours will not be pleased that the rows of media vans are back in front of Pauline's house.

Inside the family hug, Pauline finds herself pressed into kitchen cupboards, handles poking into her spine. She struggles to get free, ending up instead in John's armpit. The familiar odour makes her head spin – just like the last time, when she stood over him in bed with a pillow ready to smother him. She should've done it. She wishes she had. She's repulsed by the smell of him and struggles to fight back nausea. 'Seb, get over here,' Tilly shouts over her shoulder.

Her brother appears through the front door, a little sheeny and manic-eyed. 'Mum, you're back,' he says, slamming the front door, to shouts of protest from their not-so-adoring public.

He joins them, throwing his arms around the family unit. 'I'm so glad you're here,' he murmurs into Pauline's ear. 'Are you all right?'

She nods, wondering if her son had to cut short his course and what it was for. Even with everything that's happening, Pauline feels like she's let Seb down by not asking more about his life. The guilt pulses through her, even now. She looks away as Tilly finally releases them. 'Let's have a cup of tea,' Pauline says, moving quickly through the kitchen in case her daughter makes them touch some more.

'I think we should probably make it something a bit stronger,' Tilly says, laughing to herself. 'We're celebrating, after all.'

'Quite right,' John says jovially as Seb nods agreeably. 'Paula, get us a bottle of something special out of the understairs cupboard, will you? There's some whisky I nicked from my Christmas work party last year.'

She swallows, fear filling her. His brothers drank it at the reading.

'You gave it to Leonard,' she whispers and he frowns.

'What are you saying, Paula? Speak up, for God's sake!'

She clears her throat. 'In your . . . will,' she says, trying to be heard. 'You gave him the whisky.' Her heart races. She's still afraid of him, of his reactions. 'I think there's Prosecco?'

John's face darkens. 'Fine. Get that.' He smiles then. 'And get yourself a Malibu and Coke. I know it's your favourite.'

She wants to weep, but obliges, feeling any residual strength draining away. She's felt so strong lately and look at her now.

Meekly obeying orders. Fetching and carrying. Drinking fabric softener. But that strength she felt clearly wasn't real if it could disappear so easily, simply at the sound of John's voice.

They clink glasses, Tilly and Seb shouting, 'eyes, eyes, eyes' at each other, apparently oblivious to Pauline's discomfort. She doesn't want to look *him* in the eyes.

'The first thing I'm going to do,' John announces to the room, 'is take my family shopping!' He raises his glass again, adding gleefully, 'Since I'm now a very rich man!'

Pauline notes the *I'm*, but no one else takes much notice.

'Although,' John muses, pouting, 'I'll also have to get myself a new car pretty sharpish, since that last one got a bit dinged up.' He laughs. 'I don't even know what happened to it. Languishing in some Austrian junkyard, I expect!'

'But you were in your car when it went off the road, right?' Seb asks curiously, and his dad shakes his head, waving away the question.

'Er . . . no, no, and never mind all that now,' he booms. 'Let's just be glad it wasn't me!'

'But how did you end up in hospital then, if you weren't in the car wreck?' Seb continues, frustration in his voice.

'Shut up, Seb!' Tilly commands, looking doe-eyed at her dad. 'Who cares about all that! He's home, that's what matters.' Inspiration hits her. 'Oh! Mum bought a new car. We can go shopping in that!'

John turns to Pauline with surprise. '*You* bought a new car?' He shakes his head, turning back to Tilly. 'That's a disaster waiting to happen. She's the world's worst driver!' He laughs at this and Tilly joins in. Seb does not. 'Well,' John continues, checking his watch, 'bring me the keys then,

Paula, I better take over the driving from here on out.' He turns again to Tilly. 'With your mother at the wheel, we'd all end up dying in a fiery wreck. And I've only just escaped one!' He laughs long and hard, then dumps down his champagne flute. 'Let's get going.'

They head outside, ignoring the cameras and the shouts. John low-whistles at the sight of the brand-new Porsche parked down the road. He side-eyes Pauline. 'I never knew you had it in you,' he murmurs with something like disgust in his voice. 'Though I'd have got it in red,' he adds with self-importance.

Pauline thinks of Teddy's comment about middle-aged men driving red cars because they're too scared to buy Viagra. Though, in hindsight, she's very relieved John has always been too embarrassed to buy the blue pills he needs.

Poor Bridget, she thinks again.

John drives too fast towards London, but Pauline does not secretly delight in every speed bump, like she did in Audrey's old car. Audrey's joy in driving was infectious, while John's road rage is stressful and uncomfortable.

In the back, Pauline's adult children don't seem to notice the tension. Tilly chats happily, filling her dad in on her life over the months he's missed.

They pull up near Harrods, and Pauline's heart beats faster knowing Teddy lives so close. Are The Lottery Winner Widows Club all there together right now? Are they having fun without her? Maybe they're relieved to have lost the most broken – the weakest – of their group and now they can truly let loose and enjoy themselves.

Pauline thinks of Teddy's anger the other day, and wonders if she's been able to forgive Audrey's lies. She wishes it were possible for her. Maybe she could've moved past it if John weren't back, but she can't have two people in her life like that.

Not that there would be any point in forgiving Audrey anyway. It's not like John will let Pauline see the group anymore. He never let her have friends.

There are photographers waiting for them inside the grand department store, and it's clear John has set up some kind of publicity shoot. She didn't speak or pose at the press conference, but – look – here is the dutiful wife now, back at her husband's side. Look how happy the whole family are, enjoying their miracle. She watches John as he smiles widely for the cameras and jokes with Tilly and Seb. She tries to smile, too, channelling air steward Connie as they move around the jewellery section.

This is the most attention John's ever given their children, she realises. The most he's smiled at them their whole lives. He always said the kids were her remit, her responsibility. He had no interest in nappies or school reports. Like those things were somehow so exciting for Pauline! But look at Tilly now, basking in his attention, lapping up the praise; so desperate for his approval and love.

It makes Pauline sad.

John performatively calls his wife over now, loudly telling her – and the photographers – how he wants to buy her something sparkly.

'I know how to keep the little woman sweet,' he winks at the nearest camera. 'Happy wife, happy life, eh, lads?'

She steps towards him reluctantly and he turns. 'What do you fancy, love? A bracelet? A diamond necklace?'

She lightly shakes her head. 'No, thank you,' she says. A shadow passes across his face, a flicker of irritation.

'Don't be silly,' he says through gritted teeth. He takes her arm, moving her firmly to a glass case. 'What about that one?' He points at a delicate necklace covered in diamonds. The description says it is a White Gold and Diamond Classic Butterfly Necklace.

'There's no price,' Pauline says meekly, feeling so much like Paula and hating herself for it. She points to the small sign, reading, 'Price On Application'.

'That doesn't matter!' John says loudly. 'We've got twenty million in the bank!' He laughs again as flashes go off. The paps are loving this.

He lets go of her arm, moving off. 'Maybe I'll buy myself a watch!' he says, and Pauline breathes out, relieved. He's already forgotten about her and the ostentatious butterfly necklace. John waves at a staff member. 'That one doesn't have a price.' He points to something within the glass case. 'How much is it?'

The man smoothly removes the watch with gloves, placing it tenderly on the counter top. 'This is the H. Moser & Cie. red gold and sapphire streamliner tourbillon watch,' he says in an even voice. 'Its case is eighteen karat rose gold, with sixty baguette-cut coloured sapphires. It features a circular dial and sapphire glass. It has a seventy-two-hour power reserve and represents exquisite craftsmanship—'

'Yes, yes,' John says a touch impatiently. 'It's very nice, I'll take it. Bag it up for me. How much do you want for it?'

The man nods lightly and begins the process of carefully packaging up the gaudy thing. 'It's one-five-eight.'

When John nods and says, 'Oh, I thought it'd be more,' the staff member pauses and adds, 'Thousand. One hundred and fifty-eight thousand pounds.'

John pales, swallowing hard. He glances anxiously at the audience around him. They close in, snapping endless shots, awaiting a reaction.

'Well,' John swallows again. 'That is . . . completely fine, of course. That's what I expected. That's about how much . . . I assumed it would be. And that is fine, because I've always been a watch man, and I've always wanted a . . .' – he searches for the brand name – 'a H . . . a HMV watch. So yes, how wonderful. Wrap it up, my good man!'

Seb leans closer for a proper look. 'Wow!' he says. 'I like all the pretty pinks and reds. So cool, Dad, so modern of you that you're choosing a women's watch for yourself.'

John peers closer at the colourful watch, his face flaming red as he realises. 'Don't be ridiculous!' he stutters, trying and failing to hide his irritation. 'This is obviously – *obviously* – for . . .' – he turns, waving towards Tilly – 'my beautiful daughter. I'm buying her this . . . HMV watch for' – more swallowing – 'one hundred and fifty-eight thousand pounds.' He enunciates each number.

Tilly gasps, throwing herself at her dad for a hug. 'Oh my God, *thank you*!' she squeals. 'Thank you so much! I can't believe it!'

The staff member hovers with the bag. 'And how will you be paying today, sir?'

John's face falls. 'Oh, I hadn't thought. All my cards . . .' He glances at his emotional daughter and she grimaces.

'Sorry, Dad, we cut up all your cards when we thought you were . . .' – she swallows – 'gone. We had everything transferred into Mum's name.' John, Tilly and Seb all turn to look over at Pauline, who is hovering as far back as she's able. Behind the row of cameras.

'I've got a card,' she confirms faintly. 'I've got it.' She reaches into her handbag and John stalks over, hand out.

'Give it to me,' he half-snarls, before remembering all the eyes on him. She hands it over and his eyes travel across the card – across her name printed along the bottom. The revulsion is clear.

'We'll have to get this taken care of,' he mutters furiously. It's clear he doesn't mean a replacement card for himself. He means getting rid of hers.

John stalks back over to the counter where he indiscreetly arranges payment with the smooth-faced staff member. Pauline can see the way he gives himself a shake, and as he turns to present the gleaming box to his daughter, he's back to being Charming John, smiling winningly for the cameras.

'Man back from the dead spends his lottery winnings!' he shouts to them, offering up his idea of a headline. He grins, looking inspired. 'We should go get some cash out. I'll throw it up in the air, and you lot can take pictures of us jumping around in it.' He laughs. 'I'm doing your job for you!' Pauline catches a couple of the photographers exchanging looks.

'I think we've got what we need now, John,' one of them says, adding nicely, 'We'll get going. Thanks.'

John pouts. 'This is the story of the decade.' He points frantically over at Pauline. 'Don't you want to get a few quotes from her? From the wife? About how thrilled she is to have me back?'

Pauline's face flushes a deep red. The truth is, she would love to tell the whole world *exactly* how thrilled she is to have him back, but now's not really the time. She glances at Tilly who's beaming from ear to ear as she admires her expensive new watch.

Now's definitely not the time.

A couple of the paps are looking at her earnestly. 'Actually, yeah!' one of them says eagerly. 'We would love a few lines from you, Paula! How did it feel to get the call that your husband wasn't really dead?'

She stares down, her throat closing up. John jogs over to her side. 'Aw, my gal's a bit camera shy,' he tells them. 'But you can quote her as saying she's gassed to have me back. It's a bloody miracle and she's been bursting with happiness every minute of the day. It's a dream come true, eh, Paula?'

'It's Pauline,' she whispers, something bubbling up inside her.

'Eh? What's that?' he says, then more firmly, 'Don't get excited now.'

The bubbling stops.

'Nothing.'

'Right, good. Let's go spend some more money!' John shouts, leading the way across the marble floor. 'After everything I've been through and had to do, I reckon I deserve to buy something huge and extravagant for myself!'

Pauline nods, watching him go. After everything John's done, he definitely deserves something huge.

Like a garden spade to the back of the head.

39

'Is everything OK, Mum?' Seb is at the back door, hovering anxiously.

It's a Wednesday night and John has gone to play snooker with his friends and brothers. He will be back late. He's a local celebrity these days, and everyone wants a piece of him.

'Yes, Sebby,' she says quickly, though he has walked in on her staring into space, which must've looked a bit odd. 'I'm fine, just thinking.'

She was thinking. She was thinking that she has to find a solution to all of this. It's been over a week of everything being Back To Normal, but she's realising that she can't go Back To Normal. She needs to be Pauline again. Those months of freedom have unleashed something inside her. She misses it. And more than anything, she misses her friends in The Lottery Winner Widows Club.

John has been on his best behaviour since he's been back. He's been kind and smiley. Thoughtful even. It's probably, in part, because Tilly and Seb have been around so much. Not to mention the eyes of the world are still on them. John has done multiple media interviews, and came home yesterday talking about a meeting he'd had with a producer about an

ITV drama. Although, he told her, wiggling his eyebrows, he's holding out for a Netflix miniseries.

He's happier than she's ever seen him. There have been moments where Pauline's even thought she might be able to forget everything he's done. In time. Maybe.

Although, it might be easier to try and forget her friends and who she was around them. Forget how much she's changed.

Seb sits down across from her.

'I'm sorry I didn't defend you that day,' he tells her suddenly, with urgency. 'That day, when Tilly staged her stupid intervention.' He looks down at his lap. 'I should've stopped her. I should've spoken up. I knew it wasn't right. I'm too much of a follower sometimes, I think.' He looks up now, biting his lip. 'I should've defended you. There are so many times when I should've defended you over the years.'

She regards him curiously. 'What do you mean?' He blinks at her and she asks the question. 'Are you . . . Are you talking about your dad?'

Seb nods slowly. 'I never knew whether to say anything because I know you love him, but if I'm being honest with you, Mum, I don't . . . I don't really like the way he treats you a lot of the time.'

Something begins to unfurl in her stomach. Seb saw. He saw it. He saw her.

She doesn't know what to say. She's spent so much time denying and pretending. But she doesn't want to anymore. Whatever it might cost, she doesn't want to pretend everything is – and always was – fine. At last, she says, 'You've noticed?'

'Yes,' he nods again. 'And I'm really sorry I didn't say anything before. It's so hard to know when it's the right time to say something. I didn't know at what point I was supposed to stop being a kid with you and Dad. At what age are you meant to stand up to your own dad and go, "Hey, don't speak to Mum like that"?' He swallows. 'I've always wanted to protect you, but I didn't know how. So I just tried to stay close. I tried to look out for you and be here for you. I felt pretty useless most of the time – and I know I *am* useless in a lot of ways – but I wanted to at least be here for you. I wanted to be around if you ever needed me or wanted help.'

Pauline blinks at her son, wondering when he became an adult. Because he is now – he really is – and yet, this is the closest he's come in decades to that compassionate, astute little boy she remembers.

He's known the truth for all these years and has been trying to protect her.

A realisation hits her suddenly, out of nowhere.

The shed.

He stayed *for her.*

Her son saw who his dad really was and he stayed close. Even if it meant living in a horrible, old, spider-infested shed in the back garden. Pauline thought she'd been protecting Seb by keeping things to herself – all the while despairing of her adult son refusing to move out or find himself a real life – and the truth was that he was the one protecting *her.*

Seb sighs. 'Anyway, then y'know this huge, bananapants thing happened with him dying in this awful car accident.' He screws up his face. 'By the way, are we really supposed to believe the authorities over there just . . . got it wrong? I really don't understand what the hell went on. None of it makes any sense.' He shakes his head. 'And Tilly was so worried about you after the funeral, but I thought you seemed . . . *better.* You seemed happier. You were coming out of your shell a bit... and, to be honest with you, Mum, so was I. You were doing things that *you* wanted to do. You made those cool friends.' He brightens. 'You bought that awesome car!' Then his face falls. 'What's happening with that by the way? Are you just *giving* it to Dad? Is he keeping it?' Seb sighs. 'Whatever, I don't want it to sound like I'm sad Dad's back, but...' He does sound a bit sad his dad's back. 'I dunno... a part of me was kind of relieved he was gone.' He adds hastily, 'I didn't wish him dead or anything, y'know, but everything felt easier without him around. *You* seemed easier. And freer.' He swallows. 'I want you to be OK, Mum. And I want you to put yourself first. It's great Dad's not really dead, but you don't have to... you know. Never mind us, we're grown-ups, we're fine. You have to choose yourself. Put your own oxygen mask on first, right, Mum?'

She places her hand over his. He was relieved John was gone, just like she was. The puzzle pieces begin to fall into place. When his dad had "died", hadn't Seb started to get his act together? Without her husband around holding both of them back, Seb had finally started to live his life. Hadn't he mentioned looking at places to rent? Hadn't he started looking at job websites? Hadn't he had interviews and— oh!

'Seb!' she says with sudden urgency. 'How did your course go?'

'Ah!' he twinkles. 'The course, of course! I'm on course to do well on the course.' They both laugh, and then he shrugs, suddenly a little bashful. 'Actually, it was really, totally, bananapants amazing. I learned so much about how therapy works and what it would take to become a therapist...'

That's what the course was about!

'And I've decided it's something I really want to do. I want to be a therapist. I want to help people, if I can. It'll be a lot of work and take years to get qualified, but I feel sure about it.'

Pauline wants to cry because this is beyond perfect. Her perfect Seb. She squeezes his hand. 'I'm so proud of you,' she says in a whisper, looking at him properly for what feels like the first time in years.

He suddenly looks a bit shifty. 'OK, well, try and remember how proud you are for the next few minutes, will you, Mum? Because I may have done something you don't like.' He pauses. 'There are some people who really want to talk to you.'

'What?' Pauline sits up straight. What's he talking about? 'Not another press conference!'

He laughs. 'No, of course not!' he says. 'It's your mates! I know they've been trying to speak to you since Dad's reincarnation and you've kept ignoring them.' He shakes his head disapprovingly. 'Now, I don't want to interfere, but I really liked that lot.' He pauses. 'And I *really* liked Teddy's apartment. That was super cool. I want a go in that outdoor roof terrace pool at some point.' Pauline laughs affectionately as he continues, 'Look, I don't know what's gone down between you lot, but they're your friends, OK? I don't believe they could've done anything you can't get past. You have to forgive them. You need them around.'

Pauline considers this. Seb thinks she should forgive them? Seb can see she needs them.

She realises then that she has already forgiven Audrey. It took her a few days – those long days in a hotel bed spent feeling oh-so sorry for herself – but she has definitely forgiven her. In hindsight, it hardly feels like there was anything to forgive. Audrey gave her so much. So what if the reason they met wasn't the reason she thought? She can more than understand the impulse to protect her children.

Pauline sighs. 'I think they're the ones who probably need to forgive *me*,' she mumbles, looking down at her hands. She thinks of the tantrum she threw over Audrey's confession and flushes with shame. She thinks of all those mean things she shouted and how she stormed out of the flat. How she's ignored all their messages and phone calls. They'll probably never want to speak to her again.

'Rubbish,' Seb says happily. 'Ivy is *desperate* to hear from you. She says she misses you like crazy.'

'You've spoken to Ivy?'

A hint of redness blooms on Seb's cheekbones. 'Er . . . yeah, a bit, yeah. I got her number at Teddy's apartment that day . . . just to, like, swap some info about her cool band T-shirts.' His eyes get wide and faux innocent. 'Anyway, she told me they've been trying to get hold of you and you're being really stubborn about it.' He pauses. 'She's really nice, isn't she?' He scrunches up his nose. 'Actually, Mum, please forgive me for this. I'd hate for you to feel ambushed again, but they're all waiting for you in my shed. Like, right now. Audrey's been playing on my Nintendo. She's ruining all my high scores.'

Despite herself, this makes Pauline laugh, then gasp. 'They're here? Outside, now?' She is breathless as he nods. She leaps up, excitement filling her stomach. Her friends are here. They're really here. Oh God, she's missed them so much.

Leaving Seb in the kitchen, she rushes out into the garden. She laughs hysterically when she sees the clown car of a shed full of Audrey, Teddy and Ivy. 'Room for one more?' she asks and they collectively throw open their arms.

'Pauline!' Ivy cries, and bursts into tears.

'Babe!' Teddy grins widely, while Audrey smiles shyly.

'Please say you've forgiven me, my darling,' she asks, not waiting for a response before pulling her into a cuddle.

Pauline takes a moment before responding. She considers everything Audrey must've dealt with. How she coped, knowing Harold had done what he'd done, and then knowing her daughter had done what she'd done. Her friend must've been so frightened, thinking someone was going to knock on the door at any moment and take her child away. She inhales deeply.

'Oh Audrey, I'm so sorry, too!' Pauline cries. 'I understand why you did what you did. I'd do anything for my children, too. You must've been so scared when Nina did . . . what she did.' She draws back, finding a spot where she can just about perch on the edge of Seb's tiny single bed. 'And if Columbo ever does come to see me about Harry – about Harold – I promise you I won't say a word about your daughter. Not about any of it.'

Audrey looks like she wants to cry. 'I want you to know I am not the same as John,' she says fiercely. 'I feel so awful about what I did; I have this whole time. I'm so sorry for lying to you. To you all. I know you felt manipulated, and I completely understand why, but everything I said and did once we met *was* real. I really do love you all.' She squeezes Pauline's hand. 'And I swear I'm not here to check up on your bloody witness account! I didn't come here to make sure you won't say anything. I just came to say sorry again and make sure you knew I meant it.' She pauses, then adds hastily, 'But thank you for saying that about Nina, my darling, that means the world to me.'

They smile at one another, then reach around in a circle to hold hands. After a minute, Teddy clears her throat.

'Pauline, we have to get you away from John.'

Pauline hangs her head. 'I know,' she whispers. 'But I also don't know if I can.' She swallows hard. 'He knows. John knows about the three of you, about our club, about what you all did.' She looks up and around, eyes desperate. 'When I thought he was dead, I wrote an email . . . I told him. I told him . . . Gosh, I'm sorry, I'm *so* sorry—'

'Shush, shush,' Audrey scolds her quietly as Ivy squeezes Pauline's hand. 'Don't do that, it's not your fault.' They fall silent again, and Pauline knows with certainty that it *is* her fault. She has trapped her friends and she has trapped herself. Even as a ghost, John wasn't someone she should've ever trusted.

Teddy leans in, almost knocking over an old kettle plugged into the extension lead. 'Actually, I think I have a way to solve all of this. A way to fix all our problems.'

Ivy makes a noise. 'Oh, Teddy, not murder again? Please don't say murder.'

'No,' Teddy laughs as Pauline sighs with relief. 'I think we can all agree that we're not really murderers.'

'I am,' Ivy says gravely.

Audrey squeezes her hand. 'Yes, very well done, my darling. Your husband deserved it and there would be a strong argument for self-defence anyway. Oh, and if you do go to jail, you're only twenty-seven! You'll be out before you're even Teddy's age.'

Teddy waves her sunglasses in the air. 'Nothing much happens in your thirties, babe. You might as well skip it. Your forties are the best decade.'

Ivy laughs at this as Pauline adds quickly, 'But you don't need to worry about any of that because no one will find out!' She reaches for Ivy's hand. 'And it was just a one-off, wasn't it? One moment of fury, buried in a lifetime of helping people, not hurting them.'

Ivy nods, squeezing Pauline's hand.

'And goodness, we were *so* rubbish at murder!' Pauline exclaims, thinking back to their various attempts. All that planning, all the big, brave, vaguely psychopathic talk, and none of them had it in them. She smiles warmly at the group, then turns to Teddy. 'So what's your non-murder plan then?'

Teddy shakes her head, jangling huge pink diamond earrings. Pauline tries to focus on what her friend is saying and not obsess over the way her hair bounces lightly around her shoulders. She never did send Pauline a link to the shampoo she uses.

'So, Audrey,' Teddy begins, 'you said you'd kept the medication bottle your daughter used on Harold, right? The empty one? Just in case?' She smiles around the group, leaving a dramatic pause. 'I know we've worked our way through a lot of bad plans in the last couple of months. But if we can pull this one off, I really think it's going to take care of everything . . .'

40

Pauline leads them all inside, relieved to finally escape the shed. Yes, it was lovely making up with her friends out there, but there are too many spiders. She's glad Seb won't need to be in there much longer.

She's quiet as they sit down at the kitchen table.

'This is nice!' Audrey says, patting Pauline's hand as she takes in the room. 'It's a bit more spacious than your outside . . . garden studio.'

Pauline laughs at the diplomacy. It's not usually Audrey's style, but she's on her best behaviour. 'It's a shed! It's my son Seb's shed. There's no point pretending otherwise.' She pauses. 'But at least there's an outside toilet. I couldn't bear to share a loo with my grown-up son.'

'Having to share a loo with men at all is an abomination,' Teddy mutters.

'Seb is an absolute darling!' Audrey's eyes light up. 'A doll and a total dreamboat.'

Ivy beams. 'Personally, I thought the shed – and the outside loo! – were really sweet.'

Teddy slides into the seat beside Pauline, nudging her a

little. 'Look, Pauline, I know it's a lot – my plan – and if you don't like the idea, or need more time . . .'

Audrey leans forward. 'We'd understand if you've changed your mind about John altogether. Maybe he's a different man now he's back. Maybe—'

Pauline interrupts. 'He's not.' She shakes her head. 'He's pretending to be better, but I keep seeing flashes of the real him. I know it's only a matter of time. And I think he'll be even worse once all the attention dies down.'

'We don't want it to die down just yet,' Ivy points out. 'It's important to the plan.'

'Right,' Teddy nods slowly, 'I just mean though, Pauline, you don't *have* to make a decision right now. Obviously, the idea hinges on you having to do a lot of being very brave, and I know the last few months have been really difficult for you. Especially these past couple of weeks. If you need a bit of time to think about it, we understand. We can figure something out.'

Pauline smiles at her friend, then round at Audrey and Ivy. 'The worst part of John being back was not being able to speak to you three.'

They all smile at each other warmly. 'Same, my darling,' Audrey tells her.

Pauline makes a face. 'But also my terrible husband coming back from the dead and taking my lovely Porsche away from me.'

'We'll get that Porsche back, you'll see.' Teddy nods with determination.

'But I do need more time, I'm afraid,' Pauline admits after a moment. 'Not because I'm unsure of the plan or have any doubt it will work.' She looks to Teddy. 'I think you're a *genius* by the way! And with the lot of you metaphorically holding my hand, I think I'm capable of all kinds of bravery.' She grins, then pauses, glancing towards the rest of the house. 'It's just . . . I need a little bit of time because I have to talk to Tilly and Seb first. Before we do anything else, I need to be honest with my children. I owe them that. I owe them the truth. I've started the conversation with my son, but he needs to hear all of it.' She takes a moment. 'I've spent too long trying to protect them and I'm starting to realise that's actually quite selfish of me. Honestly, I think hiding it was actually more about protecting myself, not them. I was protecting myself from their reactions, from their pain. But they're not children anymore. They need to know the truth about their father.'

'What do I need to know about Dad?' Seb is suddenly at the kitchen door, looking worried.

Pauline turns to him. 'Oh! Hi, Sebby,' she says almost shyly. 'Come in here for a minute.'

'Tilly's on her way over,' he says quickly. 'I came to warn you.'

Pauline doesn't acknowledge this. 'You remember everyone?' She waves at the group, then pauses, recalling how he was responsible for bringing them all over here. 'Of course you do.' They all nod cheerily with familiarity. Pauline notes a lingering look between Seb and Ivy, wondering what it might mean.

He nods, 'Hi, you lot. I'm glad you've made up. Mum's been miserable without you.'

'We'll get out of your way,' Teddy says, leaping up. 'Give you a chance to talk.'

Audrey follows suit, stopping to cuddle Seb. 'Your mother is a treasure,' she tells him in a low voice. 'I want you to promise me you'll be there for her. I'm not going to tell you to look after her because she can look after herself, but you can help by being there for her, no matter what happens next. We'll see you very soon, darling boy.'

He nods dumbly, as they all file out the back door. Ivy pauses to smile sweetly at Seb. 'Thanks for helping reunite us,' she says, and Seb stares at her with something like wonder.

'You're welcome,' he replies at last.

Pauline considers how she feels about her son making puppy-dog eyes at her friend. Her friend who did, incidentally, murder her husband.

Good, she decides. She feels good. After all, there's no denying Seb also has his flaws. Ivy might be a killer, but her son sleeps in a spider-infested shed in his mother's back garden. Most people, Pauline decides, would probably take a spot of mariticide over that.

She waves them off and moments later, the front door bangs open and shut. 'Muuuuuum? Daaaaaaad?' Tilly's voice echoes through the hallway. 'Are you here?'

She appears in a flurry of coat being removed and gloves being discarded. Tilly has always filled a room upon arriving anywhere. It's something Pauline has long admired about her daughter.

'Dad out?' she asks and Seb nods.

'Snooker,' he replies and Tilly rolls her eyes with affection.

'Of course! I'm glad he's immediately found his way straight back into his old routine and old life.'

Pauline makes tea, wondering how she is going to say any of what she has to say. They deserve the truth. She deserves to *say* her truth, but those first words . . . that part where she has to start talking . . . it feels like a huge, insurmountable thing.

'Anyway,' Tilly says breezily, accepting a steaming cup of tea from her mum and making herself comfortable at the kitchen table. 'I came over because it turns out trying to get insurance on a watch worth a hundred and fifty-eight grand is really difficult.' She makes a face. 'They're saying it's going to cost me, like, three grand a year! And I don't want to be ungrateful but... um, no. You know?' She smiles sweetly at her mum. 'Unless you think Dad might be up for paying for it?'

Pauline swallows, wondering if Tilly even hears herself. She is already assuming John is the one in charge of all their money. She has slipped straight back into old patterns and old assumptions.

Nothing will change unless Pauline changes them.

'Tilly, Seb,' she begins, her voice shaking a little, 'I want to talk to you both about something important, if it's OK.'

'Wuh-oh, sounds serious!' Tilly says in a jokey voice. 'You're not going to say Dad's been in another car accident, are you?'

Seb snorts at this, though the memory of sitting around this same kitchen table all those months ago, having to tell both her children that their father was dead, will haunt Pauline for the rest of her life. To think that he willingly put her through that – and them! It is all the reminder she needs that she has to say this.

'No,' Pauline says carefully. 'It's about me and your dad.' She pauses and Seb – sensing what is coming – reaches over and takes her hand. The gesture undermines Pauline's bravery and she takes another moment to compose herself. She would rather not cry until everything has been said.

Seb squeezes her hand. 'Are you splitting up?' he asks gently and Tilly scoffs.

'Don't be ridiculous, Sebby!' she says loudly. 'Of course they're not splitting up. They're very happy together. Dad's just back from the bloody dead! This is their happily ever after.'

Seb looks at his mum with sad eyes, then turns back to his sister. 'They're *not* happy, Tills. You'd have to be a blind idiot to think that. They haven't been happy for as long as I can remember.' He pauses, looking at Pauline searchingly. 'Or, at least, *Mum* hasn't been happy. Maybe Dad was – is – I don't know.'

He noticed. Why had she always assumed he had no idea? That he was so oblivious? How awful for poor Seb to see his mother so unhappy for all these years. How could she ever have thought he'd be better off that way?

'Who are you calling a blind idiot?' Tilly says crossly. 'You're talking rubbish. Isn't he, Mum? It's rubbish, right? You and Dad are great together. You're happy. You're not getting a divorce.' She says this firmly, like she will brook no argument, but Pauline sits up straighter.

'I'm sorry, Tilly, but no, it's not rubbish.' She clears her throat. 'And yes, we probably are splitting up.' She pauses, thinking about Teddy's plan. 'Or at least... taking some time apart. I haven't been happy for a long time. Things have been... very bad. It's very difficult for me to talk about, but your father, he...' She swallows, suddenly unsure.

Maybe she should've rehearsed this, memorised what to say. Her two children wait, looking at her expectantly.

'He hasn't been kind to me,' she says at last. 'Over the years, he has been very *unkind*. And I didn't know how to put that into words for a long time. I thought I loved him, and I thought it was normal, the way he behaved. But I understand now that it's not OK. It was never OK.'

Tilly is getting red in the face. 'What do you mean? You're not saying . . .' She trails off, looking helpless. 'Are you saying he isn't a good man? What does that mean, Mum? What are you saying?'

It hurts Pauline's heart to see her daughter so helpless and uncertain like this. She knows Tilly has always been desperate to win her dad's approval – to get his attention and his love – but she has to know the truth. She nods slowly. 'I think he tries to be a good man, Tilly, in his own way. But he's taken a lot from me. He's been very controlling and jealous. He built an identity for me and I wasn't allowed much freedom outside of that.'

Tilly looks like she's been slapped, while Seb stares down at the table, something like resignation on his face. After a moment Tilly shuffles her chair closer to Pauline. 'OK, yeah, I know Dad can be a bit jealous – we've all seen that – but are you saying he's been, like . . .' She searches for the word, continuing in a whisper, 'Are you saying he's been . . . abusive?'

Pauline bites her lip as horrible silence fills the room. That word has so much power, so many connotations, and even knowing it's true, she finds she can't say it out loud.

Tilly grabs her mother's hand. 'Please say you don't mean that!' she cries desperately.

Seb wheels around in his seat, his expression angry. 'Tills, you claim to be the biggest feminist around!' he says accusingly. 'Why are you in denial about this? When it's someone you know, something that affects you personally? Why aren't you *listening*?'

'But we would've seen it, wouldn't we?' Tilly's voice is high pitched. 'I would've known! I would've been able to tell if my dad was a bad guy. He's always been there for us! For me! He came on the roller coaster ride!' Her eyes are wild, but Pauline can see the tears under there, waiting. She's desperately holding them back. 'He came to the theme park that day and he went on that ride with me even though he was terrified and it made him sick!' She waves her wrist, the watch glinting in the light. 'He bought me this!'

'People can be more than one thing, Tilly!' Seb yells. 'And one bloody day of being nice on a roller coaster doesn't make for a good dad! I can't remember him ever being anything but distant and cold with me. And *mean*! Mostly to Mum, but he wasn't exactly Danny Tanner to us, was he?'

'Who the hell is Danny Tanner?' Tilly is flummoxed.

'*Full House?*' Seb rolls his eyes. 'Never mind that! The point is we need to listen to Mum now. We need to hear her out.'

'I am hearing her out, Seb!' Tilly is hot-cheeked, her eyes dancing. 'I just don't understand! I don't underst—' Her voice cracks and she looks at her mum with desperate eyes. She's imploring her mum to take the words back. When Pauline reaches for her hand, Tilly pulls away. 'I don't know if I can . . . I don't know how to . . .' She doesn't get a chance to finish the sentence. There is a noise out in the hallway: the loud slam of a front door.

'Honey, I'm home!' John calls out in a happy, sing-song voice. He appears moments later in the kitchen doorway, looking around him with surprise. 'Tilly! Seb! You're here, are you? How nice.' He looks to his wife, not sensing the room's strange atmosphere. 'Although it's getting a bit late, you should probably head off home. Where's my dinner, eh, Paula?'

Pauline stands up now, facing him, looking at him properly for what feels like the first time. 'It's Pauline,' she says, that rebellious feeling bubbling up inside her again. And this time she's holding on to those bubbles for dear life.

He barks a laugh at this. 'Huh. I haven't heard that name in a few years,' he says dryly.

'*Pauline?!*' Seb repeats, sounding baffled. 'Who's Pauline?'

'It's me,' his mum says. 'It's my name. Your dad made me change it.'

Tilly's mouth falls open. She's looking between her parents as if seeing them for the first time. 'What? What are you talking about? Why would he do that?'

Pauline had thought she was ready to be Paula again. She thought she had no choice. But she got it wrong. She does have a choice but there *is* only one option she's ready to take: the option of not letting John have her again. She can't. She can't go back. She can never go back. Her chest is tight and heaving.

John laughs again now, a heaviness to the sound. 'Oh shut up, Paula, you're being ridiculous.'

Seb takes a step forward. He looks furious. '*You* shut up, Dad,' he says with steel in his voice. Then he walks over to Pauline, threading his fingers through hers and squeezing her hand.

Pauline squeezes it back, feeling his strength and resolve pulsing through her. 'John, we're over,' she says, and he gapes at her as she adds, 'I'm leaving you.'

There is silence in the room as the four of them all regard one another in shock.

At last John speaks. 'Don't be ridiculous, Paula,' he scoffs, sounding uncertain. 'We'll talk about this later.' He moves towards her, and Seb steps forward now, blocking his path. He stares at his father for a few seconds, then turns back to his mum.

'He faked it, didn't he?' He frowns at her. 'His so-called death? The car accident? His disappearance? All of it? It was horseshit, wasn't it? I'm right, aren't I?' Pauline looks up at her son in wonder as he continues furiously, 'None of it made any sense. I knew it didn't make sense! And we all just lapped up the lies – the excuses.'

Tilly stares at her brother. 'No!' she says in a whisper, but there are no more words from her after that. More seconds pass. More silence stretches out into oblivion. And then at last Tilly turns away from her family, walks out of the room and out of the house. She's gone.

John stares at Pauline. There is a second where she thinks he might hit her. And then she sees him for what he really is: a fearful, snivelling little coward.

All she sees on his face now is weakness.

His expression changes as he sees what she sees, and he turns on his heel. Following in Tilly's wake, he leaves the front door banging on its hinges, leaving Pauline and Seb standing alone in the kitchen.

'Well done, Mum,' Seb says cheerfully after a moment, then turns to her with a lopsided grin. 'Do you want to come play Mario Kart on my Nintendo?'

41

Pauline wakes up with a start, feeling discombobulated.

It takes her a minute to remember – not only what's happened – but where she is. She's in Tilly's old bedroom. She slept in here, on the off chance that John might come home last night.

He didn't.

And she couldn't care less. *Hopefully he's gone back to Austria*, she thinks.

Either way, it won't stop them putting Teddy's plan into action.

She retrieves her dressing gown, pulling the cord tight around her middle and heading downstairs to make a cup of tea.

'Mum?' Seb is waiting at the foot of the stairs and beckons her to follow him into the kitchen. Tilly is waiting there at the table.

She doesn't look like she's slept. Her eyes are red-rimmed and bloodshot. If Pauline didn't know any better, she'd think her daughter had got into Seb's marijuana shed stash.

'Are you OK?' she asks her softly and Tilly nods. After a moment she asks it back.

'Are *you* OK?'

Pauline smiles shyly. 'Yes.'

Tilly looks relieved, then swallows hard. 'Dad's at a hotel,' she says, though Pauline didn't ask and couldn't care less. 'He tried to come stay at mine and Misha's, but I told him to get lost.' She clears her throat. 'I talked to him after . . . what you said. He followed me and tried to insist Seb was wrong. He denied it – claimed it was all a misunderstanding about him faking his own death – but it was so obvious. I feel very stupid for having missed it. Seb was right. It was really clear right away, wasn't it? He didn't even bother trying to come up with a half-decent story, did he?' She blinks hard. 'I can't believe we – I – believed him.'

Pauline doesn't answer directly. Instead, she places a hand on her daughter's shoulder. 'Would you like a cup of tea?' she asks and Tilly nods. She heads to the counter where she fills the kettle and watches as it slowly springs to life. Seb hands her three mugs and a spoon, and Pauline takes her time squeezing the bags and adding milk. Plus Seb's four sugars.

'He really faked it?' Tilly asks, though it's clear she knows. She shakes her head like she is arguing internally with herself. 'He really did it? Are you . . . Do you really . . . ?' Pauline places a mug in front of Tilly as she finally gets out a question. '*Why?* Why would he do that? To us? To you? Why?'

'I can't answer that completely,' Pauline says sadly, taking a seat opposite her daughter. 'Because I can't comprehend why anyone would ever do such a thing. But I do know he was trying to escape me, a lot of debt, and an *entanglement* he was caught up in at work.'

'Debt?' Tilly looks flabbergasted. 'And wait, do you mean an affair?' she asks, eyes wide. They get even wider as Pauline nods her confirmation.

Seb takes the third seat in their triangle and they fall silent again, things sinking in, others falling into place.

'But things were . . . he was bad before that?' Tilly asks, and when her mum doesn't immediately answer, she adds, 'I'm so sorry for the way I stormed out last night. I need to figure out how to listen. Seb was right.' Seb playfully widens his eyes at his sister and she gives him a soft punch on the shoulder. 'Shut up, you idiot.' She turns back to her mum. 'You said . . .' She hesitates, then leans forward, looking earnest. 'Are you up for explaining? Like, when you said Dad was controlling, what did you mean? I really want you to tell us the truth. The whole truth. I'm so sorry about yesterday. I'm listening now.'

Pauline takes a deep breath, then sips her hot tea. She nods. 'Do you remember that day you came to pick me up and I wasn't here? You went looking for me and found me at my friend Teddy's apartment in west London?'

'Yes,' Tilly says quickly. 'We were supposed to be at a grief counselling session, but you were hanging out with that group of women in that gazillion-pound place in Knightsbridge.' She pauses, then gives Pauline a soft smile. 'Still kind of weird, by the way.'

Pauline nods. 'You found me by looking at that laptop over there.' She nods towards the countertop where the computer always sits. 'Via that thing you mentioned, Find My Phone?'

'Yes,' Tilly confirms, blowing on her hot tea.

'Tilly, sweetheart, I didn't set that up,' she says. 'I didn't know what that app even was until you mentioned it. I had to google it afterwards. I had no idea there was a way to track someone's phone like that. But it made so much sense, all of a sudden. That was – is – John's computer. I was never allowed one because he said I shouldn't be online too much.' She takes a deep breath. 'And now I understand how John always knew where I was all the time. He would turn up at my work randomly. If I had to go on a home site visit, he would appear out of nowhere there, to check what I was doing. I thought he was following me in his car, but I realise now that he was tracking my movements through my phone. He also kept a log with all the times and dates of everything I did.'

Seb reaches for his mum's hand, holding it gently. She feels him start to tremble.

'That's horrible,' Tilly says in a low voice, staring at the table.

'He didn't want me talking to other men, or other people at all, if I'm honest. He isolated me from any friends and family I had.' She stops, feeling a wave of remorse. 'And I'm sorry that meant you never got to know your grandparents really. They were such lovely, kind people.'

'Dad always said they were horrible, your mum and dad,' Seb says almost to himself. 'He acted like he was saving you by keeping all of us away from them. Helping you escape.'

Pauline shakes her head. 'They were very good, nice people, my mum and dad. I miss them every day. He wanted me as far away from them as possible. It's why we bought this house in Surrey all those years ago. My family lived in Carlisle which is about a six-hour drive. So of course we couldn't possibly visit.' She pauses. 'I'm sorry,' she adds simply and Seb moves his chair closer, circling an arm around her.

'It's not your fault, Mum!' he tells her earnestly. 'I'm so sorry I didn't realise how bad it was. I didn't understand.'

Across the table, Tilly looks wretched. 'This is all so confusing. I thought he was a good dad, wasn't he?' She sounds desperate. 'I know he wasn't around much, but when he was, he was nice, wasn't he?'

Pauline nods. 'Well, I suppose people can be more than one thing. Someone can do bad things at home but still go out and do charity or love their friends.'

Seb points a finger. 'Hitler was a vegetarian painter.'

'He could be a bad husband and a good dad.' Pauline ignores Seb's unhelpful input.

'That day at the roller coaster,' Tilly says mistily, and Pauline looks down, remembering the passion with which her daughter told the story during their therapy session. Tilly's favourite memories of John.

'Tilly,' she says carefully, suddenly unsure how much more honesty her daughter can survive. 'Those two memories you shared with the counsellor, Gerald ... I'm so sorry, sweetheart, but they weren't quite right. You told him about a Christmas Day with a video camera, recording *Sleeping Beauty*, and another one at the theme park, where your dad went on the big scary ride with you and got sick.' Her daughter nods and Pauline takes a deep breath. 'My love, those were me. They weren't John. They were times with me. Your dad wasn't there for either of those days, those ... memories. My parents actually sent us that video camera for Christmas. Your father was away at some snooker tournament for the whole week over the festive period. I'm the one who spent all day helping you rehearse your show. And when he came back and I told him who the camera was from, he got really cross. He smashed it up and posted the pieces back to my mum and dad. It was the last time they sent me a gift. That's why we only ever recorded *Sleeping Beauty*. You asked me for months afterwards if we could film something else and you hated me when I kept saying no. But I couldn't tell you what had really happened to that Christmas gift.' She sighs. 'And that day at the theme park, he didn't come with us. He said it sounded like hell, all those queues and all those children. I'm sorry, but I'm the one frightened by roller coasters. I'm the one who was sick afterwards but still went on again when you asked. I'm sorry, Tills. I really am. I don't want to take away any good memories and good feelings you have for your dad, but I need you to understand who he really is. And why I need to get away from him.'

Tilly shakes her head, looking bereft as she tries to take in her mum's words. She's having to reassess so much of what she thought about her own life and the memories she created. She swallows, then looks suddenly fierce. 'I wish all those idiots on the internet were right about the car crash. I wish you *had* killed him, Mum.'

Pauline reaches for her hand. 'You don't mean that.'

Beside her, Seb nods. 'I kind of agree with Tills.'

Pauline looks pensive. 'Well, since I'm being very honest with you, I'll admit I felt the same for quite a while.' She clears her throat, thinking of the pillow she'd held over John's prone body. It's back in the study. 'And I still want him punished for everything he did to me, but for now, I just needed to tell you both the truth.'

Tilly takes a deep breath. 'I'm sorry, Mum. I'm really, really sorry.'

Elly Vine

The three of them reach across the table for one another. They sit there for a few minutes, quietly holding hands, processing.

It is sad and it is joyous, and Pauline – at last – can see her way out of all of this mess.

42

Pauline is sitting in a car, outside a police station. Teddy and Ivy are – as they put it – *psyching her up*.

'You're going to be great,' Ivy says nicely. 'You don't even have to say that much. Mostly you're just telling them the truth about him faking his own death, about the affair, and about what a jealous, angry man he's always been.'

'Then you casually mention that one other thing . . .' Teddy adds encouragingly. 'You've got the bag, right?'

Pauline nods, gently patting her coat pocket. She sighs. 'I could really do with an Audrey cuddle right now,' she says and Ivy leans forward to wrap her arms around her. It's not as good as an Audrey hug, but it helps. It's funny how quickly she's gotten used to cuddles. Who knew how much strength they could give you?

'Well,' Teddy tells her in a scolding tone, 'she couldn't be here, could she? It's pretty important to the plan that no one sees you with Audrey.'

'I know,' Pauline says and then steels herself. 'OK, I'm ready. Here we go.'

They head for the station's double doors, pausing to let a couple of women exit. They're chatting animatedly about the appeal of men in uniforms.

Inside, Ivy takes a seat on a blue plastic chair as Pauline and Teddy head for the front desk. A handsome young man in uniform sits behind glass, and Pauline decides that she also sees the appeal of men in uniform.

'Hello?' she offers hesitantly and the handsome officer looks up.

'How can I help?' he says neutrally, and Pauline quivers. Beside her, she can feel Teddy mentally holding her up, and she straightens, channelling the bravado of Tina Edwina Fletcher – Teddy for short.

'I need to report a crime,' she says and her voice is clearer than it's ever been. Beside her, her friend gives her a squeeze.

The police officer asks her a few questions and pales as she fills him in.

'Just . . . er, wait a minute, will you?' he tells her, waving at the chairs. 'Have a seat, someone will be with you shortly.'

She expects to be sitting a while, but it is not long before Pauline finds herself being escorted through to an interview room by the desk officer. He introduces her to a Detective Sergeant Daveys, who tells Pauline to call him Thomas. He has a nice moustache that somehow seems sort of comforting.

'I'm Pauline Sheldon,' says Pauline.

'Tina Edwina Fletcher,' says her friend smoothly. 'I'm a friend, but I also happen to be Pauline's lawyer. I'm here to make sure everything goes the way it should.'

Pauline catches Thomas's moustache twitch, but he nods, gesturing for everyone to take a seat.

'Now, Pauline,' he begins slowly, 'can you tell me why you're here today?'

'It's about my husband, John Sheldon,' she begins nervously.

Thomas maintains a poker face. 'OK, Pauline,' he says carefully. 'If it's all right with you, I'm going to record this conversation and take an official statement.'

Pauline nods, taking a deep breath. Here we go.

Over the next half an hour, she tells Thomas with the moustache about her relationship. She tells him about the years of controlling, abusive behaviour she suffered at John's hands, about his wild jealousy, his financial abuse, and the way he tracked her movements with an app and a notebook.

Thomas tells her this is a crime, as of 29 December 2015. It's called coercive control.

She then tells him how John faked his own death several months ago and how he has now – just last week – come back to life. She is surprised to learn that this is *not* a crime. Not technically. Thomas explains that usually faking your own death involves some level of fraud, but John didn't have life insurance. He just wanted to escape his life.

Thomas leans in. 'Pauline, why do you think he did it? Why did he fake his own death? Did you say you were going to report him for the abuse? Were you going to leave him? Or was there some other kind of instigating incident that led to him faking his own death?'

Pauline looks down at her hands. She thinks of John's affair. She thinks of the loan sharks coming after him. But she doesn't say these things. 'I work in a care home, Officer,' she says at last, not quite able to call him by his first name. It's too informal for Pauline. 'As I said, John was very jealous. He was always very funny about me working with the male residents – even much older men – and he would constantly quiz me about them.' Pauline clears her throat uneasily as Teddy uncrosses her legs, then re-crosses them. 'John demanded to know the names of the residents I worked with and how much attention they gave me.' Before her, the police officer makes a note, his face thoughtful as she continues. 'There was one gentleman I looked after who was particularly handsy – though of course I told him off and asked him to stop. He was in his eighties, for goodness' sake.' Pauline tuts before picking the story back up. 'John gradually became obsessed with this man. He was always grilling me about him and asking whether he'd come near me that day. My husband even showed up at the care home to check up on me and had arguments with the old man.' She looks up, meeting the police officer's eyes. His expression is concerned, his brows knitted together. 'You can ask my colleagues there. I think they were shocked by his behaviour.' She pauses to swallow hard. She has rehearsed this speech but it still sticks in her throat, remembering the way John would humiliate her in front of her colleagues. She inhales deeply.

'Take your time, Pauline,' the nice officer says neutrally.

She nods her head. 'Not long before John disappeared – just before he faked his own death – this particular old man, he . . . well, he died very suddenly and without warning. He'd overdosed on his own heart medication. It was quite suspicious, and at the time I couldn't understand how it'd happened. Because you see' – she leans in, looking directly at the officer's moustache – 'the elderly gentleman didn't have access to his own medication. Only us – only the staff – did. I was one of only a handful of people with keys to the medication drawer.' She shakes her head, as Thomas makes more notes, his energy more frantic now. 'The resident couldn't have got in there. I couldn't believe it.' She sits back in her chair, feeling like Audrey with the smooth half-truths. 'But then the news came that John had been in this terrible car accident in the Austrian Alps and I didn't think any more of it. I was... well, goodness, a bit distracted by my grief. Grief has tentacles, don't you know?' She takes another deep breath and picks the small plastic fridge bag out of her coat pocket, sliding it across the table. 'And then yesterday I was unpacking my husband's things – he hasn't bothered to do it since he got back – and I found these items.'

Thomas leans forward, picking up the bag and examining its contents. There is a key – Pauline's medicine drawer key for the care home – and a prescription bottle for Digitalis.

The detective sergeant picks up his pen, his moustache twitching with something like excitement. 'And what was this elderly gentleman's name, Pauline? The one who died suspiciously? Can you remember?' he asks, ready to make a note.

Pauline nods, and under the table she feels Teddy's leg press urgently against her own. 'Harold Woodbead,' she tells him with Audrey-style confidence. 'We called him Handsy Harry at the home.' She pauses for dramatic effect. 'Officer, I'm worried that my husband, John, killed Harry.'

43

Pauline is asked to go over her story several more times. Detective Sergeant Thomas Daveys is recording, but he's also making notes. He seems to be taking this very seriously.

Halfway through a question about why they didn't have CCTV at the home and how her boss, Gary, complained relentlessly about the meagre budget, the door to the interview room opens. A man with his head down comes in and takes a seat in the dim light at the back of the room. The DS turns, looking irritated. The irritation turns to agitation when he sees who it is.

He clears his throat. 'Sorry, just a second,' he tells Pauline and Teddy, getting up. He steps to the man, speaking in urgent, angry whispers.

'What are you doing in here?' he hisses. 'You can't be here.'

'Shane at the front desk called me. I want to hear this. I have a right to hear this,' the man replies.

DS Daveys shakes his head. 'You've been suspended. You've got no right at all. Please leave.'

There is a moment of tension, before the man nods and stands. As he and the DS eyeball one another, Pauline supresses a gasp.

She recognises him.

Beside her at the table, she feels Teddy stiffen with shock. They both recognise him.

It's Dominic Shipman. The awful man they tried to murder. The man they reported for being drunk at the wheel. The police officer with the bungalow.

Is he here because of what they did? Because he knows they were the ones who got him in trouble? How could he know?

Pauline feels her throat constrict and under the table, Teddy's grip tightens on her leg. It's clear she's just as blindsided as Pauline. Why is he here? What's happening?

DS Daveys ushers Dominic out, still muttering furiously. He shuts the door firmly and turns back to Pauline and Teddy.

'I'm sorry about my coll—' he cuts himself off. 'I'm not going to call him a colleague, actually. He's been suspended. He never should've been here.'

He looks upset then gives himself a shake. 'Look, I've taken up a lot of your time. Let's leave it here for now. I'll be in touch with any follow-up questions in the coming days.'

He leads them out, across the foyer, stopping short of the glass doors, where Ivy joins them and DS Daveys begins to say his goodbyes. He gives Pauline a crime reference number and says he will be in touch with an update on the case as soon as he can. He adds that he's pretty sure they've got enough for a proper investigation into John Sheldon and his connection to Harold Woodbead.

'Hmm, just wait a minute.' DS Daveys pauses, looking out across the car park. Dominic is still out there. He's furiously stalking away across the grey expanse, muttering to himself. He stops for a moment, pulling on an old beige coat as he goes. It's a mac. An old beige mac.

The three of them stare out of the doors after him, something dawning on Pauline.

'Just wait until he's gone, if that's OK. I don't want him bothering you,' the DS requests in a low voice. 'I shouldn't tell you this, but he's not a good person. He's been suspended and there are criminal charges pending.' He leans in, speaking in a low voice. 'He was drunk at the wheel and then assaulted one of our colleagues when they tried to bring him in.' He looks a little embarrassed. 'I shouldn't have told you that.' He sighs. 'But honestly, I'm ashamed that he was ever a police officer. People like him give the force a bad name. There's been a big push to sort out our vetting procedures during hiring, but it's a slow process.'

'Why was he even interested in our statement?' Teddy asks, her voice thick as she stares out at the retreating back of Dominic.

DS Daveys sighs. 'I'm sorry. I think someone here called him when you came in. Dominic worked on the Harold Woodbead case. He got a bit obsessive actually. He was convinced the old man's wife was involved. Poor old thing, she's in her eighties from what I hear.'

Pauline watches the horrible little man as he disappears off into the distance. He pulls his coat closer around him in the wind. His Columbo coat.

Columbo. Dominic Shipman is Columbo.

The DS says his goodbyes, and the women step outside, heading for the car. Pauline feels dazed as Teddy turns to face her.

They stare at one another for a long minute. 'Fucking Audrey,' Teddy says. 'She's done it again.'

And then they all start laughing.

44

Detective Sergeant Thomas Daveys – who Teddy is calling Magnum PI because of his moustache – has advised Pauline not to go home, so they head back to Teddy's apartment. She's been staying there for the past few days anyway, since the conversation with her children. She doesn't want to run into John, and she needs time away from the house.

Audrey is waiting for them in the living room.

'How did it go, my darlings?' she calls out as they arrive en masse through the front door.

'You fuck!' Teddy roars out across the apartment. 'You have some explaining to do, you little sociopath.'

Audrey blinks, looking mildly surprised. 'I do? More of it?'

Teddy draws herself up to her full, imposing height, staring down balefully at the older woman. 'Columbo? Dominic Shipman? The same knobhead?'

Audrey looks thoughtful. 'Oh! I'd forgotten about him.' She shakes her head. 'He's been suspended. Surely he wasn't at the police station? I thought we'd got rid of him.'

Pauline can't help herself. She starts giggling. 'Audrey! You set us up. Again. You tried to get us to kill Columbo all those weeks ago. Why didn't you tell us?'

Ivy shakes her head. 'How did you even...' Something occurs to her. 'Hold on.' She turns on Audrey. 'You're the one who suggested I go to that particular support group! You're the one who suggested I started writing a journal about it, logging the worst of the men and their stories.' She blinks. 'Wait, now I remember – you even suggested we go after Dominic first.'

'It's just a coincidence, my darling,' Audrey says with wide, innocent eyes.

Teddy snorts. 'Why didn't you say anything when you saw him then? When we were following him around outside the pub?'

'I wasn't wearing my glasses.'

Pauline starts laughing again.

'Bullshit!' Teddy declares, but she looks like she's going to laugh as well.

Audrey shrugs, looking caught out. 'Oh, all right, fine. But if I really *promise* to stop planting things and manipulating all of you, can we just put this tiny little indiscretion behind us?'

'So you *did* set all of this up?' Ivy is goggle-eyed. 'You knew who Columbo was from the start?'

Audrey gives a mischievous grin. 'You didn't think I'd look into the dreadful police officer harassing me and my daughter? I spent months looking for Pauline, but you thought I'd let Columbo go without a thorough investigation?' She tuts. 'Turns out he was another awful, abusive, women-beating shit and his colleagues were covering for him. He really did deserve to be on our kill list. I just made sure he was at the top of it.'

'He *did* need to be stopped,' Ivy murmurs and Audrey scoops her up for a cuddle.

Teddy points a stern finger in Audrey's direction. 'Just because that cretin deserved what he got, doesn't mean what you did was right.' She sighs. 'OK, look, we'll laugh this one off, but no more of this, Audrey! Just tell us the truth. We can handle it. We still would've taken Dominic Shipman on, even if we'd known who he really was.'

'I'm rather glad I didn't know,' Pauline admits. 'I was already on the verge of breaking down half the time. Knowing we were stalking the man who was also stalking *us*, and a police officer no less, might've sent me over the edge.'

'You're welcome, my darling!' Audrey beams.

Teddy rolls her eyes. 'I think we deserve a drink.' She heads for an inbuilt fridge, reaching inside and retrieving a bottle of Dom Perignon. 'It's pink!' she adds with a grin.

'Vintage!' Audrey observes with delight grabbing for the bottle as Ivy gathers glasses. She pops the top and pours. 'Four hundred pounds a pop, this stuff!' she cackles and Teddy frowns at her.

'Audrey, just because you haven't really won the lottery, it doesn't mean you have to be gauche.'

'Actually,' Audrey laughs again, 'I meant *what a shame* we have to consume such a *pauper* drink. You should see my castle's wine cellar. We have a Domaine Leroy Corton Renardes, Grand Cru bottle of wine in there that's worth about fifty thou. There's also a disgusting Speyside Single Malt Scotch Whisky my father bought. It's from 1940 and worth two hundred and fifteen thousand pounds. My dad says he's going to drink it on his a hundred and tenth birthday.'

Pauline regards her, open-mouthed. Two hundred and fifteen thousand pounds for a bottle of booze that tastes like chargrilled soil? She'll never get used to this world. Though, when she tastes Teddy's pink champagne moments later, she makes a mental note that she would like to. It's *gorgeous*. Smooth and delicate with toasty, nutty flavours. Not a hint of fabric softener.

Ooh, maybe that's what she'll do next: become a professional champagne taster. Is that a thing?

Ivy leans forward on the huge sofa, shaking her head. 'I can't believe it might work.' She looks around at the others. 'Do you think it really did? Did it work? Did we just get rid of John and Columbo all in one go?'

Teddy shrugs. 'I guess we'll see. It'll certainly get them off our backs for a while, at least.' She smiles at Pauline. 'And even if the case goes away or gets dropped, it will definitely get leaked to the press. John is about to get exposed to the world for who he really is and everything he's done.'

'Meanwhile Columbo's on suspension.' Audrey grins.

'Hold on.' Ivy frowns. 'Didn't you say he was still harassing you, Audrey?'

She shrugs. 'A little, but I reported it. He hasn't been around since. There's no way they won't dismiss him.'

'And now our new friend Magnum PI is taking over the case, focusing all his attentions on John Sheldon,' Teddy finishes.

Pauline puts her drink down, a rush of anxiety ruining her good mood. 'Do you think John will tell them?' She swallows hard. 'About all of you, I mean? Do you think when they bring him in for an interview, he'll tell them about my email? About how you killed your husbands?'

Audrey places a hand on top of Pauline's. 'My darling, I know you've been worrying about this, but what did you *really* tell him in this email? All he has to go on is three first names of women he's never met—'

'And Teddy isn't even my real name!' Teddy announces happily.

Audrey giggles. 'And if he did work out which Audrey it is, he'd look absurd trying to accuse me of the crime he's facing charges over.'

Ivy nods. 'It would make him look very silly, wouldn't it? Trying to claim a bunch of lottery winners were in cahoots after all murdering their husbands! No one would ever buy such a ridiculous idea.'

'There's one more thing that might be a bit reassuring.' Teddy leans back into the luxury cushions of her sofa. She smiles like a cat. Her friends regard her curiously, waiting. 'I put in a call to our friend Craig and his pal.' She pauses. 'The loan sharks? Yes, they've had their money paid back in full, but, to be honest, Craig wasn't particularly happy that John was let off the hook like he was. He was *displeased* that John had faked his own death to avoid paying and didn't much like threatening poor Pauline all those times—'

'He didn't seem to mind *that* much,' Pauline points out.

'He was just doing his job,' Audrey says, full of sympathy for her fellow sociopath.

'Either way,' Teddy waves her hand dismissively, 'Craig was more than happy to receive a nice little bonus from me to message John earlier today.' She raises her eyebrows. 'He let him know that if anything gets brought up that shouldn't be, he'll be around to collect on a different kind of debt. With interest.'

Pauline gapes at her friend. 'Teddy,' she says at last. 'You are so brilliant.' She takes a deep breath. The solid mass in her chest loosens. 'I'm free,' Pauline whispers, smiling. 'I'm really, truly free.'

They clink their glasses once again, acknowledging a job well done.

Ivy sits up straighter. 'I want to help other women feel free,' she says suddenly, with urgency. 'I still want us to do something to help victims— Survivors!' She half-laughs. 'Obviously murdering isn't the way to go, but I can't help it. I need to do something to help all those women I've met in the support group. There are so many awful people in the world and I want us to be able to do something about that. We helped my friend Gemma with Dominic. And we've helped Pauline with John—'

'Pauline helped *herself*,' Teddy says proudly.

'She did,' Ivy acknowledges, smiling softly. 'And you're amazing, by the way, Pauline. In case we haven't said that enough or made that crystal clear.' She sighs. 'But there are a lot of people struggling out there. Owen the predator is still out there hurting women. All those other men on my list, they're out there doing what they do, over and over.'

Audrey rests her head on Ivy's shoulder. 'I agree with Ivy. We should be able to do something. We all have money to spend and we all believe in moral relativism.'

Pauline nods a lot, though she has no idea what moral relativism means.

Teddy cocks her head. 'So maybe we become, I don't know, facilitators of some kind? We could help women get rid of their horrible partners by any means necessary.'

The buzzer goes, and this time, Pauline is unsurprised to see her children at the door. This time they were invited.

'Come on in, my darlings!' Audrey calls out. 'We were just talking about moral relativism.'

'Moral what-ivism?' Seb looks blank and Audrey grabs him for a bear hug.

'Thank you for asking that! I only said it to sound clever and not a single one of these women asked me what it meant. Can you believe that? It's just inconsiderate when a person's so clearly trying to show off.'

'I know what it means,' Teddy says and Ivy nods in agreement.

'I've seen *The Good Place*,' she explains but is ignored because no one else knows what that is.

'Anyway, Seb darling,' Audrey continues, 'it's a philosophy I happen to be a big fan of. It says not everything is universally good or bad.' She directs this at Seb, though Pauline is also listening intently. 'So our choices should be more dependent on the context. It's all relative! Who are we to judge!' She side-eyes her friends. 'For example, just plucking this out of thin air, is killing evil rapists always wrong?'

'Kill them all!' Tilly says jovially and Teddy raises her eyebrows, looking amused.

'I happen to agree,' Audrey replies casually.

The group makes their way into the open-plan kitchen. Audrey fetches more glasses and they drink champagne together, chatting warmly amongst themselves.

Pauline watches Seb gravitate to Ivy, eyeing them as they shyly talk in low voices by the kitchen island.

'Anyway,' Audrey continues breezily. 'If we're not really allowed to kill bad people,' she says, coughing lightly, 'I think we should talk about how else we can help women who need us.'

'I've had an idea for that,' Ivy pipes up. She grins around the room, bright-eyed and excited.

Pauline takes in her friend, standing across the room, beaming. She's so different from the Ivy she met that first day at her house. Unrecognisable from the broken and small young woman who barely whispered one-word answers and couldn't make eye contact. She speaks up without encouragement now and has this shimmying confidence about her. She even seems taller these days. But she's also kept all the sweetness, the kindness and compassion she always had. She has kept all the good egg about her.

The Lottery Winner Widows Club might not have managed to murder any evil, abusive men together, Pauline realises, but what little they have achieved has obviously been enough to truly help Ivy with her pain. Pauline doubts she'll ever fully recover from what she went through with her husband, but it's clear she is doing so much better. It warms her heart.

Ivy reaches down to stroke Paula the Dog, who squats loyally at her side. 'So here's my plan,' she begins with enthusiasm. 'I want to open a dog therapy centre for survivors of sexual assault and domestic violence.' Her voice is eager. 'I've been doing a lot of research into it, and trained dogs have been hugely helpful for those who've suffered abuse or have PTSD. About a third of abuse survivors have post-traumatic stress disorder, did you know that? Having a dog around provides emotional support and reduces anxiety. Petting a dog releases oxytocin, which helps with stress. The evidence shows having a dog around actively relaxes people and can encourage them to open up.' She takes a deep breath, finding her stride. 'And I'm thinking we could also offer therapy on site, and maybe legal advice.' She nods at Teddy, who looks surprised, then nods with excitement. 'We could even have rooms above the centre. A safe house for those who need it.'

'That's such a great idea,' Tilly tells her with enthusiasm. 'If there's anything me and my wife, Misha, can do to help, I'd love to get involved.'

'Me too!' Seb says with enthusiasm. 'I'm about to start training to be a therapist, you know!'

Pauline thinks of how sweetly Ivy dotes on Paula the Dog, how she gives the pet more attention than her owner, Audrey. Of *course* dogs had to be part of her big idea to save womenkind.

Pauline smiles. 'Our twenty million is at your disposal, Ivy. Minus a bit for some luxuries, of course. I think it's high time I spent some money on myself.'

'Quite right,' Teddy nods. 'It's about time you really enjoyed being rich.'

Audrey snorts. 'I'm in, of course.' She pauses. 'Does it mean killing the odd narcissist is totally off the table?'

Tilly finds this hilarious. 'I'm also up for getting involved in all that if needed,' she jokes as the majority of the room hard-eyeballs one another.

Ivy continues to talk animatedly about her plan and about how she's going to train Paula the Dog as a service animal, even as Paula the Dog zooms around the room chasing a fly that she is trying to swallow whole.

As the others chat and drink, Tilly crosses the room to sit beside Pauline and pull her close. 'Are you OK?' her daughter asks softly.

Their conversation at the kitchen table the other day has wholly changed things between them.

Over the years, Tilly had started to mother her mother. She didn't even notice she was doing it, but Pauline saw it happen and hated it. She had become so weak and submissive around John, and she'd let herself be the same small, incapable child for the rest of the world. As Tilly grew up, she had to be the grown-up. The mother.

But that has shifted in these last few days. Tilly has stopped seeing her mum as a one-dimensional, useless, silly old woman and started trying to understand her. She sees her mum's trauma and her coping mechanisms. She sees her. Which is all Pauline ever wanted.

But of course, it will take some time for them to forgive one another. Their relationship took a dark turn there for a while, and it can't all be swept under the carpet. They're going to keep seeing Gerald, the counsellor, in an effort to work through some of the deeper issues. It will take time and effort, but for now, they're treating one another with softness and kindness. Which is pretty much all anyone can ask for from their loved ones.

'I'm fine, sweetheart. Are *you* OK?'

Tilly nods. 'Did you think any more about what we talked about?'

After Pauline confessed the truth about her marriage, she, Tilly and Seb sat around for a while longer, talking. It didn't take Tilly long to accept the truth about her father and realise she'd been in denial for a long time. In fact, Tilly was the one who'd told Pauline she should visit the police and report her dad for abuse. So he can't do it to another woman, she'd said, and it had made Pauline worry about Bridget the secretary.

'I did think about it, sweetheart.' Pauline nods. 'And I went to see the police today.' She doesn't expand. She doesn't tell Tilly how she is in the process of helping fit her dad up for murder. That conversation can probably wait.

Tilly's eyes widen. 'You did? Wow.' She puffs out her cheeks. 'God, you've really done it? That's so . . . so *brave*!'

She turns to fully look at her mum. 'I'm really bloody proud of you. Never mind proud, actually, I'm in *awe* of you. I don't know anyone who could be so strong, not after all you've been through.'

'Well, goodness.' Pauline feels herself swell with pride. 'Thank you.'

Tilly continues looking at her with admiration, then glances around the room. 'It's these women, isn't it?' she says quietly. 'It's your new friends. They've given you so much confidence. They've helped you loads, I can see that now. I was an idiot for trying to warn you away from them. They're clearly so good for you. I think they're probably magic.' She pauses, eyeing Audrey, who is trying to persuade Teddy to have an arm wrestle. 'I mean, don't get me wrong, they're all still a bunch of weirdos . . .'

Pauline arches an eyebrow. 'Aren't all the best people?' she asks and they both laugh.

'And have you noticed . . .' Tilly nudges her mum with her elbow, nodding towards the corner sofa across the room. There sit Ivy and Seb, their heads almost touching as they speak in such a familiarly intimate way.

'Oh yes.' Pauline grins, taking another sip of her drink. 'I have noticed indeed.'

'It's about time my little brother got his act together.' Tilly sounds amused. 'And I'm getting the impression she'd be well worth upgrading from the shed for.'

'I can tell you,' Pauline says, smiling again, 'she very much is.'

They snuggle into one another for a moment before Tilly speaks again in an urgent tone. 'I really am so sorry about everything, I hope you know that. I was so stubborn about seeing what you were going through.' Tilly sighs.

'I feel like it was some kind of temporary blindness, like I was wearing blinkers, and couldn't see what was right in front of me for so long.' She looks down at her own lap. 'It was like your life with Dad was a magic eye picture. Everything was so blurry and confusing – a big blur of a photo – and then when you explained it all, it suddenly came into focus. I thought I didn't really know you all this time, but it was him I didn't know. I misunderstood you both completely.'

'I'm sorry, too, Tilly,' Pauline tells her. 'I thought I was doing the right thing by keeping you in the dark. By staying with him and putting up with it.'

'I know, I get it. It's not your fault, Mum. And I hope they throw the book at him,' Tilly says darkly. 'I hope he gets everything that's coming to him.'

'I hope so too, my love,' she says, thinking of that plastic bag of evidence she'd passed across the desk at the police station. She wishes she could see his face when they brought him in.

After all, if framing someone for murder doesn't even the score for a faked death, what does?

EPILOGUE

Six Months Later

'I can't believe the police finally caught up with us!' Audrey says sombrely, regarding her partner in crime, Pauline, from across the cramped room.

'Are you two OK in there? It isn't too horrible?' Ivy calls loudly through the solid, locked door, her voice full of genuine concern.

'There's a toilet!' Audrey replies excitably, waving at the amenities. 'And a sink! It's right next to the bed. How incredibly handy. I might get one of these at the castle.'

'We're fine,' Pauline calls out. 'It's a bit grey and cramped in here, but no worse really than a private jet.'

From where she's sitting at the end of the cot, Audrey cackles.

'After everything we've been through, we really could've done without this,' Teddy shouts reproachfully, her voice muffled by the walls. She sounds a bit bored.

'It's not my fault!' Pauline cries. 'Don't blame me, it was Audrey who ran off with the pizza and refused to get out of the jacuzzi. I just happened to be there with her. They shouldn't have arrested me as well, it wasn't fair.'

'They didn't arrest you, Pauline,' Ivy calls out reassuringly.

'It's police corruption!' Audrey shouts, defiance in her voice. 'They can't just lock us in a prison cell like this.'

'I wouldn't exactly call them *police*,' Teddy says carefully. 'And I wouldn't exactly call that a prison cell.'

'Fine,' Audrey tuts. 'Well then, it's cruise ship security corruption. And they had no right to put us in the brig. I thought maritime law meant anything goes. Surely international waters mean you can do whatever you like without consequences.' She shakes her head. 'We really should've remembered that when we were in our murdering era.'

'They had every right to put you in the brig, actually,' Teddy tells her archly. 'Really, Audrey, you gave them no choice when you refused to listen to staff and do as you were told. All you had to do was stop eating pizza in the hot tub! You were getting pineapple and ham in all the jets.' She tuts. 'And instead, you had to be chased out by security, and then you both ran away to hide in the mini golf castle. There were children trying to play through.' She sighs. 'And Pauline, you really shouldn't let Audrey be such a bad influence on you. You're like Batman and Robin these days, always up to mischief.'

Pauline and Audrey look at each other and giggle.

Until this afternoon, they'd mostly managed to stay out of trouble during their Christmas cruise. But that was never going to last very long, not with Audrey around. And – as she's said more than once during their travels – it's important to get your money's worth when you're paying twenty thousand pounds a week to get seasick.

Not that Pauline would say it isn't worth the cash. Her cabin – positioned right at the front of the boat, on the port side, overlooking the ocean – must be well over eight hundred square feet. It has a king-sized bed, a huge walk-in wardrobe, its own separate living room, and a bathroom that would put most five-star hotel rooms to shame. Not to mention the private terrace, where Pauline directs the on-board butler to serve coffee every morning. She's sat out there on her own for a few minutes each morning, sipping her cappuccino and letting herself be hypnotised by the deep blue, blue water.

It has been like a dream.

Until their dramatic arrest by security, who escorted them to the brig an hour ago.

'Why didn't you just get out when they told you to?' Teddy sounds exasperated through the door.

Audrey waves her hands. 'I don't like being told what to do.'

Pauline weighs in. 'And I don't like Audrey being told what to do.'

Through the door, there are more annoyed-sounding tuts from Teddy, as Ivy giggles. It's nice that Ivy's come down to see them, given how busy she's been since they boarded the ship.

With Seb.

Kissing Seb.

Pauline's son had been rather a last-minute addition to the holiday. Ivy asked if he could join them only hours before they were due to leave, and there was a scramble to make arrangements. Luckily, he and Ivy were more than willing to share a room, which was very generous of them.

Seb knows everything.

Ivy told him about her ex-husband. And from there, the truth came out about all of it. He knows the whole lot, from the drunken beatings to the fatal trip down the stairs to all those failed attempts the group made at being murderers.

Even the truth of his dad not really murdering Handsy Harry. Everything. And – if all the kissing they're doing on this cruise is anything to go by – he is apparently fine with it all. So fine, in fact, that the pair of them are making plans to move in together in the New Year.

With Pauline's help, Seb's about to exchange on a lovely three-bed on the outskirts of Surrey. The property is surrounded by several acres of green space, as well as some nearby woods. It's ideal for him and Ivy, who have recently adopted two Great Dane puppies, Paula the Dog the Second and Paula the Dog the third.

It's all terribly confusing, and Paula the Dog – who Seb refers to as Paula the OG Dog – is apparently very jealous.

In contrast, Tilly and her wife, Misha, are already unpacked and settled in their brand-new, shiny one-bed apartment in central London – courtesy of their lottery winner mum, Pauline, who's been spending money like her life depended on it in recent months.

Pauline took a lot longer in choosing her own property, but just this week she's had an offer accepted on a beautiful country cottage about twenty minutes away from Seb and Ivy. It's a three-bedroom seventeenth-century chocolate box of a house. Tilly was horrified by the thatched roof and its EPC rating, but Pauline didn't mind any of that. Plus, it has the exact kind of stunning, huge open fireplace Pauline had so often dreamed about. She's planning on lighting it, even on the hottest of summer days. There are no suspicious stains on the kitchen ceiling and Pauline's hired a gardener to mow the grass.

The only really modern aspect of the property is the huge, renovated outbuilding round the back of the large driveway, where Pauline keeps her car. Cars plural now, actually. Last month she bought herself a Ferrari 812 GTS and she's been driving it at speed all over the UK. It's pure joy. Sometimes she and Audrey have drag races down the long private road outside Audrey's Scottish castle. It's not terribly responsible behaviour, but – as her friend regularly says – it would be a fun way to go, wouldn't it?

Of course, Seb is horrified by her 'ragging' the 'seven-speed dual-clutch automatic transmission' – whatever any of that means – but as she explained very nicely to him, it's not like it was a brand-new car. She got it second hand for a very reasonable four hundred thousand pounds.

'I'm back!' Seb calls out, sounding out of breath. 'I found the captain. He's going to let them out.' There is a pause. 'Mum, you OK in there?'

'I'm fine, sweetheart. Sorry about this.'

'Don't be sorry,' he calls. 'Kind of proud of you, to be honest.'

The gruff voice of the captain tuts. 'You shouldn't be. I've been briefed by the security team. The ladies behaved very badly. Very unbecoming.' There is a loud clunking sound as the door is unlocked and finally swings open.

'Sorry,' Pauline says with feeling to the stern-faced captain. 'We won't do it again.'

'*Probably* not,' Audrey mutters.

He huffs a little. 'You know we'd be within our rights to let the police know about all this?' he warns and Pauline gasps loudly.

'No!'

She thinks of the nice Detective Sergeant Thomas Daveys with his nice moustache. What would he think about her evading capture over a pizza-hot-tub incident on a cruise ship? He'd be appalled! And what if it affects her standing as a witness when John's case comes to trial in January?

Although, at least the prosecution would still have John's secretary, Bridget, as a witness.

Pauline thinks of her conversation with poor Bridget last week, and how surreal it had been. It turned out the secretary had been trying to reach out to Pauline ever since John's funeral. She was one of those random numbers that kept calling her. Of course, she'd never answered, assuming it was more family members wanting money. Or maybe strangers wanting money. Or even loan sharks wanting money.

A lot of people wanted money.

She and Bridget ended up talking on the phone for two long hours, dissecting everything about John and their relationships with him. They found they had a depressing amount in common. It seemed all those tears Bridget was loudly shedding at the funeral were... relief. She'd been miserable and racked with guilt, trapped in this awful affair with her boss. She'd hated herself and the way he'd treated her, but felt like she couldn't escape. That is, until he'd escaped everyone by thoughtfully *unaliving*.

While Pauline had spent those happy months making friends with The Lottery Winner Widows Club and planning murders, Bridget had – probably much more sensibly – been going through intense therapy. By the time she saw the press conference announcing her lover's return from the dead, she'd had several breakthroughs and was in the midst of improving her life-long low self-esteem that always seemed to lead to terrible romantic decisions.

It was a difficult conversation for Pauline. But nice. Cathartic. She felt better afterwards and certainly bore no ill will towards the poor woman. Hearing that she was doing well and wasn't about to let John back into her life was a huge weight off Pauline's shoulders.

Not that he could've re-entered *anyone's* life after his arrest. He's been held without bail all this time, given he's already proved to be a flight risk.

As well as the murder of Harold Woodbead, John is also facing multiple other charges, including Identity Fraud and Forgery over those fake documents he created during the whole pretending-to-die thingy, as well as Immigration and Travel Fraud for using a forged passport when travelling back to the UK. Magnum PI also promised to try to make the coercive control charge stick, for good measure, but admitted only around three or four per cent of cases result in a charge. The stats made Pauline sadder than the possibility of John getting away with it. But it felt good to have them trying to prosecute – even if it might be difficult. If no one ever tries with these cases, the men who do this will always get away with it. And Pauline wants to make things better for women if she can.

Possibly more importantly – knowing how desperate John was for them to love him – the newspapers are having a *field day*. Headlines have been screaming for months about how he staged his own fake death and fooled his family along with a nation. Then someone leaked the news about his arrest in connection with a possible murder and it became international news. Headlines everywhere have gone mad. Pauline has mostly found it amusing, though she draws the line at the one that read, '*Lottery winner faked death after murdering wife's elderly lover.*' Audrey told her if that one offended her, she *really* shouldn't look at the *National Enquirer*, who claimed Pauline and Harold Woodbead had a secret S&M room at the care home.

The angry ship captain is still scolding Audrey.

'We may issue you a fine, Mrs Woodbead—'

'Please call me Ms Swift,' Audrey interrupts, her hand up. 'I've gone back to my maiden name. Swift. No relation to Taylor.'

'All right, Ms Swift, but please take this seriously. This kind of disorderly conduct can't happen again on board, or we'll be forced to remove you at the next port. We've just passed Miami, but we could drop you off in Cuba.'

The Lottery Winner Widows Club's plan had been to stay with the ship past Mexico and Belize, until they docked in Roatan, Honduras in four days' time, where they were planning to make an on-the-spot decision about their next move – stay in Central America or find a new adventure. But Cuba doesn't sound so bad. It's not the worst threat Pauline's ever heard.

Audrey sighs, looking resigned. 'Fine, I'll be good.' She tuts. 'It really is your own fault, you know. You're the ones serving unlimited champagne with breakfast. What did you *think* would happen?'

The captain shakes his head, looking around at the group before stalking away.

'Behave yourselves!' he shouts from over a shoulder.

Audrey and Pauline eyeball each other, feeling rebellious. 'I might give him my number,' Audrey announces gleefully after a moment. 'I'm pretty sure I got what the kids call *a vibe*. I think he probably quite likes a bad girl.'

'Does that mean you've finally dumped French Antoine?' Pauline asks and Audrey sighs.

'Not yet, but he knows I'm only interested in something casual whenever I'm visiting the French Riviera.' She looks perky. 'And he's given up smoking! Isn't that wonderful? He looks ten years younger.'

'Good for him.' Teddy smiles and she flicks her glorious hair. Something glints at her roots and Pauline looks closer.

'What's that?' she asks Teddy, curiously. 'That clip thing, in your hair?'

Teddy raises an eyebrow. 'It's just where my extensions are attached, babe.' She smiles wryly as Pauline gasps in shock. 'Oh babe, you thought my hair was real? It's all fake! I've got the thinnest hair in the universe. There are, like, three strands that are real over here. The rest are glued in. Aren't they great?'

Pauline stares goggle-eyed at the locks she has envied so much for almost a year now. 'Your hair isn't real,' she whispers to herself.

'I'll take you to my hairdresser when we get back,' Teddy offers nicely and Pauline nods eagerly. She wonders if they can make her look like Sigourney Weaver. What a thrill! Something else occurs to her. 'Teddy,' she begins slowly, 'where are you *actually* from? I've wondered about your accent since that very first day we met in my kitchen.'

Teddy smiles enigmatically. 'You can't tell?' she asks, and Pauline would swear she now sounds like a character from that show she watches with Ivy and Seb – *The Real Housewives of New Jersey*.

'I haven't got a clue,' Pauline confesses.

Teddy holds a dramatic pause before grinning. 'I'm Canadian,' she admits, adding, 'But my parents were Australian-Irish and French-Italian. The accent throws a lot of people. I like it that way.' She shrugs.

'So wait.' Pauline struggles to get her head around this brand-new information. 'You're not even American at all?'

'Nope.'

Pauline gapes at her non-American, non-perfect-haired friend, as Ivy giggles, turning doe-eyed to Seb. 'What shall we do with all this freedom, after your mum and Audrey's extended incarceration?'

Pauline wonders how Ivy might look in her mother's wedding veil and whether they would consider having children. She'd love to be a grandma.

'Shall we go duty-free shopping?' Teddy suggests and everyone murmurs their agreement.

They head down to the atrium via the main staircase. Pauline's now seen it several times but she still stares around herself in awe at the grand entrance. It is exactly like that bit in *Titanic* where Kate walks down to see Leo in a tuxedo waiting for her, and for a moment Pauline feels a thrill, wondering if they might end up hitting an iceberg – wouldn't that be fun!

They pass rows of endless designer boutiques, talking about what show they'll see later that night at the on-boat theatre. Last night's performance was like seeing an episode of *Strictly Come Dancing* in real life, without the joke act MP. They pass the boat's fitness centre and all laugh at the idea of using a gym while on holiday.

'You know there's a library on deck eleven?' Teddy says and they all ooh and aah, agreeing plans to head up and find a new novel later. One they won't get round to reading beside the many on-board pools.

'Oh, by the way, Mum,' Seb says brightly. 'The solicitors have emailed. The searches are back. It's looking like we might be able to complete on the house sooner than we thought.'

'That's wonderful, sweetheart.' Pauline claps her hands.

Yes, children should be able to stand on their own two feet, but she firmly believes the world these days is skewed against the young. She and John purchased their house in the late eighties for thirty-five thousand pounds. These days that would barely be a deposit on a home! Pauline has all this money, and yes, she adores the refuge centre they've set up – and it's doing amazing things already – but she also wants to be able to do nice things for herself. And buying her children a home each is making her happier than she's felt in years.

Not least because she'll get her garden shed back.

Ivy looks pretty relieved about that part too.

They pause outside Chanel. Teddy stares longingly at a pink handbag in the window. 'I might have to buy a new flat for all my clothes,' she murmurs.

A man emerges from the shop, slamming the door aggressively. It boomerangs back in the face of a woman trailing in his wake, nearly knocking her off her feet. He doesn't notice. 'There,' he says to her, waving a small Chanel bag in her face. 'And that better shut you the hell up.' She stays silent as instructed, and Pauline watches carefully. 'You know,' he is crowing, 'I am a high value male and your body count is seriously questionable. You're hitting the wall, too, getting *old*, so just know how lucky you are I'm willing to even be here right now. I could have my pick.'

'Yuck,' Audrey says as the strangers walk away down the corridor.

'Misogynistic dog whistles,' Seb says with quiet fury. 'It's all over the internet and it's disgusting. You know, I keep getting targeted Andrew Tate-type videos shown to me in my social media feed? As if *of course* I'll be into it because I'm a man. It doesn't seem to matter how many times I click "not interested" or report it.'

'I know we're only supposed to be helping women at the refuge these days,' Audrey says thoughtfully, 'but can't we be, I don't know, *murder facilitators*? Help women kill their own husbands if they want to? Because some of them *definitely* deserve it.'

Teddy frowns. 'Is The Lottery Winners Widows Murder Facilitators Club too clunky?'

Pauline takes a few steps in the direction the couple are slowly walking. 'I think we should at least offer her the option.'

'Excuse me,' Ivy calls out to the pair. *'Excuse me!'* They turn at the end of the corridor. The man's lip curls with distaste at being addressed – by a *woman* of all things.

'What?'

'Can I talk to you?' Ivy moves closer, directing herself at the woman only. She glances anxiously at her partner and he rolls his eyes.

'Why?' he answers. 'What do you want?'

'I . . . I work for Chanel,' Ivy lies smoothly, stepping forward. 'And we'd love to do a survey on your latest purchase. You can win a ten-thousand-pound shopping spree!'

She looks at him with uncertainty and he rolls his eyes again.

'Whatever, I'll be at the fitness centre, in the cold room. Come find me when you're done.'

'What on earth is a *cold room*?' Audrey mutters.

'Like, the opposite of a sauna,' Teddy offers helpfully. 'It's horrible.'

Ivy waits for the man to be fully out of sight before she turns to the quivering young woman.

'Hello,' she says softly. 'What's your name?'

'Charlotte.' She matches Ivy's tone.

'Hi, Charlotte.' Ivy nods round at the rest of the group, all waiting and watching. 'We're the Lottery Winners Widows Murder Facilitators Club and we want to help you take back your power.'

The woman frowns. 'You're . . . *what?*'

* * *

To: John.Sheldon1960@oldmail.com
From: PaulineJeanieWilkes1964@Smail.com
Subject: Divorce finalised!

Dear John,

Finally, an actual Dear John letter! Thanks for nothing. Enjoy your time in prison.

Goodbye for ever,
Pauline

Acknowledgements

Hello you, Lucy Vine here. Hold on, let me just put on my Elly hat. I'm a whole different person as Elly – a lot meaner. Elly laughs at people who trip up, Elly doesn't care that you're hungry or tired, Elly's a hardened crime writer who doesn't even start her acknowledgements with a 'thank you'. She waits until the next paragraph.

Thank you SO SO SO much for reading this book (unless you've skipped straight to the back, which makes you an Elly kind of person). I am incredibly grateful and – if I wasn't currently in Elly mode – I would probably be feeling a little emotional about all of it. This com-crime book came about after a chance encounter with editor extraordinaire, Jack Butler, at Goldsboro Books in Soho one summer – so I have to start by saying thank you to him. I will always be your biggest fan, Jack. Thank you so much for everything you did to make this book happen. I also owe the most enormous, outsized thank you to the absolutely brilliant Rachel Hart. You are amazing and I loved everything we did together. Thank you SO MUCH to everyone at Wildfire and Headline, you've been incredible: Joseph Edwards, Helena Towers, Katrina Smedley, Amy Cox and Tina Paul. Thank you also

Acknowledgements

to Federica Leonardis for your fabulous copy-edit and to Jill Cole for your brilliant proofread!

Thank you to my incredible agent Diana Beaumont, who continues to be one of my favourite people. And thank you hugely to my friends and family, who have been so nice to me throughout all this. I love you guys.

I had the most fun writing this book, truly, and I hope it will make you lovely readers smile, too. If you caught my dedication, you might be wondering who the 'real' Ivy, Teddy and Audrey are. They're my (very silly) three dogs. When I sat down to start writing this book, I knew I had these three characters I already loved but didn't yet know. My husband, David suggested I . . . Oh wait, Elly doesn't have a husband, she's a lone wolf. So OK, this random, very hot, tall guy I know called David suggested I use the names and personalities of our three dogs. And so, I did. They inspired our little club, and it turned out to be the best cure for writer's block. Although, I should add that none of them have been through anything like what TLWWC have. Ivy does look sad all the time but it's a total put-on. DM me for photos.

LOVE YOU BYE.

© Sarah Kate Photography

Elly Vine is the pseudonym of bestselling author, **Lucy Vine**. **Lucy Vine** is the author of novels *Hot Mess, What Fresh Hell, Are We Nearly There Yet?, Bad Choices, Seven Exes, Date with Destiny* and *Book Boyfriend*. Her eighth novel is *Good For You*. Her books have been published in seventeen territories, with *Hot Mess* optioned for a TV series in America. In a previous life, Lucy was a journalist, writing for publications including *Grazia, Stylist, Heat, Fabulous, Marie Claire, Sugar* and *Cosmopolitan*. You can find her on Instagram and TikTok @lucyvineauthor. Her website is www.lucyvine.co.uk.

RAISING READERS
Books Build Bright Futures

Dear Reader,

We'd love your attention for one more page to tell you about the crisis in children's reading, and what we can all do.

Studies have shown that reading for fun is the **single biggest predictor of a child's future success** – more than family circumstance, parents' educational background or income. It improves academic results, mental health, wealth, communication skills and ambition.

The number of children reading for fun is in rapid decline. Young people have a lot of competition for their time, and a worryingly high number do not have a single book at home.

Our business works extensively with schools, libraries and literacy charities, but here are some ways we can all raise more readers:

- Reading to children for just 10 minutes a day makes a difference
- Don't give up if your children aren't regular readers – there will be books for them!
- Visit bookshops and libraries to get recommendations
- Encourage them to listen to audiobooks
- Support school libraries
- Give books as gifts

Thank you for reading.
www.JoinRaisingReaders.com